PEGG
PEGG GREEN
CLIFF HOUSE SCHOOL
PLAYING FIELDS
MEADOW
WHEAT FIELDS
CATTLE
ORCHARD
PINE WOOD
POULTRY FARM
FARMLAND
PRIVATE WOOD
MARKET GARDENS
APPLE ORCHARD
ALLOTMENTS
FRIARDALE STATION
MEADOW
Legend
FIRST CLASS ROAD
SECOND CLASS ROAD
OTHER ROADS
FOOTPATHS
RAILWAYS
CUTTING
EMBANKMENT
SAND
CLIFF
BRIDGE OVER
BRIDGE UNDER
FOOTBRIDGE

BILLY BUNTER IN INDIA

VOLUME 2

Frank Richards was the pen name of **Charles Hamilton**.

Charles Harold St. John Hamilton (8 August 1876 – 24 December 1961) was an English writer, specializing in writing long-running series of stories for weekly magazines about recurrent casts of characters, his most frequent and famous genre being boys' public school stories, though he also wrote in other genres. He used a variety of pen names, generally using a different name for each set of characters he wrote about, the most famous being Frank Richards for the Greyfriars School stories featuring Billy Bunter. Other important pen names included Martin Clifford (for St. Jim's), Owen Conquest (for Rookwood), Ralph Redway (for The Rio Kid), and Hilda Richards (for Bessie Bunter). He also wrote hundreds of stories such as the Ken King stories for *The Modern Boy*.

Amalgamated Press started a new story paper for boys called *The Gem* in 1907 and by issue number eleven, it had established a format: the major content was to be a story about St Jim's school, starring Tom Merry as the main character and written by Charles Hamilton under the pen name of Martin Clifford. This paper rapidly established itself, and to capitalize on its success, a similar venture was launched in 1908. This was to be known as *The Magnet*. The subject matter was a school called Greyfriars and Hamilton was again to be the author, this time using the name Frank Richards.

In 1915 Hamilton started a third school series for Amalgamated Press, Rookwood, this time under the name Owen Conquest and featuring a leading character called Jimmy Silver. These appeared in the *Boys' Friend Weekly,* and were shorter than the Greyfriars and St. Jim's stories.

These three schools took up most of Hamilton's energies over the following 30 odd years and make up the work for which he is best remembered. His 'golden age' is generally considered as being the period from about 1925 to about 1935. In all, he provided stories for 82 per cent of the issues of *The Magnet* and two-thirds of the issues of *The Gem*.

Following the winding up of *The Magnet* in 1940, Hamilton was not able to continue the Greyfriars saga, as Amalgamated Press held the copyright and initially would not release it. But by 1946 they changed their mind and granted Richards permission to write Greyfriars stories again. He then signed a contract with publishers Charles Skilton for a hardback series, the first volume of which, *Billy Bunter of Greyfriars School*, was published in September 1947. The series continued for the rest of his life, but with Skilton transferring rights to Cassell in 1952. In addition, Hamilton, under the pen names above, wrote further books featuring St Jim's, Rookwood, and Cliff House (the Bessie Bunter series), as well as the television scripts for seven series of Billy Bunter stories for the BBC.

Charles Hamilton died on 24 December 1961, aged 85, and was cremated at the Kent County Crematorium at Charing. He is estimated to have written about 100 million words in his lifetime (that's the equivalent of 1,200 average-length novels) and has featured in the *Guinness Book of Records* as the world's most prolific author.

The Magnet Library story arcs

Billy Bunter in India

(AKA HARRY WHARTON & CO IN INDIA SERIES PUBLISHED ACROSS MAGNET VOL XXX IN 11 PARTS IN 1926)

Illustrated by C.H. Chapman and Leonard Shields

VOLUME 2

CONTAINING PARTS 7 TO 11

Frank Richards

CHANCELLOR
PRESS

Billy Bunter in India
First published in the Magnet magazine issues as shown in the Contents page
This edition under the Chancellor Press imprint © Hachette India 2024
(Registered Name: Hachette Book Publishing India Pvt. Ltd.)
An Hachette UK Company www.hachetteindia.com

SRD. For sale only in the Indian subcontinent.

The texts in these editions in most cases have been reprinted as is, with minimal editorial changes and by and large no bowdlerizing for political correctness; though in some editions, a few words and phrases considered archaic, or those considered offensive now, along with archaic punctuation may have been modified in places to make the text more accessible to today's readers. The narratives, language, beliefs, social mores and/or cultural depictions, in these volumes are a reflection of their times and must be viewed as such. They may also contain certain cultural, racial and gender prejudices and stereotypes that may be outdated or clearly wrong then and wrong today; but their removal would be tantamount to claiming these prejudices never existed. The Publisher does not endorse or support those depictions or stereotypes; and these books have been made available for a discerning audience that will read it for entertainment value and a chronicle/record of popular fiction of past times.

The Bunter books are being reissued for the adult nostalgia market and not as a children's series given that today there may exist concerns of sensitivity.

Cover design by Priya Singh. Cover illustration and Magnet logo simulation from the original Magnet library magazines and/or reprinted collections.

Series note: Some of the books in the series (unless otherwise credited) may have cover or inside illustrations from the original Magnet magazines, and while full restoration has been attempted, some images may be grainy or faded due to the condition of the original material. The end notes or bonus material or blurb details (if any) included in volumes may have been sourced from the public domain or free use publications such as Wikipedia and attribution is hereby made also allowing similar free use reproduction from here. Sources requiring further specific attribution may write in and further detailing and/or corrections shall be made in subsequent printings/editions.

Reprint specifications may be subject to change including but not limited to finishes, paper, colour sections.

ISBN: 978-93-5731-682-8

Hachette Book Publishing India Pvt. Ltd. 4th & 5th Floors, Corporate Centre, Plot No. 94, Sector 44, Gurugram - 122 003, India

Typeset in Times New Roman 11/13 pt by Manipal Technologies Limited, Manipal

Printed and bound in India by Manipal Technologies Limited, Manipal

Contents

Billy Bunter in India; published in VOLS XXX in 1926
in 11 parts across Issues 960-970

Part 7 Issue 966 | Bound for Bhanipur!

Part 8 Issue 967 | In the Heart of the Himalayas!

Part 9 Issue 968 | The Terror of the Jungle!

Part 10 Issue 969 | The Nabob's Rival!

Part 11 Issue 970 | From India to Greyfriars!

PART 7. BOUND FOR BHANIPUR!

76

Looking After Bunter!

"DELHI next stop!"

"Better wake up, Bunter!" grinned Bob Cherry.

Billy Bunter was snoring.

His deep and far from musical snore mingled with the rattle and roar of the train.

If there was one thing that Billy Bunter could do, and do well, it was sleeping. The voices of Harry Wharton & Co. did not disturb him; neither did the rattling and jolting of the train.

The soft Indian evening had closed in; a myriad of stars glimmered in the sky.

The Famous Five, of the Greyfriars Remove, were tired with their long journey. But they did not think of closing their eyes; the sights and sounds of Central India were new and strange to them, and of endless interest. But William George Bunter, regardless of the sights and sounds of mysterious Hindustan, was sleeping as if he was in the old Remove dormitory at Greyfriars school.

"Bunter!"

Bob Cherry leaned over the fat junior and shook him vigorously by the shoulder.

"Groogh!"

"Bunter!" bawled Bob.

Billy Bunter's eyes opened wide behind his big spectacles.

"Ow! Beast! 'Tain't rising bell!"

"Ha, ha, ha!"

"Next stop, Delhi!" said Bob Cherry.

"We get out at Delhi, Bunter."

"Oh!"

Bunter scrambled to his feet.

His deep snore no longer echoed through the car. The silence was both grateful and comforting.

"I say, you fellows, wait for me!" exclaimed Bunter.

"We'll wait!" said Johnny Bull, with a chuckle.

"The waitfulness will be terrific, my esteemed Bunter!" said Hurree Jamset Ram Singh.

"Where's my hat? Where's my bag? I say, you fellows, where's my things? You might lend a fellow a hand!" howled Bunter. "Just like you to leave me behind in the train, just like you left me behind at Bombay, you beasts! I believe you want to leave me in the train."

"My esteemed Bunter—"

"Oh, shut up! Where's my hat?" roared Bunter.

"Here you are!" grinned Frank Nugent. "You've been sitting on it, old fat bean!"

"Beast!"

Bunter took the pith sun hat, and punched it out into the shape of a hat again and jammed it on his head.

"Where's my bag?"

"Here you are!" said Harry Wharton.

"Where's my rug?"

"Catch!" said Bob Cherry, and he tossed Bunter his rug.

"Whooop!"

Billy Bunter caught the rug with his head, and it folded up round his fat features.

He dragged it off and gave the playful Bob a withering glare through his big spectacles.

"That the lot?" asked Bob cheerily, quite unwithered by the glare.

"Yes, you rotter!"

"What I like about Bunter," said Bob, "is his graceful, polished way of thanking a fellow for lending him a hand."

"Ha, ha, ha!"

"Ow! Wow!" roared Billy Bunter. "You rotter, leggo! You—oh! Ow! Wow! Yooop!" In the sinewy grasp of Hurree Jamset Ram Singh the Owl of the Remove was whirled along the carriage floor and out on to the platform, where he landed with a thump! "Ha, ha, ha!" roared Harry Wharton & Co.

"I'm ready now," growled Bunter.

The fat junior blinked round him. From the windows of the car there was no sign yet of a station. At the other end of the car, Colonel Wharton sat smoking a cigar and reading the "Pioneer." Harry Wharton & Co. had not yet started to gather up their paraphernalia.

Bunter looked perplexed.

He stood, with all his possessions, ready to disembark; but the train rattled on without a sign of stopping.

"Cherry, you beast!"

"Yes, old bean?"

"Didn't you say Delhi was the next stop?"

"Certainly!"

Bunter blinked at the windows again. Still there was no sign of a station. He blinked round at the grinning faces of the Famous Five.

It began to dawn upon his fat brain that his leg had been pulled.

"When do we get into Delhi?" he demanded.

"Can't say exactly," answered Bob Cherry cheerily. "Somewhere about half an hour or an hour, I fancy."

"You—you—you—" gasped Bunter.

"You told me it was the next stop."

"So it is."

"You—you silly chump!" roared Bunter. "Was there any need to wake me up if we don't get in for an hour?"

"Not at all!"

"You burbling fathead! What did you wake me for, then?" bawled Bunter.

"Fed-up with your snoring, old bean."

"Ha, ha, ha!"

"You—you—you—" gasped Bunter.

The expression on Billy Bunter's fat face seemed to have an exhilarating effect on the chums of the Greyfriars Remove. They roared.

"Beasts!"

William George Bunter disposed of his hat, his bag, and his rug, and sat down again and settled himself once more to balmy slumber.

Fortunately—for Bunter, if not for his travelling companions—he was able to drop into slumber at a moment's notice.

Snore!

"Going it again already!" said Bob Cherry. "Jevver hear such a thumping row?

"The snorefulness is terrific!" said Hurree Jamset Ram Singh.

"Let him rip!" said Harry Wharton, laughing. "He's less trouble asleep." And Billy Bunter continued to snore contentedly until the train glided into Delhi, under the lamp-lights.

The train stopped at last.

Harry Wharton & Co. had arrived at the ancient Mogul capital on their long journey to Bhanipur, the native home of Hurree Jamset Ram Singh.

Colonel Wharton rose to his feet.

"Delhi!" he said. "Come, my boys!"

Snore!

"Better wake Bunter again!" grinned Bob Cherry. "Even Bunter will want to be woke up now we're at Delhi. Bunter! Bunter! Bunter!"

Snore!

"Bunter!" roared Bob.

"The wakefulness is essential, my esteemed Bunter," said Hurree Jamset Ram Singh, shaking the Owl of the Remove by the shoulder.

"Groogh!"

"My esteemed snoreful Bunter—"

"Leggo!"

"Delhi, my esteemed fatheaded.

Bunter!" said the nabob, shaking the Owl of the Remove again.

"Wake up!"

Bunter opened his eyes.

He blinked quite furiously at the face of the Nabob.

"You beast! Leggo! Let a fellow snooze!"

"My esteemed idiotic Bunter—"

"Shut up!"

Billy Bunter closed his eyes again. Evidently the Owl of the Remove took it for granted that his fat leg was being pulled again. But the other fellows had followed Colonel Wharton out of the car now, and Hurree Jamset Ram Singh gave the sleeping beauty another shake.

"Bunter—"

The fat junior opened his eyes again and gave Hurree Singh a glare of concentrated ferocity.

"Can't you let a fellow sleep?"

"My esteemed Bunter, we have arrive-fully reached Delhi, and—"

"Take that, then!"

"Ow!" roared the nabob as Billy Bunter landed out with a fat fist.

Hurree Jamset Ram Singh "took" it. He had no choice about that. He took it on his dusky nose, and sat down in the carriage.

"Now leave a fellow alone!" growled Bunter.

"Ow!"

Hurree Jamset Ram Singh staggered to his feet.

The dusky nabob was one of the best-tempered fellows in the Greyfriars Remove. But the best of tempers was bound to fail under the strain of William George Bunter.

Bunter settled back to sleep again, apparently considering the incident closed. Two dusky hands grasped him.

"Ow! Wow!" roared Bunter. "You rotter, leggo! You—Oh! Ow! Wow! Yoooop!"

Bunter whirled along the carriage in the sinewy grasp of the nabob of Bhanipur. He hardly realised whether he was on his head or his heels as he was whirled along.

He went out upon the platform with swoop.

Bump!

Bunter sat down.

He sat and roared. Harry Wharton & Co. burst into a roar, though of a different kind.

"Ha, ha, ha!"

"Ow! Wow! Yooop!'" roared Bunter. "My hat! I—I'll—I'll slaughter him! I—I—I'll—?

"Bunter!"

Colonel Wharton rapped out the word.

"Ow! Yes! Ow!" gasped Bunter.

"I'm hurt!"

"Be quiet!"

"Oh, my hat!"

Bunter blinked at the colonel, almost overcome with indignation.

"You fat duffer!" growled Johnny Bull. "Did you want to stop in the train and be shunted into a siding?"

Bunter blinked round him.

"Oh! Is this Delhi?" he stuttered.

"Did you think it was Clapham Junction?" asked Bob Cherry.

"Ha, ha, ha!"

"Beast!"

Billy Bunter picked himself up and rolled after the Greyfriars party.

77

Harry Wharton & Co. in Delhi!

"SHA'N'T want rocking to sleep tonight!" yawned Rob Cherry.

The Greyfriars fellows were tired after their long railway journey from Bombay. After supper in the Delhi hotel they were shown up to their room—a large, airy apartment, with windows looking on a court where graceful palm trees waved and swayed in the starlight. Pandy Din, the colonel's kitmutghar, was making up their beds, with the help of the peon servant. Billy Bunter sat down and watched them with a dissatisfied face. Travelling in India was not precisely like travelling in Western countries, and Bunter did not consider that he was receiving all the comforts and attentions to which so important a personage was entitled.

"I say, you fellows!" he grunted.

"Hallo, hallo, hallo! What's the grouse now?" inquired Bob.

Bunter blinked at him through his big spectacles.

"I'm not grousing, you beast!"

"Not grousing?" asked Bob in astonishment. "What's the matter, then? Are you ill?"

"Oh, really, Cherry—"

"Bunter didn't have enough supper," said Johnny Bull, shaking his head. "He ate only enough for a couple of elephants."

"Oh, cheese it!" said Bunter. "I've been thinking "What's the good of beginning that, at your time of life?" demanded Bob. "And what are you doing it with, anyhow? Gammon!"

"I've been thinking," roared Bunter. "Travelling in India seems to be quite different from travelling in England."

"It's a different country, you see," explained Bob. "Look on the giddy map and you'll see—"

"Oh, don't be an ass! It seems to be the custom here for travellers to take their own servants to wait on them in hotels," said Bunter. "Now, I don't see why this journey should be done on the cheap."

"Not when we've got a millionaire in the party," assented Bob. "You can send wireless telegrams from here, I believe. What about sending to Bunter Court for a few thousand pounds?"

Bunter did not need that suggestion.

"Inky's got lots of money," he said. "It was understood that my exes would be stood, of course. But I'm not the fellow to be under any obligation to anybody, I hope. Any small sums that are advanced to me will be settled later."

"Are you expecting a postal-order in Delhi?" asked Bob.

And the juniors chuckled. Since leaving Greyfriars School much less than usual had been heard of Billy Bunter's celebrated postal-order.

"As a matter of fact, I rather think that a good many remittances will have accumulated at Greyfriars by this time," said Bunter. "But of course, that's neither here nor there. We're in Delhi now.'

"The remittances are neither here nor there, that's a cert!" said Bob, and the juniors chuckled again.

"To come to the point," continued the Owl of the Remove, "we're travelling with only two servants. When I'm home for the holidays at Bunter Court I'm accustomed to a host of menials."

"Go it!"

"You fellows are not accustomed to the decencies of life," explained Bunter. "It's different with me. You can take a whack in that blinking kitmutghar and that blinking peon, but I think I'm entitled to a servant to myself. I think it's my due."

"Go ahead, then," said Bob. "I don't suppose the colonel would object; and there are plenty of native servants to be engaged if you want them. You've only to go to an agent—there's an agent's office at the Kashmir Gate, not very far from this hotel. Walk round in the morning and engage a whole army of 'em."

"That's what I was thinking of," said Bunter. "I don't want a lot of attention. I can rough it, I hope. But I shall want a servant to myself, and unless I have one I don't see how I can consent to come any farther with this party. It was my intention to see Inky safe to Bhanipur; but something is due to oneself, you know."

"You're not thinking of deserting us?" ejaculated Bob.

"I am!" said Bunter firmly. "Unless I'm treated decently I shall chuck the whole thing."

Bob looked round.

"Where's my handkerchief?" he asked. "Somebody lend me a hanky. I'm going to cry!"

"Ha, ha, ha!"

"This is a serious matter," hooted Bunter.

"My mistake. I wasn't aware of that," yawned Bob. "Now, if Bunter's done talking, you fellows, let's turn in. I'm sleepy, and Bunter's entertaining conversation makes me sleepier."

"The drowsiness is terrific," remarked Hurree Jamset Ram Singh.

"I say, you fellows, I haven't finished yet," howled Bunter.

"We'll turn in, all the same," said Harry Wharton, laughing. "You never have finished wagging your chin, you know."

"I mean what I say," said Bunter. "I'm going to engage a native servant in the morning, to look after me specially. If there's any mean and sordid argument about the fellow's wages I leave it to you. If you choose to swindle him I can't stop you."

"Oh, my hat!"

"That's final," said Bunter. "After brekker tomorrow I'm going round to the agent's to engage an ayah."

"A—a—a what?" ejaculated Wharton.

"An ayah," said Bunter.

"You're going to engage an ayah?" exclaimed the captain of the Remove, staring at Bunter blankly.

"Yes. Native servants here are called ayahs," Bunter condescended to explain. "I've picked up some Hindustani, you know. Not like you dense duffers; you never pick up anything! It's a just crackjaw language—"

"My esteemed Bunter—" murmured Hurree Singh.

"Idiotic, if you ask me," said Bunter. "Fatheadedest lingo I've ever heard, Inky! Blessed if I know how these natives understand one another! But I've picked up some of it all the same, and I happen to know that a native servant is called an ayah."

"Ha, ha, ha!"

"What are you cackling at?" demanded Bunter.

"Oh, my hat!" gasped Bob. "You're going to engage an ayah to look after you, are you?"

"Yes!" hooted Bunter.

"Well, perhaps you need one," said Bob. "Go ahead with it."

"Ha, ha, ha!"

"You can cackle!" said Bunter contemptuously. "Blessed if I ever saw such a jealous lot—jealous of a chap because he picks up a language that is too stiff for you! Yah!"

"You silly ass!" roared Johnny Bull. "Don't you know that—"

"Shush!" interrupted Bob Cherry. "Don't you begin teaching Bunter things, Johnny. Bunter's the man who knows."

Johnny Bull stared.

"But he can't engage an ayah!" he ejaculated.

"Why not?" chuckled Bob. "Bunter knows best. Let him get on with it, if it's his lofty will and pleasure."

"Oh!" said Johnny Bull, and he chuckled. "Well, let him, as he knows best."

"Ha, ha, ha!"

"I should jolly well think so!" said Billy Bunter warmly.

"Like your check, I think, Bull, to say that I can't engage an ayah. I can jolly well tell you that I'm going to engage an ayah first thing in the morning."

"Ha, ha, ha!" roared the juniors.

Bunter, in his wisdom, was aware that an ayah was a native servant. But it was obvious that he was not quite aware of the kind of native servant an ayah was.

However, the juniors did not enlighten him. Bunter was not in want of instructions, and the chums of the Remove did not give him the instruction he did not want.

"Let's turn in, now Bunter's done his funny turn," said Frank Nugent; and the juniors proceed to bed.

Pandy Din and the peon had gone. Colonel Wharton glanced in from the adjoining room.

"You boys comfortable here?" he asked.

"Quite, sir!" said Bob cheerily.

"The comfort is terrific, esteemed sahib."

The colonel smiled.

"Well, good night! Pandy Din will be on the watch; but I do not think we shall see anything tonight of the enemy. Good night!"

"Good night, sir!"

The colonel went back to his room. Harry Wharton & Co. settled down to sleep, but Bunter's deep snore was not immediately heard. Bunter had put in a great deal of sleep that day, so perhaps he was not quite so much in need of slumber as the other fellows. Five juniors had dropped off into slumber when the Owl's voice was heard.

"I say, you fellows—"

No answer.

"Wharton! I say, Wharton!"

Harry Wharton opened his eyes.

"What's that?"

"I was speaking, Wharton—"

"Don't, then!"

"Oh, really, Wharton—"

"Shurrup, and let a fellow go to sleep!" murmured the captain of the Remove drowsily.

"I can hear somebody moving outside the door!" said Bunter.

"Fathead!"

"I tell you I can hear somebody!" said Bunter. "If it's that beast Nally, Das, with a knife or something, I—"

"You ass, it's Pandy Din, the kitmutghar; he's watching."

"Oh!" said Bunter.

Wharton settled down again. Billy Bunter blinked to and fro in the shadows uneasily. Bunter had not forgotten his experiences in Bombay, when he had fallen into the hands of Nally Das.

"I say, Wharton—"

Silence.

"Bob, old man—I say, Bob—"

"Is that Bunter burbling?" came Bob Cherry's exasperated voice. "Can't you let a chap snooze? We weren't snoring all the way in the train, you fat differ, and we want to sleep o' nights. Shut up!'"

"That's all very well!" growled Bunter. "But if one of those kidnapping rotters was to butt in—"

"Nobody wants to kidnap you, anyway; they're after Inky: I jolly well wish somebody would kidnap you and shut you up somewhere safe!"

"Beast!"

"Dry up!"

"Old Wharton won't let me carry a revolver," said Bunter peevishly. "I don't feel safe without a revolver."

"We jolly well shouldn't be safe if you had one, fathead!"

"Yah!"

Bob Cherry slumbered again, and for a time there was silence. A soft breeze came in from the palm-gardens through the light curtains at the windows. Bunter closed his eyes, but opened them again.

"I say, you fellows—"

Deep breathing answered him. The Famous Five were all asleep.

"Wharton!" shouted Bunter.

"Oh, my hat!" Wharton awoke again

"Is that Bunter? What is it now, you fat duffer?"

"I was thinking of snakes—"

"What?"

"Are there any snakes in Delhi?"

"I wish there was a boa-constrictor, and that he had you in his inside!" said the captain of the Remove in concentrated tones. "If you wake me up again I'll scalp you!"

"Beast!"

Once more there was silence and, slumber. But a few minutes later the voice of William George Bunter shattered the silence.

"Wharton! I say, Wharton! Don't he a selfish beast. you know! Look here, Wharton—"

"Eh?" Harry Wharton's eyes opened.

"What about tigers?"

"Tigers?"

"Yes, tigers. Can't tigers get in here?"

Harry Wharton did not give his opinion on the possibility of tigers getting into a Delhi hotel. He groped for a boot.

Whiz!

"Oh, my hat! Yaroooh! Whoooop!"

"If you want another boot, Bunter I'll—"

"Ow! Wow! Beast!"

And the voice of Bunter was heard no more, and at long last there was peace.

78

A Morning in Delhi!

COLONEL WHARTON and the Famous Five breakfasted cheerily in the sunny morning at a table set among the palm-trees in the hotel gardens. Billy Bunter was not down yet; he was putting in a little extra sleep, doubtless feeling safe from makes and tigers in the day-time. The absence of Bunter did not detract from the cheeriness of the breakfast-party—rather the reverse. There were a good many guests at the Delhi hotel, and many were breakfasting in the garden in the cool of the morning, and innumerable native servants came and went, soft-footed and silent. Pandy Din waited on the juniors, with a cheery, brown face.

The juniors looked about them a good deal, interested in their new surroundings. At Bombay they had stayed in a bungalow, and since then they had been on the Indian railways, and this was their first experience of hotel life in India. It was a matter of keen interest to them, that they were in the ancient capital of the Mogul Empire, the city that had seen such desperate fighting in the days of the Mutiny. The Indian Mutiny, hitherto, had been little more than a section of history to the Greyfriars juniors, but now they were among some of its scenes—within a walk was the famous "Ridge" whence the British operations were carried on—close at hand were the places where the British troops had closed in desperate strife with the mutineer sepoys.

Naturally, the juniors wanted to see something of those historic scenes, as Colonel Wharton easily understood. Hurree Jamset Ram Singh had been in Delhi before, but it was new and strange to his comrades.

"You would like a trot through the city, of course?" the colonel remarked, with a smile, when breakfast was over.

"What-ho!" said Bob Cherry.

"I have to take Hurree Singh to call upon the Governor-General," said Colonel Wharton. "There will be no harm in your taking a stroll through the city, with Pandy Din to look after you. Keep together, and do not get out of Pandy Din's sight."

"We'll be jolly careful, uncle," said Harry.

And when the colonel and the nabob were gone, the four Removites of Greyfriars prepared for their "trot" through the historic city, to see as much as could, be seen in a day; for on the morrow early the party were resuming the journey by railroad to Lahore.

Bunter was not yet down, and Wharton went to call him. He found the Owl of the Remove snoring.

"Bunter!"

"Groogh! Gerrout!"

"We're going out—"

"Go, then, and be blowed!"

Wharton grinned.

"Don't you want to come, fathead? It's the only chance of seeing something of Delhi."

Bunter gave him a sleepy blink.

"Blow Delhi!" was his answer.

"It's an interesting place to see, you know."

"I don't think much of it! Buzz off!"

And the captain of the Remove buzzed off, leaving Bunter to have his sleep out.

"Isn't Bunter coning along?" asked Bob Cherry.

"No. He's putting in an extra snooze."

"Good old Bunter! There's times when a fellow feels quite obliged to him."

"Ha, ha, ha!"

And under the care of Pandy Din, the juniors walked out of the hotel and started their inspection of the Mogul city. Billy Bunter went on sleeping contentedly; and till quite a late hour in the morning his deep snore was to be heard. When Bunter turned out at last, and came down to breakfast, he found the peon, who informed him that the colonel sahib and the juniors and Pandy Din were gone. Bunter grunted.

"Just like the rotters, to clear off and leave a fellow on his own," he growled. "Well, give me some brekker, anyhow."

And a breakfast of considerable dimensions having been disposed of, Bunter ordered the peon to guide him to the agency at the Kashmir Gate, where he was quite resolved to engage the "ayah" for his own personal service—a much more important business, in Bunter's opinion, than seeing any of the sights of the great city.

In fact, nothing could transcend the importance of William George Bunter's personal comfort being properly looked after. Had the Viceroy of India taken that matter under his especial care, Bunter would doubtless have considered that an eminently proper state of affairs. At least, he was going to have a special native servant of his own, and Bunter had little doubt that the native would become devotedly attached to him—recognising what a great sahib Bunter was, and admiring him accordingly. He would be, in fact, the "faithful native" Bunter had read about in books—and Bunter was assured that he had personal qualities calculated to inspire faithfulness in a "native."

A faithful native who should rejoice in Bunter's smile, and tremble at his frown, was exactly what the Owl of the Remove wanted. As for the paltry question of the native's wages, Bunter was prepared to leave that little detail to be managed by his comrades. Sordid details of that kind were beneath him.

Bunter rolled importantly into the agency by the Kashmir Gate, where almost anything could be obtained, from railway tickets and rickshaws and round tours, to bearers and guides and timetables and telegrams. There were plenty of tourists going in and out, mostly with red faces under white topes, and some with guide-books under their arms. A drowsy young man sat up and took notice when Bunter inquired of him whether he could engage a native servant there, and he answered that Bunter could, but on learning that the native servant required was an ayah, the young man, with a jerk of his pen, directed Bunter to another department.

Bunter rolled into that department, and found it in charge of a fat, perspiring Eurasian gentleman, who fanned himself considerably, and inquired in a languid voice what Bunter wanted. The Eurasian gentleman being half-Hindu, did not really feel the heat so much as he pretended, but he felt that it was due to his European half to affect to be quite overcome by it.

"Yes," he told Bunter. "We can recommend a good ayah—a reliable ayah who has served in good families."

"That's what I want," said Bunter. "Nothing second-class for me, you know. And at once, you know."

The Eurasian gentleman fanned himself again, and opened a book. In that book he wrote Bunter's name, and the address of the hotel.

"Will convenience be consulted adequately if I shall send ayah to hotel this evening?"

"That's all right."

"The question of salary—"

"Never mind that," said Bunter. "If I get what I want, I don't mind paying well for it."

"Sahib can rely upon ayah recommended by this agency. We have on our list only those with worthy recommendations of good families."

"Good!" said Bunter.

And he rolled out satisfied.

Outside, he looked for the peon. He had not told the man to wait, but had expected him to do so. The peon, however, was gone.

"Cheeky native!" grunted Bunter.

But Bunter did not mind very much. He decided upon a stroll through the city on his own, and he rolled away cheerily, his fat face crimson with warmth, his spectacles gleaming under the shade of his topee. But it was very hot in the city by the Jumna, and Bunter was soon tired of exertion. He rolled down the famous Chandni Chauk, and looked round for somewhere to rest. Having found a seat under a big, shady tree, Bunter sat down, and for some minutes watched the people passing and re-passing. Finally his head nodded forward, and his eyes closed behind his big spectacles, and he dozed; and the snore of William George Bunter was added to the other interesting sounds of the ancient Mogul capital.

79

The Sleeping Beauty!

"LOTS to be seen here," remarked Bob Cherry.

"Oh, lots!" agreed Nugent.

"The lotfulness is terrific as Inky would say if he were with us," said Harry Wharton, with a smile.

"But it's jolly hot!"

"It is—it are!" agreed Johnny Bull.

Pandy Din had acted as guide to the juniors, and they had seen a great deal of the ancient capital on the banks of the Jumna. They had a look at the celebrated Jami Masjid, and at several of the scenes of the fighting in the old days of the Mutiny; and now they were strolling along the Chandni Chauk, feeling pleasantly tired. They stopped under the shade of a leafy tree out of the blaze of the sun, A low, rumbling sound came to their cars as they stopped, but they did not for the moment observe it. Bob Cherry mopped his brow, fanned himself with his sun-hat, and put it on again. Undoubtedly it was warm in Delhi.

"About time we got back to the hotel," said Wharton. "My uncle will be back before this with Inky."

Bob glanced up at the cloudless sky.

"Storm coming on, I fancy," he said.

"Don't you fellows notice the thunder in the distance?"

The juniors listened.

A whirring rumble came to their cars, distinctly like the muttering of distant thunder.

"I suppose they have sudden thunderstorms in this heat," remarked Harry Wharton.

Johnny Bull grinned.

"If we were in the old dorm at Greyfriars, I should say that that was Bunter snoring," he remarked.

"Ha, ha, ha!"

Wharton called to Pandy Din, who was standing like a bronze statue at a little distance, waiting the pleasure of the sahibs.

"Is there going to be a storm, Pandy Din?"

"I think not, sahib."

"Isn't that thunder?"

The kitmutghar grinned.

"No thunder, sahib—it is one that sleeps!" he said. He made a gesture towards a seat on the other side of the big shady tree.

"Oh!" said Bob, with a chuckle.

"Some giddy tourist taking a nap in the heat of the day."

"It is the little fat sahib!" said Pandy Din.

"What? Bunter?"

"Han, sahib."

The juniors moved round the big tree towards the seat and stared at the sleeper thereon.

It was William George Bunter.

He was fast asleep, with his fat little legs stretched out and his head leaning forward under his sun-hat. His snore was deep and incessant.

"My only hat!" ejaculated Bob. "It's Bunter, turned up like a bad penny! I wonder if he's engaged his giddy ayah yet?"

"Ha, ha, ha!"

Harry Wharton frowned.

"He ought not to be out alone," he said. "He knows jolly well that be ought not. The fathead should have come with us, or stayed in the hotel. He caused trouble enough at Bombay by wandering off on his own against orders."

"Let's gather him now," said Johnny Bull.

"Bunter!" shouted Bob.

Bunter did not wake.

He was tired and he was sleepy. He was plunged deep into slumber, dreaming of the tuckshop at Greyfriars and unlimited jam-tarts. Even Bob's stentorian shout did not awaken him.

"My hat! He's going it!" said Nugent.

Rumble, rumble. rumble!

Bunter certainly was going it. For quite a considerable distance along the Chandni Chauk is sonorous snoring could be heard. Tourists who passed him glanced round and stared; natives grinned at him; and Bunter slept and snored on unheeding.

The juniors contemplated the groaning Owl of the Remove with grinning faces.

Rumble, rumble, rumble!

"Better wake him," said Harry. "We can take him back with us. My uncle would be waxy if he knew that the fat idiot had wandered out by himself."

"Bunter!"

"Bunty!"

"Fathead!"

The Owl of the Remove snored on.

"Hold on a minute!" said Bob Cherry, with a grin, as Johnny Bull was about to grasp the fat junior by the shoulder and shake him.

"What's the game?" asked Johnny Bull.

"Only a little jest on the giddy 'sleeping beauty'!" said Bob. Evidently the torrid Indian climate had not undermined Bob's exuberant spirits. His chums watched him as he proceeded, a dusky grin dawning even on the bronze face of Pandy Din.

Bob had a copy of the "Allahabad Pioneer" under his arm. He detached the leaves of the newspaper and proceeded to pin them round Bunter's topee in a pyramidal form, changing the topee into an enormous conical top-hat of paper.

The remains of the newspaper he twisted into sections, attached to a estring like the tail of a kite.

The string was tied to the back of Bunter's hat.

Bob Cherry stood back to survey his handiwork with a satisfied grin. There was a chuckle from the other juniors.

"Bunter ought to make a sensation, got up like that!" said Bob. "Well, he likes making a sensation—he loves the limelight! He will get lots when he walks round Delhi like that."

In his tall paper hat, with the kite-tail stringing behind it, Billy Bunter strolled down the Chandni Chauk. A plump Eurasian, coming towards him, stared and then backed away, with alarm in his olive face. The expression on the fat gentleman's countenance plainly indicated that he had fallen in with a lunatic!

"Ha, ha, ha!"

Still Bunter was sleeping peacefully. But it was time for him to awaken now, and Bob prodded him vigorously.

"Groogh!"

Bunter's eyes opened behind his spectacles.

He sat up and blinked at the Greyfriars juniors.

"You fellows!" he ejaculated.

"We've found you, old fat bean!" said Bob cheerily. "Your snore guided us, you know. It can be heard for miles."

"Oh, really, Cherry—"

"You ought not to have come out alone, Bunter," said Harry Wharton.

"Rats!"

"You fat duffer—"

"I want you to get it into your head, Wharton, that I'm jolly well going to as I jolly well like!" said Bunter independently. "You may be captain of the Remove at Greyfriars, and no end of a big gun, in your own estimation—though I never thought much of you. But here you're nobody—less than nobody, in fact."

"You silly owl!" said Harry. "You may butt into danger, wandering around by yourself."

"Oh, rats! Those natives bagged the at Bombay because they wanted to find out where Inky was," said Bunter. "They know where Inky is now, and they've got their eye on him, so it's all right. I'm safe enough. Besides, I don't care for danger—not funky like you fellows!"

"Oh, my hat!"

"We're going back to the hotel now, with Harry. "You'd better come along with us, Bunter."

"Go and eat coke!"

"Look here—"

"Rats!"

Bunter had not awakened in a good temper.

"We could dribble him back," suggested Bob Cherry. "Let's kick him it turns, you know, and we'll got him as far as the hotel—if he doesn't burst!"

"Oh, really, Cherry—"

"Look here, Bunter," said Harry Wharton impatiently, "it's true that circumstances here are different from Bombay, but you know that my uncle does not want us to go out alone."

"Blow your under!"

"What?" roared Wharton.

"Too uppish for me," said Bunter. "I saved his life on the train when that native, Nally Das, was after him. It he grateful? Not he! I've jolly well saved all your lives, one way or whether! Especially

Inky's. You're an ungrateful lot! You even keep me sort of money! There's going to be a sordid argument about the wages of my ayah—I know that!"

Wharton jumped.

"You haven't really engaged an ayah, you fathead?"

"I jolly well have!" said Bunter scornfully. "My ayah's coming to the hotel this evening to be taken on."

"Oh, my hat!"

"Ha, ha, ha!"

"You can cackle—even that native's cackling!" said Bunter, with a disdainful blink at the grinning face of Pandy Din. "Well, cackle as much as you like—and be blowed to you! I'm not under your orders, Wharton! You can go and eat coke! And I'll jolly well come back to the hotel when I jolly well like! see?"

And, to assert his independence, Billy Bunter rose and rolled away, giving the Greyfriars juniors a final disdainful blink as he went.

Harry Wharton & Co. gazed after him.

Bunter was blissfully unconscious of the change Bob Cherry's playful hands had made in his appearance help of the Indian newspaper.

In his tall paper hat, the kite-tail stringing behind him, his aspect was remarkable and striking, not to say extraordinary and amazing.

"Ha, ha, ha!"

A contemptuous snort came back from Bunter, and he rolled off down the Chandni Chauk, satisfied that he had put the cheeky juniors in their place, and satisfied with things generally.

A plump Eurasian gentleman, coming towards him, caught sudden sight of Bunter and jumped. The plump gentleman stopped, stared, and backed away, with alarm in his olive face. The expression on the Eurasian's countenance plainly indicated that he supposed that he had fallen in with a lunatic. Bunter blinked at him arrogantly and rolled on. A party of American tourists stopped to stare at him.

"Some guy, I guess!" Bunter heard one of them remark in nasal tones.

Bunter blinked at him disdainfully and rolled on, leaving the tourists staring andlaughing.

"On the whole, I think we're well out of a walk home with Bunter!" chuckled Johnny Bull. "It looks to me as if Bunter is going to make a sensation."

Bunter was taking one already.

There were plenty of people in the Chandni Chauk, and they all seemed interested in the Owl of the Remove. They stared, or grinned, or laughed, and some of then backed out of his way, obviously thinking that it was a case of sunstroke, or lunacy.

"It's too had!" said Harry Wharton, laughing.

"My dear chap, Bunter asks for these things," said Bob Cherry. "He ought to have come back with us. If he prefers to go alone he can go like that. Let's hook it; Bunter's getting a mob already."

"Ha, ha, ha!"

And the chums of the Remove walked away with Pandy Din, leaving William George Bunter to continue his sensational progress along the Chandni Chauk on his independent own.

80

Bunter Astonishes the Natives!

BILLY BUNTER was astonished.

It was true that he loved the limelight. Bunter never let a chance of the limelight like the sunbeams pass him by.

Still, in some ways it was possible to have too much of a good thing.

Bunter was getting too much now.

A distinguished-looking fellow like Bunter, handsome and, in fact, stately, might be expected to attract a second glance. Bunter realised that, and did not, of course, mind. It was natural—in Bunter's opinion—for the male sex to glance at him with envy, and the gentle sex with admiration in their glad eyes.

But even Bunter, with all his fatuous self-satisfaction could not think that it was admiration he was exciting now. He was getting much more attention than he was accustomed to, but it really did not seem to be of the admiring sort.

People looked, and looked again, and turned round their heads to look a third time. Native boys gathered to follow him. Possibly they supposed that Bunter was some kind of a showman, and was going to give a performance. Little black and brown and bronze urchins of all ages and sizes gathered in the wake of Billy Bunter, and he found himself leading quite an army as he turned out of the Chandni Chauk and headed for the hotel.

Bunter couldn't understand it.

There were plenty of things that Bunter never could understand, but this was the greatest problem of all. It beat him.

Certainly if there had been a looking-glass at hand and he could have seen himself he would have understood.

There were all sorts of costumes in the streets of Delhi—many of them strange and remarkable. But it is safe to say that there was no pedestrian abroad that day as remarkable as William George Bunter. A fellow who walked abroad with a conical paper hat nearly two feet high, and a kite's tail dangling down his back, would have attracted attention anywhere, in any city from China to Peru.

Delhi, like all Eastern cities, swarms with idlers and loafers with nothing particular to do, and quite a large number of them acquired an interest in this remarkable sahib, who was apparently either mad or playing an extraordinary trick. They walked round and after Bunter, watching him, and the mob of sightseers grew and grew. Many voices called out to him; but as they spoke in the native tongues Bunter did not comprehend. He would have been startled to learn that he was looked on by some of his followers as a new kind of fakir; by others as a conjurer, or a showman; and by still others as a wandering lunatic.

Bunter marched on haughtily, his fat little nose turned up in contempt, and his fat red face growing more and more crimson. Limelight to this extent was neither grateful nor comforting.

"The silly owls!" he murmured, in perplexity. "Anybody would think I'd landed on a cannibal island, where Englishman had never been seen before? There are lots of other white men here—and they seem to stare at me as much as the natives! What the thump does it mean?"

A big Punjabi policeman stopped and stared at Bunter, and stepped into his path. Bunter halted.

"Sahib!" murmured the policeman deprecatingly.

"What do you want?" snapped Bunter.

"If the sahib suffering from sunstroke—"

"What?"

"If it being sunstroke—"

"Don't you be a cheeky ass!" said Bunter, and he rolled round the policeman and progressed, leaving the big policeman who would have been willing to take him to the hospital, where sunstroke cases are promptly treated. But the sahib was entitled to have his own way. Even a fat little sahib in a tall paper hat and a kite's tail was a sahib.

Bunter rolled on, quickening his pace: He desired very much to leave his army behind.

But they were not to be left. They followed on, grinning and chattering in many tongues, and their numbers grew and grew. It seemed to Bunter that all the idlers in Delhi were gathering in his wake. An American tourist stared at him and tapped him on the arm.

"Say, what's the game?" he inquired.

Bunter blinked at him.

"Eh?"

"Is it a bet?" asked the Transatlantic gentleman, staring at Bunter through his horn-rimmed glasses.

"Is what a bet?" snapped Bunter. "What do you mean?"

"I guess I mean—are you doing it for a wager?"

"Doing what?" shrieked Bunter.

"This stunt!"

"Go and eat coke!" said Bunter, and he pushed past the tourist and rent on his way.

"Waal, carry me home to die!" said the Transatlantic gentleman. "This is the queerest stunt I've seen in India so far. This beats it!"

Bunter rolled on, to an accompaniment of laughter and chatter. He was more than fed-up, and he looked round for a vehicle to finish his journey.

A carriage was crawling by, with a native driver looking for a hire, and Bunter waved a fat hand at him as a signal. The native driver stared back and seemed to hesitate. He was looking for a passenger, but probably not for so remarkable a passenger as W. G. Bunter in his present guise.

"Stop!" shouted Bunter. "Here!"

The man drew up the vehicle, with some reluctance in his manner. Bunter blinked angrily at his staring, uneasy face.

"Speak English!" he snapped.

"I am speaking English," said the driver. "Desires the sahib to be drive to hospital?"

"Hospital?" gasped Bunter. "No, You idiot! I want to be driven to the Palm Hotel."

Bunter's numerous followers gathered round. Two or three dozen of them entered into conversation with the carriage driver at once, amid gurgles of laughter. The remarks that were made upon Bunter would have made his hair curl, could he have understood any of them. The mob seemed to be satisfied by this time that he was not a fakir, or a conjurer, or a street dancer, and had settled that he was insane. Sunstroke seemed to be a reasonable explantation of Bunter's conduct.

That he did not know how he was got up was, of course, not likely to be guessed.

"What's the fare?" demanded Bunter suspiciously.

"Twenty rupee."

"You mean two!" snarled Bunter.

"Meaning twenty," said the driver calmly. The native did not mean to carry a lunatic about at the ordinary fare.

Bunter hesitated a moment; and then it occurred to him that he could leave the question of the fare to be settled by somebody else, once he was safe at the hotel.

"All right!" he growled.

He stepped into the open cartilage.

The driver whipped up his horse end Bunter sat in state, with a burning face under his topee, crowned by the high paper that.

"Quicker!" he called in the driver. "Leave that gang of cheeky natives behind. See?"

The whip cracked again.

But the cheeky natives were not to be left behind. Two or three of the younger sort clambered behind the carriage and hung on; others trotted, to keep pace. The Delhi loafers were not to be deprived of this unusual entertainment by so simple an expedient as taking a carriage; and a breeze from the Jumma fluttered out the kite's tail behind Bunter with striking effect.

The fat junior was glad when the hotel was reached. He caused quite a sensation there.

Men smoking their cigars on the veranda jumped up to stare at him. Native waiters, and bearers, and kitmutghars stared and cackled. Bunter almost wondered whether he was on his head or his heels by this time. Never had he created so immense a sensation in his fat career.

From a window above, five juniors locked out, and roared with laughter as they spotted Bunter in the carriage. The colonel and Hurree Jamset Ram Singh had returned from the Governor-General's palace some time before Harry Wharton & Co. had arrived at the hotel, and the nabob was with his chums again. Hurree Singh's dark eyes almost started from his head at the sight of Bunter.

"The esteemed and idiotic Bunter is quite potty," he said. "Look at him, my worthy chums."

"Ha, ha, ha!"

"Bunter! And he's still got it on!" shrieked Bob Cherry. "Oh, my hat? He's got half Delhi after him!"

"Ha, ha, ha!"

"Hallo, hallo, hallo! There's the colonel!" said Bob. "He doesn't seem to think it's funny. He's the only one that doesn't."

"Except Bunter," grinned Nugent.

"Ha, ha, ha!"

Colonel Wharton had been smoking a cigar on the veranda with some old acquaintance he had encountered in Delhi. The sight of Bunter made the colonel jump; but it did not make him laugh. He strode out to the carriage at once.

"Bunter!" he exclaimed. "What does this mean?"

Bunter blinked at him. "Blessed if I know!" he stuttered. "All these scoundrels have followed me from the Chandni Chauk. I don't know why."

"Are you mad?" boomed the colonel.

"M-in mad?" stuttered Bunter.

"Is it sunstroke, or what?"

"What do you mean?" yelled Buster.

"The question is, what do you mean?" snorted the colonel. "How dare you get yourself up in that ridiculous manner and parade the streets? If you are not out of your senses what do you mean? Do you wish to make an absurd show of yourself to a mob of natives?" Bunter gasped.

"What what—I don't understand. What—what the thump do you mean? What have I done?"

"Surely it is not possible that you have been drinking!" exclaimed the colonel, aghast.

"D-d-drinking?" stuttered Bunter.

"Take it off at once!"

"Eh?"

"Take it off!" thundered the colonel.

"Take what off?" spluttered the Owl of the Remove helplessly. He wondered whether all Delhi had gone mad, the colonel included.

"That ridiculous paper hat."

"Pip-pip-paper hat?"

"Take it off, you absurd young ass!"

"How can I take off what I haven't got on?" shrieked Bunter. "I think you must be potty. I'm not wearing a paper hat, am I? I'm wearing my topee, same as usual. Are you blind?"

Colonel Wharton stared at him speechlessly. How Bunter could be wearing an enormous paper hat without knowing it was a mystery to him. He grabbed at the paper hat, but it did not come off. It was pinned securely round the topee. He jerked it of the topee.

Then Bunter saw what most of Delhi had already seen. He stared at the conical paper hat attached to his topee with bulging eyes.

"What—what—what's that?" he stuttered.

He blinked at the paper hat and the kite's tail like a fellow in a dream. Even Bunter realised that in that guise he had been calculated to cause a sensation in Delhi, or anywhere else.

"Is it possible that you did not know that this was on your head?" demanded the amazed colonel.

"Beast!" roared Bunter.

"What! You dare to call me—"

"I don't mean you. I mean that other beast—one of those beasts! They must have done this when they found me asleep on the seat under the tree!" yelled Bunter. "I was taking a nap when those rotters found me, and they must have fixed me up like that while I was asleep. Beats!"

"Good gad!" said the colonel.

"Ha, ha, ha!" came in a roar from the window above. Colonel Wharton glanced up at five laughing faces. Bunter shook a fat fist at them.

The colonel's stern face broke into a grin. He realised that the ancient Mogul capital of India had been the scene of a jape more suited to the Remove passage at Greyfriars.

"Well, well, get in, Bunter!" he said "You have attracted enough attention I think, for one day. Get into the hotel and stay there. Pandy Din, pay the driver. Go in at once, Bunter!"

Billy Bunter was too glad to roll into the building and hide his blushes. For once that limelight had palled on the Owl of the Remove, and he was glad to get out of it.

81

Bunter's Ayah!

STARS glimmered in the dark blue sky; through the scented dusk "soft breeze" came from the wide water of the Jamuna. In the palm garden of the Delhi hotel Harry Wharton & Co. rested in long cane chairs, and took their case after their evening meal. Through the dusk of the gardens cigar ends glimmered red, from strolling smokers. Here and there was a murmur of voices and a drowsy hum of insects. The Famous Five were feeling very content and cheery, as they sat and sipped coffee or sherbet, and chatted idly. Colonel Wharton had left them there. He had business on hand connected with the journey on the morrow northward to Lahore. In the distance hovered Pandy Din, the kitmutghar, brown and good-tempered, with a keen eye open. So far, the Greyfriars party had seen nothing of their enemies since their arrival at Delhi, and they wondered whether Nally Das, the desperate emissary of the Rajah Baji Rao, had given up his task of kidnapping the nabob and preventing him from reaching his home at Bhanipur. Certainly Nally Das could not have shown himself in Delhi without being taken by the police; his attempt upon Colonel Wharton's life in the train had booked him for a term of years at the Andaman islands, if he was caught. But when Bob Cherry suggested that Baji Rao's agents had given up the thing as a "bad job," Hurree Jamset Ram Singh shook his dusky head.

"My esteemed relative, Baji Rao, will not allow me to arrive safefully at Bhanipur if he can preventfully stop me," he said. "Once I am in the palace of my fathers, the worthy and disgusting rascal will be played out, like a tooth that is drawn. He will never be nabob in my place, if once I secure fully join my uncle, the Jam Bahadur. But in Delhi we have nothing to fear—the excellent colonel has the aid of the police, and the esteemed rascals are looked for. But when we leave—" Harry Wharton nodded, as the nabob pursed.

"They're getting desperate," he said. "At first they tried to kidnap Inky—now they've gone further, and my uncle came very near to falling under Nally Das' knife on the train from Bombay. I think we shall see something more of them after we leave Delhi. And when we are beyond Lahore, we shall be in wild country—Bhanipur is rather off the map, isn't it, Inky?"

"The excellent railroad does not run reachfully to Bhanipur," said Hurree Singh, "and in the hills on the frontier there are dacoits—"

"What are dacoits?" asked Bunter.

"Robbers, my esteemed Bunter."

"Fancy having a brush with Indian dacoits!" said Bob cheerily. "Worth coming all this way for, what?"

"We shall be all right if the colonel will let me have my revolver," said Bunter peevishly. "You can rely on me to protect you—as usual."

"If that's all we have to rely on, old fat bean, our number's up!" said Job, with a chuckle.

"Ha, ha, ha!"

"I've seen you through safe so far," said Bunter. "Didn't I save Inky at Marseilles? Didn't I save time on the steamer in the Mediterranean? Didn't I butt in at the right moment when Nally Das was after the colonel on the Bombay train? What?"

"You've come in useful a few times, by a series of accidents," said Johnny Bull. "Not in any other way. Can it!"

"Oh, really, Bull—"

"Give your chin a rest, old fat man!"

"I'm accustomed to ingratitude," said Bunter bitterly. "After all I've done for you, all you can think of is playing tricks on a fellow when he's asleep–"

"Ha, ha, ha!"

"Yah!"

Billy Bunter relapsed into indignant silence. He had not yet forgotten the incident of the paper hat and the kite's tail; and the comic side of that incident was quite lost on him. He groped in his pocket and drew out a packet of cigarettes, and put one in his mouth. The Famous Five looked at him—whereupon Bunter lighted the cigarette with a flourish. Colonel Wharton was absent, and it was a case of the mouse playing while the cat was away.

"You fat duffer," said Bob. "Chuck that away!"

"Rats," said Bunter contemptuously. "I'll stand you a fag all round, you fellows, if you like. Why not? No masters or prefects here to rag a fellow. Be men, like me!"

"Fathead!"

Billy Bunter snorted, and smoked his cigarette. He hoped that the guests sauntering in the dusky gardens would notice that he was a man of the world, a fellow who knew his way about, and not an ordinary schoolboy like the rest of the party. If anyone noticed Bunter, however, it was probably not with admiration.

A Hindu waiter came along the garden, looking round, and stopped at the little table round which the juniors sat, and on which stood their coffee-cups, He salaamed to the young sahibs.

"Sahib Bunter—"

"Hallo!" said Bunter carelessly.

"One ayah come and saying to see Sahib Bunter."

Bunter sat up.

"That's right," he said. "I was expecting an ayah. I engaged one this morning at the agency."

The waiter peered at him.

"Young sahib engage ayah?" he asked.

"Yes; it's all right."

The Hindu waiter did not seem to think, somehow, that it was all right. He appeared puzzled.

"Me showing ayah to garden to see Sahib Bunter?" he asked at length.

"Yes, and don't dawdle."

"Han, sahib."

The waiter disappeared, and Billy Bunter gave his companions a lofty, vaunting look. They were all grinning.

"You can cackle," he said, "but I've engaged a native servant, and

I'm jolly well taking him with me when we leave Delhi tomorrow, see?"

"Him!" murmured Wharton.

"The harmfulness is not terrific," gurgled Hurree Singh.

Bunter blinked at them, not understanding.

"If there's any sordid question about the man's wages, I shall decline to discuss the matter," he said. "It was understood—clearly understood—that my exes would be paid, if I consented to come to India to protect Inky. I shall not condescend to enter into any mean argument about money."

"My esteemed Bunter—"

"It's up to you, Inky," said the Owl of the Remove. "I shall expect you to stand the ayah's salary."

"My worthy and ludicrous Bunter, if you shall take the esteemed ayah with you, I shall please fully pay the wages."

The juniors chuckled. They did not think that Bunter would want to take the ayah with him—when he saw the ayah.

"Well, that's decent of you, Inky, at least," said Bunter. "Of course, it's up to you. Hallo, who's this?"

The Hindu waiter was returning, and he was showing the way to the juniors' table, to a stout lady dressed in white, rather voluminous garments, with a long white veil over her head and face. She was a native lady, and rather fat, and of uncertain years. The waiter spoke to her in his own tongue, indicating Bunter, and retired, leaving the plump lady bowing gracefully to the perplexed junior, while Harry Wharton & Co. tried hard to suppress their smiles.

"What do you want?" asked Bunter.

"I come to see you, sahib."

Bunter blinked at her. Bunter would not have been surprised to receive the "glad eye" from an Indian damsel; he, at least, was quite well aware what an attractive fellow he was. But this good dame was not less than forty, so it could scarcely be a case of the "glad eye." Bunter could not guess what it meant.

"You came to see me?" he asked.

"Han, sahib."

"Who are you, then?" demanded Bunter.

"Name being Aoudha," said the visitor. "I come from the agency by the Kashmir Gate."

"Oh! I see," said Bunter. "About the ayah. Aren't they sending my ayah, this evening after all?"

Through the veil, the features of the dame could not be very clearly seen. But the juniors could see that she looked puzzled.

"Yes, sahib! Ayah being send," she answered.

"Where is he, then?" asked Bunter.

"I being ayah."

Bunter jumped.

"You!" he ejaculated.

"I, Aoudha, being ayah," said the visitor, bowing and smiling. "I am recommend by honourable Major Smith, and honourable Miss Wilkins, with writings in English. I serve for rupees one hundred a month, and am customed to care of children."

"Children!" said Bunter faintly.

The ayah eyed him. No doubt she had expected to find the Sahib Bunter a gentlemen of much more advanced years than the Owl of the Remove, and a married gentleman with a family. Otherwise, it was difficult to guess what he wanted with an ayah, an ayah's duties being those of a nurse, or lady's maid, or both combined.

The ayah was not likely to guess that Bunter, in his sublime ignorance and self-satisfaction, had engaged an ayah thinking that "ayah" was a manservant.

"But the little sahib is a boy," said Aoudha. "He is not married?"

"Married!" stuttered Bunter.

"The sahib do not marry, as boys, like the people of Hindustan," said the ayah.

"Oh, my hat!"

"But perhaps the sahib is sick, and needs the care of an ayah?" asked Aoudha. "It is a new duty to me, but I am willing. I have nursed the sick before. But for that I shall ask one hundred and twenty rupee."

Bunter blinked at the ayah, and blinked at the juniors, who were almost suffocating in their efforts to preserve their gravity.

"What does she mean, you fellows?" stuttered the Owl of the Remove.

"What does she say she's an ayah for?"

"She is an ayah, fathead!" gasped Bob Cherry.

"Rats! Isn't an ayah a man servant?" demanded Bunter.

"Ha, ha! No."

"An ayah is of the gentle and feminine variety," explained Hurree Jamset Ram Singh.

"Gammon! If that's so, why couldn't you tell a fellow?" snorted Bunter.

"You wouldn't let us tell you!" chuckled Bob. "You knew best, you know. Don't you always know best?"

"Ha, ha, ha!"

The ayah looked puzzled.

"The sahib is satisfy?" she asked. "I showing sahib my writings in English, recommend from honourable major and honourable miss. Is it to be engage?"

"Oh, no!" gasped Bunter.

With all his desire for the services of a faithful attendant, Bunter did not want a woman-servant. Even Bunter drew the line at engaging a lady's-maid or nurse for himself.

Aoudha frowned.

"But why?" she asked. "Sahib was not yet looked at my writings, and he say no. Why he say no?"

"I—I—I—" stuttered Bunter.

"Tell her it's a mistake, and that you're only a blithering idiot that doesn't know his way about," suggested Johnny Bull.

"Ha, ha, ha!"

"You answering me," said the ayah, showing signs of anger, which was not surprising, in the circumstances. I have best of recommend from honourable major and distinguished English miss, likewise recommend from Agency. All duties I shall perform to satisfaction. Speak English, and no objection to leaving India. You answering me why you say no?"

"Oh, crumbs!" gasped Bunter. "You—you see I—I— It's all a mistake! I—I don't want you! P-p-please go way!"

"Why you no want?"

"Oh dear! Tell the waiter to come back and shift her, you fellows?"

Aoudha's eyes flashed through her veil.

"You no pukka sahib!" she exclaimed. "I make one journey to see sahib, I pay money for rickshaw, and sahib say there is mistake. But you engaging ayah at agency, and there is no mistake. You engaging me, and I coming. No mistake!"

"I—I tell you—" gasped Bunter.

"You no wanting ayah?"

"No!" stuttered the hapless Owl of the Remove. "That's it, I—I don't want an ayah! Good-evening!"

"You wasting by time and money on rickshaw and you no want?"

"That's it! Goodbye!"

"If I were that ayah," said Johnny Bull, "I'd jolly well smack his cheeky head!"

"Ha, ha, ha!"

The ayah looked as if she were going to act upon that tip from Johnny Bull. Naturally, she was extremely annoyed, being only able to conclude that she was the victim of a thoughtless practical joke on the part of an inconsiderable schoolboy.

Bunter jumped up in alarm as the plump lady moved towards. him. He did not like the gleam of her black eyes through the veil; still less did he like the swing of her plump hand towards him.

"Here, you keep off!" he roared. "Keep her off, you fellows! Oh, my hat!" Bunter dodged round the effectible. "I say, you follows, back me up! Keep her off while I hook it!"

"Ha, ha, ha!" roared the juniors.

Billy Bunter fairly bolted, streaking for the hotel buildings as if his fat life depended on it.

"Ha, ha, ha!"

Harry Wharton jumped up, and interposed as the ayah was pursuing Bunter. "Hold on, madam!" he exclaimed. "We'll make it all right. You shall lose nothing by coming here. That fat duffer made a mistake—"

"No mistake! He engage ayah—I being good ayah—" Wharton dragged.

"Yes, yes, but—" Wharton dragged handful of rupees from his pocket. "Will that make it right, madam?"

Apparently it made it right, for the ayah smiled serenely at once. "You pukka sahib," she said.

And having been indemnified for her loss of time and the expense of her rickshaw by twenty rupees, the plump dame bowed and retired. The juniors were glad enough to see her depart. Bunter had vanished into the hotel, and retired to the juniors' room—extremely uneasy lest the ayah should pursue him there and insist upon being engaged, or smack his head in lieu of an engagement.

"Good old Bunter!" chuckled Bob Cherry.

"The fat ass!" said Harry. "It would have served him right to let him deal with the ayah himself. She looked as if she had a temper."

Hurree Jamset Ram Singh grinned.

"My esteemed chums, a wheezy good idea has occurred to me brainfully," he said. "The worthy and ridiculous Bunter insisted upon engaging an ayah and he does not know that the ayah has taken her honourable departure. Suppose the ludicrous ayah follows Bunter to his room, and insists upon attending on his honourable person?"

"But she's gone," said Nugent.

"It is easy to obtain a white dress and a white veil, my esteemed chum, and the esteemed short-sighted Owl would not see any difference."

The juniors stared at Hurree Singh for a moment, and then burst into a roar.

"Ha, ha, ha!"

"Good egg!" chortled Bob Cherry. "He would have an ayah, and he wouldn't be happy, till he got it! Let him keep it now he's got it!

"Ha, ha, ha!"

The juniors left their coffee unfinished. Pandy Din was despatched to secure an ayah's dress, and in the kitmutghar's room Hurree Jamset Ram Singh put it on. Billy Bunter was not finished with his ayah yet!

82

The Ayah on Duty!

"I—I SAY, you fellows!"

Billy Bunter was sitting on his bed in a very uneasy frame of mind, and he blinked nervously at the juniors as they came in. Wharton and Bob Cherry, Nugent and Johnny Bull had come up to bed, but the nabob was not with them. The nabob was still putting some final touches to his ayah's attire, with the help of Pandy Din. "I—I say, is she gone?"

"Your ayah?" asked Bob.

"She isn't my ayah!" hooted Bunter. "I don't want an ayah, and I'm jolly well not going to have an ayah! I—I thought an ayah was a manservant, you silly idiots, like a kitmutghar."

"Ha, ha, ha!"

"You ought to have told me that an ayah was a blinking female!" hooted Bunter.

"You wouldn't let us tell you!" chuckled Bob. "Now you've engaged an ayah, you're for it. You can't expect ayahs to come along here and be satisfied when they're told it was a mistake. Be reasonable. Besides, she says she's accustomed to children, and you need looking after like a baby. You admit that, Bunter?"

"No, I don't!" roared Bunter.

"Well, there it is, whether you admit it or not. You can't engage a native servant and sack her at a moment's notice without any cause of complaint."

"D-d-do you mean to say she isn't gone?"' gasped Bunter.

"I don't know where she is; but as we came upstairs, I saw somebody who looked jolly like an ayah."

"Oh, crumbs!"

"I dare say you'll find her useful, Bunter," said Harry Wharton laughing. "She looked a hefty sort of ayah, and being accustomed to children—"

"Smack him, ayah!" chortled Bob Cherry. "A jolly good smacking is what he wants!" Billy Bunter made a jump to escape, but the ayah—with a very powerful grasp- jerked him back. Smack! "Yarooooh!" wailed the Owl of the Remove. "Leave off! I—I I won't be put to bed by a woman!"

"Beast! She doesn't know which is our room," gasped Bunter.

"I suppose she'll inquire, if she's looking for her employer," said Johnny Bull.

"I'm not her employer!" shrieked Bunter.

"You are, old man—you are! You engaged her at the agency this morning," chuckled Bob. "You can't deny that you engaged an ayah."

"I—I thought—"

"What you thought isn't evidence, that's good law," said Bob. "Dash it all, we all advised you not to engage an ayah; and you would have your own way. What are you grousing about?"

"I won't pay her any wages—I won't pay her an anna—I—she won't stay without wages!" gasped Bunter.

"Inky will see to that; you told him it was up to him."

"Ha, ha, ha!"

"You—you beasts!" gasped Bunter. "Mean to say that I've got to have a blinking ayah if I don't want a blinking ayah?"

"You will have to settle that with the ayah. If I were an ayah I wouldn't be sacked like that for nothing."

There was a tap at the door. Pandy Din put in a grinning face.

"Ayah ask to see honourable sahib Bunter."

There was a yell from Bunter.

"Keep her out! She can't come in here."

"What rot!" said Bob. "An ayah's duty is to put the children to bed. She's going to do her duty, now you've engaged her."

Bunter spluttered.

"You—you—you awful rotter! You can let her put you to bed if you like she's not going to put me to bed!"

"I haven't engaged her," chortled Bob Cherry. "If I engaged an ayah, I should expect her to do her duty, which would be putting me to bed."

"Ha, ha, ha!" shrieked the juniors.

Bunter jumped up and made a rush for the door, with the intention of locking out the ayah. But he was too late. A figure in white, with a rather thick white veil descending over head and face, sailed into the room. Billy Bunter backed away.

"Sahib Bunter!" said a soft voice from under the veil.

"Go away!" gasped Bunter.

"Little fat sahib engage ayah—"

"No!" yelled Bunter. "I don't want an ayah! Turn her out, you fellows. Shove her out of the room. Never mind if you hurt her."

"Dear man, we're not handling a lady to please you," said Wharton. "You engaged an ayah, and here's a giddy ayah. What's the trouble?"

"Beast! Turn her out! Call the manager! Call the khansama! Call the porters! Oh dear!"

"Ha, ha, ha!"

"I being good ayah, and putting the little fat sahib to bed," purred the soft voice under the veil.

"No!" yelled Bunter.

He backed away from the ayah–till he came in contact with the edge of his bed, and sat down suddenly. As Bunter sprawled on the bed, the ayah kneeled down before him, and began to take off his shoes.

"Go away!" yelled Bunter.

"No going away!" purred the ayah. "You engaging me, and I doing duty. If you no liking me, you send me away tomorrow."

"Take her away, you fellows!"

"Ha, ha, ha!"

"I'll jolly well kick you if you touch me!" raved Bunter. "I won't be put to bed! Keep off!"

And in sheer desperation, Bunter lunged out with his foot. But the ayah was on the look-out. A brown hand grasped Bunter's ankle and twisted it aside, with a grip that was very powerful. Bunter gave a howl. His fat ankle felt as if it had been in a grip of steel. "You behaving yourself better with a lady!" said the ayah severely."

"You being bad boy, I smacking you."

"Oh lor'!"

"Smack him, ayah!" chortled Bob Cherry. "A jolly good smacking is what he wants. You see, he's a wilful kid, and doesn't know his own mind. First he wants an ayah, and then he doesn't want an ayah. I don't believe he really knows what he does want."

"I looking after him, and if he is bad, smacking him!"

"Ha, ha, ha!"

Bunter's boots were off now, and the ayah began to drag off his socks. The socks came off, and then the ayah began to remove his collar and tie. Bunter made a jump to escape; but the ayah—with a very powerful grasp—jerked him back, and then :

Smack!

"Yaroooooooh!"

"Ha, ha, ha!" yelled the juniors.

"Oh, crumbs! Oh dear! Go away!

Leave off! I—I—I— won't be put to bed by a woman I" wailed Bunter.

"Ha, ha, ha!"

"I say, you fellows, make her go away!"

"Ha, ha, ha!"

Bunter's jacket came off, and then his purple cummerbund. Then the ayah unbuckled his belt. Certainly, a genuine ayah would not have been likely to proceed thus; but Bunter knew nothing about the manners and customs of ayahs, and he had not the remotest idea that the thick veil concealed the grinning features of Hurree Singh.

"Leave off!" he gasped, clutching at his trousers with desperate hands. "I—I—I— Help! Help!"

"Ha, ha, ha!"

The communicating door of Colonel Wharton's room opened, and the kind, bronzed face of the colonel looked in.

"You boys seem very merry tonight," he said. "Why—what—who—" The Colonel stared blankly at the ayah.

Bunter gave a howl. "Make her go away, sir! Turn her out! Ow!"

"What on earth—" exclaimed the astonished colonel.

"It's Bunter's ayah," said Bob Cherry, wiping away his tears. "Bunter engaged an ayah this morning, thinking that an ayah was a manservant."

"Good gad!"

"The ayah came, and Bunter sacked her on the spot," said Bob. "He didn't seem to want her after all."

"Ha, ha, ha!"

"So, as we thought he was entitled to an ayah, we rigged up Inky for the job," said Harry Wharton.

"What?" yelled Bunter.

The ayah threw her veil aside. The grinning dusky features of Hurree Jamset Ram Singh were disclosed.

"Inky!" he stuttered.

"My esteemed self," said the nabob, cheerily.

"Ha, ha, ha!"

"You—you—you japing idiot!" roared Bunter.

Colonel Wharton broke into a laugh.

"I think you are the most ridiculous boy I have ever seen, Bunter," he said. "But really, you should not play these tricks on a lad so obtuse as Bunter."

"Oh, really, sir—"

"You had better go to bed now," said the colonel, laughing, and he went back to his room.

Hurree Jamset Ram Singh threw off the ayah's dress. Billy Bunter eyed him as if he could eat him.

"You—you cheeky rotter!" he gasped, "Pulling my leg all the time?"

"That's actually dawned on him!" said Bob Cherry. "What a brain!"

"Ha, ha, ha!"

"Beast!"

And Billy Bunter turned in, glowering with wrath, but considerably relieved to find that he was not, after, all, to have the attentions of an ayah.

83

Awful!

DELHI was left behind by the Greyfriars party the next morning. Billy Bunter, at least, was not sorry to quit the famous city of the Moguls; his adventures in Delhi had not proved grateful or comforting. Northward the express bore the party, by Saharunpore and Amritsar, and then on towards Lahore. Hurree Jamset Ram Singh's face wore cheery smiles as he drew nearer and nearer to his homeland.

To the other fellows of Greyfriars Bhanipur was a distant unknown spot, no more than a name; but to the nabob it was home, where his earliest years had been spent, and which he had never forgotten. In cheery tones the dusky junior told them about Bhanipur, which, according to his description, was the most delectable spot in the famous Land of the Five Rivers. And Harry Wharton & Co. were very keen to see that delectable kingdom of the hilly north. Even Billy Bunter detached his thoughts a little from sleep and tuck, and pictured himself swanking in a marble palace surrounded by bowing and admiring natives.

In a few days more the juniors were to see Bhanipur, and Inky's uncle, the Jam Vahadurmand, the wise old moonshee who had taught him his remarkable English; and the nabob promised them a tiger-hunt, and they quite thrilled at the thought of tracking the tiger in his native jungle.

But many a long mile lay as yet between them and the nabob's palace in the little hill-locked kingdom of Bhanipur. Although under the protection of the British Raj, Bhanipur was an independent State, and it was rather a new idea to the Co. to think of Inky as a "giddy monarch," as Bob described it, sitting in state upon a golden throne, and giving commands to innumerable guards and retainers.

Billy Bunter was quite startled to learn that it was in Inky's power, once he stood in his palace, to give orders to armed guards to "chop a fellow's head off." Certainly the good-natured and amiable nabob, known at Greyfriars as the best-tempered fellow in the Remove and a crack cricketer, did not seem much to resemble a dusky despot of the East. It. was not likely that there would be any chopping off of heads at Bhanipur under the rule of Hurree Jamset Ram Singh; and yet the juniors sometimes wondered a little whether they knew their Indian chum quite so well as they had supposed.

When he mentioned the Rajah Baji Rao, his ambitious kinsman who was seeking to rob him of his throne, the nabob's kindly face hardened, and a glitter came into his eyes, which savoured more of the East than of the West. And it was borne in upon the minds of the Co. that it was quite probable that there would be shedding of blood while they were the guests of their Indian chum in the mountain kingdom. Once at Bhanipur, Inky would come to grips with the disloyal kinsman whose emissaries had dogged him all the way to India, and whose attempts had shadowed the journey with incessant danger.

At Amritsar, where the train stopped, Billy Bunter laid in a supply of fruit and sticky cakes from the merchants who thronged along the train, and when the express rolled on towards Lahore he prepared to enjoy himself. He sat, happy and sticky, for quite a long time till his supply was gone. Where he put it all was a puzzle to the other fellows; but when it was all gone Bunter, like Alexander of old, looked round for new worlds to conquer. The other fellows had bought cakes, and had not yet eaten them, and Bunter eyed those cakes for a long time.

"I say, you fellows—" he said at last.

"Hallo, hallo, hallo! Bursting?" asked Bob Cherry.

"Oh, really, Cherry—"

"If the esteemed Bunter is feeling ill—"

"Oh, don't be an ass!" said Bunter peevishly. "I'm not ill—I'm hungry!"

"Great pip!"

"If you fellows don't want those cakes I'll polish them off," said the Owl of the Remove. "We shall be in Lahore in an hour or two now, and you can get some more!"

"Go it!" said Harry Wharton, laughing. "You can have mine."

Wharton's cake vanished, and Bob Cherry's followed it. Nugent's cake went next, and then Bunter eyed the cake belonging to Johnny Bull. Johnny Bull seemed a little less accommodating than his comrades. He picked up the cake and munched it.

"I was going to eat that cake!" said Bunter, in an injured tone.

"Go hon!"

"If there's anything I dislike it's selfishness," said Bunter. "You knew jolly well that I wanted that cake!"

"Quite!" assented Johnny, munching cheerfully.

"If I'm going to be treated with this rotten greedy selfishness all round—" began Bunter warmly.

Hurree Jamset Ram Singh pushed his cake towards the fat junior.

"Pile infully, my esteemed Bunter!" he said.

Bunter grabbed the cake.

"Well, a fellow expects something to eat!" he said, with his mouth full. "This climate seems rather to make me hungry."

"Is there any climate that doesn't?" snorted Johnny Bull.

"Oh, really, Bull—"

"Let the esteemed Bunter rip!" said Hurree Singh cheerily. "In my country there is a belief in re-incarnation, and Bunter is a proof of it!"

"Eh—how do you make that out?" asked Bob.

"It is the esteemed belief that one does not live only one life," said the nabob seriously. "The same person is born and born again, under a variety of forms. I think it probable that my excellent relative, Baji Rao, was a tiger or a serpent in a previous state of existence!"

"Oh, my hat!" said Wharton. "You don't really believe those things yourself, Inky?"

The nabob smiled. How much he believed or discarded of the weird mythology of his native land the junior never knew. Perhaps the nabob did not quite know himself.

"But is not Bunter a proof?" he said.

"How's that?"

"You have seen, in the Indian cities, the pariah dogs that roam the streets and eat up everything that they can discover?"

"Yes," said Harry.

"All is grist that comes to their mill," said the nabob gravely. "They will eat up anything and everything, and leave nothing. It occurs to my esteemed mind that Bunter, in his former state of existence, was a pariah dog—and he has not changed very much in his re-incarnation as a fat bounder!"

"Ha, ha, ha!"

"Why, you cheeky beast!" gasped Bunter.

If Bunter had believed in the weird theory of successive incarnations he would certainly have believed that in his previous existence he had been a monarch or an emperor, or a duke at least. Certainly he was not flattered by the idea that he had lived before as a pariah dog.

He glared at the nabob in wrathful indignation, while the other fellows roared.

"My hat! There must be something in it!" said Bob Cherry. "Why, the resemblance is really striking!"

"It leaps to the eye!" grinned Nugent.

"The pariah dog will eat anything," said Bob. "Well, Bunter will eat anything! It's always on the hunt for food. Well, Bunter's always on the hunt for food! It howls when it's kicked out of the way, and you fellows know how Bunter howls when he's kicked."

"Ha, ha, ha!"

"So that point's settled," said Bob. "There's something in the jolly theory of re-incarnations, and Bunter was a pariah dog last time he lived on the earth. I wonder what he will be next time? A shark, perhaps!"

"Ha, ha, ha!"

"A slug, perhaps!" suggested Johnny Bull. "Perhaps a snail!"

"You cheeky rotters!" roared Bunter.

"Ha, ha, ha!"

Bunter munched the cake, and blinked at the chuckling juniors in great indignation. But he found comfort in the cake.

"You can cackle!" he said. "I'd like to know what would have happened to Inky, that time on the Mediterranean steamer, if I hadn't mopped up his lemonade for him! It was drugged, and I got the drug instead of Inky! Catch you fellows sacrificing yourselves for a pal like that!"

"You didn't know Inky's lemonade was drugged when you bagged it," growled Johnny Bull.

"Oh, really, Bull—"

"You're always bagging a fellow's tuck," said Johnny. "That time it happened to come in useful. That was all."

Bunter sneered.

"I'm accustomed to being run down and belittled by jealous fellows," he said. "You wouldn't have done it. Of course. I did it for Inky's sake, to save him. I don't expect you to acknowledge it. I don't expect any gratitude from Inky. But there it is."

"You fat chum—"

"Shakespeare says that ingratitude is sharper than a thankless child's tooth!" said Bunter.

"Ha, ha, ha!"

"Did you bag Inky's cake just now to save him over again?" asked Bob Cherry, with a chuckle.

"Oh, rats!"

Hurree Jamset Ram Singh closed one eye at his chums, unseen by the Owl of the Remove.

"My esteemed chums, did you notice the man who sold me that cake?" he asked.

"Nunno."

"You did not notice that he bore a resemblance to the esteemed and rascally Nally Das?"

"Oh, my hat!"

The juniors stared at Hurree Jamset Ram Singh. They had not specially noticed the cake merchant at Amritsar Station. But the cheery wink of the nabob reassured them. They realised that he was pulling the fat leg of the Owl of the Remove.

"The esteemed Bunter has eaten my cake," said Hurree Singh. "If it is poisoned he has saved me over again."

Bunter's fat jaw dropped.

"Pip-pip-poisoned?" he stuttered.

"The esteemed Bunter is noble and devoted, and he does not hesitate to take my terrific dangers upon his own excellent self," said the nabob. "The obligefulness is terrific!"

"Good old Bunter!" said Bob, entering into the jest. "If Bunter bagged your cake, suspecting it to be poisoned, of course, that alters the case. It was really kind."

"Noble!" said Nugent.

"Splendid!" exclaimed Wharton.

"Do you feel any pain yet, Bunter?"

"Eh?" stuttered Bunter.

"If Inky's cake was poisoned, old chap, you'll soon be feeling the effects," said the captain of the Remove. "You will have saved Inky over again, same as you did on the steamer at Marseilles. I must say I never expected this devotion from Bunter!"

"I admit I never did," assented Bob. "Wants some pluck to eat a poisoned cake for another fellow's sake."

"Well, that's where Bunter comes out strong. We all know his pluck. He's told us all about it lots of times."

The expression on Bunter's fat face by this time was extraordinary. He sat with his mouth open, gasping and blinking at the grave faces of the juniors in horror and dismay. They regarded him with great solicitude.

"Feeling bad yet?" asked Bob.

"Ow!"

"Of course, very likely the cake wasn't poisoned," argued Bob. "There's no actual proof—"

"Wow!"

"If the esteemed Bunter feels the deleterious effects we shall soon know," said Hurree Singh; "and if he has swallowed the disgusting poison intended for my esteemed self he has saved my unworthy life, and the obligefulness is terrific."

"Groogh!"

"Anything wrong, Bunter?"

"Ow! Wow! You!" Bunter staggered to his feet. "Stop the train! Call a doctor! Help! I'm poisoned! Yoop! Yaroooooooh! Help!'

84

Not Fatal!

COLONEL WHARTON dropped his newspaper and jumped up. The wild yells of Billy Bunter rang through the train and the colonel was naturally startled. Bunter collapsed on the floor, roaring.

"Good gad! What is the matter?" exclaimed the colonel.

"Yarooooh!"

"Bunter!"

"I'm poisoned!"

"Poisoned?" exclaimed the colonel.

"Ha, ha, ha!"

"Beasts!" roared Bunter. "You don't care if I'm poisoned. You don't care if I expire at your feet. Yooop!"

"What is the matter with you, Bunter?" exclaimed the colonel testily. The laughter of the other juniors was a fairly convincing proof that there was nothing serious the matter with Bunter.

"Stop the train!"

"Nonsense!"

"Call a doctor!" yelled Bunter.

"Absurd! What is the matter?"

"I'm poisoned!"

"Bunter's eaten a little too much, I think, sir," said Bob Cherry demurely.

"He feels as if he were on the Channel again."

"Very probable," grunted the colonel. "Have you eaten all those foodstuffs that I saw you buying at Amritsar, Bunter?"

"Ow! Yes. Wow!"

"Then it is no wonder that you feel ill," said the colonel severely. "You should be more temperate in a hot climate, Bunter. You must endeavour to control this greediness."

"Yaroooh! I'm poisoned!" howled Bunter. "I ate Inky's cake, and it was poisoned. I believe he gave it to me on purpose!"

"Don't be absurd!"

"Help!"

The colonel scanned the grinning faces of the juniors.

"I suppose this is some jest on Bunter?" he exclaimed.

"Hem! Something in that line, uncle," admitted Wharton. "There's nothing the matter with him, really."

"I'm dying!" howled Bunter. "I can feel frightful pains all over me. Like daggers! Ow!"

It was very probable that the Owl of the Remove was feeling a little inward trouble. His feed on the train was likely to have caused trouble, even to Bunter's ostrich-like inside.

"He looks ill," said the colonel. "What is the pain you speak of like, Bunter?"

"Like burning daggers!"

"What?"

"And red-hot pincers! Yarooooh!"

"Where do you feel it?" demanded the colonel.

"Everywhere—all over! It's all over Yow-ow-ow!"

"If it's all over, old bean, there's nothing to worry about, is there?" asked Bob Cherry.

"Yow-ow! Beast! I mean it's all over me. Head to foot. Frightful pains, like red-hot daggers and burning needles—yarooooh! Call a doctor! Stop the train! I'm not going to be poisoned to please you!"

"But you wanted to take on Inky's danger, you know," chuckled Bob. "It's just in your line."

"Beast! Help!"

"What has put it into his foolish head that he is poisoned?" asked the puzzled colonel.

"I thinkfully consider that some remarkfullness of my esteemed self put the idea into Bunter's idiotic head," murmured the nabob of Bhanipur. "It was a little jokefullness to subtract the swank from the fat and ridiculous Bunter."

Bunter sat up.

"You—you beast—"

"Ha, ha, ha!"

"Mean to say that your cake wasn't poisoned?" roared Bunter.

"Not to my knowfulness, my esteemed fat Bunter."

"You—you—you—" gasped Bunter.

"Ha, ha, ha!" roared the juniors.

William George Bunter scammed to be experiencing a sudden recovery. He staggered to his feet, blinking at the laughing juniors with an infuriated blink.

"You rotters!" he howled. "You jolly well knew that Inky's cake wasn't poisoned!"

"So would you have known it if you hadn't been a silly funk!" growled Johnny Bull.

"The funkfulness is terrific."

"Ha, ha, ha!"

"Come, come!" said the colonel, laughing. "You seem to be all right, Bunter. Please make a little less noise."

And Colonel Wharton went back to his seat and his newspaper. Bunter sat down again, eyeing the Famous Five furiously.

"You rotters! Taking me in—"

"Giving you a chance to show your jolly old devotion, same as you did on the steamer, old fat bean!" grinned Bob Cherry.

"Ha, ha, ha!"

"Beast!"

The juniors grinned cheerily as the train ran on to Lahore. Billy Bunter sat silent for a time; even Bunter had nothing to say. But as Lahore Station came in sight the fat junior recovered himself.

"You fellows thought you were pulling my leg!" he sneered.

"We jolly well did!" agreed Bob.

"The thinkfullness was terrific."

"Well, you jolly well didn't!" said Bunter. "I knew it was a lark all the time—see? I jolly well made you think I was scared."

"You did!" chuckled Bob. "We certainly thought you were frightened out of your silly wits. And we think so still."

"Yah!"

The Greyfriars party alighted at Lahore, and Bunter blinked

round him in the lamplight, glimmering through the dusk of the Indian evening.

"Where's the hotel?" he asked.

"Echo answers, 'Where?' "answered Bob Cherry.

"The wherefulness is terrific," said the nabob.

"I suppose we're going to put up at an hotel?" exclaimed Bunter. "I'm tired. Hungry, too!"

"Oh, my hat!"

"Frightfully hungry and tired out," said Bunter. "I want a meal next, then a bed, I say, sir, hadn't we better get off at once to the hotel?"

Colonel Wharton was speaking to a porter. He turned back and glanced at Bunter.

"What hotel?" he said. "What do you mean, Bunter? We are not staying in Lahore."

"Not staying in Lahore?" ejaculated Bunter.

"No."

"Then what the thump are we doing?"

"We are taking the train for Rawalpindi."

"Not this evening?"

"In twenty minutes," said the colonel.

"I'm tired!"

"Indeed!"

"And hungry."

"Well?"

"Well," spluttered Bunter, "I object to going on tonight! I object to sleeping in trains! I object—"

"Very good," said the colonel, unmoved. "My boys, come with me. Bunter, you may remain where you are."

"Eh?"

"Goodbye, Bunter!" chuckled Bob Cherry. And the Famous Five walked away with the colonel, followed by Pandy Din and the peon, and porters with their baggage, leaving Bunter rooted to the platform.

The Owl of the Remove stood and stared after them. It dawned upon his fat mind that as he had stated his vigorous objections to going on that night on the railway, the colonel was leaving him to his own devices. He gasped with wrath and dismay.

"Oh dear! Rotters! Oh!"

Bunter certainly had no mind to remain on the platform of the Lahore railway-station on his lonesome own. As the party moved off, without even turning their heads, Bunter made a rush after them.

"I say, you fellows, hold on!"

The Greyfriars fellows did not "hold on." The colonel was proceeding with rapid strides, and they were walking quickly to keep it with him. Bunter had to race after them, his fat little legs fairly twinkling. He overtook them at last, and arrived with them in a breathless state at the train which was waiting to carry the passengers on into the hills of Rawalpindi.

Bob Cherry grimed at him as he rolled on to the train.

"Hallo, hallo, hallo! Changed your mind, old fat man?"

"Coming on tonight, after all?" asked Johnny Bull.

Bunter answered only with a snort. His objections seemed to have been overcome somehow, or perhaps he felt that he could not deprive the travellers of the benefits of his fascinating society. At all events, he was still with the Greyfriars party when the train pulled out of Lahore and rattled on to Rawalpindi.

85

The Spy at Rawalpindi!

"IT'S c-c-cold!"

"Kik-kik-cold!" stuttered Bunter.

"That must be due to a change in the temperature," said Bob Cherry gravely; and the juniors chuckled.

Bunter blinked morosely.

After the heat of the day, the cold was rather keen. The juniors were far in the North of India now, and though the days were hot, the nights were cold enough. Bunter's teeth chattered as the train pulled on among shadowy hills. Far away in the light of the stars the snow-clad summits of the Himalayas could be seen—and it was with a thrill that the Greyfriars fellows realised that they were looking at the famed Himalayas. But Bunter was not bothering about the Himalayas. He was, as usual, bothering about W.G. Bunter.

There had been a feed on the train, and even Bunter was satisfied with it. But he did not like the cold. Having groused long and often about the heat, he had now another topic for grousing—the cold. Bunter was never likely to be long at a loss for a topic for grousing.

Bedding was unpacked by Pandy Din—warm blankets and pillows and wadded quilts called razais; essential articles for railway travelling in India. The juniors rolled themselves up and slept cheerily, undisturbed by the rattle and rear of the train. Bunter, having annexed more than his share of bedding, made himself comfortable, and his dulcet voice was silent at last, being changed for a deep snore.

In the morning the Greyfriars party were at Rawalpindi.

They turned out cheerily enough, in sharp cold. But the heat revived as the sun rose higher, and Bunter ceased to grouse about the cold and groused once more about the heat.

"I say, you fellows, I'm jolly well not going on any farther today!" he told the juniors. "I'm going to rest a day here at least."

"Bow-wow!"

"I tell you I'm jolly well not going in another train!" hooted Bunter.

"The trainfulness is now finished, my esteemed fat Bunter," said Hurree Jamset Ram Singh.

Bunter blinked at him.

"Rot!" he said. "The railway runs right on the Peshawar."

"The railway does, my esteemed Bunter, but we do not!" chuckled the nabob. "We leave the railroad at Rawalpindi. Our route lies a way from the railway into the hills."

"Oh!" said Bunter. He blinked towards the mighty Himalayas, barring the horizon to the East. "Blessed if I think much of your kingdom, Inky, there isn't even a railway there?"

"The disdain of the esteemed Bunter is crushfully humiliating," said Hurree Jamset Ram Singh sorrowfully. "Should his words be heard in my kingdom, all the inhabitants will cover their heads with ashes and hide their faces from the sun."

"Ha, ha, ha!""

"Oh, don't be an ass!" growled Bunter. "Look here, if there isn't any railway, how the thump are we going to get to Bhanipur? I suppose we're not going to walk up the Himalayas, are we?"

"I thinkfully opine that the honourable colonel will proceed by car for a great distance."

"Oh! That's all right," said Bunter. "If it's a good car, with plenty of grub on board, I don't mind. But after that?"

"After that, the excellent horse back!"

"Lucky I'm a jolly good rider!" said Bunter.

"Lucky if you are!" grinned Bob Cherry. "It won't be so easy as your stunts on the donkeys at Margate!"

"Of course, I'm accustomed to riding at home, at Bunter Court," said the Owl of the Remove with dignity. "I don't suppose Inky's got at his palace any gees like those my pater keeps in his exclusive stables at Bunter."

"I don't suppose he has!" agreed Bob, with a chuckle.

A carriage was waiting at the station to the Greyfriars party. Evidently, their arrival had been arranged for and expected. They drove from the station, down the Mall, Pandy Din following in a conveyance with the baggage. The peon had been left behind at Lahore—considerably to Bunter's disgust. Only the kitmutghar remained now to serve the party; but, fortunately, Harry Wharton & Co. were rather accustomed to taking care of themselves, and did not require all attentions which Bunter considered his due. Perhaps Bunter missed the innumerable menials of Bunter Court; or perhaps he liked spreading himself on a journey where he had no bills to foot.

A military gentleman, an officer of the Rawalpindi garrison, welcomed the travellers at a bungalow on the Mall, where the juniors learned that they are to stay that day and the night, starting into the mountains the follow morning. They were keen enough to start, and they in were not at all sorry to have the railway behind. The chums of the Remove were quite ready to rough it indeed, they were looking toward with the keenest anticipation to their journey into the lower ranges of the mighty Himalayas.

After tiffin Colonel Wharton took his young comrades out for a ramble through the town. Besides the extensive cantonments, there was little to be seen, but the juniors looked at the memorial statue of Queen Victoria and the public park and the golf-links through their eyes often turned away towards the great mountains barring the eastern sky.

"We're being followed, sir!" Bob Cherry said to the colonel after a time. Colonel Wharton glanced down at him with a smile.

"Do you think so?" he asked.

"I'm sure of it, sir," said Bob. "See that ragged beggar yonder—skulking by the park wall?"

"Yes? A wandering mendicant—a jogee!" said the colonel, with a nod. The juniors glanced at the man.

He was a brown-skinned, gaunt native, with black, matted hair, clad in little more than a loin cloth, and that dirty and ragged. They had seen swarms of much wandering beggars since arriving in India, and there was nothing specially to remark about this one.

"He was hanging about the bungalow, sir, when he came out," said Bob. "He has been hanging on our track all the time and never losing sight of us.

"Then we will give him another walk," said the colonel.

"Oh!" said Bob, a little puzzled.

The party walked on. Several times the juniors glanced about them, and they did not fail to spot the jogee, hovering in the distance—never looking directly towards them, but never letting them out of his sight. They left the town behind, and the juniors noticed that Pandy Din, who had been following, had disappeared. The colonel had spoken a few words to the kitmutghar in its own tongue, incomprehensible to the Greyfriars fellows, though Hurree Singh had started a little as be heard. Pandy Din had vanished a few minutes afterwards.

From the town the colonel led the way with long strides by a road shaded with trees and turned off at last into a path through a wood. The juniors followed him, and, glancing back as they entered the wood, they noticed the jogee in the distance.

It was clear enough that the man was shadowing them, and they wondered at the colonel's imperturbable calmness. The fact that they were watched brought clearly to their minds the peril that still haunted them; for they did not need telling that the jogee as one of the spies of Nally Das.

It was a long walk; and, fortunately, Bunter had remained behind to rest in the bungalow on the Mall. Bunter had declared warmly that he was not going to tramp about in the sun, and that he was going to have a snooze; and the Famous five had been quite pleased to leave him snoozing. Certainly, this long walk would have made the fat junior perspire. The famous Five were sturdy and fit; but they were feeling fatigued when they emerged from the wood at last and followed another road back to Rawalpindi..

They looked behind a good many times but nothing more was seen of the jogee.

"We've dropped that spy!" said Harry Wharton.

"Must have left him behind in the wool?" remarked Bob.

Colonel Wharton smiled.

"Quite so," he said. "Now, my boys. the road is direct from here to Captain Ferrer's bungalow, and I can return quite safely by yourselves. I have some little business to attend to."

Leaving the juniors on the road, the colonel turned back to the wood and disappeared among the trees.

Harry Wharton & Co. exchanged puzzled glances.

"Something's up!" said Bob sagely.

"There's something on!" agreed Harry Wharton. "Blessed if I quite know what it is, though!"

"Perhaps-fully I can enlighten my worthy claims," murmured if Hurree Jam-et Ram Singh. "I heard what the esteemed Colonel Sahib said to Pandy Din when he dismissed him."

"I forgot you understood the lingo, old bean," said Harry. "But what did—"

"What has Pandy Din to do with it?"' asked Johnny Bull.

The nabob smiled.

"The colonel sahib ordered Pandy Din to lose no time in getting to the wood and to wait there," he said. "The esteemed kitmutghar was to take cover in the wood and wait for us and the spy."

"We didn't see him," said Nugent.

"Neitherfully, I think, did the see," said Hurree Singh. "But he was there, my esteemed chums, and I thankfully opine that that is why the jogees followed us no further than the wood.

Bob Cherry gave a prolonged whistle.

"My hat! Then we took that jolly long walk really to lead that spying rotter into a trap!" he exclaimed.

"Just that!" grimed the nabob.

"And Pandy Din has bagged him in the wood!" ejaculated Nugent.

"I think so, my esteemed Franky."

"Good!"

And the juniors, understanding at last how the matters stood, walked of cheerily to the bungalow on the Mail, where they found Billy Bunter awake and getting anxious about supper.

86

News of Nally Das!

COLONEL, WHARTON strode by a shadowy path through the wood, a prim expression on his bronzed face. The juniors, accustomed to the kindly expression of the colonel, would hardly have known him now, so grim was his sunburned face. He had returned to the wood where the kitmutghar had lain wait for the spy with business on hand which the Removites of Greyfriars were not to witness.

A low whistle sounded softly among the trees, and the colonel turned from the path and plunged into a thicket. He came in a few minutes to a deep glade shaded by banyan-trees in the heart of the silent wood. Pandy Din, standing erect as a bronze state, saluted him. At the feet of the kitmutghar lay the jogee, bound hand and feet, his dark, dirty face under its dirty turban alive with feat and apprehension.

The colonel hooked down at him grimly. "You have done well, Pandy Din," he said.

Panty Din salaamed, with a faint grin on his brown face.

"It was easy, sahib. This dog followed the traces of my master into the wood. The sahib gave me ample time to reach the place and lie in ambush. I was ready for this son of a dog. He drew a knife when I seized him; but—"

The kitmutghar shrugged his shoulders.

"Speak, you dog!" said the colonel, his eyes on the apprehensive face of the jogee. "Your name?"

The man shook his head to signify that he did not understand English.

"You will make him speak, Pandy Din."

The kitmutghar grinned, and drew a hidden knife. The black eyes of the jogee rolled wildly.

"Mercy, noble sahib!"

"You have found your tongue, then," said the colonel contemptuously. "Listen to me, you dog! You watched me arrive in Rawalpindi; you watched me at the bungalow of Ferrers Sahib; you listened, concealed as you thought, while I talked with the chauffeur about the journey tomorrow by car; you followed me in the town; you followed me to this wood. All the time you were yourself watched. You understand?"

"Sahib, I swaer—"

"Silence! You are no jogee; you are a paid spy of Nally Das!" said the colonel.

The man started at the name.

"Your life hangs on a thread," continued Colonel Wharton. "You are not now in Bombay, or Delhi, or even Lahore; you are in the hills of Rawalpindi, where life is cheap. What has Nally Das paid you to spy on me?"

"I swear—" stammered the jogee huskily.

"At the first lie you are a dead man! Take care!"

Pandy Din made a movement with his knife, his ruthless eyes gleaming at the spy; and the man shuddered.

"Sahib, I was paid two hundred rupees."

"I will give you twice as much for the truth! The truth, mind! One false word will cost you your life!"

"I will tell the sahib the truth," muttered the wretched man through his chattering teeth.

"You learned that I leave Rawalpindi tomorrow with my companions and the Nabob of Bhanipur."

"Han, sahib."

"You learned that we travel by car by a lonely road through the hills. You sent word of this to your master."

"It is true."

"Where is Nally Das?"

"In the hills above Rawalpindi," faltered the jogee. "My messenger was to reach him by the ruined temple in the hills."

"He knows, then, my plans for tomorrow?"

"He knows."

"In the hills of Rawalpindi there are many dacoits," said the colonel, his keen eyes fixed on the man's shrinking face. "It is easy for Nally Das to gather there a hand of ruffians for any desperate deed. Speak!"

"My life is worth nothing if Nally Das learns that I betrayed him," muttered the jogee.

"Your life is worth less than nothing if you do not speak. If harm befalls the Nabob of Bhanipur on the road tomorrow, what do you think will be the value of your dog's life—you, left a prisoner in the hands of Ferrers Sahib at Rawalpindi, to be hanged as soon as news is received that Nally has succeeded?"

The wretch trembled.

"I will tell you all, sahib. Where the road passes the ruined temple of Kalee, Nally Das will be in waiting with a hundred of the dacoits of the hills. He has long made his preparations, and I was to wait and watch for the colonel sahib, and send him word. I have sent word; and if the colonel sahib takes the road tomorrow he will be slain, and the Huzoor Nabob will be taken a prisoner."

"You can tell me no more?"

"Sahib, I have told you all."

"Ach-cha!" said the colonel. "I believe you now. Pandy Din, you will take this man back to Rawalpindi, and leave him secure. Kill him if he attempts to escape!"

"On my head be it!" said the kitmutghar.

"Jogee, if you have told the truth, tomorrow night you are free, with four hundred rupees for your reward. If you have spoken falsely you will be hanged tomorrow at sunset!"

"Sahib, I swear—"

"Enough!"

Colonel Wharton turned and strode away, leaving the prisoner in the hands of Pandy Din.

Harry Wharton & Co. gave the colonel somewhat curious glances when he rejoined them at the bungalow on the Mall in Rawalpindi. But the colonel's face wore its usual kindly smile and gave no inclination of his thoughts. In the evening the juniors sat in the moonlit garden chatting, before turning in, when a familiar sound of whirring and droning came to their ears.

"A giddy aeroplane!" exclaimed Bob Cherry, looking up at the clear sky.

The juniors stared up at the plate with interest. Strange enough it was to see the machine circling against the stars of the Indian sky, in the shadow of the Himalayas—the last word of Western invention in the heart of the changeless East.

"A fighting plane!" said the colonel, glancing up. "You may see it again, my boys—and perhaps hear the machine. gun going. You must be prepared for strange sights and sounds now that you are on the Indian frontier."

He paused and knocked the ash from his cigar.

"Hurree Singh I am bound to take with me," he went on. "But if any of you boys would choose to remain here in Rawalpindi, instead of going on into the mountains—"

"No fear!"

"No jolly fear, sir!"

"Then you must prepare for grim sights," said the colonel gravely. "We are going through hill-roads infested by dacoits—ruffians who watch for a chance to murder a soldier for his rifle, a dancing-girl for her earrings. Tomorrow you will see something of an India that you have seen nothing of so far—if you come."

The Famous Five felt a thrill. It was danger—and they knew it. But they did not falter.

"We're jolly well coming!" said Bob Cherry sturdily.

"And what do you say, Bunter?"

Bunter blinked at the colonel. In the quiet, moonlit garden, under the deodars, it was difficult to visualise danger. Bunter grinned. He was not to be "done" so easily as all this.

"I'm coming," he said. "Danger's nothing to me—in fact, I revel in it. I'm not funky—like some fellows."

"The danger is real," said the colonel quietly.

Bunter winked at the circling aeroplane.

"That's all right, sir—if there's danger I feel bound to come and see these fellows through. Leave it at that!"

"Oh, my hat!" murmured Bob. And it was left at that.

87

A Bolt from the Blue!

"IT'S a good car!" said Bunter, deigning to approve.

It was a good car, there was no doubt about that. It was a roomy one, too, with ample space for the colonel and the Greyfriars juniors. It rolled out of Rawalpindi in the sunlight of the morning, a second car laden with baggage following, in the charge of Pandy Din.

Rawalpindi was left behind, the cantonments disappeared from sight, and the great lonely hills encompassed the gliding car. The road was good, and the pace was rapid. Bunter settled down in a corner seat with a bag of sticky cakes, though he had given rather a startled glance at the rifles that stood ready in the car, and at the revolver which lay beside the colonel on the seat.

It dawned upon Bunter's fat mind that there was danger on the road, as the colonel had told him—that the thought of an attack on the car in the solitudes of the hills was what was in Colonel Wharton's mind. But by the time that dawned on Bunter the party were twenty miles out of Rawalpindi, and return was not to be thought of. Billy Bunter comforted himself with sweet, sticky cakes and hoped for the best.

Mile after mile glided under the wheels of the car, the native chauffeur driving on steadily, and wilder and wilder grew the mountain scenery round the travellers.

It was close on noon when Colonel Wharton looked sharply from the car and fixed his eyes upon a mass of ruined buildings by the roadside some distance ahead. It was the ruined temple of Kalee. Backward swept the colonel's glance, and it rested upon a moving object in the sky. Harry Wharton, following his glance, made out the aeroplane against the blinding blue.

"The plane!" he exclaimed.

The gang of savage decoits, armed to the teeth, swept towards the car with a wild rush. "My hat!" said Bob Cherry. "We—" Whirrrrar! Something, that seemed like a huge bird, darkened the sky for a second. Then, like a bird of prey rushing upon its quarry, the fighting plane swept down. The yells of the dacoits were answered by the rattle and bang of the machine-gun above.

"You will keep in cover here," said the colonel quietly. "You see that ruin by the roadside—"

"Yes."

"Nally Das is lying in wait there, with a hundred dacoits of the hills."

"Wha-a-at?"

"They may open fire," said the colonel, unmoved. "But it is more likely that they will rush the car, as they seek to take Hurree Singh alive, and dare not shed his blood if they can help it."

"A hundred!" repeated Johnny Bull.

"Or more."

"Then we're done for!" said Bob Cherry. "We can't handle a hundred of them, sir. But we'll jolly well die game!"

Colonel Wharton smiled.

"I have not brought you here to die in a trap," he said. "You will see! But take care; the danger is real enough, although every precaution has been taken."

Crack!

It was a signal shot from the ruined temple.

With a howl of terror, Billy Bunter rolled off his seat and plunged into the bottom of the car. But no one heeded Bunter.

Forth from the ruined temple—only a few moments before still and silent as the grave—rushed a wild crew—dark-skinned men in turbans, armed with tulwars, spears, and long knives—a gang of the desperate robbers of the hills of Rawalpindi. A hundred of them at least, brawny ruffians, armed to the teeth, and they swept towards the car with a wild rush. Ahead the road was blocked by a fallen tree.

The car jammed to a halt. From the shattered gateway of the temple the fierce face of Nally Das looked, watching the attack of the savage dacoits.

"My, hat!" said Bob Cherry... "We are—"

Whirrrrrr!

Something that seemed like a huge bird darkened the sky for a second. Like a bird of prey rushing upon its quarry, the fighting-plane swept down.

The yells of the dacoits were answered by the rattle and bang of the machine-gun above.

"'The plane!" shouted Bob.

"Hurrah!"

Then the juniors understood as they stared from the car with tense faces. The trapper was trapped, the biter bit. A tearing hail of bullets from the plane swept through and through the gang of robbers, and the savage rush of the dacoits stopped and broke, and their threatening yells changed into shrieks of pain and terror.

From the ruined temple Nally Das watched, his dark face convulsed with rage. He watched for a few moments, and then he vanished—fleeing—knowing only too well that he had failed, and that only flight could save him.

But the mob of dacoits rushing in the open broke and fled in vain; the storm of searching bullets rained on them, and man after man rolled over, yelling and screaming.

With white faces the Greyfriars juniors watched the terrible scene that unfolded before their eyes like a scene at the theatre.

Of all the desperate gang that had rushed the car, sure of their prey, only one came within a dozen yards, and he only to fall before a sharp shot from the colonel's revolver. The rest, torn right and left by the rain of lead from the machine-gun above, scattered and darted wildly for safety among the rocks.

The juniors' rifles were ready, hut they were not needed. Half the desperate gang lay, groaning, or terribly still, on the sun-baked rocks; the rest, yelling with terror, fled in all directions, casting away their tulwars and long-barrelled guns for greater speed. And as they fled the raining bullets still searched them among the rock.

It was over!

The road was cleared, the car glided its way; and behind the Greyfriars party the vultures gathered from far and near, and the hyenas came creeping out of their lairs. Without a backward glance Harry Wharton & Co. dashed on their way, with nothing to fear from the dacoits of Rawalpindi.

PART 8. IN THE HEART OF THE HIMALAYAS!

88

In the Indian Hills!

"JOLLY, isn't it?" said Bob Cherry.

"Topping!"

Hurree Jamset Ram Singh grinned a dusky grin, and remarked that the topfulness was terrific.

The Famous Five, of the Greyfriars Remove, were all looking, and feeling, merry and bright.

Even Billy Bunter looked cheerful, and had a contented grin on his fat face.

Harry Wharton & Co. were far from Greyfriars now. Greyfriars School was on the other side of the round globe.

Camping out in the pleasant summer weather was always agreeable. But camping in the shadow of the mighty Himalayas was, as Bob remarked, "no end of a catch."

The chums of Greyfriars, on their way with Hurree Singh to his native home in Bhanipur, were drawing near their journey's end.

It had been a long and adventurous journey; and danger had dogged the way, by the Mediterranean, the Red Sea, Bombay, and Delhi, and Rawalpindi.

Rawalpindi, and the railroad, lay behind them now; the snort of the iron horse had never been heard in the mountain passes through which the journey now lay.

White with snow, even in the blaze of the summer sun, the great peaks of the Himalayas barred the horizon to the east. In the clear atmosphere of the hills, the mighty peaks seemed quite near at hand; but many a long hundred miles lay between the Greyfriars juniors and those soaring peaks that pierced the clouds.

The Greyfriars party had halted, in the heat of noon, for rest and refreshment. The car that had brought them up from Rawalpindi stood on the white road; the juniors were camped under a great spreading tree, whose vast branches could have sheltered a battalion.

Colonel Wharton was pacing to and fro at a little distance, in the shade, smoking his after-lunch cigar. The Punjabi chauffeur slept in the car. Pandy Din, the khitmutghar, had disappeared with a rifle under his arm, looking for game, or perhaps for an enemy. Harry Wharton & Co. sat with their backs to the big trunk of the tree, in the cool shade, and enjoyed a rest, and gazed at the scone about them. Mountain range rose on range, rising to the far-off mighty mass of the Himalayas. It seemed to the juniors that they were on the roof of the world.

"Jolly, and no mistake," said Johnny Bull. "It was no end of a wheeze to come along with old Inky. This is the rippingest holiday we've ever had, you chaps."

"Yes, rather," assented Nugent. "Why, even Bunter isn't grousing, for once."

Billy Bunter's eyes had closed behind his big spectacles. He opened them to blink at Frank Nugent.

"Oh, really, Nugent—"

"The topfulness must really be terrific, as Inky says, when Bunter isn't grousing," remarked Harry Wharton.

"Ha, ha, ha!"

"Oh, really, Wharton—"

"Had enough lunch, Bunter?" grinned Bob.

"Well, I haven't done badly," said Bunter. "It was rather thoughtful of the colonel to have a good supply of grub packed in the car. I must admit I've done pretty well. Not like the lunches, at home, at Bunter Court, of course."

"Of course not," assented Bob gravely.

"But not bad!" said Bunter tolerantly. "If the grub is going to be like this all the time I shall be satisfied. It's a good car, too—though not, of course, like my pater's Rolls."

The juniors chuckled.

"Taking it all in all, I'm not sorry I came," said Bunter generously. "You fellows haven't treated me really well; but, after all, I got used to your bad manners at Greyfriars."

"Oh!"

"Even Inky isn't really grateful enough, though I've travelled all this way to protect him," said Bunter, blinking at the Nabob of Bhanipur.

"My esteemed fat Bunter—" murmured the Nabob.

"Now, don't deny it, Inky!" Bunter wagged a fat forefinger at the dusky junior. "You're not grateful."

"The admitfulness of the soft impeachment is terrific, my esteemed Bunter."

"You're an ungrateful lot, in fact," said Bunter. "Still, as I said, I got used to your selfishness at Greyfriars. When a follow doesn't expect much, he doesn't get disappointed. See?"

"Fathead!" said Bob Cherry politely.

"Oh, really, Cherry—"

"We shall be at Bhanipur tomorrow," remarked Harry Wharton. "Then we shall see Inky in all his glory, with a giddy crown on his jolly old napper, riding the elephant of state."

The Nabob grinned.

"I suppose we shall put up at the palace?" asked Bunter.

"Quite so, my esteemed fat one."

"With slaves to wait on us?" asked Bunter.

"As many as the esteemed Bunter may like."

"And plenty of grub?"

"The grubfulness will be terrific."

Billy Bunter's fat face expanded in a cheery smile. Even Bunter was satisfied at the prospect.

"But we don't get to Bhanipur till tomorrow," he said. "There's tonight to be considered. What sort of an hotel are we likely to find tonight in these blinking mountains?"

"Ha, ha, ha!"

"Do not stir," whispered Inky. "Not a movement! Bunter, keep still, on your life!" Billy Bunter caught his breath. "What do you mean?" he gasped. "Keep up your esteemed courage," said Hurree Jamset Ram Singh, softly. "It is a snake - and if you move he will strike!"

"Blessed if I see anything to cackle at," said Bunter. "I suppose we're getting to an hotel for the night."

"Better suppose again!" chuckled Bob Cherry. "They must have forgotten that you were coming, Bunter, for they neglected to build a grand hotel in the mountains for you. It was an oversight."

Bunter stared.

"Mean to say that there isn't any hotel?" he demanded.

"Ha, ha! No."

"But we can't camp out," exclaimed Bunter excitedly.

"The days are beastly hot here, but the nights are beastly cold. In fact, it's a beastly country altogether; if you don't mind my mentioning it, Inky."

"Not at all, my esteemed Bunter. I am accustomed to the exquisite politefulness of the fat Bunter."

"Ha, ha, ha!"

"Oh, really, Inky—"

"There's a dak bungalow, where we shall put up for the night, Bunter," said Harry Wharton, laughing.

"What on earth's a dak bungalow?" said Bunter peevishly. "I can jolly well tell you that I want a roof over my head tonight. I think it's up to you to make a fellow comfortable, when he's travelled half round the world to protect you from danger. I—What the thump are you blinking like that for, Inky?"

A sudden change had come over Hurree Jamset Ram Singh's face.

"Do not move, my esteemed Bunter!" he said in a low voice.

"I don't mean to move," grumbled Bunter, who was reclining in a more or less graceful attitude, half-buried in fallen leaves. "But what—"

The gaze of the Nabob was fixed on the thick bed of leaves in which Bunter was sprawling. Harry Wharton & Co. followed his glance, and drew in their breath quickly. From the dead leaves a strange glitter caught their eyes, and a stealthy movement. A sinuous head, green and gold, with eyes that glittered like jewels, moved stealthily in the leaves, only a foot from the unconscious Owl of the Remove.

Hurree Jamset Ram Singh's face was set and hard. He understood, better than the other fellows did, the fearful danger that had suddenly come upon the fat junior.

"Do not stir!" he whispered. "Not a movement! Bunter, keep still—do not stir or speak—on your life!"

Bunter caught his breath.

"What do you mean?" he gasped.

"Keep up your esteemed courage," said the Nabob softly. "It is a snake and if you move, he will strike! Silence, and keep still—still as the grave, if you would live!"

89

In Deadly Peril!

BILLY BUNTER sat motionless, as if petrified.

Indeed, he was almost petrified by sheer terror.

His round eyes, bulging behind his big glasses, turned towards the winding head of the snake, as it emerged from the leaves,, and fixed on it in a glassy stare. A faint moan of terror came from Bunter, and that was all.

Harry Wharton & Co. did not move. They were several feet from Bunter, and they dared not startle the snake. A single movement might have caused the horrible creature to strike, and Bunter was well within reach of the poisoned fang.

Instinctively, the Greyfriars juniors left the matter to Hurree Jamset Ram Singh. He had told them not to stir, and they did not stir; but they watched the snake's winding head with fascinated eyes, all the colour forsaking their cheeks as they watched.

The Nabob's face was set hard; he was cool and collected. He made no movement of any kind; and, fortunately, Bunter was too terrified, too utterly petrified with fear to move.

"Colonel sahib!"

Hurree Jamset Ram Singh called in a soft, subdued voice just loud enough to reach the ears of Colonel Wharton pacing under the big tree a dozen fact away.

The colonel halted, and glanced round taking his cigar from his lips.

"Colonel sahib, look at Bunter—and, for his life's sake, do not startle the snake, sahib!"

"Good gad!"

Colonel Wharton muttered the word through his teeth, as his startled eye turned on Bunter, and he discerned the green and golden head that wound stealthily out of the leaves close by the fat junior.

"Do not stir, any of you!" came the colonel's quiet voice.

The juniors remained silent and motionless. But in the stillness of the hot noontide they heard the faint sound of the colonel taking out his revolver.

Bunter's eyes had closed behind his spectacles. The Owl of the Remove had fainted.

Harry Wharton & Co. did not venture to look round at the colonel; they sat like statues. The green and gold sinuous body of the snake was winding out the dead leaves, and one coil lay across Bunter's elbow—the hideous head was only a few inches from his side. Was the thing about to strike? It seemed so—and it was certain to happen if the reptile was startled. They knew that the colonel, from his distance, was quietly taking aim with his revolver and upon the sureness of a shot depended the life of Billy Bunter. There would be no time for a second shot if the snake was merely wounded—no time before the poisoned fang had done its deadly work on the helpless Owl.

It seemed an age to the juniors before the shot came—a century of waiting, and the anguish of their anxiety was almost more than they could bear. Yet it was only a few seconds before the ring of the revolver awoke the echoes of the rocky valley.

Crack!

Wharton, whose fascinated stare was fixed on the snake, saw one of the greenish, glittering eyes darken suddenly, like a candle that was extinguished. The bullet, fired with unfailing aim, had blotted it out.

There was a sudden hissing and writhing, and the snake's head fell back in the dead leaves.

In an instant Hurree Singh, quickest of the horrified party to move, had leaped up and seized the insensible fat junior and dragged him away.

The coils of the snake were writhing and wriggling wildly in the leaves. The reptile was dead, killed instantly by the bullet that had smashed its head; but the tenacious life still lingered in the coiling body.

"Oh!" gasped Bob Cherry, white as a sheet.

Wharton sprang up and grasped his rifle, that leaned against the trunk of the big tree. The butt crashed down on the reptile's head.

"Oh crumbs!" murmured Frank Nugent, wiping the thick perspiration from his brow.

"Bunter!" muttered Johnny Bull. "He's fainted!"

"The faintfulness will not hurt the esteemed Bunter," said Hurree Singh.

"But the narrowfulness of the escape was terrific."

Colonel Wharton hurried up.

The old soldier's face was set and grim.

"Bunter's only fainted, sir," said Bob.

"Thank goodness that shot did it! If it had missed—"

He shuddered.

"You must take more care, my boys," said the colonel quietly. "We are not now in Delhi or Lahore. We are in the wilds now, and our lives are in our own hands. Any bed of leaves in this valley may hide a poisonous snake. Bunter should not have lain there without first stirring out the leaves to make sure."

"We'll be jolly careful—after this!" murmured Nugent.

"Yes, rather?"

There was a deep, quavering sigh from Billy Bunter, and his eyes opened behind his spectacles. He blinked round dizzily at the juniors.

"I—I say, you fellows, what's happened?" he stammered.

"All serene now, old chap," said Bob reassuringly.

"Safe as houses, old man," said Harry,

"I—I thought—" Bunter gasped with terror. "I saw a-a snake—aa—" He scrambled to his feet and jumped away at the sight of the coiling body on the leaves. "Ow! Help! Keep it off!"

"It's all right, now, fathead—"

"Yaroooh?"

Bunter did not stop to learn that the snake was killed. He made a wild rush for the ear.

"It's all right now, fathead!" roared Bob Cherry. "The danger's over, ass!"

"Ow!"

Bunter plunged headlong into the car. There was a howl from the Punjabi chauffeur, who was taking a nap in the car in the shade. Bunter plunged in right on him, and awoke the native most unpleasantly by stumbling over him and plunging a fat elbow into his eye.

"Oh! Ow! Wow!" roared Bunter. "Gerraway! You silly native, wharer you mean by tripping me up! Ow! There's a snake after me! Wow!"

The Punjabi stared at him, and shoved him aside, and left the car. Bunter collapsed on a seat and gasped.

Harry Wharton & Co. came over to the car. They were grinning now. The party had been very near a tragedy; but Bunter had turned the scene into comedy immediately.

"You fat duffer!" said Bob Cherry. "Don't I keep on telling you it's all right? 'The snake's killed."

"Ow!" gasped Bunter.

"You can get out of the car, fathead. I tell you it's all safe."

"I jolly well won't get out of the car!" roared Bunter. "I'm staying here till we start. I'm not going to be bitten by poisonous snakes to please you!"

"You silly ass—"

"Beast!"

"Stay in the car if you like," said Harry Wharton, laughing. "But there's nothing to be afraid of now, you duffer!"

Bunter recovered himself a little.

"Sure the snake's killed?" he asked.

"Quite, ass! You wouldn't be here now, sitting up and taking notice, if it hadn't been."

"Oh!" gasped Bunter. The missfulness is as good as the milefulness!" said the Nabob of Bhanipur reassuringly.

"If you fellows think I was frightened—" began Bunter.

"Oh, my hat! It did look like it—just a little bit!" said Bob.

"Just a few!" grinned Nugent.

"Nothing of the kind, of course. I hope I've got too much nerve to be frightened by a snake," said Bunter. "A snake isn't much. I should have taken it by the tail, you know, and knocked its head against the tree, and—and polished it off, you know. There was nothing for you fellows to be alarmed about."

"Well, we were alarmed—for you," said Bob.

"For yourselves, you mean," said Bunter. "I daresay you were scared—you would be, at a snake. Not my style."

The juniors gazed at Bunter. As he had fainted from sheer terror, while the reptile was alive, and fled in a blue funk from its dead body, his present attitude was even more Bunterish, so to speak, than usual. The Owl of the Remove gave them a scornful blink.

"If there's any more snakes, just call me," he said. "I'll stay in the car—not because I'm afraid of snakes, but—but because these seats are jolly comfy for taking a nap. If you fellows are frightened at a snake again, give me a call, and I'll come and protect you."

"You—you—you—" gasped Bob. "Why, you fat villain, you fainted from pure unadulterated funk!".

"I didn't faint!" roared Bunter. "I—I may have nodded off for a minute or two. A fellow gets drowsy in this heat. I was simply taking a nap."

"Taking a nap!" yelled Johnny Bull.

"Taking a nap—with a poisonous reptile crawling over you!"

Bunter nodded.

"Exactly," he said. "My nerve, you know! You'll always find me cool and collected in the moment of danger! Not like you chaps!".,

"Oh, my hat!"

"Great Scott! What's that wriggling near Bunter's foot?" exclaimed Bob Cherry suddenly.

As a matter of actual fact, nothing was wriggling near Bunter's foot. But the words were enough for Bunter. He did not stop to look. He came out of the car with a flying leap—so suddenly that he crashed into the group of juniors at the door, and sent them spinning right and left. Bob had not expected that outcome to his little joke. There was a roar as the juniors were knocked flying by

Bunter's terrific weight being suddenly hurled at them. Bob rolled over, and Bunter rolled on him, yelling.

"Good gad!" Colonel Wharton strode up hurriedly. "What is it?"

"Help!"

"But what—"

"Snakes!" yelled Bunter. "Snakes in the car! Help!"

"Gerroff!" shrieked Bob Cherry. "You're squashing me! Yarooh! Dragonoff!"

"Snakes!" yelled Bunter. "Save me! Snakes!"

"You fat idiot?" roared Wharton. "There's nothing in the car! Bob was pulling your silly leg, you fat dummy!"

"Oh! Ow! Wow!" gasped Bunter. A heavy shove sent him rolling off Bob Cherry, and he rolled on a prickly plant what grew by the roadside. He reposed on that plant for about a millionth part of a second, and then he leaped to his fret as if electrified.

"Ow! I'm stung! I'm bitten! I'm killed! Whooooop!"

"Bunter!" roared the Colonel.

"I'm stung by snakes! I'm bitten by cobras! I'm poisoned! I'm dying! l'm expiring! Yaroon!"

"You absurd boy! You are not hurt. Be quiet! You have scratched yourself on some thorns, that is all."

"Oh!" gasped Bunter.

Colonel Wharton, with a snort of impatience, strode away. Billy Bunter blinked at the Famous Five, who were grinning. He rolled back to the car. This time he peered all over the interior of the vehicle before he ventured to stretch his fat limbs on the cushions. Then he settled down to repose, and the old familiar sound of his deep and resonant snore was heard, till it was time for the party to proceed.

90

Not to be Chucked!

THERE was a thoughtful frown on the fat brow of William George Bunter as the big car glided along the road through the hillpasses. The long, white road wound on, seemingly endless, here passing through the thick shades of a forest, there winding along a rocky valley where hardly aherb grew; and again climbing a high ridge, snorting with exertion, and then whizzing down at great speed on the farther slope.

The road was good, the work of the engineers whose unending labours are opening up the remote spaces of India. It ran where, in olden days, a camel track had run—days not so very far back, when the only communication between Bhanipur and British India had been by caravan and ox-wagon.

Even yet the railroad had not penetrated as far as Hurree Singh's native state, but well-laid roads opened up an easy passage for motor-cars. By strange, wild, and gorgeous scenery the car glided on, the Punjabi chauffeur sitting like a bronze statue at the wheel; the baggagecar following, driven by Pandy Din, the khitmutghar.

The incident of the snake had made the juniors rather serious for a time, and it had been a warning to them that they were now in the wilderness, and needed to be on their guard. But it had not affected their spirits, and it was a cheery party that crowded into the big car. Colonel Wharton sat outside with the chauffeur, with a rifle across his knees, and his keen eyes on the alert. The juniors had their rifles with them, too. Peril after peril had cropped up in their path, and they were ready for anything that might happen. But William George Bunter was looking unusually thoughtful, and he unburdened himself of his thoughts at last.

"I say, you fellows—"

"Hallo, hallo, hallo! Any more snakes?"' asked Bob cheerily.

"Now, don't jump out of the car because I say snakes, Bunter! We're going too fast for your acrobatic stunts!"

'Oh, really, Cherry! The fact is, I'm not satisfied," said Bunter.

"That's no news, old fat man," said Bob. "Are you ever satisfied? "But what's the special trouble now?"

After we got out at Rawalpindi in the car, we were attacked by a gang of dacoits," said Bunter. "Of course, I hid in the bottom of the car while the trouble was on; but you were only looking for a pin you'd dropped, or something of the sort—what!"

"Ha, ha, ha!"

"Now we've got among poisonous snakes and things," said Bunter. "I tell you I don't like it! There may be a tiger next."

"Are there any tigers in these parts, Inky?" asked Bob.

The nabob grinned.

"Lots!" he answered. "In fact, my esteemed chum, the lotfulness is terrific. And if a tiger should see the esteemed Bunter, he would follow him for miles. Tigers like nice fat pigs—"

"Ha, ha, ha!"

"Bunter would be an esteemed and excellent morsel for a hungry tiger," said the nabob blandly.

"Oh, really, Inky—"

"And there are wild elephants in the forests," went on Hurree Jamset Ram Singh.

"Sometimes they wander out into the roads. Wild elephants are very ferocious. It is fortunate for our excellent selves that we have Bunter with us to protect us."

"That's all very well," said Bunter, "but I can't say I like it. Mean to say we might run into a herd of wild elephants?"

"Certainfully."

Bunter looked more thoughtful than ever. His thoughts did not seem to be wholly pleasant ones.

"You shouldn't have come, old fatman," said Bob. "The colonel left you behind in Bombay, you know, and you would follow on. He offered to fix you up at Rawalpindi, till we got back from the hills. If you haven't any sense, old bean, you should try to cultivate a little pluck."

Snort from Bunter.

"I've got more pluck than any other fellow here, and chance it," he said. "All the same, I don't like it, and I tell you plainly that I don't like it. I've a jolly good mind to go back to Rawalpindi. You fellows can't complain. You're ungrateful and disrespectful. Considering everything, you can't expect me to stick to you."

"Think of the grub at Bhanipur!" said Bob Cherry encouragingly.

"Oh, blow Bhanipur! I don't think much of Inky's country, if it's anything like this!" said Bunter peevishly. I could make myself quite comfortable at Rawalpindi. How far have we come?

"About a hundred miles, I fancy. Rather a long walk back for you, Bunter, if you leave us in the lurch!" grinned Bob.

"Look here, WWharton—"

"Well, ass?"

"Mean to say that your uncle wouldn't turn back and land me at Rawalpindi and leave me out of this beastly journey?" demanded Bunter.

Harry Wharton laughed.

"You can ask him!" he said. "My opinion is that he wouldn't!"

"You fat duffer!" growled Johnny Bull. "Do you think we're going to lose two or three days' journey because you're in a funk?"

"That does it!" said Bunter savagely. "I'm going back!"

"Fathead!"

"I'm not going to be trampled on by wild elephants, and bitten by poison onsnakes, and torn to pieces by savage tigers, to please you!" hooted Bunter. "I'm not going to be murdered by dacoits, either, see?"

"All those things won't happen to you, old bean," said Bob consolingly. "If a tiger gets you, he won't leave anything for the snakes, the elephants, or the dacoits."

"Ha, ha, ha!"

And on the other hand, if an ant tramples on you, there won't be a shiny spot left for the tigers, the snakes, and the dacoits," argued Bob; "and if it's the snakes that finish you off, the elephants and tigers, and dacoits wouldn't touch you afterwards.".

"You—you—you—" gasped Bunter, while the juniors chuckled.

"Step out of the ear, Bunter," said Colonel Wharton. Bunter blinked at him. "No need to get out," he said. The colonel did not reply. Bunter suddenly felt himself seized by the collar. Next moment, he was jerked out of the car and stretched across Colonel Wharton's knees. Smack! Smack! Smack! "Yaroooh! Whoop! Help!" roared Bunter, as the colonel spanked him with a heavy hand.

"If you're chopped up by dacoits," continued Bob cheerily, "even you needn't worry about elephants and tiger afterwards. A chap can only die once, old bean. Isn't that a comfort?"

Bunter did not seem to derive much comfort from that undoubted fact. Apparently he did not want to die even once.

"I'm going back!" he howled. "I'm chucking this—see? You fellows have only got yourselves to thank."

"We'd try to bear it," grinned Nugent.

"The sorrowfulness of calamity would be averted by the strength of fortitude," said Hurree Jamset Ran Singh.

"Don't be an ass, Bunter," said Harry Wharton. "There's no going back now. Screw up your courage, if you've got any, and stick it out."

"I tell you I'm going to chuck it!" roared Bunter.

Billy Bunter glared at the Famous Five. Bunter had been doing an unusual amount of thinking, and the outcome was, as he had stated, that he did not like it. He had been told, even before leaving Greyfriars, that the journey would be a dangerous one. But Bunter feared no peril that was far off. But though his fat intellect worked slowly, it worked. It had penetrated into his podgy mind at last that the danger was there, and that it was very real. The affair of the snake had put the lid on, so to speak. Bunter had made up his fat mind that he was fed-up, and that he was going to chuck it. He declined to recognize the undoubted fact that it was too late.

"Call out to your uncle to stop the car, Wharton!" he snapped.

"What for, ass?"

"To turn back!"

"Fathead!"

Billy Bunter rapped on the glass screen that separated the juniors from the driver and the colonel. The latter turned his head, and looked into the car inquiringly.

"Stop!" shouted Bunter.

"What?"

"Stop!"

The colonel stared at him through the glass.

"I want to go back!" roared Bunter.

"What?"

"I'm chucking it!"

Colonel Wharton gave him a fixed stare, with quite an extraordinary expression on his bronzed face. Then he turned his back on Bunter again, and though Bunter rapped his knuckles loudly on the glass, and roared, the colonel gave no further heed. Bunter turned his spectacles angrily on the captain of the Remove.

"Has your uncle gone deaf, Wharton?" he bawled.

"I think not," said Harry, laughing. "I think you'd better shut up, Bunter. It's too late to turn back."

"Don't I keep telling you I'm chucking it?" roared Bunter.

"Ass!"

Bunter turned to the glass screen again, with a ferocious glare.

He rapped on it again and again, and at last the colonel turned his head once more.

"Silence!" the juniors heard him rap out.

"Sha'n't!" roared Bunter.

"What?"

"I'm going back!" yelled Bunter. "I'm fed-up! I'm jolly well sick of it, and, if you want to know, I'm jolly well sick of you, too! Put that in your pipe and smoke it, and be blowed to you?"

The colonel gave the Punjabi chauffeur a sign, and the car jammed to a halt. Bunter grinned triumphantly at the junior.

"I thought that would fetch him," he said. "I'm jolly well not standing on any ceremony with your blessed uncle, Wharton. Stiff old military stick! Yah!"

Colonel Wharton stepped down, and opened the car door. The Famous Five sat silent, reading more in the colonel's grim face than the Owl of the Remove read there.

"Step out, Bunter!" said the colonel quietly.

Bunter blinked at him.

"No need to get out," he said. "I'm going back in the car, of course. Tell that native to turn round."

The colonel did not reply. He reached into the car, and gripped Bunter's collar with a powerful hand. Heavy-weight as he was, Bunter found himself jerked out of the car like a cork from a bottle.

"Ow! What—"

Colonel Wharton sat on the step of the car, and Bunter found himself sprawling face down on the colonel's knee.

Smack, smack, smack!

"Yaroooh! Whooop! Help!" roared Bunter.

"Ha, ha, ha!"

Smack, smack, smack!

It seemed like a horrid dream to William George Bunter. He was being spanked—actually spanked, by a hard and heavy hand that smote with terrific vim. There was a sound like the beating of a carpet as the colonel spanked, and from William George Bunter came sounds resembling the voice of the Bull of Bashan of olden time.

Bunter was set on his feet, yelling.

"Now get into the car!"

"Sha'n't!" gasped Bunter.

"What?"

"I—I—I mean—yes—all right! I'm getting in, ain't I!" yelled Bunter, as the colonel made a movement towards him.

And he got in, sprawling in his haste. The door slammed after him, and Colonel Wharton resumed his seat beside the chauffeur. In the car, Bunter picked himself up from among five pairs of feet, and blinked with an infuriated blink at the grinning chums of the Remove.

"If—if that beast thinks I'm going to stand this!" he gasped.

"Not going to stand it?" asked Bob.

"No!" roared Bunter.

"Sit down, then!"

"Yarooh!"

Bunter sat down again, hard.

When he picked himself up once more Bunter resumed his seat, and did not state any more of his thoughts. Judging by the expression on his fat face, his thoughts were ferocious, if not homicidal. But Bunter decided to keep them to himself. One thing was clear to his fat mind. He had decided to chuck the journey; but the journey, at this stage, was not to be chucked. In spite of dacoits, snakes, tigers, and wild elephants, Billy Bunter was booked for Bhanipur.

91

The Dak Bungalow in the Hills!

"THAT'S it!" said Bob Cherry. It was the dak bungalow.

The car halted, and the Greyfriars juniors turned out, glad to stretch their legs again.

The sun was setting, the sky ablaze with crimson and purple and gold. The long hot day was drawing to a close. Already the cold of the mountain night was creeping in, and the juniors had donned their coats, mindful of the danger of chills in the sudden change of temperature at sunset.

Billy Bunter blinked disparagingly at the dak bungalow.

Even the Owl of the Remove could scarcely have expected to find a first-class hotel in the wild wastes of the Himalaya foothills. Possibly he had expected a handsomely-appointed bungalow like that of Ferrers Sahib, in which the party had stayed a night at Rawalpindi. But the dak bungalow was a building of the plainest description; it afforded a shelter from the night, and little or nothing more.

"Stopping there, are we?" asked Bunter, with a snort, as he blinked at the low buildings.

"Just there, old fat man," said Bob.

"Looks to me a good bit like a cattle-shed."

"Go hon!"

"I'm not going to stand this sort of thing, I can tell you!" said Bunter morosely.

"Fathead!"

Snort from Bunter. The fat junior was in a sulky temper.

Many times during the long journey from Greyfriars to the Indian frontier Bunter had threatened to quit the party; and always he had had the chagrin to find that such threats were received with equanimity, if not indeed with enthusiasm.

Certainly, Bunter had never meant to quit. He had been left behind at Bombay, and had followed on. He had had the offer of being left in ease and comfort at Rawalpindi, to be picked up on the party's return; and he had refused the offer. Any fellow but Bunter would have considered, after that, that he was booked for the journey, and would have ceased from troubling, and let the weary be at rest. Not so Bunter.

At long last it had dawned upon the Owl's obtuse brain that the dangers and discomforts of the journey were very real, and much greater than he had realized; and he had made up his fat mind that he did not want any more conclusion, when it was no longer possible for him to quit.

Certainly, he could not walk back a hundred miles by the hill-passes, of which he did not know a yard of the way. Still, more certainly, Colonel Wharton had no intention of turning back and losing two or three days' time to please him.

Bunter did not seem to realize that having made his bed, he must lie on it. He was, at long last, in grim earnest in his desire to quit the part; and he took it as an immense grievance that he could not do so.

It was only one day more to Bhanipur where the fat Owl could expect to roll in case and lazy comfort. But one more night, and one more day, in the savage hills were exactly one night and one day too much for Bunter. He still shuddered at the remembrance of the rushing gang of dacoits who had attacked the car in a lonely pass. But the dacoits had been out to pieces by machine-gun fire from the aeroplane which had followed the car, and what was left of the gang had fled for life.

Bunter had recovered, to some extent, from that scare. But the poisonous snake, in the dead leaves upon which he had unthinkingly sprawled, had put the lid on. In a country infested by dacoits and poisonous reptiles, there was no comfort for W. C. Bunter—and he wanted to chuck it. And his indignation was absolutely boundless when he learned that "chucking" it was out of the question.

He rolled after the party to the dak bungalow, with a morose and frowning face.

He had made up his fat mind very late in the day; but he had made it up. He was going to "chuck" it. How was the question; and Bunter was determined to find ways and means.

In the meantime, he was in need of rest and refreshment, especially refreshment. But he was not going to keep on this rotten trip in the Indian hills; he was determined on that.

The khansama came out of the bungalow to greet the travellers salaaming profoundly to the colonel sahib. The Greyfriars party entered with curious eyes on their surroundings. They had heard a good deal of the dak bunglows of India; but this was the first they had stayed in on their long journey. Only in the large cities of India is the hotel accommodation anything like that of Western countries; in the provinces, and on the long country roads, the dak bungalow takes the place of the hotel or inn of Europe.

A thoughtful Government provides the dak bungalow for the convenience of travellers, where otherwise there would be no shelter; and these rest houses are found all over the Indian peninsula. But the traveller must take his own bedding, and generally his own food and servants; and when travellers are many on the road a room may be kept only for twenty-four hours. The keeper of the dak bungalow is called the khansama, which may mean butler or steward, the literal meaning being "master of the household arrangements."

Generally the khansama can speak English—the rather decorative English of the Indian native. Colonel Wharton and the Remove fellows were greeted in their own language—as nearly as the khansama's flowery Eastern mind could get to the plain language of the West.

"Being greatly delighted to welcome noble sahibs. Honorable sahibs condescend to enter unworthy dwelling."

The honorable sahibs condescended to enter.

Fortunately, the khansama had been in earlier days cook in the English cantonments at Rawalpindi, and he was able to provide the travellers with an excellent supper, which he helped Pandy Din to serve with his own plump, dusky hands.

Billy Bunter, morose as he was, did full justice to the supper.

Indeed, the khasama's pilau was so excellent that Bunter did it more than justice, and the quantity he stowed away made the keeper of the dak bungalow open his eyes wide.

After supper Pandy Din carried beds and blankets from the car to the rooms assigned to the party in the dak bungalow.

"Better turn in. Bunter, old top!" said Bob Cherry. "You must be tired out."

Bunter blinked at him.

"No more tired than you fellows!" he grunted. "You've come as far in the car as I have."

"But we didn't go so far with the pilau!" grinned Bob.

Colonel Wharton was speaking to Pandy Din, in the khitmutghar's own tongue. The juniors noticed that Pandy Din left the dak bungalow, with his rifle under his arm, and they could guess that he was going to see out.

Since the fight with the dacoits nothing had been seen of the enemy; Nally Das had vanished in the hills. But the colonel evidently thought it possible that the Rajah Baji Rao might make yet one more attempt, through his emissaries, to prevent Hurree Singh from reaching Bhanipur. It was the last chance of the plotting rajah; for, on the morrow, the Nabob of Bhanipur would be encircled by armed guards.

"Jolly night, isn't it?" said Bob Cherry, looking out of the doorway at the dark, velvety sky strewn with stars.

"It's cold!" growled Bunter.

"It isn't warm," agreed Bob. "But if it was you would be grousing because it was, old fat man. Keep smiling."

"I shouldn't wonder if there was a tiger hiding in those magnolias," said Bunter.

"Half a dozen, perhaps," said Bob genially. "Go and look."

"Ha, ha, ha!"

"Hallo, hallo, hallo! More giddy travellers?" said Bob.

There was a clatter of hoofs on the road.

In the bright starlight a troop of horses and horsemen came in sight, winding down the mountain road from the East.

The juniors watched them curiously.

"That lot must be coming from Bhanipur," said Harry Wharton. "Are they your people, Inky?"

Hurree Jamset Ram Singh was regarding the approaching party with keen interest. He shook his dusky head.

"It is an Afghan horse-dealer and his troop," he said. "Bhanipur is famous for its breed of horses, my esteemed chums; like Jodhpur, in the south. Many merchants come to Bhanipur to buy horses, and lead them away to sell in the markets at Lahore and Lucknow. I have seen that horseman years ago—he is a well-known horse trader; his name is Dost Hamid."

"A giddy old acquaintance!" said Nugent.

The nabob smiled faintly.

"There is no acquaintance between a nabob and a horse-dealer, my esteemed Nugent. I am in my own country now. Moreover, Dost Hamid the Afghan is a Mohammedan—that is to say, an infidel dog, from the point of view of a Hindu. While the worthy horse-dealer would regard me, prince of the country as I am, as a dog of an unbeliever."

"Oh, my hat!"

Dost Hamid rode at the head of his troop, evidently an important man, in his own eyes and the eyes of his followers.

He was a tall, powerful man, with a face the colour of mahogany and a thick beard, dyed red. His dark, flashing eyes looked out keenly from under thick, black brows.

Following the Afghan came more than a dozen men, leading strings of horses. There were more than sixty horses in the troop. most of them handsome animals. The Greyfriars fellows realized that they were getting a glimpse of the export trade of the little State of Bhanipur.

Dost Hamid halted before the dak bungalow, glanced at the group there, but did not salute them.

"A curse upon all unbelievers!" he said aloud, in his own tongue—fortunately, incomprehensible to the juniors.

Then he dismounted.

"Did he speak to us?" asked Nugent. "If he's saying good-evening in his own lingo, it would be only civil to answer."

The nabob grimed.

"He was greeting us politely, my esteemed Franky."

"What did he say?" asked Johnny Bull.

"You would not care to hear, my worthy Johnny!"

"Oh rats! Give it a name," said Bob. "You're our giddy interpreter in these parts, you know."

"The excellent and ludicrous Dost Hamid was kindly cursing us as misbelievers," explained the nabob.

"Oh, my hat! The lot of as?" asked Wharton.

"Certainly; both the Englishman and the Hindu, are unbelievers to the Mussulman."

"Cheeky ass!" growled Johnny Bull.

"The cheekfulness is terrific," agreed the nabob. To The Afghan Mohammedan is different, not really Indian. he is an intruder, like—" Hurree Jamset Ram Singh broke off quite suddenly.

"Like what?" asked Bob unsuspiciously.

"Nothing, my esteemed chum."

"Great pip!" ejaculated Johnny Bull. "Were you going to say like the jolly old Englishman, Inky?"

Hurree Jamset Ram Singh's face coloured faintly.

"My esteemed chums must excuse me," he murmured. "But here I am in my own country, and the thoughts that arise in my mind are not always the same thoughts as at Greyfriars."

It came again into the minds of Harry Wharton & Co. that they did not know their Indian chum quite so thoroughly as they had supposed. There was a "native" side to Hurree Singh's mind, which had never been in evidence at Greyfriars.

The khansama went out to greet Dost Hamid, though with much less graciousness than he had displayed to the colonel sahib. But his manner was respectful, and, to the juniors, it seemed tinctured with fear. They were not surprised at that for the Afghan looked what he was—a lawless man. likely to be as ready with his knife as with his fist, and as ready with his fit as with his tongue.

"So that crowd are coming away from Bhanipur?" asked Billy Bunter with a thoughtful blink at the horse-dealers.

Hurree Singh nodded.

"Then they will be going down to Rawalpindi?" asked Bunter.

"That is so."

"Good!" said Bunter.

The juniors glanced at the Owl of the Remove. Something, evidently, was working in the Owl's fat brain.

"What about it?" asked Bob.

"Oh, nothing!"

Bunter rolled out into the starlight. Whatever his thoughts were, he did not seem to intend to communicate them to the Famous Five.

"What has that fat duffer got in his silly noddle now?" asked Bob, staring after the fat junior.

"Goodness knows!"

"Luckily, it doesn't matter," said Bob.

And the juniors continued to watch the horse dealers camping under the trees, dismissing William George Bunter from their minds.

92

In the Dead of Night!

"SPEAK English?"

Dost Hamid sat on a heap of saddle-bags under a tree, smoking his hookah after his supper. Like dim shades, his men could be seen camped among the rising horses under the stars.

The burly horse trader turned his head and stared at Billy Bunter. He stared at him hard, without answering. Bunter blinked at him.

He was far from understanding the haughty pride and savage disdain of the Afghan. To him, the horse trader of Kabul was simply a "native," like the Bengalee of the south. Bunter was never likely to learn to distinguish between one inhabitant of India and another. Between the Afghan and the sleek native of Bengal there is less similarity than between the Englishman and the Italian. But to Bunter's mind all men with dark skins were "blinking natives "; merely that and nothing more.

"Do you speak English?" he asked irritably

Dost Hamid nodded surely.

"Why the thump don't you answer, then?" snapped Bunter. "Look here, I hear that you're a horse trader, taking your horses down the hills to Rawalpindi."

Another nod. The Afghan was a man of few words, and he did not seem to desire to waste any of the few upon Billy Bunter.

"I want a lift down to Rawalpindi," explained Bunter.

The Afghan stared.

"I've come up here with a lot of rotters," the Owl of the Remove further explained. "I want to go back, and I want a lift. See? I'll pay you twenty rupees to take me back to Rawalpindi."

"I am no driver of a tonga," said the horse trader surlily.

Bunter did not know what a tonga was, though he could guess that it was a conveyance of some kind.

"I suppose you could fix me up on a horse?" he said. "Fix up some sort of a palanquin on a horse, and that will be all right. I'll make it twenty-five rupees."

The Afghan's eyes glittered for a moment.

"A curse upon all unbelievers!" he said. That seemed to be his favorite remark. "The little sahib talks of rupees. Where are the rupees?"

Bunter frowned.

For a "blinking native" to doubt his word in this way was really intolerable. Bunter was inclined to kick the horse trader for his impudence. But the Afghan looked rather too hefty a man to be kicked. It was extremely fortunate for Bunter that he decided not to deliver the kick; for assuredly a thrust of Dost Hamid's Afghan knife would have been his reward.

"Look here, blow you!" growled Bunter.

He drew out a handful of rupees to show the trader. Billy Bunter was quite well supplied with cash. Hurree Jamset Ram Singh had been his banker since he had arrived in India; and Bunter, when he ran out of money, always succeeded in drawing a fresh supply from the nabob.

The Afghan's eyes glittered again.

"The little sahib can pay," he said. "Be it so."

"When do you start?" asked Bunter anxiously.

"One hour."

"Good! You're not staying here the night, then?"

"I stay to feed my horses and my men," said Dost Hamid. "In one hour we take the road down the mountain."

"That's all right. I'll come with you," said Bunter. "Those rotters will be fast asleep then, and the old fool, too."

Dost Hamid looked at him inquiringly.

"You see, they can't do without me," said Bunter. "They won't let me go back if they can stop me. I'm going, all the same."

The horse trader smiled—a smile that might have alarmed the Owl of the Remove had he been less short-sighted.

But Bunter had no doubts.

To the Owl of the Remove a horse trader was a horse trader, and he did not suppose there would be any danger in getting a lift from the Afghan. In fact, he supposed that danger would be over once he was quit of the Greyfriars party. Hurree Singh was in incessant danger from some attempt by his ambitious kinsman, Baji Rao. The attack of the dacoits had been on Hurree Singh's account. Once parted from the nabob, Bunter had nothing to fear from Hurree Singh's enemies. Nally Das and his associates would not waste a thought on him. So far, Bunter was right, and it did not occur to his fat mind that he might be getting out of the frying-pan into the fire; that Dost Hamid, the horse trader, might have other avocations as well as trading in horses; and that it might be as safe to meet a dacoit in the hills as to meet the Afghan in a solitary place.

"Mind, not a word to the colonel sahib," said Bunter anxiously. "He wouldn't let me go if he knew."

The horse trader grinned.

"Not a word," he agreed.

"Not a syllable to those other fellows, either."

"On my head be it!" said Dost Hamid gravely.

"That's all right, then. They won't part with me if they can help it," said Bunter. "But I know I'm jolly well not going to be bitten by snakes, and murdered by dacoits, to please them! I'll come out here in an hour's timewhat?"

"Be it so."

"That's settled, then."

Billy Bunter rolled away in the shadows, quite satisfied. Dost Hamid stared after him, and grinned over his hookah. Bunter, from sheer funk, was running into a danger from which a courageous fellow might well have shrunk. He was not aware of it yet, and the horse trader certainly did not mean to tell him.

"Hallo, hallo, hallo! Here's Bunter!" said Bob Cherry, as the fat junior came into the dak bungalow. "Where have you been, old fat top?"

"That's telling," said Bunter mysteriously.

"Eh?"

"Mind your own business," said Bunter.

Bob Cherry stared at him.

"You fat idiot—" he began.

"Go it!" said Bunter, with a sneer. "You'll feel a bit different when I'm gone, I can tell you. I've stood by you fellows a jolly long time, but I can tell you I'm fed-up with your ingratitude, and I'm done with you. I wash my hands of you."

"Well, they can do with a wash, I dare say," said Bob.

"Bah!"

Bunter rolled away to his room. The juniors were going to bed now. Johnny Bull shared Bunter's room; but Johnny was a sound sleeper, and Bunter did not anticipate any trouble with him when he made his start. Johnny Bull, when he turned in, noticed that Bunter's snore was not echoing as usual; but he was tired with the day's journey, and he was soon asleep. It did not even occur to him that Bunter was remaining awake.

Bunter, as a matter of fact, dared not sleep. Once his eyes had closed in slumber it was fairly certain that he could have snored on till morning, in which case his little scheme would have been knocked on the head. Dost Hamid and his troop would be gone before morning. So, though it cost him tremendous efforts, Bunter remained awake and waited.

As soon as Johnny Bull's steady breathing assured him that Johnny was fast asleep, Bunter rose and dressed himself in the glimmer of starlight from the high window. He packed his bag in which he had already placed a good supply of eatables. Bunter had learned little of the manners and customs of Hindustan, but he had learned, at least, that it was always judicious to take a supply of food on a journey. That was an important matter which was not likely to escape Bunter's notice. He put on a warm coat—the night was extremely cold. Indeed, it was so cold that Bunter was inclined to abandon his little scheme and remain in the shelter of the dak bungalow. But his resolution remained firm.

He was done with the ungrateful juniors of Greyfriars, and he was going. He was done with the stern old colonel, who had spanked him—spanked William George Bunter! He would have liked to blink into the colonel's room and tell him that he was done with him, and that he was going; but he did not venture to do so. He did not want to be spanked again; both his dignity and his fat person suffered from such an experience.

Bunter did not even realize that, had there been some safe method of sending him back to Rawalpindi, the colonel would willingly have taken advantage of it. Little as Bunter enjoyed the colonel's company, the colonel enjoyed Bunter's still less. It was true that, by a series of curious chances, Bunter had more than once proved useful on the journey, and for that reason the old military gentleman would have tolerated him patiently. But Bunter was quite mistaken in thinking that Colonel Wharton had any objection to his departure. Quite the reverse was the case.

But the plainest of plain English was not enough for Bunter on such a subject. He found it very hard to realize that any person could willingly forego the delights of his company.

If the colonel was willing to let him go, too, why didn't he arrange with the horse traders to take him down to Rawalpindi instead of Bunter having to make the arrangement surreptitiously?

Certainly, the colonel could have made that arrangement easily enough with Dost Hamid.

It did not occur to Colonel Wharton to do so, for the simple reason that the lawless Afghan was not to be trusted, being a man who did not value a human life at ten rupees.

All that, however, was quite hidden from Bunter. To his obtuse mind Dost Hamid was a horse trader, who would naturally give a fellow a lift for a reasonable tip.

Bunter did not like natives, or trust them, but he quite failed to see any difference between one native and another. To his fat and fatuous mind, Pandy Din, the faithful khitmutghar, and Dost Hamid, the horse trader, were much of a muchness; indeed, he did not see much difference between them and Hurree Jamset Ram Singh himself.

Bunter was destined to learn that there were considerable differences in these matters.

He stole quietly to a window—the unbarring of the door would have made too much noise. Bunter was assured that if his intended flight was discovered it would be stopped. That undoubtedly was the case; Colonel Wharton would never have allowed him to risk his life in the company of the lawless horse traders. But Bunter did not understand the reason; he only knew that his flight would be stopped, and he was determined that it should not be stopped.

The open, unglazed window was covered by a netting. Billy Bunter opened his knife and cut away the netting.

Then he dropped his bag into the magnolias outside the window, and clambered after it.

There was a stirring from Johnny Bull. Some sound had reached his ear's and disturbed him.

Bunter paused, and remained motionless at the window. Johnny Bull grunted, turned his heal on his pillow, and slept peacefully again.

"Beast!" murmured Bunter.

He dropped from the window after his bag.

His fat heart was beating fast as he picked himself up and picked up his bag.

In the distance, under the dim trees, he could see moving shapes as the horse traders prepared for their journey. Bunter scuttled across to the camp of the Afghan.

There had been no alarm. Bunter had escaped from the dak bungalow undiscovered. The die was cast now.

93

Like a Lamb to the Slaughter

HIGH over the mountain the moon sailed in silver splendour, streaming down light upon mighty forest and towering rock and plashing stream. From the dak bungalow the troop of horse traders went winding down the mountain, Dost Hamid riding ahead grim and silent on his big black horse, his men following him with the strings of animals, clattering, plunging, whinnying, amid a muttering of Afghan threats and curses.

Behind the red-bearded Afghan came a horse with a fat figure on its back that blinked to and fro through glimmering spectacles.

Bunter was on route.

Once or twice Dost Hamid glanced at him, with a cruel, sardonic grin, but otherwise he gave no heed to the Owl of Greyfriars.

Bunter was far from being a good rider. But he was able to cling on to the back of a horse, and he clung on, feeling extremely uncomfortable, and with growing indignation. He had bargained for a palanquin, in which he might have travelled quite comfortably, and, in fact, fast asleep. He had been given a horse, and he did not like it. He was determined to have that little matter out with the horse trader, but he decided to let it wait for a time; he was anxious to go away from the vicinity of the dak bungalow as fast as he could. It was firmly impressed upon his fat mind that the Greyfriars party would not lose him if they could help it, and that if they discovered his evasion they would be after him.

As soon as the promised palanquin was provided, Bunter would be able to take it quite easily, sleeping and eating by turns during the journey down the mountain. Those rotters—Harry Wharton & Co.—could keep on over the passes if they liked, among dacoits and poisonous snakes and tigers. Bunter was fed-up with it. And if they landed in some serape through being left without Bunter's advice and assistance—well, serve them jolly well right. They deserved it for their black ingratitude!

About a mile from the dak bungalow Bunter decided that it was high time to settle the question of the palanquin. The jolting of the horse was making him quite uncomfortable.

"I say, you know!" he called out.

Dost Hamid did not turn his head.

"Do you hear me?" hooted Bunter.

The Afghan glanced round darkly.

"What about that palanquin?" demanded Bunter.

Dost Hamid pulled in his horse. He signed to Bunter to pull to the side of the road and let the troop with the strings of horses go by. Bunter obeyed, and the traders went clattering by, some of the dark faces turning on Bunter with curious looks.

"Well, what about it?" demanded Bunter impatiently. "We agreed on a palanquin—what you call a palkee in your beastly language, you know; I can't stick on this beastly horse much longer! A bargain's a bargain! I can jolly well tell you that I sha'n't pay you if you don't keep to it!"

Dost Hamid did not answer. He waited in silence till the whole troop had gone by and disappeared beyond a winding of the road.

Bunter and the horse trader remained alone on the road under the glimmer of the moon.

Bunter was too short-sighted and too obtuse to mark and read the expression on the Afghan's dark face. He did not even realise that a man like Dost Hamid was a dangerous character. A native who dyed his beard red was, in Bunter's eyes, more a figure of fun than anything else. But, in spite of his blissful ignorance and his fatuity, a feeling of uneasiness came over Bunter as the sounds of the troop died away down the winding mountain road.

The spot was a solitary one, the dak bungalow a mile off, and no other building within fifty miles. On either side of the road dark forests climbed the slopes of the hills—shadowy, grim, impenetrable. Bunter found his heart beating faster; he did not know why.

"Well, where's the palanquin?" he exclaimed, and there was a quiver in his voice. It was as if his nerves understood more than his intelligence. "I don't see it! What are we waiting for?"

"Dismount!" said Dost Hamid.

Bunter dismounted. The Afghan did the same and proceeded to tether both horses by the roadside.

"Follow me!" he said.

He strode off the road into the shadow of the trees. Bunter followed him, concluding that the palanquin was awaiting him there. A dozen yards from the road the Afghan halted. Bunter stopped.

"The little fat sahib has left his friends!" said Dost Hamid grimly. "They do not know that he has travelled with the men of Kabul!"

"No," said Bunter.

"They never will know!" said Dost Hamid. "Give me the rupees!"

"Oh, really, you know," protested Bunter, "I'm jolly well not going to pay you till we get to Rawalpindi, you know!"

"Give me the rupees!"

There was a growling tone in the man's savage voice that sent a thrill of terror through the Owl of Greyfriars.

"I—I say—" he stammered.

He caught the glittering, threatening glance of the Afghan's dark eyes and stopped. The man's thick red beard, which had struck Bunter as ridiculous before, looked terrible now in the glimmer of the moon through the thick branches overhead. A shiver ran through Billy Bunter from head to foot.

Without another word, he groped in his pocket for the rupees.

"All of them!" said Dost Hamid.

"Look here—"

The Afghan laid his hand upon a long-barreled, silver-mounted pistol in his girdle.

"Every rupee!" he said grimly.

"D—d—do you mean that—that you're going to rob me?" gasped Bunter, the truth-part of the truth, at least-dawning upon his fat brain.

"A curse on all unbelievers," said Dost Hamid. "The death of an infidel is always meriting the blessing of the Prophet!" Bunter's fat legs refused to support him. He fell helplessly on his knees, A moment more and the shot would have sped. Crack! It was not the report of Dost Hamid's pistol; it was the clear, sharp ring of a rifle close at hand. There was a sudden yell from the Afghan, and his right arm dropped to his side.

"Dog of an unbeliever, are yon to keep me waiting?" said the Afghan. "Give me the rupees, son of a thousand pigs!"

Bunter, with a trembling hand, passed over the rupees to the horse trader. He dared not keep back a single coin. There were more than a hundred rupees in all, and the horse trader's black eyes glittered with greed as he grasped them and thrust them away into his punch.

"That is all?" he snarled.

"Yes!" gasped Bunter.

"A curse on all unbelievers!" said the Afghan.

"I—I say, look here! You'll jolly well get into trouble for this, you know!" gasped Bunter. "Do you think I'm going to let you rob me like this? I'll jolly well report it at Rawalpindi, I can tell you! You won't be allowed to keep my money!"

"Does the little fat sahib think that he is going to Rawalpindi?" asked the horse trader, with grim irony.

"You awful rotter!" gasped Bunter. "Mean to say that you've brought me here to rob me, and mean to leave me stranded?"

The Afghan laughed.

Bunter was afraid of the man—terribly afraid now. But his rage for the moment was stronger than his fear. He had been duped, and instead of a comfortable journey down to Rawalpindi, he had the prospect of finding his way back up the mountain road alone, past midnight, encompassed by the dangers of the Indian night, to rejoin the party they had left. His little round eyes glittered through his spectacles.

"You—you awful rascal!" he spluttered. "You scoundrel! You won't get away with it, all the same! Colonel Wharton won't let me be robbed like this by a black thief!"

Had there been any thought of mercy in the Afghan's savage mind, Bunter's words would have banished it. To the Afghan, as proud of his blood and descent as any English sahib could be, the term "native" was a deadly insult, to be wiped out only in blood. Even in the streets of Rawalpindi, or in the bazaar of Lahore, Dost Hamid would have answered such an insult with a shot from his pistol or a stab from his knife. His sinuous fingers closed almost convulsively on the silver-chased butt of the long pistol stuck in his broad Bokhara belt.

"But the colonel sahib does not know that you travelled with the horse traders!" he said grimly.

"He will know when I tell him!" howled Bunter.

"But the little fat sahib will not tell him!"

"I jolly well will!"

Bunter broke off suddenly as the horse trader drew the, long-barreled pistol from his belt. With a rush of understanding, the terrible truth came into his mind. He had been brought there into the lonely forest by the mountain road, not only to be robbed, but to be murdered!

Bunter gave a terrified gasp, and his fat knees knocked together. His eyes dilated behind his big spectacles as the Afghan raised the pistol and the long barrel was pointed at him.

"A curse on all unbelievers!" said Dost Hamid. "The death of an infidel is always meriting the blessing of the Prophet!"

Bunter's fat legs refused to support him. He fell helplessly on his knees.

A moment more, and the shot would have sped.

Crack!

It was not the report of Dost Hamid's pistol. It was the clear, sharp ring of a rifle close at hand.

There was a sudden, terrible yell from the Afghan. The long-barreled pistol crashed to the earth, still undischarged, and Dost Hamid's right arm dropped to his side, streaming with blood, smashed at the elbow by the bullet that had sped from the shadows of the forest.

94

For Life or Death!

BILLY BUNTER was still on his knees, his brain swimming. In his utter terror, he did not know what was happening. He fancied that the Afghan had fired and it was some moments before he knew that he was not hurt, and realized that Dost Hamid was staggering like a drunken man, clasping his shattered right arm with his left hand, and howling out curses mingled with cries of pain. Bunter blinked round him dazedly.

A figure that seemed familiar was emerging from the trees, running swiftly to the spot, a smoking rifle in hand. The newcomer was a native, and there was something familiar in his look, but Bunter was too dazed to recognize him in the dim light that filtered through the branches.

Dost Hamid turned a glare of fury on him. His dark face was convulsed with pain and rage. His left hand released the shattered arm, and groped for the long Afghan knife in his belt.

The man with the rifle came up, panting.

"Stand clear, little sahib!" he panted.

"Pandy Din!" gasped Bunter.

It was the khitmutghar.

Bunter remembered, though he had hardly heeded that Pandy Din had gone out with his rifle from the dak bungalow, to keep watch during the night for Hurree Singh's enemies. The watchfulness of the khitmutghar had been fortunate for Bunter.

"You getting out of the way?" rapped out the khitmutghar.

Bunter staggered to his feet.

He understood that the matter was not at an end; his life still depended on the khitmutghar.

He tottered to a tree, and stood leaning against it, gulping for breath, staring on the scene in terror.

Dost Hamid's right arm hung helpless, blood streaming down it and dropping from his dusky fingers. But the long Afghan knife was flashing in his left hand. His injury was a terrible one, and many a strong man would have sunk under it; but the man from the Kabul mountains was virile all through, tough and wiry as a wild beast.

Bunter did not understand, but the Afghan understood that he was not to escape with his wound. Bunter knew nothing of the blood-feuds of the Indian hills; but Pandy Din knew. Not for his life would Pandy Din have dared to let the African live. The blood-feud of Dost Hamid and his kindred would have followed him, dogging his footsteps with the danger of death, till sooner or later he fell under a bullet from behind a rock or a knife-thrust in the dark.

With set teeth, snarling like a wild animal, Dost Hamid closed in on the khitmutghar, the long Afghan knife gleaming in his left hand. The rifle-butt crashed on him, and he staggered. The knife clattered on the ground. But a moment more, and the Afghan had dodged the whirling rifle, and closed on Pandy Din and grasped him.

Bunter, watching breathlessly, understood that the khitmutghar had intended to crush in the Afghan's skull with his rifle-butt; but Dost Hamid had been too quick for him. The khitmutghar had to drop the rifle now, and use both hands to struggle with the man from Kabul.

Dost Hamid had one arm against two; but he was a much more powerful man than the khitmutghar, sturdy as the latter was. His left arm was wound about the khitmutghar, crushing him to the Afghan's brawny chest, and he received without heeding a rain of fierce blows in his face. Pandy Din grasped him with both hands and struggled striving to throw him down. The terrible agony of his wound did not seem to affect the Afghan, or only to drive him to mad fury. The two men struggled furiously and savagely, reeling to and fro, watched by the hapless Bunter's terrified eyes. The fat junior stood petrified under the tree.

The Afghan seemed to be failing, when Pandy Din's foot caught in a trailing root, and he went over.

He crashed to the ground, with the Afghan above him, and in an instant the horse trader's brawny knee was planted on his chest. Dost Hamid's left hand changed its grip to the khitmutghar's throat, and his grip was like that of a band of steel.

Fiercely the fallen man struck, and struck again, unheeded. He strove to get at the hunting-knife in his belt, but his belt was under the gripping knee of the Afghan, and he could not reach it.

Pandy Din's eyes rolled horribly as the savage grip tightened on his throat.

Only a couple of feet away from him lay the long Afghan knife which Dost Hamid had dropped. But it was beyond his reach, though his desperate fingers groped for it.

The Afghan's eves were blazing with savage triumph now. His right arm, streaming crimson, hung like a broken branch; but his left hand closed ever more tightly on the khitmutghar's throat. Pandy Din's despairing eyes turned on the Greyfriars junior under the tree.

Bunter shuddered.

He knew that his rescuer was at his last gasp—that a few minutes more would see the khitmutghar a dead man in the choking grip of the horse trader And then—

Bunter tried to pull himself together. His terror was so great that he was shaking from head to foot. He dared not approach the Afghan, though his life and the khitmutghar's depended on it. But the despairing eyes of Pandy Dir stirred him, and he moved from under the tree. His trembling hand picked up the long Afghan knife, and he thrust the handle of it into the hand of Pandy Din.

There was a flashing gleam of steel as the knife swept in the air, a desperate yell from Dost Hamid, and the horse trader rolled off his victim.

Pandy Din, his throat released from the choking grasp that had been crushing out his life, lay panting and gasping for breath. By him, in the herbage, lay the Afghan horse trader.

Pandy Din did not heed him. He had struck once, with the long

Afghan knife, and he knew that he need not strike again. One deep groan came from the horse trader of Kabul, and then no other sound. The burly body lay still.

For several minutes the khitmutghar lay panting. But he rose to his feet at last. Bunter's terrified eyes turned on the still figure of the horse trader.

"He is—is—is—" he stuttered.

Pandy Din did not answer, but he smiled grimly. The silver-mounted handle of the Afghan knife was sticking out of Dost Hamid's loose garments; from its position, Bunter knew that the long blade must be buried to the hilt in the ruffian's body. He shuddered, and turned away.

Pandy Din picked up his rifle. He reloaded it, and then looked round and listened. There was no sound, save the distant howl of a jackal in the forest.

"Little sahib, the others are gone?" asked Pandy Din.

"Long ago," said Bunter, with chattering teeth. "That brute—I—I mean he sent them on, while he kept me behind, to—to—" He broke off, gasping. The khitmutghar understood.

"At the next camp the horse traders will miss their chief," he said. "If they return for him they will find what the jackals have left."

"The jackals!" muttered Bunter.

Pandy Din made a gesture, and Bunter glanced round. From the shadows of the forest two or three pairs of shining eyes looked at the scene; the scavengers of the hills were already gathering. The wretched Owl shuddered from head to foot. That would have been his fate but for the intervention of the khitmutghar. That, as it had chanced, was to be the fate of the greedy horse trader. If his men came back in search of him they would find a few bones, picked clean, and nothing to tell them how he had come by his death.

"Little sahib, you should not have wandered so far in the night," said the khitmutghar; "I will take you back to the dak. But—he robbed you—"

Pandy Din moved towards the still body of the horse trader.

Bunter shuddered.

"It's nothing—it doesn't matter! I don't want to touch the money now!"

"As the little sahib wishes. Follow me."

Bunter was only too glad to follow the khitmutghar from the scene of the tragedy.

As they went he heard behind them the savage snarling of beasts of prey that had gathered for the horrid feast.

He hurried on.

For once Billy Bunter exerted himself. Pandy Din stooped to cast loose the two horses that the Afghan had tethered, and to start the animals trotting down the road the way the troop had gone. Then he went on with rapid strides, towards the dak bungalow, Bunter's little legs going like clock-work to keep pace with him.

Only a short time before Bunter had crept out of the dak, expecting and hoping never to see it again. Now he was longing for the sight of it—longing to creep within the shelter of its walls. Every shadow of the forest, every gleam of the moonlight on the rocks had terrors for Bunter; the shadowy night was peopled with foes to his terrified imagination. And when at last the dak bungalow was reached, and the khansama opened to the knock of Pandy Din, Bunter staggered in, almost fainting with relief.

95

Bunter Changes His Mind!

"WAKE up, fatty!"

Snore!

"Wake up, ass!"

Snorrrrrre!

Billy Bunter was going strong.

Having lost most of his sleep the night before, the Owl of the Remove was making up for lost time.

Harry Wharton & Co. were up, in the sunny morning; the last stage of the journey was to be done before the heat of day came on. But Billy Bunter was not prepared to turn out.

After the khitmutghar had brought him back to the dak bungalow, Bunter had dropped into bed, and immediately into slumber. He had hardly stirred since; and Johnny Bull, on awakening, had heard the old familiar sound of his snoring. The Famous Five did not know, as yet, of Bunter's adventure in the night.

"The giddy sleeping beauty seems to be growing stronger than usual!" grinned Bob Cherry. "But he's got to wake! I'll squeeze a sponge over his chivvy!"

"Gerrrroooooggh!" spluttered Bunter, as he woke up quite suddenly, under the application of the wet sponge. He sat up and blinked.

"'Tain't rising-bell, you chaps! Let a fellow sleep!"

"Ha, ha, ha! Do you think you're back at Greyfriars?" roared Bob Cherry. "We've got to get on to Bhanipur this morning, fathead."

"I'm tired."

"It must be catching," said Bob. "You make me tired, too."

"Turn out, Bunter," said Harry Wharton, laughing. "We've got to get on the road, you know, and the khansama has breakfast ready."

"Blow the khansama!"

"Do you want to be left behind, fathead?" asked Nugent.

Bunter was about to answer "Yes," when the recollection of the previous night's terrible experience came with a rush into his mind. He started up, gasping.

"Don't you leave me behind, you beasts!" he spluttered. "I sha'n't be long. "ll be ready in a tick!"

"Right-ho! You didn't seem so keen on coming on to Bhanipur yesterday," said Wharton in surprise.

"Blow Bhanipur!" snarled Bunter. "Bless Bhanipur! I'm not going to be left alone among these murdering natives, I can tell you!"

"My esteemed Bunter—" murmured Hurree Jamset Ram Singh.

"A rotten lot of murdering natives!" howled Bunter. "I'm not going to be robbed and murdered to please you, though. I was jolly nearly done in last night by a villain."

The juniors stared at him.

"Last night?" repeated Bob.

"Ow! Yes."

"Too much supper, I suppose," said Bob. "You've been dreaming, Bunter. It was a giddy nightmare."

"Yah!"

"It was the pilau that did it!" grinned Johnny Bull. "The khansama made up a ripping pilau, and you overdid it, Bunter. You had enough for nine or ten. You can't really do with more than enough for six."

"Ha, ha, ha!"

"Nothing happened last night, old bean," said Nugent reassuringly. "Pandy Din was on guard all night, and there was no alarm."

"I tell you—" roared Bunter.

"Oh, come along to brekker, and tell us your dreams afterwards!" said Johnny Bull.

And the Famous Five went out to breakfast set among the shady trees. Bunter joined them in a few minutes, looking peevish and sulky, and still tremulous. The khansama and Pandy Din waited on the breakfasters; Colonel Wharton had already finished, and was standing by the car with the Punjabi chauffeur.

Bunter breakfasted in sulky silence.

He was in a tremor with what he had been through; it had been more than enough to shake the nerve of the Owl of the Remove. And, he was by no means thinking of deserting the party now. The mere thought of getting out of sight of English faces threw him into a cold perspiration. He would not have accepted a lift on a Royal elephant from the greatest native prince or king in Hindustan. No inducement would have made Bunter trust himself alone among the natives again. Fortunately, his alarming experiences had not affected his appetite. His breakfast was as Gargantuan as usual, and made the khansama regard him with wondering admiration. But he kept his eyes wide open on his companions; he was not going to be left behind. At the first sign of starting, Bunter was prepared to leave even his breakfast unfinished.

"The horse traders are gone," Bob Cherry remarked, with a glance towards the spot where Dost Hamid and his men had camped the night before.

Bunter shuddered. The mere recollection of the red-bearded Afghan was enough to make him tremble.

Colonel Wharton came through the trees, and stopped at the table. His eyes fixed sternly on Bunter.

"G-g-good-morning, sir!" stammered Bunter.

He knew that Pandy Din must have reported the night's happenings to the colonel sahib, and he was uneasy as to how the colonel would take it.

"You had a narrow escape last night, Bunter," said the colonel quietly.

"I—I know."

"It was utterly foolish and reckless to leave the dak in company with natives whom you did not know," said Colonel Wharton.

"I—I know," mumbled Bunter. "I offered to tip that villain Dost Hamid for a lift down to Rawalpindi. I—I never knew—"

Harry Wharton & Co. stared.

"Did anything happen in the night, uncle?" asked Harry.

"Yes. Bunter started for Rawalpindi with the horse traders, and but for Pandy Din he would have been murdered by Dost Hamid for his rupees."

"Oh!" gasped Wharton.

"I—I thought it was all right," mumbled Bunter. "The villain was just pulling my leg; getting me away from here so that he could knock me on the head and bag my rupees. Oh dear!"

"You utter idiot?" growled Johnny Bull.

"Oh, really, Bull—"

"The idiocy of the esteemed Bunter is marvellous!" said Hurree Singh, staring blankly at the fat junior.

"It appears, Bunter, that you do not desire to finish the journey to Bhanipur," said Colonel Wharton. "You should have stayed behind at Rawalpindi, as I advised you. But if you wanted to go back you should have told me; there was no need to be surreptitious. I should have been only too glad to make arrangements to send you back in safety."

"Oh!"gasped Bunter.

He blinked at the colonel.

"You wouldn't let me go back when I wanted to," he stuttered. "I—I thought I—I—"

"Certainly I should not have turned back myself, as you had the impudence to ask!" snapped the colonel. "That was a different matter. Are you absolutely obtuse, Bunter?"

"That's it!" grinned Bob Cherry. "Brains were left out of Bunter, sir; he got an extra allowance of fat instead."

"Oh, really, Cherry—"

"I think you are the most obtuse boy I have ever seen, Bunter," said the colonel. "You are certainly the most troublesome. However, as no harm has resulted from your folly, to you, at least, we need say no more about it. I shall arrange for you to be taken back to Rawalpindi, and you will remain at Captain Ferrers' bungalow there till we return from Bhanipur. You are quite unfitted to travel in this country, and it was foolish of you to come. I will engage a reliable man to take you—"

"A Englishman?" gasped Bunter.

"Do not be absurd! We are the only Europeans for fifty miles n round here. I shall find a reliable native."

"I won't go with a howled Punter, in alarm. "I'm not going to be murdered!"

"Silence! I tell you I shall find a reliable man, and he will take care of you till you reach Rawalpindi!" snapped the colonel.

"I won't go with a native!" roared Bunter.

"You will go with a Rajput trader who is expected here shortly. And I advise you not to call him a native, Bunter, or you may not reach Rawalpindi without receiving the chastisement you deserve for your ignorance and insolence."

With that Colonel Wharton turned and strode away, apparently having no more time to waste on William George Bunter.

Bunter turned a helpless blink on the Famous Five.

"I say you ffollows—"

"It's all right, Bunter," said Harry Wharton soothingly. "You can depend on my uncle to see that you will be safe."

"The esteemed Rajput may be trusted, my worthy, funky Bunter."

"Anyhow, you've asked for it!" growled Johnny Bull.

"I won't go with a native!" howled Bunter. "I was nearly murdered last night by a villain of an Afghan. Why can't you all come back with me to Rawalpindi, and go on to Bhanipur later?"

"Fathead!"

"I say, you fellows, you talk to the old codger," said Bunter anxiously.

"Tell him I want to come to Bhanipur—in fact, I'm awfully keen. See? You talk to him, Wharton; the old codger is your uncle, you know."

The captain of the Remove looked at Bunter.

"As you're leaving us today I won't punch you," he said curtly. "But if you speak of my uncle like that again, look out for trouble!"

"Beast!"

"You're booked, old fatty!" said Johnny Bull. "What the thump are you grousing about? You want to go back, don't you?"

"I'm not going with a murdering villain ", yelled Bunter.

"You will be safe enough, you silly owl!"

"Rats! Rot! Besides, I—I want to come on to Bhanipur!" gasped Bunter. "Now I come to think of it, I want to come with you, Inky."

"The wantfulness is all on your side, my esteemed Bunter."

"I'm coming on to Bhanipur!" groaned Bunter. "I—I don't mind dacoits and—and snakes and—and—and tigers. In fact, I—I like 'em"

"He, ha, ha!"

"You fix it up with the old—I mean with the colonel, Wharton! Remember all I've done for you, old chap!"

"It's settled, you ass!"

"Oh, really, Wharton—"

The Famous Five left the breakfast able. Bunter was left—still eating—but at the same time blinking after them, in alarm and dismay. To be left at the dak bungalow, to wait there for the Rajput trader to arrive, and to travel a hundred miles with the Rajput, was a prospect that made Bunter almost cringe with terror. The khansama had been polite and attentive; but he was a native, and after the colonel was gone he was quite capable—in Bunter's terrified opinion—of poisoning the fat junior in a pilau, or knocking him on the head and burying him under the magnolias. Even if the khansama did none of those awful things, the Rajput trader would undoubtedly—so it seemed to Bunter's scared mind—shoot him through the head for his watch and chain, or the clothes he stood in. What difference was there between a blinking khansama and a blinking Rajput and a blinking Afghan horse trader?

Bunter could see no difference, and he was determined that he was not going to trust himself out of sight of a Englishman's face. He almost suspected the colonel of really wanting him to be knocked on the head by some ferocious native in those awful mountains.

One thing was settled in Bunter's mind—he wasn't going to be left behind. But as it was settled by all the rest of the party that he was to be left behind at the dak bungalow, it was evident that the Owl of the Remove had a very difficult problem to solve, and that his fat wits were likely to have some unaccustomed exercise in the solving of it.

96

Missing!

"BUNTER!"

"Where's Bunter?"

"Hallo, hallo, hallo! Bun. Bunty! Bunty! roared, Bob Cherry.

It was time to start.

The cars were ready; the baggage was packed on the baggage-car; Colonel Wharton had completed his arrangements with the khansama with regard to William George Bunter. The Famous Five looked for Bunter to say goodbye to him, and the colonel desired to see him to give him some necessary advice, and to hand him a sufficient sum of cash for his needs at Rawalpindi. And Bunter was not to be found.

Harry Wharton & Co. had left him still breakfasting. Evidently Bunter had finished breakfast—he was gone.

Supposing that he had gone into the dak for a nap, the juniors sought him there. But he was not there.

They sought him up and down the gardens, but he was not to be seen. They shouted to him, but there came no answer.

The Owl of the Remove seemed to have vanished into thin air.

"Where on earth can the fat chump be?" exclaimed Johnny Bull, in exasperation. "Is he hiding somewhere, to give us a lot of trouble for nothing?"

"He can't have gone out," said Wharton. He's too jolly scared to go out alone after what happened last night."

"Then where is he?"

"Echo answers—where?"

"The wherefulness is terrific."

"Let's ask the khansama," said Bob, impatiently. "Bother the fat duffer! The giddy khansama may have seen him.

But the khansama knew nothing.

"Not seeing the little fat sahib," he said. "He walking out on road, but afterwards not seeing him."

"He went out on the road?" exclaimed Harry.

"Han, sahib! Not seeing him after."

"Well, my hat!"

The juniors returned to the car, where Colonel Wharton was waiting for them with growing impatience. The colonel eyed them grimly.

"Why have you not brought Bunter? I must speak to him before we go."

"Can't find him, sir," said Bob.

"What?"

"The khansama says he went out on the road after brekker," said Harry Wharton, puzzled and perplexed. "Goodness knows why! I—I suppose he hasn't got into any fresh trouble?"

The colonel knitted his brows.

"Pandy Din!"

The khitmutghar came up from baggage-car.

Colonel Wharton gave him a few words in his own tongue, and the khitmutghar salaamed and hurried away.

"I—I suppose we're waiting, uncle, till we know what's become of Bunter?" asked Harry hesitatingly.

"Pandy Din will search for him for an hour," said the colonel curtly. "If he is not found in that time, he must take his chance. Doubtless he has only gone for a walk, and will return to the dak. But whatever foolish thing he may have done, we cannot wait long. We have an appointment to keep at the frontier of Bhanipur, and we must cover a good distance before the heat of the day comes on."

"After all, nothing could have happened to him," said Bob. "He was too jolly scared last night to think of going far from the dak."

"It's a silly trick to bother us!" growled Johnny Bull. "He's changed his silly mind, and doesn't want to be left behind. I shouldn't wonder if he's hiding in the gardens all the time."

"Let's look, anyhow; we may as well, while we are waiting."

Harry Wharton & Co proceeded to search for the Owl of the

Remove and down and round they went, calling to Bunter; but there was no reply, and they did not find the fat junior.

It seemed probable that Bunter was concealing himself somewhere, in the belief that the party would not go while he was missing. It was, in fact, exactly one of the fatuous devices that might have been expected of Bunter. In the gardens surrounding the dak there were endless nooks where the fat junior might have lain hidden.

Whatever might be the explanation, he was not found. The juniors returned to the car at last, exasperated and a little troubled in mind. They found Pandy Din there. The khitmutghar had been equally unsuccessful.

Colonel Wharton looked at his watch.

"We can wait no longer," he said. "I will give instructions to the khansama to take every care of Bunter, and to have him searched for if he does not return soon. Word will be sent to us at Bhanipur. You need have no anxiety. Get into the car."

There was nothing else to be done, and the Famous Five stepped in. The throb of the engine echoed among the Indian hills.

The khansama came bowing and salaaming to take leave of his distinguished guests. He bowed and salaamed all the while he was receiving colonel's instructions with regard to Bunter.

"On my head be it!" he said solemnly.

Colonel Wharton stepped into the car, and the khansama stood bowing and salaaming as the party started. When the juniors looked back he was still "going it," as Bob Cherry expressed it, and he disappeared from sight at last, still bowing and salaaming as if he had a spring in his back.

Colonel Wharton had entered the car with the juniors, instead of sitting beside the chauffeur as on the previous day. They noticed that he kept his revolver in his hand, and he bade them keep their rifles loaded and ready. The Punjabi chauffeur had a revolver on the seat beside him; and Pandy Din, driving the baggage-car behind, had his weapons at hand. It was clear that the colonel looked for danger on the "last lap" of the journey to Hurree Jamset Ram Singh's kingdom.

The road ran like a long white ribbon up the valley, amid towering hills thick with forest. The colonel's keen glance watched on either side, incessant, unresting.

"The last danger will be over in a few hours," he said. "We must be on our guard until then."

"The dacoits?" asked Harry.

The colonel shook his head.

"The lesson the dacoits received from the fighting-plane has been more than enough for them," he answered. "I doubt whether Nally Das could bribe a single one of the robbers of the hills to attack us again. There is no danger from the dacoits. The danger is now from the retainers of the Rajah Baji Rao—Nally Das and his own associates. I do not think they would venture upon an open attack so near the frontier of Bhanipur, and, in fact, Baji Rao would not venture to let his own men be seen engaged in such an attempt. He dare not let it become publicly known that he is plotting against the Nabob of Bhanipur. But—"

Colonel Wharton knitted his brows.

"So far, only attempts have been made to kidnap Hurree Singh," he said. "Baji Rao hesitates to shed the blood of a nabob of Bhanipur. He knows that he is suspected, and if his guilt should be proved, it means his ruin. But now that the game is nearly lost, now that Hurree Singh is about to enter his kingdom, I fear that he may take more desperate measures. He would not dare to order his men to attack us openly. Kidnapping Hurree Singh is no longer possible for him. But he might quite probably place everything on a last throw of the dice, and take the risk of assassination. A mark-man hidden by the road might—"

The colonel broke off, his keen eyes sweeping the road.

The juniors breathed more quickly.

They understood that the situation had changed. Hurree Jamset Ram Singh was no longer threatened by the kidnappers. He was safe from that, secure now, unless his desperate kinsman should use the last resource of assassination. If the nabob was threatened now at all, it was his life that was threatened.

"My hat!" murmured Bob Cherry. "We'll look after you, Inky,

old man, and see that you don't, get potted before you get to Bhanipur."

The nabob grinned.

"The serenefulness is terrific!" he said. "It is the last chance of the worthy and treacherous Baji Rao, and I thinkfully opine that something will happen yetfully before we reach the border of Bhanipur, where my guards wait us. But as the English proverb says, it is the cracked pitcher which goes to the well and saves a stitch in time."

The car sped on by the mountain road.

97

In Ambush?

AND where was Billy Bunter?

Harry Wharton & Co. would have been surprised could they have seen the Owl of the Remove. It did not cross their mind for a moment that the fat junior had not been left behind at the dak. As a matter of fact, Bunter, so far from being left behind, was ahead of the Greyfriars party.

It was firmly fixed in Bunter's fat mind that he wasn't going to be "left." To be left alone among "natives" was too terrifying; Bunter could not and would not realise that all would be well for him under the arrangements made by the colonel. Every face was, for him, the face of a possible or probable robber and assassin; every native was more or less of a Dost Hamid. But he knew that Colonel Wharton had made up his mind, and that if he stepped into the car when it started he would be lifted out again and handed over to the khansama.

To the uneasy and terrified Owl, it seemed that his valuable life was at stake. The terrors of the road, dacoits, snakes, tigers, wild elephants, were as nothing compared with the catastrophe of being left alone among natives. He did not want to go onward; but much, much less did he want to go back. And in that difficult position Bunter's fat brain had labored at high pressure, and he had evolved a plan.

So while the Greyfriars party were making their preparations for departure, Bunter had slipped quietly away. The Khansama had seen him go out upon the toad, but had seen no more of him. That was not surprising, as Bunter had turned his back on the halting-place, and gone tramping forward towards the border of Bhanipur at his best pace. The well-laid road, winding over the mountains, was a certain guide; even Bunter was not capable of missing the way. He kept to the middle of the road, with fearful eyes blinking on either side, for dacoits, tigers, Afghan horse traders, wild elephants, and other fearsome creatures. And he covered the ground with unusual speed, dreading every moment to hear behind him the buzz of the Greyfriars car. He did not want to hear that—yet; not while he was still near enough to the dak bungalow to be sent back there.

Bunter's stratagem was, he flattered himself, a masterly one. He was going as fast and as far as he could ahead of the party. When they came up with him, they would simply have to let him step aboard again; they could not refuse to let him hook on, as it were. To pass him by and leave him stranded on the mountain road, miles from the dak, miles from anywhere, was really impossible. And Colonel Wharton would not turn back in the car and lose time.

Bunter knew that a messenger had been sent forward overnight from the dak bungalow to announce the hour of the Greyfriars party's arrival at the Bhanipur border. Some time would be lost when Bunter was missed, at the start. That was fairly certain. After that there would be no more time to lose. If he was overtaken half a mile, or a mile, from the dak, the colonel might turn back with him. But at a greater distance it was extremely unlikely that he would do so.

Willed he or nilled he, so to speak, the colonel would have let the fat junior look on again.

It seemed quite a masterly scheme to the Owl of the Remove.

He tramped on as fast as he could, making the most of his time, hoping that his absence would cause a long delay at the dak.

"The beasts!" he murmured. "The rotters! They couldn't possibly leave me stranded on the road, to walk back six or seven miles. They're hound to pick me up when they come up. Simply bound to! The old codger may think I could walk back alone, but the fellows will put in a word for me. Besides, I shall be worn out—and hungry, too! Even that stiff old codger must have some human feelings somewhere. He's a beast, but he's not beast enough to leave me to expire on the road. I'll make out that I've sprained my ankle, too, and can't walk."

Bunter grinned.

Only a hundred yards ahead, at the opening of the gorge, the hidden assassin waited. Bunter's heart thumped. He did not venture to call out as he stepped into the road. Trembling In every fat limb, with perspiration streaming down his fat face, Bunter raised his hands aloft as the car containing Harry Wharton & Co. came in sight.

"As soon as I hear the car I'll sit down, and then they can come up and find me crippled—unable to walk. It will be up to them then. Beasts!"

Bunter tramped on valorously.

When the road ran down an incline he broke into a trot. The success of his masterly scheme depended on being a good distance from the dak when the party overtook him. If it meant only a short time to be wasted, he more than suspected that the colonel would run him back to the bungalow in the car.

There were drawbacks to the scheme, of course. Bunter was in a state of palpitating funk at finding himself alone on the mountain road, even in the bright sunshine of the morning. But he had, only the choice between two evils—of trying on this dodge, or allowing himself to be left alone among "natives." And the latter alternative was not to be thought of.

He blinked right and left, watchful for dark faces, and the sight of a native sent him scuttling in terror behind a tree. The native was only a coolie, tramping along the road with a bundle on his back. But Bunter remained in cover, palpitating, till he was out of sight, and then resumed his way, blinking round watchfully for another possible enemy.

The road wound mostly downward, the summit of the pass having been cleared the previous afternoon. Bunter made quite a good speed, and mile after mile vanished under his tramping feet. Whether the car had started yet from the dak bungalow he did not know; but there was no sound of it, so far, on the long, white road behind him.

Bunter halted at last.

The sun was high in the heavens now, and the heat was growing. The road before him ran on through a narrow rocky gorge, shadowy even in the blaze of the Indian sun. The shade would have been welcome enough to Bunter, but the high rocks, shutting in the view on all sides, scared him. In the wide valley he had been able to observe the approach of any possible enemy; there were broad spaces on either side of the road. But once within that narrow gorge, a score of dacoits might have been hidden unseen within a dozen feet of the road. Snakes, and tigers, and elephants, for all Bunter knew, might be lurking in those rocky recesses, waiting for a chance to spring out on him. He stopped, and blinked into the deep gorge into which the white road descended, and shook his head. He would have preferred to cover a greater distance before stopping to wait for the car, but his fat heart failed him.

"Beasts!" he murmured, referring, perhaps, to the possible denizens of the rocky gorge, or perhaps to the Greyfriars party.

He sat down in the shadow of a huge boulder by the roadside, after carefully inspecting the spot for snakes.

There he waited, occasionally blinking back the way he had come for a sign of the car.

It was certain, by this time, that the party must have waited at the dak to search for him, for there was no sign yet of the party on the road. Bunter began to hope that they had not waited too long. The solitude of the mountain road, the deep silence of the hills, had a terrifying effect upon him, now that he was waiting. It seemed to Bunter that he was alone in a vast solitude, and yet, to his uneasy imagination, every rock and boulder hid a fierce enemy.

In the deep stillness of the mountains a slight sound and movement at a little distance sufficed to set his nerves twittering. He was blinking back along the road, but the sound came from the other direction. Bunter turned his eyes towards the rocky gorge ahead, and his heart almost died within him at what he saw.

From the shadows of the gorge a man had emerged.

The man was a native, which alone would have been sufficient to scare the Owl of the Remove in his present frame of mind. But that was not all. The man was Nally Das!

More than once Bunter had seen the Hindu who had attempted to kidnap Hurree Singh in far-off England, and who had dogged the party on their journey, besetting their path with perils. Bunter crouched lower in the shadow of the great boulder, scarcely daring to breathe. He knew what to expect if Nally Das saw him. The Hindu's presence showed that another attempt was to be made on the nabob, almost on the border of his kingdom; and had Bunter been discovered there, certainly he would not have been allowed to live to give a warning. Once more the Owl of the Remove, in his cunning fatuity, had thrown himself into fearful peril.

But the Hindu was not looking towards him, and Bunter was almost hidden by the great rock that loomed over him by the roadside. Nally Das stood on a rock and stared away up the road, his shoulder turned in Bunter's direction. Bunter watched him in breathless terror. He knew that the Hindu was looking for the Greyfriars car. The Greyfriars party were watched for in the shadowy gorge ahead.

For a full minute Nally Das stood motionless on the rock, his eyes searching the vacant road. Then he turned and disappeared.

Bunter breathed again.

Silently, with terrified caution, he crawled round the base of the great boulder, to place it between him and the Hindu, if Nally Das should return to scan the road again. From beyond the rocks he heard a voice calling—the voice of Nally Das.

"Kalouth!"

Bunter knew the name of the Hindu's confederate. Kalouth had been with Nally Das in England, when Wibley of the Remove had fallen into the hands of the kidnappers.

There were sounds of footsteps. Bunter lay and trembled. If the two Hindus came round the big boulder, they could not fail to discover him, and that was—death! But the footsteps increased and he heard a murmur of voices.

He recognized the Hindustani without understanding it. From the tone of Nally Das' voice, however, he guessed that Baji Rao's chief emissary was giving, instructions. Kalouth replied only with a grunt or two of assent. Then there was silence. Footsteps died away in the gorge.

They were gone.

Bunter moved at last. Keeping in the cover of the big rock, he blinked desperately out on the road. He would have given all the treasures of the East to see the colonel's car in the distance. But it was not in sight. Still keeping in cover, he blinked towards the gorge. Far in the distance he had a glimpse of a Hindu's back. One of the Hindus was departing, and though Bunter could not see clearly at the distance, he was sure that it was Nally Das. The man was going, but he had left his confederate somewhere among the rocks at the mouth of the gorge.

Bunter backed away silently.

His idea was to scramble away among the boulders, and strike the road again at a safer spot, nearer to the dak bungalow. Cautiously he went, blinking back every moment, and keeping well away from the road. And suddenly he saw Kalouth from behind.

The man had climbed to the top of a large rock at the opening of the gorge, and lay there, on his face. Before him, on the rock, lay a rifle and Kalouth was watching along the barrel. Bunter saw little more than his legs and the back of his turban; but the man's attitude told him everything. Kalouth lay there, watching the road, with rifle ready, to fire into the car from cover as it came by. In such a position, with a magazine-rifle, a good marksman might have picked off every member of the Greyfriars party before he could have been dislodged,

One blink at the ambushed assassin was enough for Bunter. But for the necessity of silence, he would have taken to his heels. But he dared not risk causing the Hindu to turn his glance towards him. Silently, cautiously, Bunter picked his way among the boulders, ant hardly breathed till he had placed a hundred yards between him and Kalouth.

There he was safe, screened by the great boulders piled ruggedly along the roadside.

"Oh dear!" gasped Bunter.

The perspiration was streaming down his fat face.

Whirrrrr!

"The car!" panted the Owl of the Remove.

The Greyfriars car was coming at last. Bunter scrambled among the rocks to the roadside; in the distance he saw the coming car, with the baggage-car behind. And only a hundred yards ahead, at the opening of the gorge, the hidden rifleman waited.

Bunter's heart thumped.

At that spot the winding road was hidden from the watching Kalouth. Not till the car was within twenty yards would he see it. Bunter realized that he was safely out of sight of the watching assassin, and he stepped into the road.

He did not venture to call out.

Trembling in every fat limb, with perspiration streaming down his face, he stood in the middle of the road, and raised his fat hands to the Punjabi chauffeur; and, with a grinding of brakes the car came to a halt.

98

Clearing the Road!

"BUNTER!"

"That fat idiot!"

"Here, of all places!" ejaculated Bob Cherry.

"Where the thump did he spring from?"

Harry Wharton & Co. stared in amazement at Bunter. They had wondered what had become of him; but it had never crossed their minds that he was ahead of them on the mountain road. Bunter rolled to the door of the car as it stopped, and met the surprised stares of the juniors, and the grim frown of Colonel Wharton.

"So you are here!" said the colonel quietly.

"Yes," gasped Bunter.

The old military gentleman's lip curled.

"I think I understand. You came on ahead, while you were being searched for at the dak."

"Yes; I—I—I—" stammered Bunter.

taking Bunter Sahib to the dak," said the colonel. "You will then follow on as speedily as you can."

"On my head be it, sahib."

"Get into Pandy Din's car, Bunter."

"I-I say, you fellows—"

"Nothing doing, old fat bean," said Bob, Cherry. "You really shouldn't be such a troublesome passenger, you know.

"Goodbye, Bunter!"

"The farewellfulness is terrific, my esteemed fat Bunter!"

Bunter grabbed hold of the door of the car.

"I—I tell you—" he spluttered.

"You are wasting time, Bunter," said the colonel.

"I—I—I tell you—"

"Stand back, Bunter, and step into Pandy Din's car," said Colonel

Wharton curtly. "Do you hear me? I have no more time to waste on you!" Bunter splattered.

Harry Wharton & Co. remained silent. They would hare relented towards the fatuous Owl of the Remove, certainly, and allowed him to hook on again. But it was for the colonel to give orders; and they did not think of arguing with him. But Bunter though his little scheme had been a lamentable failure—had a card up his sleeve that neither the colonel nor the juniors suspected. He had not, indeed, realised himself that he had a trump card to play. He hung on to the door of the car and spluttered.

"I say, you fellows—look here, Colonel Wharton, I've got something to tell you—danger——"

"Hook it, old man!" murmured Bob Cherry soothingly.

"The hookfulness is the proper caper, my fat, ludicrous Bunter."

"I've seen Nally Das!" yelled Bunter desperately.

The colonel's bronzed hand was about to jerk him back from the car.

"Nally Das!" ejaculated Wharton.

"And—and Kalouth!" gasped Bunter.

"Oh, my hat! The jolly old enemy are on the road, then," said Bob Cherry. "They're the two blighters who tried to kidnap Inky at Greyfriars."

Colonel Wharton gave the Owl of the Remove a keen, searching look. Bunter was full of prevarication and trickery, as he had discovered very early in their acquaintance. But the fat junior was evidently in earnest now; his terror was unmistakable, and the colonel realised that it was not wholly due to his fear of being sent back among "natives," Something had happened on the mountain road while Bunter was there ahead of the car.

"Explain yourself, Bunter!" the colonel said sharply.

Bunter spluttered out his story.

Pandy Din stood back, waiting for orders; but there was a glitter in his black eyes, and the juniors noticed his hand seeking the hunting-knife in his belt. The khitmutghar was ready to deal with the ambushed assassin on the mountain road. His eyes were on the colonel's face, waiting for a sign.

"My hat!" murmured Harry, gazing at the Owl of the Remove in wonder. "It seems to be Bunter's jolly off destiny to come in useful on this trip. Who'd have thought it?"

Hurree Singh nodded.

"The esteemed Kalouth would give me the finishing potfulness, as the car passed," he remarked. "It is Baji Rao's last card."

"More likely to miss, though, with the car going at a good speed," said Johnny Bull.

Colonel Wharton compressed his lips.

He had been keeping a watch, as the car glided on, with the keenness of an eagle; but he was well aware that the ambush described by Bunter might have been successful. Kalouth, in cover on top of the high rock, commanding the road with his rifle, might not have been spotted in time—indeed, it was most likely that he would never have been discerned before he had time to fire at least one shot. And it was certain that he was a good marksman—he must have been selected for that.

With the car going slow, he could have picked off the nabob, or any other victim to chose; with the car going fast, he could have shot the chauffeur, and sent the car rushing to sudden destruction on the rocks.

The risk was one that the travellers had to take in the wild passes of the Indian frontier; only watchfulness could have saved them, and it was likely enough that in this instance it would not have saved them, but the warning given by the Owl of the Remove was enough.

The colonel asked a few questions, drawing out of Bunter all the information he could give. Then he glanced at Pandy Din. The khitmutghar had listened attentively.

The glance from the Colonel Sahib was enough.

"On my head be it!" said the khitmutghar.

He stepped away from the road, and disappeared among the boulders and scrub of the hillside.

The cars remained motionless. Harry Wharton glanced at his uncle.

"We stop here?" he asked.

"Until we receive a signal from Pandy Din that the road is clear," answered Colonel Wharton.

The juniors waited in silence. Bunter leaned on the car and gasped, but he did not speak.

Even Bunter understood that there was tragedy in the air. The juniors' hearts beat almost painfully. Kalouth, the hidden assassin, watching for his prey, like a hyena, among the rocks, deserved no pity or mercy. But the moments were terrible to the Greyfriars fellows, unused to the ruthless warfare of the Indian frontier. And they were not without anxiety for Pandy Din. The khitmutghar had vanished—no sign or sound betrayed his existence to friend or foe.

The juniors knew that he was creeping stealthily among the strewn boulders of the hillside, to approach the ambushed assassin from behind, and take him by surprise. They knew what would happen if he succeeded. But Kalouth must have heard the car before it halted. The halt, out of his sight, might make him suspicious; he might be watching for a surprise attack. The ring of his rifle might tell that Pandy Din had gone, not to success, but to death.

In deep silence, their hearts almost aching with the intensity of their anxiety, the Greyfriars party waited—minute followed minute, and each silent minute seemed an age to them as they listened.

There was a sound at last—a sudden, strange sound from the distance. It was a hoarse, desperate cry.

The juniors started, and exchanged glances. Colonel Wharton's bronzed face alone remained unmoved.

It was a death-cry that the juniors had heard. In that tense moment a life had gone out like a candle that is snuffed. But who had perished, out of their sight, among the sun-baked rocks? They waited, in anxiety that had grown intolerable, till footsteps rang on the states, and a dusky, smiling face looked at them from the road. It was the khitmutghar.

He salaamed to the colonel.

"The road is clear, sahib."

"Ach-cha!" said the colonel, with a nod, and the khitmutghar went back to the baggage-car.

"I—I say!" gasped Bunter.

The colonel gave him a look.

"You may get in, Bunter."

Bunter scrambled into the ear.

The engine throbbed again. The Punjabi chauffeur drove on. Pandy Din, still with a smile on his face, followed with the baggage-car. No more was said of Kalouth. The khitmutghar had done his work silently but surely. And if the juniors needed any witnees of the assassin's fate, they soon had it. A dark shadow for a moment hovered overhead, shadowing the sunshine.

It was a vulture settling down among thin rocks. Another and another of the obscene birds came speeding to the spot, as the car dashed on at a high speed by the road through the gorge.

99

Welcome to Bhanipur!

"What—"

"What-"

"Yarooob! Help! Whooop! Help! Niggers! Help!" yelled Billy Bunter.

Harry Wharton & Co. started up in amazement and alarm.

The Greyfriars party had halted at noon, their journey nearly over. They had stopped in a wide, green valley, and camped under spreading trees. In the distance ahead, on the long, white road, glimpses of tall buildings could be seen—the towers of the frontier fortress of Bhanipur. Hurree Jamset Ram Singh was in sight at last of his native land.

After tiffin, the juniors rested in the shade of the trees; and, as the heat of noontide passed, they waited to hear the colonel's word that it was time to proceed. But the colonel, pacing at a little distance with a cigar, gave no word, and the juniors waited. Hurree Jamset Ram Singh's face was wreathed in smiles. It was long since the school-boy nabob had seen his own country, and the home-coming was joyful to him.

The little kingdom locked amid the mountains of the Indian frontier was home to him, and the usually calm and impassive nabob was bubbling with satisfaction. Billy Bunter, having lunched, as usual, not wisely but too well, had taken a nap, and now he had awakened, and gone to the car to rummage for lemonade and a soda syphon. And all of a sudden he came rushing back to the party under the trees, yelling with alarm.

"Help, help, help!" he yelled.

"What's the row, you thumping ass?" roared Bob Cherry.

"Natives!" yelled Bunter. "Thousands of 'em! Savages-natives-murderers! Oh dear! I wish I hadn't come! Why couldn't you leave me at the dak, you beasts? Yarooop!"

Hurree Jamset Ram Singh chuckled.

"My esteemed Bunter—"

"Yow-ow! Help! Run for it?" roared Bunter.

"But what—" exclaimed Wharton.

He broke off, as a sound of many hoofs reached his cars. There were horsemen on the road—by the sound, many scores of them. The tattoo of innumerable hoofs echoed along the valley.

The juniors ran into the road.

From the distance towards Bhanipur a numerous cavalcade was advancing. A gigantic elephant, in gorgeous trappings of scarlet and gold, towered high, surrounded by a troop of armed horsemen. There were a hundred native troopers, armed with carbine and tulwar, with officers in resplendent native uniforms. Almost every hue of the rainbow shone from the troop in the bright sunshine. Over all towered the great elephant, with a howdah on his back, in which sat a little fat gentleman with a face under a turban that gleamed with precious stones.

"Who—what—" stuttered Bob Cherry.

"We're done for!" yelled Bunter. "Run for it!"

And the fat junior art the example, running for his life. He fairly flew, till he pitched into a sunken ditch a hundred yards from the road, and landed there with all the breath knocked out of his fat body. Breathless and terrified, Bunter lay in the ditch, gasping, expecting every moment to see a ferocious face and a gleaming weapon above him.

But the Famous Five did not heed Bunter.

They did not share his alarm. That numerous cavalcade, advancing from the direction of Bhanipur, had startled them for a moment, but they realised very quickly that they were friends, not foes. The ecstatic grin on Hurree Jamset Ram Singh's face would have reassured them, had they needed to be reassured.

"My esteemed chums, it is my excellent avuncular relative, the noble Jam, with the guards of Bhanipur," said Hurree Singh. "They have come to escort us to the palace."

"Oh!" ejaculated Bob.

"Some escort!" grinned Johnny Bull.

"It is the Jam Bahadur, Hurree Singh's uncle," said Colonel Wharton, his eyes fixed on the little fat brown gentleman in the howdah. "My messenger reached the Jam Bahadur last night, and he has come to meet the nabob."

With a clatter, the cavalcade arrived, and halted to a blare of trumpets and a clash of cymbals.

The huge elephant came to a halt. At a touch from the mahout, the driver perched on its neck, the gigantic animal knelt. Dusky officers in gorgeous raiment assisted the little brown gentleman from the howdah. With great curiosity the Greyfriars juniors gazed at the Jam Bahadur, Hurree Singh's uncle and regent, of whom they had often heard the nabob speak at Greyfriars. He was a little gentleman, and he was fat and brown, but he had a great air of dignity, and his brown, plump face was wreathed in happy smiles as he greeted his nephew and nabob.

Hurree Jamset Ram Singh embraced the gorgeous Jam, with a rush of words in his own tongue of which his comrades understood nothing. Then the Jam greeted the colonel, an old acquaintance, and then the Famous Five were presented. They found that the Jam Bahadur spoke English—an English that was very like his nephew's.

"Already being acquainted with honourable youthful sahibs letterfully by nephew and lord," said the Jam graciously. "I happy in being servant to noble friends of lord and master. Welcome to kingdom of Bhanipur in name of lord and nabob."

And the juniors grinned politely, very favorably impressed by the hospitable Jam, though his gorgeous attire struck them as being really more suitable for a circus than a palace.

The Jam, though he was Inky's uncle and guardian and regent, and evidently in affectionate relative, treated the schoolboy nabob with the deepest respect; while the guards regarded him with awe, and the officers knelt to touch his feet with their foreheads. Harry Wharton & Co. had often wondered what old Inky's manners and customs were like in his own Kingdom, and now they saw for themselves. The dusky prince, who received the homage and awed respect of the Jan Bahadur and the officers of the guard, hardly seemed the same fellow who had been treated with Lower Fourth unceremoniousness in the Remove passage at Greyfriars.

"My only hat!" Bob Cherry murmured to Wharton. "Is this the same old Inky we've always known? Blessed if I shall thump him on the back, or buzz a boot at him while we're in Bhanipur. I should expect one of these johnnies to slice off my napper!"

Wharton chuckled.

"My esteemed friends, we are now about to enter Bhanipur," said Hurree Singh, beaming. "You will be my guests at the palace, which we shall reach this evening. Will the excusefulness be terrific if I leave you for short time, to travel on elephant with Jam? The longfulness since I have seen any esteemed uncle is great."

"That's all right, old bean!" said Harry. "Hem! I suppose I'd better not call you old bean now. I'll make it Highness."

"Fathead!" said the Nabob of Bhanipur. "In my kingdom and at esteemed Greyfriars the samefulness is the proper caper. To my subjects I am Huzoor, which is to say Highness; but to my esteemed and ridiculous friends the old beanfulness is still terrific."

"Good old Inky!" chuckled Bob.

Respectful hands and bent backs assisted the Nabob of Bhanipur to the howdah on the huge elephant. The Jam Bahadur joined him there. There was another clash of cymbals and a blare of trumpets. The nabob was coming home, with musical honors, as Bob remarked to his chums.

The juniors turned to the car.

"Hallo, hallo, hallo Where's Bunter?" exclaimed Bob Cherry.

"Bunter! Bunter!"

"Oh, my hat!" exclaimed Nugent. "He's bolted! He doesn't know yet that these johnnies are an escort from Bhanipur."

"Ha, ha, ha!"

"The absurd boy!"exclaimed Colonel Wharton, laughing. "Look for him at once—he cannot have gone far."

"Little fat sahib fall in ditch," said Pandy Din, pointing.

"Ha, ha, ha!"

"The absurd boy!" exclaimed Colonel Wharton, laughing. "Look for him at once—he cannot have gone far."

"Little fat sahib fall in ditch," said Pandy Din, pointing.

"Ha, ha, ha!"

They cut across towards the ditch—fortunately a dry one—in which the terrified Owl of the Remove was sprawling. Bunter had almost recovered his breath, but he had not ventured out of the ditch; he hoped that he might lie unseen there—as indeed he had, by all but the khitmutghar. Every sound he heard from the direction of the road filled the Owl of the Remove with fresh terrors. He had no doubt at all that the Greyfriars party had been cut to pieces by overwhelming numbers of "natives." That was serious enough; but the most serious matter was—what was going to happen to Bunter himself? He lay in the broad ditch and quaked.

The sound of footsteps came to his ears, approaching his hiding place, and he quaked afresh.

A grinning face looked down at him.

"Ow! Keep off!" yelled Bunter. "Mercy! I'm not here! Ow! Wow! Keep off! Yaroooh!"

"You fat idiot!"

"Ha, ha, ha!"

"Bunter, you frabjous ass—"

Bunter blinked at the juniors. He was amazed to recognise the familiar faces griming down at him.

"You!" he gasped. "Have you got away?"

"You fat duffer!"

"Cut off!" panted Bunter. "Don't stop here and draw the brutes on me! Run for it!"

"Ha, ha, ha!"

"You burbling ass!" roared Bob Cherry. "There's no danger; it's an escort from Bhanipur. It's Inky's uncle, the Jam, and a troop of giddy guards. Catch on now, fathead!"

"Oh!" gasped Bunter.

The fat junior scrambled up. Harry Wharton & Co. grasped him and dragged him out.

Bunter blinked round him anxiously.

"I—I say, you fellows, you—you're sure?" he gasped. "I—I say, I—I don't like the look of those natives!"

"Fathead!"

The chums of the Remove marched Bunter back to the car. The fat junior was still uneasy; but he was somewhat reassured when he saw the face of Hurree Jamset Ram Singh grinning down at him from the gorgeous howdah on the back of the big elephant.

"Oh! I—I suppose it's all right!" gasped Bunter.

"Yes, ass! Come on!"

"I say, you fellows, I'm not going on that beastly elephant?" exclaimed Bunter. "He looks jolly dangerous—"

"You frumptious ass, you wouldn't be allowed on the bullifant!" said Bob Cherry. "It's a Royal bullifant—a bullifant of State—only glorious Jams and Nabobs ride on that bullifant. You're going in the car."

Bunter sniffed.

"That's all very well!" he said. "But I don't see why we can't go on the elephant, if it's a special sort of thing. I suppose we're as good as blinking natives."

Evidently the Owl of the Remove was hard to satisfy.

But the juniors did not trouble about satisfying him. Bunter was keeping the procession waiting.

Bob Cherry grasped him and up-ended him into the car. That settled the matter.

Bunter landed in the car with a roar.

"Take your seats!" said the colonel, laughing.

"Ow! Wow! Wow!"

Bunter scrambled up and took his seat; the Co. followed his example; the colonel sat down; and the car moved on. Behind the gigantic elephant the Punjabi chauffeur tooled the car along at a walking pace, Pandy Din following in the second car, and round the party the cavalrymen of Bhanipur rode with clattering hoofs.

With a burst of music, a tattoo of many hoofs, a jingling of bridles and accoutrements, the cavalcade moved on to Bhanipur. In great state the procession passed under the arched gateway of the frontier fortress of Hurree Singh's kingdom, and along a street crowded with acclaiming natives, amid louder and louder blasts of barbaric music.

"Some reception!" grimed Bob Cherry.

Then by a road shaded by great trees, mile after mile, till the capital city of Bhanipur was reached, in the blaze of the sunset, and the procession halted at the palace of Hurree Jamset Ram Singh.

The Greyfriars party had reached their destination at last; after many perils and strange adventures, Hurree Jamset Ram Singh, the Nabob of Bhanipur, welcomed them to the palace of his fathers!

PART 9. THE TERROR OF THE JUNGLE!

100

The Fall of the Mighty!

"JAMES!"

"Han, sahib!"

"Palkee!" said Billy Bunter, with great dignity.

The dusky naukar salaamed.

Bright sunshine streamed down upon the great court of the palace of Bhanipur.

It was warm—there was no doubt that it was very warm in Hurree Jamset Ram Singh's native kingdom. But the warmth was tempered by a cool breeze that came from the distant snow-clad summits of the Himalayas.

Harry Wharton & Co. had turned out that morning in great spirits.

The long, long journey from England and Greyfriars was over, and the chums of the Remove were in Bhanipur at last. To the Greyfriars juniors the palace in the white-walled city of Bhanipur was something like a scene from the"Arabian Nights."

Hurree Jamset Ram Singh—more familiarly known as "Inky" in the Remove at Greyfriars—was scarcely recognisable by his old chums, now that he was once more a great and glorious Nabob in his native land.

In spotless white linen, with priceless jewels gleaming in his turban, a gem encrusted scimitar at his side, Hurree Singh looked like anything and anybody but Inky of the Lower Fourth. But his good-natured face and his cheery, cordial grin were unchanged.

And it was difficult for the chums of the Remove to get used to the awe and respect with which old Inky was treated by officers, guards, naukars, and the other innumerable dusky individuals who swarmed in the palace.

At Greyfriars, Inky had been simply a fellow in the Lower Fourth, merely that and nothing more. At Bhanipur, he was monarch of all he surveyed. A thousand tulwars would have leaped from their scabbards at his bidding. Unnumbered retainers basked in his smile, or trembled at his frown. His orders were obeyed swiftly and without question; his lightest wishes anticipated. Inky was a great man in Bhanipur. The Lower Fourth at Greyfriars had, as Bob Cherry remarked, entertained a terrific potentate unawares.

But there was no "swank" about Inky. To officials and officers, guards and retainers, servants and slaves, he was a mighty Nabob. To his schoolboy chums he was still the cherry and unaffected Inky of old.

Harry Wharton & Co. came down the great marble steps in a merry group. They were enjoying life as guests of the Nabob of Bhanipur. Even Billy Bunter was cheery and contented. The "grub" at Bhanipur was more than satisfactory. Bunter had been rather anxious on this point—a very important point. But his anxiety had been relieved. The grub was not only unlimited, but it was excellent. A stately apartment had been assigned to the Owl of the Remove. More dusky servants than he could count waited on him. The fat junior admitted that it was quite up to the style of Bunter Court. And Bunter spread himself and was contented.

Bunter rolled out of the palace after the Famous Five, his big spectacles glittering under his topee. As a guest of the great Nabob, Bunter was receiving attentions and respect to which he was little accustomed—even at Bunter Court. That, of course, was exactly as it should have been; Bunter was, he considered, only getting his due, which he never did get in the Remove passage at Greyfriars. It was like the king coming into his own again!

Bunter's manner was lofty and dignified. Loftiness and dignity were, he considered, needed to impress the natives—whom Bunter, with characteristic manners and taste, generally referred to as "natives."

"Hallo, hallo, hallo! Enjoying life, fatty?" boomed Bob Cherry, with a slap on the back as a friendly greeting to Bunter.

"Yaroooh!"

Bunter dodged away angrily.

"Chuck that, you silly ass!" he hooted. "I don't want any of your Lower Fourth larks here, Bob Cherry!"

"Dear man!" said Bob Cheerily.

Bunter turned away to give orders to the "naukar" who hovered at his elbow.

Bunter had picked out that naukar as his special attendant from the crowd who waited on him. He liked the man's manners, which were deeply respectful. Deep respect was a new thing to Bunter, and he liked it. He even made a mental note, to borrow a handful of rupees from Hurree Singh, to tip this respectful naukar.

"James!"

"Han, sahib!"

"Buck up with the palkee!"

Salaam.

"What the thump do you call the man James for, Bunter?" asked Johnny Bull, as the naukar salaamed himself away. "His name can't be James."

"Blessed if I can remember his name," said Bunter. "I call him James because I can remember it."

"Oh, my hat!"

"James," said Bunter, with dignity, "is the name of my special footman at Bunter Court."

"Go hon!" murmured Nugent.

"So I call this chap James, see—sort of home—like," said Bunter. "Reminds me of Bunter Court. We do things rather in style there."

"I don't think!"

"Oh, really, Nugent—"

"Does the esteemed Bunter prefer to travel in a palkee?" asked Hurree Jamset Ram Singh. "There is a horse at his service, if the esteemed and ludicrous Bunter would like to ride with his friends."

"Hallo, hallo, hallo!" roared Bob Cherry. "Look out! Bunter's going!" Crash! The Hindu bearers stood firm. The poles on their shoulders remained supported on their shoulders, but the body of the palanquin collapsed, and the bottom fairly dropped out of it—and along with that, of course, Bunter dropped! "Yaroooh!" roared the fat junior.

Bunter shook his head.

"Palanquin for me," he said. "Of course, I'm a splendid rider—later on I'll show the people here what riding is really like. But I think I'll trot on in a palkee today."

"Not so likely to fall off it?" suggested Bob Cherry.

"Yah!"

"Well, we're riding," said Harry Wharton. "You can follow on in a giddy palanquin, Bunter, and go to sleep—and see the sights of Bhanipur with your eyes shit."

"Ha, ha, ha!"

"The esteemed horses are ready," murmured the Nabob; and the cheery Removites crossed over to the group of handsome steeds held by dusky grooms in waiting for them.

"James!" roared Bunter, blinking round through his spectacles for the naukar, whose name was Kasi Jee, but whom Bunter preferred to call James—as a reminder of the footman at Bunter Court—perhaps!

"Han, sahib!"

The naukar was at Bunter's elbow.

"Oh!" growled Bunter. "Here you are, then! Where's that blinking palkee?"

"Palkee come, sahib."

"Hallo, hallo, hallo, here it is!" chuckled Bob Cherry. "Hefty job for four men—carrying Bunter! Hadn't you better have an elephant, Bunter? More suited to your weight."

"Oh, really, Cherry—"

"The elephants of Bhanipur are large and powerful, and quite capable of bearing the terrific weight of the esteemed Bunter," said Hurree Jamset Ram Singh solemnly.

"Ha, ha, ha!"

"Bring that palkee here," said Bunter loftily, to the bearers. "Bring it up to the steps, you chumps."

The bearers, who naturally did not know a word of English, blinked at him with their black eyes inquiringly. Kasi Jee, who had some English, explained, and the palanquin was brought up to the marble steps. Bunter stood on the lowest step, ready to get in. Harry Wharton &Co., holding their horses by the bridles, did not mount for the moment; they were interested in watching the proceedings of Billy Bunter. The fattest fellow of Greyfriars School was undoubtedly a good weight, as Bob had remarked, for even four sturdy bearers.

The palanguin, which looked like a sort of oblong box shaded by an awning, rested on poles, which passed over the shoulders of four bearers. The Hindu bearers looked at Bunter, looked at one another, and braced themselves to receive his weight.

"What's the odds they don't crumple up?" murmured Bob Cherry, and the juniors grinned.

Bunter stepped in, and sat down in the palkee.

Terrific weight as he undoubtedly was, the four bearers were, as a matter of fact, more than equal to it. They braced themselves under the strain, and bore it nobly. But the palanquin itself, constructed lightly for a weight that was nowhere near Bunter's, creaked and groaned.

Bunter blinked out under the tasseled awning at the Famous Five.

"This is quite comfy, you chaps," he said,"and an advantage of a palkee is, that you can carry some grub in it without a lot of trouble. James!"

"Han sahib!"

"Shove in that basket!"

A well-loaded basket was placed in the palanquin. Bunter, evidently, had taken his precautions against any mischance on the Bhanipur roads during the morning excursion.

It is said to be the last straw that breaks the camel's back. The lunchbasket was a good weight, and possibly it was the little-too-much that did it. Or perhaps no palkee constructed of light Indian wood could ever have stood the strain of Bunter's avoirdupois for long. Bunter waved a fat hand as a sign to start; the bearers moved off towards the great embattled gateway that gave on the street; and as they went, there was a rending, grinding sound of breakage.

Hallo, hallo, hallo!" roared Bob Cherry. "Look out!"

"Bunter—"

"Great Scott!"

"He's going—"

"Going—going!" gasped Bob Cherry.

"Gone!"

Crash!

Bump!

The Hindu bearers stood firm. The poles on their shoulders remained supported on their shoulder. But the body of the palanquin collapsed, and the bottom fairly dropped out of stand along with that, of course, Bunter dropped. The coffin of Mahomet said, in the East, to be suspended mid-way between earth and heaven, without any visible means of support; but Mahomet's coffin is able to perform that remarkable feat. Billy Bunter could not follow its example. As soon as he lost his visible means of support the ordinary law of gravitation took control; and Bunter shot downward toward the centre of the earth, obedience to that well-known law.

He did not, of course, reach the centre of the earth. The surface of the earth, stopped him.

It stopped him suddenly, and hard. There was a terrific bump as Bunter landed on the globe.

"Yarooooh!"

"Ha, ha, ha!"

"Whoop! I'm killed!"

"Oh, my hat!"

"Yow—ow—ow! Wow!"roared Bunter Help! Whoop! Yarooop!

There was a rush to pick Bunter up. Dusky attendants swooped on him from all sides, and dragged him from the earth. Bunter clung to Kasi Jee and spluttered for breath.

"Ow! Wow! Wow! Ow! Yow silly black brute, what do you mean by it? I'm killed—I mean, nearly killed Wow!"

"Thousand pardons, sahib—the palkee breaking under great sahib's honorable weight—" gasped the dismayed naukar.

"Wow! Ow!"

Bunter turned on Kasi Jee, ferociously. It was scarcely Kasi Jee's fault that the palanquin had failed to sustain the terrific weight of the Owl of the Remove. But Bunter was hurt, and he was annoyed by the roar of laughter from the Greyfriars fellows, and by the grins of many faces. He wanted to take it out of somebody; and Kasi Jee was handy. So he proceeded to kick Kasi Jee; and the dismayed naukar dodged and dived and fled, and Bunter rushed after him, still kicking.

"Ha, ha, ha!"

"Oh, crumbs!" gasped Bob Cherry, wiping his eyes. "Bunter will be the death of me, some day. I know he will."

"Ha, ha, ha!"

The naukar vanished across the court, dodging round fountains and palm trees, with the infuriated Bunter in pursuit. Harry Wharton & Co. mounted their horses, still laughing and rode out into the street with Hurree Jamset Ram Singh.

101

The Face of Nally Das!

"SOME style!" grinned Bob Cherry. The Famous Five trotted down the wide street, shades by great trees, towards the great gateway of the city.

Hurree Jamset Ram Singh rode with his friends.

But at a short distance behind the schoolboys, twenty men of the palace guard rode, with carbines under their arms, and tulwars by their sides.

Certainly, the chums of the Remove seldom travelled in such style.

Hurree Jamset Ram Singh, glanced back at his escort, and a slight frown came over his face.

"It is the wishfulness of my esteemed uncle, the Jam Bahadur, that I should never die without guards," he said. "It is not for the stylefulness, but for the safety of my esteemed neck, my ludicrous Cherry! The dangerfulness would not worry me, but I would not make the Jam anxious."

"Quite right, old bean," said Bob. "You can't be too careful. You got into dangers enough on the way here from England."

"All the samefully, I am tempted to order the soldiers back," said the nabob. "It is enough to be a nabob in my palace; but in the ridiculous company of my chums I would preferably like to be Inky of the Remove."

"Don't!" said Wharton quickly. "The Jam knows best, Inky; besides, my uncle thinks you should never ride outside the city unguarded; and Colonel Wharton knows what's what."

"Yes, rather!" said Bob. "Stick to the jolly old guards! Can't be too careful, so long as your affectionate relative Baji Rao is outside the stone jug!"

The juniors rode out under the great stone arch of the city gateway, saluted respectfully by the soldiers of the guard there. Then their way lay through vast rice-fields, and behind them, as they trotted cheerily on, the escort trotted with jingling accoutrements.

"But if there was really danger still for old Inky, here in his own kingdom?" asked Frank Nungent.

Hurree Jamset Ram Singh nodded.

"It is more than suspected, that my cousin Baji Rao was at the bottom of the attempts to kidnap me," he said. "The kidnapper, Nally Das, is in his service; and Baji Rao was the leader of a rebellion in Bhanipur many years ago. He has only recently returned from Russia; and the Jam is convinced that the Bolshevists have their eye on Bhanipur, and would use Baji Rao as a tool in their hands. That is why the Jam wished me to return home, to be safe under his eye. But now that I am here, I do not thankfully believe that the Rajah Baji Rao will leave me in peace. He desires to become Nabob of Bhanipur; and I stand in his esteemed way."

"Then why not bag him, and put him where he can't do any mischief?" asked Bob Cherry:

"It is not so easy to do as to say, my esteemed Bob. Baji Rao is a rajah; his little principality is not so large as my city of Bhanipur. His castle and his lands were given him by my father's father; he is a vassal of Bhanipur, but he governs his own little principality without interference. He could be seized, and his lands confiscated; but—"

"But what?" asked Bob.

"But there is no proof that he has conspired against me," said the nabob. "The Jam is assured of it, and I do not doubt; but the actual proof does not exist."

"I think I'd chance it," said Bob.

The nabob smiled.

"The Jam Bahadur would chance it, like my esteemed chum," he said. "Our ways in India are not the ways of the West. The Jam would have him seized and brought to the palace, and his head struck off."

"Oh, my hat!"

"'That would be a bit drastic!" grinned Johnny Bull.

"Well, that would be rather thick," said Harry Wharton. "You're a Greyfriars man, Inky, as well as an India nabob, and you can't have people's heads chopped off in the Eastern style at a moment's warning."

Hurree Jamset Ram Singh turned a rather strange look on the captain of the Remove.

"At Greyfriars I am a Greyfriars man," he said. "Here in Bhanipur I am in Indian prince!"

Wharton looked a little startled.

"But, Inky, old man—"

"My esteemed chum, the Jam Bahadur would not strike off the head of Baji Rao without my authority," said Hurree Singh. "Now I am here, he has counselled me to order the death of the conspirator. It is for me to sign the order."

"Not without proof!" exclaimed Wharton.

"What proof will he give?" asked Hurree Singh. "It is known that his servants have attempted to kidnap me. Did they act so without the esteemed rajah's order? It is not likely."

"But—"

"But the proof will be forthcoming," said the nabob. "It is my esteemed intention to return to Greyfriars later; but I shall not leave Baji Rao to stir up strife in my kingdom, as a tool of the Russians; neither shall I take the risk of kidnapping at the school. While I am in Bhanipur I shall deal with Baji Rao. Without proof of his guilt—proof that will satisfy the British Raj—I will not send him to death. But perhaps he will himself give that proof. Perhaps-fully he will betray himself, in his eagerness to take my esteemed place as nabob. We shall see."

The juniors were silent.

It was clear to them that Hurree Jamset Ram Singh, with all his kindness of heart and smiling good-humour, had some plan in his mind for dealing with his ambitious kinsman, and that Baji Rao had no mercy to expect when the time came.

To the chums of the Remove it was a new and strange thought that their old pal Inky had the power, and perhaps the will, to send a man to death—to order his kinsman to execution.

It was not a pleasant thought to them. They realised that Hurree Singh had a dual nature; he was a Greyfriars man, a keen cricketer, a cheery junior of the lower Fourth, but he was also an Indian prince, a powerful nabob in a land where life was cheap.

"But let us not waste time thinkfully considering the esteemed and disgusting Baji Rao," said Hurree Singh cheerily. "His time will come. Now we are going to entertain ourselves joyfully."

"Hear, hear!" said Bob.

The juniors rode on in a cheery mood. Ryots working in the rice-fields looked up as the clattering hoofs passed, and salaamed to the ground at the sight of the nabob and the sahibs.

The cultivated fields were left behind, and the juniors rode by a path under spreading branches, through a shadowy forest.

The sun was approaching the zenith now, and the heat was great. Harry Wharton & Co. were glad of the shade of the great forest trees.

Hurree Jamset Ram Singh pointed ahead at last.

"That is our excellent destination," he said.

In the midst of the forest was an open expanse, and in the middle of it great masses of masonry marked where a temple once had stood. Part of the building was intact, but the greater part was in ruins. Trees grew among the ruined mason-work; thick creepers and rank grasses choked the crevices in the dismantled walls.

"What's that show?" asked Bob.

"It is an old temple of Shiva," said the nabob. "A hundred years ago it was destroyed in a raid of the Afghans. We are stopping there for our esteemed tiffin, my worthy chums."

"Good!" said Harry.

The juniors had covered a good many miles from the white-walled city of Bhanipur. They were quite ready for a rest, in the heat of noontide, and for lunch. They rode on cheerily towards the massive ruins. By a wide crevice in the old wall a gigantic tree grew, with wide-spreading branches that gave a deep and grateful shade. Harry Wharton & Co. rode under the shade of a great tree.

Hallo, hallo, hallo! There's somebody in the place!" exclaimed Bob Cherry.

He pointed with his riding-whip.

In the fissure of the old temple wall a white turban glimmered, and a face looked out. It was the face of a Hindu.

The next moment Harry Wharton gave a shout.

"It's Nally Das!"

"By gum!" ejaculated Bob. "So it is, the jolly old kidnapper! What is he doing here?"

Hurree Jamset Ram Singh fixed his keen, dark eyes on the face that looked out of the tissue in the wall. He recognized Nally Das, the chief of the gang of kidnappers who had dogged his footsteps all the way from England to Bhanipur. Nally Das, the agent of Baji Rao, the chief tool of the ambitious rajah. For a second Hurree Singh stared at the face. After a second it was gone. Hurree Singh leaped from his horse, and his scimitar fleshed in his hand as he rushed to the dismantled gateway of the old temple.

The juniors had a glimpse of his face as he went. It was not the cheery, good natured face of their old chum, Inky of the Remove. It was the grim, hard face of an Eastern seeking his enemy.

"After him!" exclaimed Harry Wharton.

And the juniors rushed into the temple.

102

The Haunted Temple!

"HALLO, hallo, hallo!"

"Where is he?"

The stone pavement of the old temple was cracked and broken, thick with rank weed, and grasses. Masses of fallen masonry lay here and there, fragments of broken idols or images. Amid the ruins, Hurree Jamset Ram Singh was seeking, his scimitar gleaming in his hand, his dark eyes gleaming from his set face.

Harry Wharton & Co. joined him quickly. They were keen enough to seize the kidnapper. But Nally Das was not to be seen.

Up and down amid the ruins, the Famous Five sought him, but he was not to be found.

They paused at last.

Nally Das had been in the old temple, that was certain. For what reason the rascally Hindu had been hiding there they could not guess, but all of them had seen the dark, savage face, and had read the startled expression on it as he recognized them. But he was gone. The great fissure in the wall was vacant; not a sign of the man was to be seen among the ruins. Nally Das seemed to have vanished into thin air.

"Gone!" said Wharton, stopping at last, greatly puzzled.

"The gonefulness is terrific."

"But where on earth has he gone?" exclaimed Bob Cherry. "We were after him jolly quick. He seemed to have evaporated."

There was a trampling of hoofs outside the building. The escort that had followed the juniors from Bhanipur had arrived.

Hurree Jamset Ram Singh turned towards the horsemen.

He called out to their officer sharply in his own language, in words that were quite incomprehensible to his English chums.

Half the party dismounted at once, and, with drawn swords,

began to search the ruined temple from end to end. The rest rode round the building, searching outside the shattered walls for Nally Das.

"The rotter must be hiding about here somewhere," said Johnny Bull.

"Anyhow, he can't have got far," remarked Nugent. "The horsemen will ride him down."

The juniors unpacked their lunch and sat down amid the ruins of the old temple of Shiva to a picnic. It was, as Bob Cherry remarked, like one of their old picnics in the priory ruing near Greyfriars. But the scene was very different; the juniors in white drill and topees, Hurree Singh in gorgeous Eastern garb; the dark Indian forest surrounding them, and in the distance the snow-capped line of the mighty Himalayas. But they enjoyed their lunch, and rested in the shade of the great tree, while the very air about them quivered with the heat.

The horsemen came trampling back. But they came without Nally Das. The subadar who commanded the escort came salaaming to Hurree Singh report. He made his report in Hindustani, and only Hurree Singh understood him. But when he had dismissed the subadar, the nabob explained to his chums. The soldiers had searched for a mile around the old temple of Shiva; they had beaten every thicket; they had explored every path, but they had not found Nally Das. The kidnapper had given them the slip.

"Lots of nooks where the rotter could hide himself," said Bob Cherry may have climbed a tree. But I wonder what he was doing here? I suppose Nally Das isn't keen on giddy antiquities?"

The nabob smiled and shook his head.

"Perhapsfully he has been in touch with his spies in the city, and this was the meeting-place," he said. "At all events, he is gone now."

"What would have happened to him if he'd been caught?" Nugent could not help asking.

Hurree Singh's face was grim for a moment.

"He is a kidnapper. He has dared to lay hands on a nabob!" he answered. "His head would be struck off!"

"Oh, my hat!"

"We're in Bhanipur now, and no mistake!" murmured Bob Cherry.

The juniors wondered a little whether they were quite sorry that Nally Das had escaped. Villain as the man way the unscrupulous tool of an ambitions schemer, they did not quite like the idea so calmly enunciated by Hurree Jamset Ram Singh. The drastic system of Bhanipur was not exactly in accordance with Greyfriars ideas.

However, the man was gone, and there was an end of the matter, so far as Harry Wharton & Co. were concerned.

They rested, and chatted cheerily after their lunch, and as the red sun sloped downward in the sky, and the heat abated, they strolled about the ancient temple, examining the place with curiosity. The Afghan raid of a century before had wrecked the mighty building but some of the old walls had been tor massive for the raiders, and still remained. In a paved court, shaded by trees and giant shrubs that had once been cultivated, but had long grow wild and rank, a bronze statue lay over turned from its pedestal. The bronze was hacked and injured, but otherwise intact; it had defied savage blows from the Mahomedan raiders, to whom a statue of the Buddha was an idol of the unbelievers.

Harry Wharton & Co. regarded it with interest.

As they stood looking at the fallen, defaced statue, a faint sound came to their ears, and they glanced round.

No one was stirring in the sunlit ruins save themselves. The subadar and his men were camped outside the old temple.

"What was that?"asked Harry.

Hurree Jamset Ram Singh cast glances to left and right, and it seemed to his chums that there was an uneasy expression on his face.

"I heard something," said Bob Cherry, "like a giddy echo. There it is again!"

Again the faint sound came to the ears of the juniors. They could not define what it was, neither could they guess from which direction it proceeded.

They listened intently, but there was no repetition of the sound.

"I suppose the giddy place isn't haunted?" said Nugent, with a smile.

"The ryots of the country believe that it is haunted by the spirits of the priests who were slain by the Afghan raiders," said Hurree Singh.

"Oh, my hat!"

"It is said that their voices may sometimes be heard echoing among the ruins," said the nabob. "For that reason the place is avoided. It is very seldom that these old stones are trodden by human feet. I of course, do not believe such a wild tale. We learn better thing at Greyfriars, my esteemed chums."

"I hope so," said Johnny Bull, with a grin.

"But after all it is time that we take horse," said the nabob. "If you have seen enough, let us departfully go."

"Right—ho!"

The juniors followed Hurree JamsetRam Singh from the ruins of the temple of Shiva. They could not help smiling as they went. In spite of his Greyfriars education, and his disbelief in the legends of his country, Hurree Singh seemed rather in haste to get out of the temple. The superstitious side of the native was not quite left out of him.

The Greyfriars party remounted their horses and rode away, with the subadar and his men following at a respectful distance.

For many a long mile they rode, till Hurree Jamset Ram Singh pulled in his horse, and raised his hand to point. In the distance, black against the setting sun, an embattled building crowned a hill, with a flag flapping idly from a tall flagstaff on the tower.

"What is that?" asked Harry.

"That, my esteemed chum, is the castle of the Rajah Baji Rao," said Hurree Singh, "my kinsman, cousin, and enemy. That, doubtless, is whither Nally Das fled after we scared him from the haunted temple."

The juniors gazed with deep interest at the fortress—palace of the ambitious rajah. In the clear air they could see guards pacing on the high, thick walls.

"Better not give him an afternoon call, I suppose?" said Bob Cherry, with a grin.

The nabob chuckled.

"We should not leave him with our lives," he said. "Baji Rao is still safe in his castle; but not, perhapsfully, for long."

Hurree Jamset Ram Singh sat still upon his horse, and stared steadfastly at the thick walls and high tower of his rival and enemy's dwelling. The look that came over his face made his comrades exchange glances. It was such a grim look as they had never seen on Inky's face at Greyfriars.

"Inky, old man!" muttered Nugent.

The nabob started, glanced at his friends, and smiled.

"My' esteemed chums, in my own land there are moments when I forget Greyfriars," he said. "Let us get back to Bhanipur. We shall reach the city by the setting of the esteemed sun."

And the Greyfriars party wheeled their horses for the ride home.

103

In the Saddle and Out!

"KASI JEE—I mean, James! Come here—idhar do!" shouted Banter, who had picked up that much Hindustani.

Kasi Jee, otherwise James, approached the fat junior rather cautiously.

He seemed uneasy.

That was not surprising, considering the manner in which Bunter had handled him after the breakdown of the palanquin.

Kasi Jee was not, perhaps, wholly unaccustomed to kicking. But a kick with Bunter's weight behind it was no joke. Kasi Jee was an obedient naukar, and had been brought up in the way in which he should go, doubtless under a heavy hand. If an angry white sahib kicked Kasi Jee, it was written in the stars that Kasi Jee should be kicked, and that was all about it. Still, probably Kasi Jee did not like it.

"Idhar do!" roared Bunter.

The naukar came up almost wriggling. But Billy Bunter was not thinking of further kicking. He was tired. He had rather over-exerted himself already on Kasi Jee's account.

"Salaam, sahib!" said the naukar submissively.

"I've been calling you!" prowled Bunter, blinking at the naukar through his big spectacles. "Are those rotters gone? I mean, my friends?"

"The great nabob and the white sahib have ridden forth from the city," said the naukar.

"Cheeky rotters! Leaving me behind, as usual!" grunted Bunter. "Nice sort of treatment for a fellow who's travelled half over the world for their sakes. Do they think I'm going to hang about the place all day?"

"Kasi Jee know not the thoughts of the sahibs."

Right up to the ruins the runaway dashed, and then all of a sudden the horse stopped. It seemed to Bunter as if a giant's hand plucked him from the saddle. Before he knew what was happening he shot over the horse's head and landed in a bush. "Yooooop!"

"You silly Owl, I don't suppose you do. Those beasts were talking about a picnic in a blinking temple or something. Do you know where the place is?"

"Han sahib!"

"That means yes, I suppose? I don't want their company, and I don't want their picnic. But I'm going, just to show them, the rotters!" growled Bunter. "I know they were jolly glad of that accident to leave me behind. But I'll show 'em!"

"Palanquin ready for honorable sir," said the naukar. Kasi Jee had prepared a new palkee for the fat sahib.

Bunter shook his head prompts.

Having fallen through the bottom of one palanquin, he did not feel disposed to trust his fat person in another. The new palanquin might have borne his weight. On the other hand, it mightn't. William George Bunter did not mean to take the risk.

"Blow your silly palkees?" he said. "I'm going some other way, James, tell me of some other way."

"Shall Kasi Jee order an elephant for the sahib?" asked the naukar. "His highness has given instructions that everything is at the disposal of his honorable guests."

Bunter shook his head again.

He did not intend to confide the fact to Kasi Jee, but he was extremely nervous of elephants at close quarters.

Certainly, an elephant would not have been likely to collapse under his weight as the palanguin had done. Even Bunter's weight would have been nothing to the mighty beast. But it was not a mode of transit that appealed to the Owl of the Remove.

"Is there anything else?" he demanded.

"There are many fine horses in the stables of the Huzoor."

Bunter grunted.

He could ride—at all events he could stick on a saddle if the horse let him; a horse was safer than an elephant, he considered. But Bunter did not want to mount one of the mettlesome steed such as the nabob had handed out to the Co.; Bunter wanted comfort.

"Con you find me a quiet animal?" he asked.

"At the sahib's order," said kasi Jee, with a peculiar gleam in his eyes for a moment.

"I don't want to go racing about, you know, like those silly chumps," said Bunter. "I want a quiet ride. Find me a good horse—quiet, you know; agree that I can jog on. If I'm not satisfied, I'll jolly well kick you again, see?"

"On my head be it."

"Buck up, then! Don't hang about!" snapped Bunter.

In a position of authority all the charming characteristics of William George Bunter came out very strongly. He had no politeness to waste on "natives," Whether Kasi Jee had any feelings or not was a matter beneath his notice. He liked giving orders, and he liked giving them in a dictatorial manner. With power in his hands, Bunter liked to spread himself, and he spread himself accordingly.

Possibly it would have been a little more to his profit, in the long run, had he treated Kasi Jee with a little more civility. With all his fawning submissiveness, the naukar did not like being kicked, and he did not like being bullied. But his face expressed nothing of his thoughts, as he proceeded to carry out the orders of the Owl of Greyfriars.

Bunter waited frowningly for the horse to be brought.

He was extremely annoyed at being left behind in the excursion. He suspected that the Famous Five had been quite pleased to start without him. They had been gone two or three hours. After the accident with the palkee, and the kicking of Kasi Jee, Bunter had felt that he needed a rest, and he had taken one, drowsing in a hammock, fanned by the punkah. But it was like Bunter to feel injured because the other fellows had not hung about the greater part of the morning waiting for him. How could a fellow be better occupied than in awaiting Bunter's convenience?

Bunter was not specially keen on an excursion, neither was he specially keen, for once, on a picnic. An immense variety of tuck awaited his commands at all hours in the palace. But the suspicion that the Greyfriars fellows were glad to leave him behind made him keen on going. The beasts should jolly well see!

A groom led up a horse—a powerful, handsome animal—and Bunter eyed it morosely. It looked quite enough, he considered—and Bunter believed himself to be a judge of horseflesh. He allowed Kasi Jee to help him into the roomy saddle, and settled down there comfortably.

"James!" he snapped.

"Sahib!"

"You've got the bag of grub?"

"Han, sahib!"

"Follow me, then. And show me the way!"

"As my lord wills."

The horse obeyed Bunter's hand, rather to his relief. The palace court was crowded, as usual, and Bunter would have been extremely annoyed had the horse dropped him off under the stare of hundreds of native eyes. He did not want the "natives" to grin at his horsemanship. As a matter of fact, they did grin, when the sahib's back was turned. Bunter rode rather after the fashion of a sack of coke, and he was never likely to "witch the world with noble horsemanship."

Colonel Wharton was riding in as Bunter rode out. The old soldier glanced at him, with a faint smile on his bronzed face. Bunter frowned, and rode on to tire city gateway, with Kasi Jee clattering behind.

Outside the city Bunter condescended to allow the naukar to range up alongside. He needed the naukar's guidance.

Kasi Jee respectfully indicated the route, and Bunter trotted on. He had his steed well in hand, or supposed that he had. The pace was slow. Bunter was not a rapid rider. Under his topee his face was crimson in the heat, and his temper grew worse and worse. Having slacked so long in his hammock, he had let the cool hours of the morning slip by, and had started his ride at an hour unusually late for the climate. He was riding now in the heat of noon, and it was not pleasant. That consideration occurred rather late to his fat mind—as things generally did. He scowled savagely at Kasi Jee, as if it was the hapless naukar's fault that the stun was so hot, and the dust to stinging.

Bunter was glad enough to get into the shade of the forest in the midst of which lay the ruined temple which was his destination. Only one thought consoled him for his discomfort—his arrival would be displeasing to the cherry picnickers at the ruins of the temple of Shiva. That they had lunched and gone did not yet occur to Bunter. His powerful brain did not assimilate more than one thought at a time. He was glad of the shade of the forest, but he blinked round uneasily into the shadows of the great trees.

"Sure this is the way, James?" he snapped.

"It is the way, sahib!"

"Are there any tigers in this forest?"

"So near the city, sahib, no tigers."

"Any snakes?"

"Many snakes, sahib."

"Oh!" growled Bunter, "Beastly country, packed with tigers, and snakes, and dacoits, and dashed natives! Fool to come here! Where's that rotten old temple you told me about?"

"It is straight by the path through the forest, sahib."

"Oh, all right! You can fall behind!" growled Bunter.

Kasi Jee drew in his horse for the lordly sahib to ride ahead. As Bunter passed on, Kasi Jee leaned over with something in his hand, and touched Bunter's horse behind the fat rider. There was a sudden start from Bunter's steed, and he threw up his head and broke into a sudden gallop.

"Ow!" gasped Bunter.

It was almost by a miracle that Bunter was not thrown to the ground as the naukar had doubtless intended when he startled the horse with a sudden prick of his knife.

But the fat junior held on, clutching at the saddle with both hands, and letting the reins go.

"Ow, wow! Stop!" spluttered Bunter. "You awful beast, stop! Oh! Ow! Help! Great pip! I shall he killed! Wow! Stop him, James—stop him, Kasi Jee. You scoundrel, I'll tan your hide if you don't stop him. Help!"

The horse galloped on, feeling himself uncontrolled. Kasi Jee sat in his saddle at a halt, and grinned. Bunter had not the faintest suspicion that the naukar had deliberately caused the horse to bolt. It did not cross his fat mind that this was retaliation for his fascinating manners and customs.

Had Kasi Jee desired to stop the runaway, it was doubtful whether he could have done so. As he did not desire it, he made no attempt. He sat his horse motionless, grinning, and Bunter vanished in the winding path through the forest.

Thud, thud, thud!

Bunter clung frantically to the saddle as the runaway raced on.

His fat face streamed with perspiration; his little round eyes bulged with terror behind his glasses.

He did not even attempt to control the horse; he could not do so. He only kept his seat by his desperate clutch of the saddle. And the animal raced on regardless of his rider. Bunter's fat brain swam as he was borne helplessly onward.

Thud, thud, thud!

The trees raced by Bunter. Several times be dodged instinctively to avoid a low branch. Thud, thud, thud! With his heart in his mouth, Bunter clung to the runaway, expecting every moment to be hurled to the earth.

An open space in the forest appeared ahead of him. Dizzily he sighted the ruins of the old temple, baking in the afternoon sun. He comprehended that this was the ruined temple where the picnic was taking place—or had taking place—and where he had intended to halt. But it was not in his power to halt now. That depended on his horse.

Right up to the ruins the runaway flashed, and then, all of a sudden, the horse stopped.

It seemed to Bunter as if a giant's hand plucked him from the saddle.

Before he knew what was happening. He shot over the horse's head and landed in a bush.

"Yoooop!"

Bunter sprawled and howled. The horse stood staring at him for a moment or two, and then swerved and trotted away, and vanished, with dangling reins and stirrups, into the forest.

104

The Secret of the Temple!

"YOW—OW—OW—OW—OW—OW!"

Thus William George Bunter.

The fat junior struggled breathlessly out of the bush. His clothes were torn, and his topee had fallen off. The thick bush, fortunately, had broken his fall; and to judge by the sounds that proceeded from Bunter, he was broken, too.

"Ow! Ow—ow—ow—yow—wow!" spluttered Bunter.

He gasped and spluttered helplessly for some minutes. But he realized it last that he was not hurt, save for a few scratches and a bump or two. He fielded his topee, and jammed it back on his perspiring head.

"Oh, dear!" he gasped.

The horse had vanished. Bunter did not mind that very much—he was fell up with that horse. There was no sign of Kasi Jee; and that was more annoying. If Kasi Jee was following him, he was undoubtedly doing so at a less rapid pace. But possibly he was not following. That was serious, because Kasi Jee had the basket of lunch with him. Bunter was getting hungry. He wondered savagely whether Harry Wharton & Co, had anything in the grub line left. It would be just like them to finish their lunch to the last crumb, regardless of the fact that Bunter might blow in. That painful doubt had to be settled at once, and Bunter rolled into the ruined temple in search of the Famous Five.

"Wharton! Bob! Beasts! Where are you? Rotters!"

Only the echo of his voice answered him.

"Why, the—the awful rotters!" gasped Bunter, in consternation, as it dawned upon his fat mind that the chums of the Remove were no longer there.

He stood and blinked round him in dismay.

He might have foreseen it—had Bunter ever foreseen anything. Harry Wharton & Co. had lunched long ago, and really they were not likely to hang about the place all the afternoon on the chance that Billy Bunter might possibly turn up after all. As a matter of fact, they had forgotten the existence of Bunter, and had not bestowed a thought on him since riding out of Bhanipur. The chums of the Remove had not really expected to enjoy Bunter's company that day; for it had not been their intention to proceed at a walking pace to suit the slow progress of a palanquin, had Bunter started with them. Bunter had expected it; but that was only one of Bunter's many expectations that would never have been realized.

Anyhow, they were gone now, there was no doubt about that. Bunter found the signs of the picnic in the ruins, but he did not find the Famous Five.

His feelings were almost too deep for words.

He was hungry, and there was no lunch, unless, and until, Kasi Jee came up with the basket. And it was very late for tiffin—very late indeed. True, Hunter had had several lunches since breakfast. But he was ready for another, and that was the important point.

"The awful beasts!" he gasped. "Leaving a fellow stranded! After all I've done for them, too! Frightful rotters!"

Bunter rolled out of the temple and blinked along the path for Kasi Jee. But the winding path through the forest was silent and vacant, so far as the Owl of the Remove could see. The fat junior rolled back into the temple, for shade from the blazing sun. Lizards crawled on the old masses of masonry, which were hot to the touch. Buster blinked round him warily for snakes. The old ruin was likely to be an abiding place for reptiles. There was nothing for it but to sit down and rest, and wait for Kasi Jee to arrive with his lunchand Bunter sought for a shady spot.

He found one in the old paved court where the bronze Buddha lay on the earth, blackened and disfigured on the old cracked stones. Bunter gave the defaced statue a carless blink in passing. Near it, a portion of the old wall stood intact, and barred off the hot rays of the sun, and scrubby tamarinds grew thickly. Between the tamarinds and the old wall, Bunter found shade, and he lay down to rest, after very carefully inspecting the spot for snakes.

He sat with his back to the wall, the tamarinds in front of him, and through interstices in the thicket he could see the bronze Buddha glistening in the sun. He rested there and listened, hoping every moment to hear the beat of a horse's hoofs, announcing the arrival of the naukar. But no sound broke the silence of the forest.

Bunter began to doze in the heat.

He started suddenly into wide wakefulness.

A faint sound had come to his ears—a sound that seemed near at hand.

The fat junior sat upright his ears strained to listen, his fat mind full of thoughts of snakes, tigers, and dacoits. The sound was repeated; and it seemed to Bunter that it was a hollow echo under the cracked pavement of the floor. He wondered whether there were vaults below the old temple, perhaps the haunts of wild beasts.

Suddenly he caught his breath and his gaze became fixed.

Through the interstices of the tamarinds before him he could see the bronze Buddha, lying as it had fallen long ago on the large flat stones of the paved court. One of the great stones, close by the Buddha's head, was in motion.

Bunter blinked, wondering whether he was dreaming.

The stone floor seemed, to the gaze, as solid as the earth itself. Yet one of the great flat stones was rising as if propelled by some hidden force from below. It was no dream, no strange fancy; the great slab rose slowly, but surely, till it stood on end, and a dark orifice in the temple floor was disclosed.

Bunter sat very still.

He was frightened—he hardly knew why. Not for worlds would he have betrayed his presence. He scarcely breathed as he continued to watch from his hiding-place.

A head rose into view from the opening in the paved floor; a face glimmered, and two flashing dark eyes stared searchingly round.

Bunter dared not breathe.

It was the face of Nally Das that he saw, scarcely three yards away from him!

His heart beat almost to suffocation.

There was a weapon in the Hindu's hand—a long knife that gleamed in the sun. The weapon, and the suspicious searching of his eyes, showed that he was on the look-out for foes. And Bunter, with a sickness at his heart, knew what would happen if Nally Das discovered him. One thrust of that flashing steel, and all things would be at an end for the Owl of the Remove. Bunter's eyes were wide open—fixed behind his big spectacles as he crouched in his hiding-place, dumb with terror.

Nally Das emerged from the opening and stood in the temple. Still his black eyes searched about him, and he listened intently. But the silence reassured him; he drew himself upright, and breathed freely. Evidently he had not the slightest suspicion that there was a hidden watcher—hidden only a few yards from him by the tamarinds. It was Harry Wharton & Co, and the subadar and the soldiers of whom Nally Das was thinking. But be was assured now that the visitors to the temple were gone.

He stepped over to the opening, and called out something softly in his own tongue. Evidently, he had companions in that mysterious recess beneath the old temple.

The slab of stone sunk back into its place; the floor was closed, and gave no sign of having been opened.

Nally Das, with a light tread, hurried a way.

He vanished from Bunter's sight.

The fat junior was deeply relieved to see him disappear.

His life had hung on a thread, and he knew it.

But the man was gone; silence had fallen on the old temple again. But below, it some strange recess beneath the cracked stones of the floor there were others—at least, one other, as Bunter knew. The Owl of the Remove realized that the sooner he was gone the better. But he did not venture to move till a quarter of an hour had elapsed since the last light footfall of Nally Das had died away.

Then he picked himself up, and trod away on tiptoe.

His heart was thumping as he crept out of the ruined temple and emerged into the forest. Hardly stopping to blink round him, he tramped away, heading back the way he had come.

It was hot—very hot; and Bhanipur was far away. But Bunter

was only anxious to get away from the dangerous neighborhood of Nally Das lurking place.

He tramped on as fast as his fat little legs could carry him. He was nearly a mile from the temple, when he sighted a horseman on the path, coming towards him at a walking-pace. For a moment Bunter's heart leaped into his mouth. Then be recognized Kasi Jee. It was the naukar, evidently not hurrying himself to overtake the fat sahib.

Bunter waved a hand to him.

"James, you cheeky rotter!"

Kasi Jee jumped down and salaamed before Bunter.

"I have found my great lord!" he exclaimed. "The heart of Kasi Jee has been heavy with distress. He has been seeking the sahib—_"

"Cut it short!" growled Bunter. "You could have jolly well found me before this if you'd wanted to, you conformed native!"

"The sahib's slave has been seeking for—"

"That's enough! My horse has run away!" growled Bunter. "I shall take your horse, and you can jolly well walk. See?"

"Kasi Jee is the sahib's servant."

"Help me up!" grunted Bunter.

He squatted in the naukar's saddle. "Not that way!" he snapped, as the naukar was about to lead the horse on towards the temple.

"Is not my lord going to the old Temple of Shiva?"

"Mind your own business! Get me out of this rotten forest as soon as you can," growled Bunter. "I've had enough of it. Get a move on!"

"As the sahib wills."

Kasi Jee led the horse back towards the plain. Bunter rode out of the forest into the blaze of the afternoon sun. He was glad enough, however, to leave the shadows of the forest behind him.

"Now find me a shady place for lunch!" he snapped.

"Han, sahib."

And at long last Bunter sat down to his delayed feed under the shade of a banyan-tree, with the wide rice-fields stretching before him. It was a large lunch and Bunter disposed of it to the last crumb; it did not occur to his fat wind to leave anything for the naukar. And having disposed of the lunch, Bunter stretched himself to slumber in the shade of the banyan, with a greasy and contented smile on his fat face; and Kasi Jee, squatting on the ground waiting the pleasure of his white lord, listened to the deep and rumbling snore of the Owl of the Remove.

105

An Indian Night's Entertainment!

"I SAY, you fellows—"

"Cheese it, old man!"

"Quiet!"

Bunter breathed hard with indignation.

The full, round moon sailed over the city and palace of Bhanipur; in the silvery light, roofs and towers glimmered white, and the tall palm-trees of the palace court stood out like tall black shadows. It was a beautiful Indian night; the heat of the day was gone, and all was peace and calm. The many windows of the palace of Bhanipur gleamed with lights; hurrying feet of silent attendants passed and re-passed; the great palm court, upon which the state apartments of the palace looked, was lined with soldiers on guard. Strains of barbaric music echoed and rang among the palm-trees and the tinkling fountains.

Harry Wharton & Co, were home from their day's ride, a little tired, but very cheery. Now they were enjoying one of the many entertainments of the palace of Bhanipur.

On a golden throne, backed by gigantic peacock-feathers worked in precious gens, sat Hurree Jamset Ram Singh in robes of state. By him, on a lower throne, sat his uncle, the Jam Bahadur, with a bright smile on his little brown face. On the other side of the nabob sat Colonel Wharton, a guest whom the ruler of Bhanipur delighted to honour.

Harry Wharton & Co. were accommodated with comfortable couches, in which they reclined luxuriously. Other guests, of dusky hue, were there in considerable numbers; the hospitality of the nabob was unbounded. The seats were arranged on either side of the nabob's throne in a semi-circle. Before them was the entertainment—jugglers, conjurers, snake-charmers, nautch-girls.

An Indian night's entertainment, resembling the "Arabian Nights" to the Greyfriars juniors.

It was entertaining enough to the juniors, new to the sights of the Indian peninsula. But every now and then they looked away from the show to glance at the nabob on the golden throne. They could hardly believe that this stately nabob, in his jewel-encrusted robes was the same old Inky of the Remove passage at Greyfriars—the fellow who had joined unceremoniously in the rough-and-tumble life of the Lower Fourth. But when he caught their glances, the nabob grinned with the same old familiar dusky grin they knew.

Behind the seats, the punkahs swayed, kept in constant motion by the dusky wallahs. Overhead, the moon sailed in cloudless splendor, and a myriad of stars glittered like points of silver.

A tall, bronze-skinned snake-charmer clad only in a linen loin-cloth, was giving a performance with his snakes, when Billy Bunter dawned on the scene.

Bunter had got back late. His nap under the banyan had lasted till sunset. Having awakened, he had kicked Kasi Jee—not for any special reason, but on principle—and ridden back to the city with the naukar.

On his arrival at the palace, Bunter found the entertainment in the palm court in full swing. And he was indignant. Besides the Greyfriars juniors, there were thirty or forty native guests.

But it seemed to be Bunter's idea that the thing ought not to have started before his arrival. Bunter rolled up to the Greyfriars seats and blinked at the juniors, careless of the disturbance he made by his late arrival.

The juniors made room for him.

"Sit down, old fat bean," said Bob Cherry.

"I say, you fellows—"

"Shut up, old man," said Nugent,"and get out of the light! Can't see through a porpoise, you know!"

"Oh, really, Nugent—"

"Sit down, Bunter."

"How long has this been going on?" shorted Bunter.

"About half an hour. Sit down."

"Couldn't wait for a chap, of course!" sneered Bunter.

"Fathead!"

"Oh, really, Wharton—"

"Shut up and sit down!"

Bunter grunted, and sank down on the soft silken cushion. He turned his big spectacles on the show.

The sap-wallah, or snake-charmer, was going strong. He stood like a figure of bronze, with the terrible reptiles twined round him, the hideous heads passing and reposing close to his face. The hissing and writhing of the snakes were incessant. And the juniors knew that the cobras that twined round the sap-wallah were poisonous reptiles; their bite death to the victim. At every instant, it seemed to them, the sap-wallah was chancing a fearful fate; yet he was evidently quite at home with the fearful creatures. They obeyed the murmur of his voice, writhing and gliding and circling at his command.

"I say, you fellows, I hope those blinking snakes are safe!" muttered Bunter, "I suppose they don't bite?"

"They jolly well do!" said Wharton. "The man must have an iron nerve. But I suppose he's used to them."

"Mean to say they're poisonous?" gasped Bunter.

"Yes, ass!"

"I—I say, suppose one of them got away, and wriggled over here?" stuttered the Owl of the Remove.

"Then we should rely on you to collar it, Bunter, and protect us!" grinned Bob Cherry.

"Oh dear!"

Bunter watched the sap-wallah and his snakes, with his little round eyes bulging behind his glasses. He was relieved when the turn was over and the snake-charmer and the reptiles were gone.

"Rotten!" grunted Bunter. "Not that I'm afraid of snakes, of course."

"Not now they're gone!" agreed Bob.

"Of course, if one of them had got among us, I should have collared it at once. Easy enough to deal with a snake, if you've got the nerve," said Bunter. "You take it by the tail, you know, and dash its head on the ground, and there you are! Nothing to be seared about if you've got the nerve. That's where I come in. It's a bit different with you fellows. I noticed you looking a bit sickly, Bull."

"Did you?" said Johnny Bull, in a deep, sulphureous voice.

"Yes, old chap—nervous—what? You were shaking a bit, Nugent."

"Ass!"

"My dear chap, you needn't deny it," said Bunter. "Snakes are pretty dangerous things, and every fellow hasn't my nerve. But you needn't be afraid, with me here, you know."

Something touched Bunter's fat ankle as he was speaking he gave a start.

"What—what's that?"

"Is it a snake?" asked Bob Cherry, peering down. "Quick, Bunter—take it by the tail?

"Yaroooh!"

"And dash its head on the ground!"

"Help!"

"Easy enough for a fellow with nerve!"

"Whoooop!"

The fat junior made a wild leap upon the seat. He stood there blinking round him in terrified alarm, spluttering wildly.

"Ow! Help! Take it away! Kill it! Drag it off! Help!"

"Ha, ha, ha!"

"Bunter!" came Colonel Wharton's deep voice. "Sit down at once! What do these antics mean, you young donkey?"

"Help!" roared Bunter. "I'm not going to be bitten by poisonous snakes! Yarooooh!"

"Silence!"

"Little sahib being in alarm?" asked the Jam Bahadur. "But there is no danger befalling little sahib."

"Help! Snakes! Yooop!".

"What is the matter with Bunter, Harry?" called out the colonel, greatly annoyed.

"Only funk," answered Harry.

"There's a snake under the seat!" yelled Bunter.

"It's all right, sir!" called out Bob Cherry. "I touched Bunter's ankle with the toe of my boot, and he seemed to think it was a snake,"

"Ha, ha, ha!"

"Wha—a—at?" spluttered Bunter.

"Sit down at once, Bunter! Behave yourself!"

"Oh!" gasped Bunter.

The fat junior collapsed into his seat, bestowing a ferocious blink on the grinning juniors. He realized that Bob Cherry had been pulling his leg.

"You—you—you—" he gasped.

There was a burst of wild music from cymbals and tambourines, and a troupe of nautch-girls danced into the scene. Bunter sat down—even Bunter was not afraid of nautch-girls. With a musical jingling of the silver bells fastened to their brown ankles, the nautch-girls danced to the tambourines under the glimmering moon, that made the palm court as light as by day. There were more than a hundred of the dancers, clad in gorgeous colours, glistening with gems, winding in the mazes of the Indian dance. The dance was led by a graceful, brown-limbed damsel, whose dark eyes lingered sometimes on the youthful nabob, and sometimes on the Greyfriars juniors as she passed before them again and again in the windings of the dance. Doubtless the nautch-girl was interested in the Europeans, and desired to note the effect upon them of her performance. But that was not Bunter's idea.

Bunter dug a fat thumb into Bob Cherry's ribs.

"I say, Cherry—"

"Hallo, hallo, hallo, fatty! Don't puncture me!"

"That's a jolly-looking girl!" said Bunter.

"Eh? Oh, ripping!" said Bob.

"She dances well," said Wharton. "That's Lakme, the queen of the nautch-girls, Bunter."

"You fellows noticed her looking at me?" said Bunter, with a smirk.

"Eh?"

"What?"

Bunter grinned complacently.

"I dare say she did," remarked Johnny Bull. "She may have wondered what we've got a porpoise here for."

"Oh, really, Bull—"

The dancer passed again, and again her dark eyes lingered on the Greyfriars juniors, and she smiled with a flash of white teeth.

Bunter smirked.

"I suppose you fellows noticed that, anyhow?" he said. "You needn't think she was looking at you, Wharton."

"Fathead!"

"I'm accustomed to jealousy," said Bunter calmly. "A really good-looking and attractive fellow has to get used to it."

"'Oh, my hat!"

"I must speak to her after this is over," said Bunter. "After all, why shouldn't a fellow be civil? This sort of thing isn't in your line, you fellows; but I'm used to getting the glad eye."

"You unspeakable idiot!" said Bob Cherry.

"Oh, really, Cherry! I've had that sort of thing from you before, at home!" said Bunter disdainfully. "You never did like it when Marjorie Hazeldene gave me the glad eye."

"What?" breathed Bob.

"You never liked it—you can't say you did," said Bunter. "The Cliff House girls were fond of me—it was natural. The jealousy I got from you fellows was rather thick. Don't begin it all over again here, just because that jolly girl is mashed. It's rather sickening, you know."

"I can't kick you here," said Bob, after some thought.

"Oh, really, you know—"

"But if you mention Marjorie again, I shall kick you and chance it!"

"Yah!"

Bunter did not mention Marjorie again. In fact, his fat attention was quite taken up with Lakme, the nautch-girl. Bunter had not the slightest doubt that the nautch-girl had noticed his uncommon attractions—indeed, how could she fail to notice them? Her glances at the Greyfriars party, to Bunter meant only one thing—the queen of the nautch-girls was greatly attracted by him, and was giving him what he elegantly termed the "glad eye." And Bunter smirked back whenever Lakme came near, and had not the slightest doubt that his fatuous smirks achieved the conquest of the dusky damsel's heart.

Bunter unexpectedly found himself enjoying the entertainment, and he was sorry when it was over and the nautch-girls trooped away. As he rolled back into the palace there was a fatuous grin on Bunter's fat face. He was thinking of the graceful and beautiful Lakme, and he had not the slightest doubt that she was thinking of him. On that point there was, in Bunter's mind, not the shadow of a doubt—not a possible, probable shadow of doubt—no possible doubt whatever.

106

The Glad Eye!

"FRANKY!"

Nugent yawned.

"Franky, old chap—"

"What's the row now?" asked Nugent. "Haven't you had enough supper?"

"Oh! really, Nugent—"

"You ate only enough for six," said Nugent. "Anything the matter with your appetite?"

"I say, old chap, be serious!" urged Bunter. "I want you to help me."

"You had a good many helpings," said Nugent. "And how can I help you now supper's over?"

"I don't mean that, you ass," said Bunter peevishly. "Look here, here, Franky, we're pals, ain't we?"

"Are we?" asked Nugent doubtfully.

"You're not such a clumsy, heavy footed ass as Bob Cherry—"

"Not such a rude, ill-mannered pig as Bull—"

"What?"

"Or so stuck up as Wharton—"

"What the thump—"

"That's why I've picked you out to help me," said Bunter, blinking seriously at Nugent through his big spectacles.

Nugent stared at him. Undoubtedly Frank Nugent was the most easygoing member of the Co. Probably that was why he had allowed Bunter to lead him out mysteriously into the moonlit gardens of the palace after supper. He was no keener on Bunter's company than the other fellows, but he had good-naturedly submitted. What Bunter wanted he could not guess, but he was willing to give the Owl of the Remove his head, so to speak.

"What on earth do you mean, Bunter?" he asked. "If you're not talking out of your silly hat, give it a name!"

"You remember that girl—"

"What girl?"

"Lakme, the nautch-girl."

"I remember," said Nugent. "What on earth about her, Bunter? Are you wandering off your rocker?"

"You remember how she gave me the glad eye during the dance?" urged Bunter.

"Oh, my hat! Did she?"

"You must have noticed it," said Bunter warmly. "Well, I want to make her acquaintance."

"Great pip!"

"All these people have their quarters in a different part of the palace," said Bunter. "But of course, that can be worked. Lakme practically asked me to make an appointment and speak to her—that's what her glances meant."

"Phew!"

"You wouldn't understand, Nugent," said Bunter condescendingly. "You aren't used to these things. I can tell you that when I've been on the pier at Margate, I've had dozens of girls looking at me and smiling."

Nugent chuckled.

"I'm not surprised to hear that," he admitted.

"You're not a jealous ass like Cherry, are you old fellow?" said Bunter. "You know how it is. I don't brag, as you know, but if a fellow's attractive, he's attractive, and that's all there is about it."

"Ye gods!" murmured Nugent.

"Now, I want you to help me," said Bunter. "There's difficulties in the way. Do you think Lakme understands English?"

Lots of the nautch-girls do, I believe," said Nugent. "But—"

"If she does, it's all right. I could send her a note."

"A—a—a note? Do you mean a bank-note?"

"No, you ass." said Bunter irritably. "I mean a billy-dooks."

"A what?" gasped Nugent.

"A billy-dooks. Don't you know what a billy-dooks is?"

"Blessed if I do," said Nugent blankly. "Is it a Hindustani word?"

"You silly ass! It's a French word, and it means a love letter."

"Oh, a billet-doux!" said Nugent, comprehending at last. "I—I see! You want to send Lakme a billet-doux."

"You can call it a billy-doo if you like—I call it a billy—dooks," said Bunter, "You don't know much French, Nugent. But never mind that now. I want you to help me."

"I can't help you in French if I don't know much French, can I?" said Nugent gravely.

"I don't mean that; I mean, help me in sending a billy-dooks to Lakme!" snapped Bunter.

"You frabjous ass!"

"Oh, really, Nugent—"

"If you get nosing into places where you've no business, you may get your silly head chopped off!" said Nugent.

"Well, you see, I was thinking of that," said Bunter. "They've got a lot of queer customs in this country that want a lot of understanding. They keep women shut up and veiled, and all that. I don't know whether they're so particular about nautch-girls; but, of course, I don't want to run into some Johnny who might out up rusty. Still, I want to see Lakme, naturally, when she's mashed on me."

"Oh dear!"

"Well, will you take a billy-dooks to her?" asked Bunter. "If she can read English, it will be all right, and I'll make an appointment in the palace gardens, see? I ask it as a pal Franky. You're not a rotter like those other chaps. Do it."

Nugent blinked at him. Apparently, as a pal, he was to penetrate to the quarters of the nautch-girls, and carry Bunter's billet-doux, taking upon himself the risk of meeting a Johnny with a dagger who might cut up rusty.

Bunter eyed him anxiously. Johnnies with daggers were extremely disagreeable johnnies to meet : but somehow Bunter did not seem to think that that mattered so far as Frank Nugent was concerned. He was very particular about the safety of his own fat skin; but

Nugent's skin was so very minor a consideration that Bunter did not think of it at all.

Frank Nugent was silent for a minute or two. Then a glimmer came into his eyes, and he smiled.

"Got the billet-doux ready?" he asked.

"Here it is, old chap," said Bunter effusively. "I've written it. Rather poetical, you know—something in the Eastern style. I begin, 'The light of your starry eyes —' "

"Don't read it out," said Nugent. "I'm not a giddy nautch-girl I've never noticed that you were a good-looking and attractive chap."

"Oh, really, Nugent—"

"Hand it over," said Frank. "Mind, I don't promise anything. I'll see what can be done. That's all I can say."

"Do your best, old fellow," said Bunter anxiously.

"I'll do the best I can for you, Bunter," said Nugent. "I can say no, more than that."

"That's all right, old fellow. I'll wait for you here, under this mango tree," said Bunter. "Don't lose time."

"Not a tick!" said Frank.

And, leaving George William Bunter waiting under the shadow of the mango tree. Frank Nugent put the billet-doux into his pocket and went back into the palace.

He preserved his gravity, though with difficulty, till he was out of sight and hearing of Bunter. But he was chuckling as he rejoined his chums. Harry Wharton & Co. were supping sherbet in a little pagoda in the gardens, to the sweet strains of a string band, hidden somewhere behind the palm tree Hurree Jamset Ram Singh was with his friends—unbent from the stately magnifiers of the Huzoor Nabob of Bhanipur, and once more the familiar lnky of old. The juniors looked inquiringly at Frank as he came into the pagoda, and a black slave brought a wicker chair and another a glass of sherbet on silver tray for the newcomer.

"My esteemed chum seems tickled," remarked Hurree Jamset Ram Singh. "What is the excellent jokefulness?"

"Bunter!"chuckled Nugent.

"I noticed that the fat duffer dragged you away after supper," said Harry. "What is it this time?"

"I'm going to tell, you fellows," chuckled Nugent. "It's a chance to pull that fat idiot's leg and teach him a lesson about handing out the glad eye. But I don't know whether I ought to let you into it. Inky."

"And whyfully not?" inquired the nabob.

Nugent grinned.

"I'll let you into it as Inky of the Remove, but not as the Nabob of Bhanipur," he explained, "As old Inky you can help us pull Bunter's leg, but as Nabob of Bhanipur you might be called upon to order his fat head to be cut off."

"Oh, my esteemed hat!" ejaculated Hurree Singh. "My worthy and ridiculous chum, please regard me as the familiar Inky of the school and leave the giddy nabob out of the esteemed question.

"Done!" said Frank. And, that point having been settled, he proceeded to explain the fatuous antics of the Owl of the Remove.

There was a general chuckle in the pagoda. It was often Bunter's fate, seriously as the fat junior took himself, to afford comic relief. But Billy Bunter giving the glad eye to an Indian beauty was really the limit. Bunter mashing the nautch-girls really put the lid on, as Bob Cherry remarked.

"I told him I'd do the best I could for him," concluded Nugent, "And the best thing we can do for him is to give him a lesson, isn't it?"

"Yes, rather!" said Wharton, laughing.

"The burbling chump!" growled Johnny Bull. "I'd have thumped him if he'd sprung this on me, instead of you, Franky."

"You see, he picked me out," explained Frank. "He told me it was because I wasn't a pig like you, old chap—"

"What?"

"Or a heavy footed ass like you Bob."

"Eh?"

"Oh stuck—up, like you, Harry—"

"The cheeky owl," exclaimed Wharton.

"Being my nice, agreeable self," continued Nugent, "I'm picked out to run the risk of meeting a Johnny with a dagger while delivering what Bunty calls his billy-dooks—"

"Ha, ha, ha?"

"And now the question arises, how are we going to make the fat idiot give up the glad eye and chuck up playing the goat," said Nugent. "Glad even in India are jolly risky, ain't they, Inky?"

Hurree Jamset Ram Singh nodded.

"Extreme fully so, my worthy chum," he answered. "The idiotic and fatheaded Bunter might very soon find himself with six inches of steal in his fat, or a bowstring round his esteemed and worthless neck."

"Well, we want to keep him from that," said Bob. "I don't suppose even a mausoleum like the Taj Mahal would really console Bunter for being buried in India."

"Ha, ha, ha! "

"He must be warned off the course," said Bob. "He can keep the glad eye for his next holiday at Margate. What did you have in mind, Franky?"

"I was thinking of a spoof appointment, and dropping him into a well, or something," said Frank. "Not a deep one, of course."

The nabob's eyes glimmered.

"That is what I was thinking of, my esteemed chums," he answered.

The juniors started.

"Wha—a—at?" ejaculated Wharton.

The chums of the Remove eyed Hurree Jamset Ram Singh a little anxiously. Since they had been in India the Indian side of Inky's character seemed to have developed more and more. And they knew that any Englishman butting into the "zenana" department of an Eastern household did so at the risk of his neck. Certainly, Bunter was only a fatuous ass, and not to be taken seriously; but for a moment the nabob's words made the juniors feel uneasy. But his cheery grin reassured them.

"The esteemed executioner will make the excellent and ludicrous Bunter jump," explained the nabob. "I will give him the careful and meticulous instructions, and he will not harm the fat idiot."

Hurree Jamset Ram Singh touched a silver gong. A gorgeously-attired attendant came up, salaaming.

The nabob gave him instructions in Hindustani, and he salaamed to the ground and disappeared. Hurree Singh rose.

"Let us proceed to open the watchful eye upon the excellent Bunter," he said. And the grinning juniors proceeded.

107

Bunter's Doom!

BILLY BUNTER waited under a mango tree, impatiently.

Occasionally he looked out into the moonlight of the gardens and smirked.

It was quite a pleasant and flattering thought to Bunter that the queen of the nautch-girls had been struck by his uncommon good looks, and his distinguished manner, and other attractions.

Jealous fellows denied that he bad any of these attractions, and indeed, chuckled at the idea. Nevertheless, the fact remained—or Bunter thought it did—that he was the only member of the party who had made a conquest of this sort during the trip to India. He had "mashed" the beautiful Lakme, and he had no doubt at all that she was keen on a meeting with him, and was indeed longing to hear the music of his voice.

It was quite an adventure for Bunter to add an Eastern beauty to the list of his conquests. He was vaguely conscious that there was a certain amount of risk in these mashing affairs in an Eastern country; but as Nugent was taking that risk for him it was not a matter of much moment. If Lakme was able to read his bullet box he was sure she would come; and he was going to spread himself and display his many perfections, like a peacock spreading its gorgeous tail. He smirked with satisfaction as he waited.

There was a step in the gardens at last.

Bunter blinked anxiously through his big spectacles and discerned a white-robed figure advancing towards him in the moonlight. He grinned. The queen of the nautch-girls was coming! But as he gave a second blink he realized that this figure was too tall for Lakme's. And as the newcomer came nearer the Owl of the Remove discerned that it was a powerfully-built man, with a crimson sash round his white robe and a fold of crimson in his white turban. His face was dark—almost black—and far from handsome. And he carried bare, under his arm, an enormous scimitar.

Bunter blinked at him uneasily.

He supposed that the man was some official of the palace, but he did not like the look of that huge, bare scimitar. You never could trust natives, was Bunter's opinion, and he was rather anxious for the big man to pass on his way and disappear.

Instead of which, the big man with the scimitar came directly towards the mango-tree where Bunter stood. The Owl of the Remove felt a tremor. The man was coming to him. What on earth did he want? The great scimitar, gleaming in the moonlight, caused cold chills to run through Bunter. He backed deeper into the shadow of the mango tree, palpitating. Surely this frightful looking "native" could have no business with him—surely—

"Sahib!"

"Ow! Yes?" gasped Bunter.

The Hindu held out a note. Bunter, in amazement, recognized the "billet-doux" he had handed to Frank Nugent for delivery to the queen of the nautch-girls.

"You send?" asked the Hindu in his limited English.

"I—I—I—" gasped Bunter.

"You sending to Lakme?"

"Yes!" gasped Bunter.

"Ach—cha! You must die."

"What?" yelled Bunter.

"It being the law of Bhanipur!" said the Hindu. "Little sahib breaking law of the zenana."

"Oh, my hat! I—I—I mean— here, keep off! Keep that sword away!" roared Bunter, in great alarm.

The Hindu had taken the great scimitar from under his arm and had grasped it in both his sinewy hands. It seemed to be his intention to cut Bunter down where he stood.

"Little sahib being ready?" he asked.

"Yarooh! Help!"

"Breaking the law of the zenana, it is to die!" said the Hindu. "Little sahib being ready?"

"Breaking the law of the zenana, it is to die," said the Hindu. being ready?" Bunter made a spring to escape. In a moment a sinewy grasp was upon him, and he was jerked to his knees. "Yarooooh! Keep off Help!" yelled Bunter, terrified. There was a chortle from behind a clump of deodars, and four grinning faces peered out.

Bunter made a spring to escape. In a moment a sinewy grasp was upon him, and he was jerked back. In the powerful grasp of the executioner Bunter was an infant. One swing of that strong arm threw him upon his fat knees.

He collapsed on the ground, yelling with terror.

"Yarooh! Keep off! Help!"

"My esteemed Bunter—" It was the soft, purring voice of the Nabob of Bhanipur. Never had Bunter been so glad to hear a familiar voice.

"Inky!" he yelled. "Inky, old chap! Keep him off! Ow! Wow!' Help!"

Hurree Singh signed to the executioner to stand back.

"What is the esteemed row, my worthy Bunter?" he inquired.

"Keep him off!" yelled Bunter.

"In my palace you are safe as houses, my worthy fat Bunter. All things you are free to do, exceptfully to break the law of the zenana. But that you have not done, I am sure!"

"Oh dear!" gasped Bunter. "I—I—I— Certainly not! It—it's all a mistake! I—I—"

Hurree Jamset Ram Singh spoke to the executioner in his own tongue, and then turned to Bunter with a very grave face.

"My esteemed Bunter—"

"Send him away?" moaned Bunter.

"Is it true that you have written messages to the nautch-girls?" asked Hurree Jamset Ram Singh.

"Yes! No! I—I mean no! It—it was only a lark!" groaned Bunter. "I —I was only—only j—j—joking."

"In such matters, my esteemed Bunter, the jokefulness is not permitted in my excellent and ridiculous native country," said the nabob. "I am sorrowfully sad that I cannot help you."

Bunter spluttered.

"Ain't you boss here?" he howled. "Can't you do as you like? Send that beast away! Ow! I won't do it anymore! Wow!"

The nabob shook his head sadly.

"Even a nabob my esteemed Bunter, is bound by the law of his country," he said. "The zenana law is most strict. The worthy glad eye, which is quite the thing on the pier at esteemed Margate is forbidden in India, and to break the law is death. I regretfully think that I cannot interfere."

"Help!" yelled Bunter.

"My esteemed Bunter—"

"Yaroooh! Help! Oh, my hat! Help! Keep him of!" shrieked Bunter. "I won't do it again! It was only a j—joke! Oh crikey! Where's Wharton? Where are those beasts? Oh crumble, keep him off!"

"I regret terrifically—"

"Yah! Beast! Help!"

Billy Bunter squirmed away on his fat knees, and suddenly leaped to his feet and ran for it. Strange to relate, the executioner did not pursue him. At a sign from the nabob the terrible official vanished in the shadows. There was a chortle behind a clump of deodars, and four grinning faces emerged into well. Bunter, going at top speed, disappeared in the direction of the palace.

"Ha, ha, ha!" roared Bob Cherry.

The nabob grinned.

"I do not thinkfully opine that the esteemed and fatheaded Bunter will hand out any more glad eyes in Bhanipur," he remarked.

"Ha, ha, ha!"

The chuckling juniors went to their rooms to bed. They looked into Billy Bunter's room, but the fat junior was not to be seen there. Apparently the Owl of the Remove was in hiding somewhere. The man with the scimitar was still looming large in his terrified imagination. Hurree Jamset Ram Singh had gone to the State apartments of the Nabob of Bhanipur; but the other fellows gathered in Harry Wharton's room for a chat before turning in, when there was a tap at the door, and it opened to show the bronzed face of Colonel Wharton. The colonel was marching Billy Bunter along, with a heavy hand on his collar, and the fat junior was blinking with apprehension, his fat knees knocking together. The chums of the Remove jumped up.

"What does this mean, Harry?" asked the colonel, eyeing his nephew rather severely.

"Hem! What, uncle!" asked the captain of the Remove.

"I found Bunter hiding under my bed.

"Oh, my hat!"

"He has told me some wild story about his life being in danger, and his being condemned to death," said the colonel.

"Ha, ha, ha!"

"I suppose it is some absurd joke?" said Colonel Wharton.

"I—I say, you fellows, it's true!" groaned Bunter. "Save me! Stand by me, you know! That beast Inky won't protect me! He was handing me over to the executioner, when I bolted. Oh dear! I wish I was back at Greyfriars."

"Well, what have you done, Bunter?" asked Bob Cherry, with a chuckle.

"I—I haven't done anything. It was really a joke!" groaned Bunter. "You know it was a joke, Franky!"

"I?" exclaimed Nugent.

"I—I never meant you to take that billy-dooks to the nautch-girl really!" gasped Bunter.""It—it was only my fun, you know."

"What?" ejaculated Colonel Wharton.

"You didn't mean me to take it to Lakme?" asked Nugent, grinning.

"Nunno! Nothing of the kind!" gasped Bunter. "You tell that beast Inky so, and he can tell the other beasts. See?"

"That's lucky," said Nugent. "Because I didn't take it to Lakme. See?" Bunter jumped.

"You didn't?" he howled.

"Ha, ha! No!"

"Then how did that beast of an executioner get after me?" yelled Bunter.

"The executioner was spoof, you silly owl!" roared Bob Cherry. "If you weren't the fattest and silliest funk that ever funked you'd have guessed it."

"Oh!" gasped Bunter.

"Ha, ha, ha!"

Colonel Wharton stared at the juniors and stared at Bunter. Then he quitted the room without further remark. Billy Bunter remained there, blinking angrily at the grinning chums of the Remove. At long last it dawned upon his fat brain that his leg had been pulled once more.

"You awful rotters!" he gasped. "You—you beasts! You—you—you—" Words seemed to fail Bunter.

"Go it!" said Bob Cherry encouragingly. "You'd laugh, two, old fat bean, if you knew what you looked like in the garden when the jolly old executioner bagged you."

"You were there?" yelled Bunter.

"The therefulness was terrific, as Inky would say," chortled Bob.

"We were behind the deodars, dear boy, watching you. Your face was worth watching."

"Ha, ha, ha!" roared the juniors.

The expression on Bunter's face was worth watching still.

"You—you—you—" spluttered Bunter.

"Ha, ha, ha!"

For a full five minutes Bunter stood and told the chums of the Remove what he thought of them. And the more he told them the more they roared. The fat junior gave it up at last, and tramped savagely away to his own room. There he found some solace in kicking Kasi Jee, who came to take his boots off. It was a relief to Bunter to learn that he was not, in point of fact under sentence of death. But the fright had been enough for him, and, as the nabob had remarked, it was not likely that Billy Bunter would indulge the "glad eye" again during his sojourn in Bhanipur.

108

The Tiger Hunt!

"WE shall want Bunter," said Bob Cherry gravely.

It was the following day. The sun was rising over the great hills, and at an early hour the Greyfriars. Palace of Bhanipur were astir. It was the day of the tiger-hunt arranged by Hurree Jamset Ram Singh of his guests, and the Remove fellows had been looking forward keenly to it. Billy Bunter had professed great keenness; indeed, he had declared his intention of taking home a tiger-skin for use as a rug in Study No.7 at Greyfriars. It would, Bunter had said, make Toddy open his eyes; and certainly Peter Todd, of the Remove, would have opened his eyes very wide indeed at the news that W. G. Bunter had shot tiger and brought home the skin.

But now that the morning of the hunt had dawned Bunter had not turned out early. He seemed to prefer an extra to the excitement and peril of the hunt.

"Better wake him," said Johnny Bull, with a chuckle. "Bunter mustn't miss this; it may be the only time we get after a tiger. It will be exciting."

"Still more exciting if the tiger gets after us," remarked Nugent. "Bunter really ought to come—the tiger would rather bag him than any of us. He would go down like an oyster."

"Ha, ha, ha!"

Bob Cherry tramped away to Bunter's room. Kasi Jee met him at the doorway with a dusky finger at his lips.

"Hush, sahib! He sleeps."

"That's all right, Jamesy," said Bob cheerily. "I've come along to wake him."

"The little sahib giving order he no wake," explained Kasi Jee.

"He's forgotten the tiger-hunt," chuckled Bob. "Can't leave old

Bunter out of such a treat. He was grousing yesterday at being left behind. We'll be more careful this time. Bunter! Bunter! Hallo, hallo, hallo!"

Snore!

Bob Cherry's voice, on its, highest gear, so to speak, might have awakens Epeminides, or Rip Van Winkle, or the Seven Sleepers of Ephesus. But it did not awaken Bunter. Bunter snored more vigorously. Perhaps he had forgot the tiger-hunt—or perhaps be hadn't.

"Bunter! Bunter! Bunter!" roared Bob.

Snore!

Bob Cherry chuckled, and Kasi Jee grinned a dusky grin. Bob leaned over the sleeper, took a fat little nose between finger and thumb, and shook Bunter—by means of his nose. Bunter awoke then—if he really was asleep. He woke with a spluttering how!

"Gurrrrggh!"

"Hallo, hallo, hallo, old top!" said Bob genially. "Turn out! We're getting ready to start."

"Beast! Let a fellow sleep."

"You've forgotten the tiger-hunt, old bean."

"Blow the tiger-hunt! I'll go another time. Go and eat coke. Get out!" yelled Bunter.

"But there mayn't be another time," urged Bob. "We don't want to leave you behind, Bunter."

"You left me behind yesterday, you beast! After that, I refuse to come with you today."

"But we want you to come with us and protect us, old bean."

"I refuse to do anything of the kind."

"The nabob has invited all of us, you know. You can't turn down a greedy royal invitation."

"After the way Inky treated me last night, I decline to accept his invitation. It would be beneath my dignity."

"But what about us?" urged Bob. "Frightful danger in a tiger-hunt. We want you to protect us. If the tiger goes for us we can all hide behind you. There's just about room for five to hide behind you, Bunter."

"Beast!"

"Then you won't come?" grinned Bob.

"No, I won't! I decline!"

"Not afraid of the tiger?" chuckled Bob.

"No!" roared Bunter. He blinked round for the naukar. "James!"

"Han, sahib."

"Turn that fellow out of my room."

Kasi Jee looked dismayed. Turning the sturdy and hefty Bob out was a task rather beyond the powers of the slight Hindu, even had he dreamed of laying disrespectful hands on a sahib.

"Do you hear me?" roared Bunter. "Turn him out!"

"Oh, my lord!" gasped Kasi Jee.

"Don't trouble, Jamesy, I'm going," chuckled Bob. "Only staying a minute to pillow that fat ass for his cheek."

"Yaroooh!" roared Bunter, as Bob grasped a pillow from the bed and pillowed him rigorously. "Ow! Oh! Stopped. Yooop! Beast! I was only j—j—joking! Yaroooh!"

"So, am I, old man. No end of a joker," said Bob, and he tossed the pillow at Bunter and walked away, leaving the Owl of the Remove roaring.

It was quite a little while before Bunter settled down again to slumber.

Bob Cherry joined his comrades in the palace courtyard. Great preparations were going on there for the hunt.

The hunters were to go on elephants and a number of the huge animals were standing ready in charge of the mahouts A crowd of shikarees had gathered, to a on foot, as well as an immense number of beaters. And there was an escort of some hundreds of the Bhanipur cavalry, who were to guard the nabob against any attempt of his enemies during the hunting.

"Bunter not coming?" asked Harry Wharton, with a laugh.

"No. He's not afraid of the tiger, but he declines to come," grinned Bob. "Ha, ha, ha!"

"We shall have to face the giddy danger the best we can without Bunter to protect us," said Bob. "Hallo, hallo, hallo! Here come the great guns!"

A gorgeous palkee was borne out of the palace, and from the silken curtains Hurree Jamset Ram Singh nodded and grinned to his friends. From the palkee, raised high on the shoulders of his attendants, the youthful nabob stepped into the howdah on the back of the royal elephant. The Jam Bahadur followed him. Colonel Wharton, who preferred to go in the saddle, mounted his horse, and Pandy Din, the khitmutghar, came over to the juniors. With the Khitmutghar's assistance, Harry Wharton & Co. mounted into the howdah on a towering elephant. There was room for the four juniors in the howdah, though if Bunter had come there would scarcely have been room for him.

With a blare of trumpets and cymbals the procession started from the palace.

The elephants trod heavily away, almost shaking the earth with their mighty tread. Crowds of the inhabitants of Bhanipur thronged the street, to stare at the hunters and salaam reverently at the passage of their nabob.

Outside the city the procession followed a well-laid road to the north, towards the far-off snowy line of the Himalayas.

They entered the path through the forest where the juniors had picnicked the previous day. Harry Wharton & Co. glanced at the ruined temple of Shiva as they passed it. The massive ruins lay silent and deserted, shimmering in the blaze of the sun. They glanced at the fissure in the old wall, whence the savage face of Nally Das had looked out the previous day, but there was no sign of life about the haunted temple now. They were aware that the kidnapper was still being searched for, and wondered whether he was still within the borders of Bhanipur. It was probable that lie was hiding in the castle of Baji Rao, probably plotting with the perfidious rajah. Since the arrival of Hurree Jamset Ram Singh in his native kingdom the scheming rajah had not been seen in the city of Bhanipur; he was keeping within the walls of his own castle on his own lands.

The old temple was passed, and the hunting-party followed the path through the forest for many a long mile. The cultivated lands were left behind them now, and at noon they halted on the edge of the jungle that clothed the lower slopes of the hills. According to the news brought in by the nabob's shikarees, a man-eating tiger lurked in this region, the terror of the native villages of the district. Harry Wharton & Co. felt rather a thrill when the hunters had arrived at the domain of the tiger, and realized that the terrible animal was probably quite near at hand, hidden in the recesses of the pathless jungle.

The hunters camped under the mango trees, on the edge of the jungle. Stately tent was set up for the nabob and the Jam Bahadur, and their royal elephant knelt before the tent, while richly-attired officers helped the Jam and his nephew to descend. They vanished into the tent, screened from common eyes; but Harry Wharton & Co. were honored with an invitation to tiffin with the nabob and the Jam were honoured with an invitation to tiffin with the nabob and the Jam.

While the tiffin was going on, the shikarees and the crowd of beaters disappeared into the jungle. From the distance, the juniors could hear the din of cymbals and tom-toms. The beaters of whom there were hundreds, had spread out in an immense circle round the jungle where the tiger had lately been traced. The clashing of cymbals, the beating of tom-toms, was intended to scare the tiger out of his lair, and drive him to a central spot where the hunters were to wait for him.

After lunch, the hunters left the camp.

Huree Jamset Ram Singh mounted the royal elephant, the Jain Bahadur salaaming him out of the tent. The little, old, brown gentleman was remaining in the camp, probably preferring a nap to a tiger-hunt in the warm drowsy afternoon.

The nabob of Bhanipur occupied the howdah on the royal elephant in solitary state. He waved a dusky hand to the Greyfriars juniors, ns the great animal started, surrounded by limiters ant guards.

Harry Wharton & Co. remounted their elephant and followed. Colonel Wharton and Pandy Din went on foot now, with rifles under their arms. The juniors had their rifles ready in the howdah. The colonel glanced up at their eager faces.

"You will be safe on the elephant, I think," he said. "If you see the tiger shoot; but take care you do not leave the howdah."

"We shan't see mush of the fun, stuck up here, sir," said Bob Cherry.

You will probably see quite is much as is safe for yan," said the colonel.

"But a fellow doesn't go on a tiger hunt to be safe," urged Bob. "We're ready to take our chances along with the shikarees."

"Yes, rather," said Harry.

Colonel Wharton smiled and shook his head. He had no intention of allowing the juniors to get to close quarters with a savage, man-eating tiger, if he could help it.

The heavy elephants tramped on, nine or ten of them, all the howdahs crowed with hunters. Along with them tramped the shikarees. They arrived at the spot in the heart of the jungle which had been marked out by the nabob's chief shikaree, ant halted. In the distance, on all sides, sounded the incessant din of cymbals and tom-toms and horns, closing in slowly but surely. I breathless shikaree arrived with the news that the tiger had been seen, stealing along in the high grasses; he was within the circle of the beaters, and the terrifying uproar was driving him towards the open space in the heart of the jungle, where the hunters now waited.

"He is coming!" the colonel called up to the juniors. "Take care!"

Bob Cherry gave a grunt.

"He can't burt us up here, I suppose, sir," he answered. "We're not giving him much of a chance."

"You have never seen a tiger-hunt, my boy!" said the colonel. "I tiger may spring upon an elephant, and climb into a howdah."

"Oh, my hat!"

There was a sudden shout.

"Hallo! hallo! Hallo! Iook!" yelled Bob, in great excitement.

From the high, jungly grass, scarce fifty yards away, a great, tawny head and two fierce, glittering eyes scanned the group of elephants and hunters.

It was the tiger.

The circle of beaters, closing in on him with deafening din, had startled him out of his lair, and driven him, slowly but surely, to the clearing where he was waited for.

"The tiger!" breathed Nugent.

The juniors fixed their eyes on the tawny head and great jaws that were flecked with foam.

Their hearts beat faster.

There was a sudden spluttering of hasty fire, and bullets rattled in the high grass round the tiger. From the royal elephant came the crack of Hurree Jamset Ram Singh's rifle, and it was answered by a roar from the tiger, as the bullet tore along the tawny neck.

"He's hit!"

The head was instantly withdrawn—the tiger vanished again in the jungle.

A trumpet rang out.

It was a signal; and the whole parts, elephants and shikarees, trampled on in the direction of the tiger, trampling down the grasses and thickets, at close quarters now with the king of the jungle.

109

The Luck of Nally Das!

CRACK! Crack! Crack!

The rifles were ringing.

The great tiger, scared and daunted by the din of cymbals and tom-toms, and by the blaze of rifle-fire, had backed into the jungle, crouching low in the thick grass. But the heavy trampling hoofs of the elephants drove him out, and a long sinuous body was seen to leap away among the high grasses, and a score of bullets whizzed as it leaped. The roar of the wounded tiger answered, echoing like thunder back from the hills.

The tiger vanished into the jungle again, and a loud scream was heard from a native shikaree who had ventured too near. The man was running, with blood streaming down from his shoulder where the tiger had clawed.

"There he is!" shouted Bob Cherry, as he sighted the tiger again from the elephant's back.

Harry Wharton's eyes were on the huge, striped body—and he pulled the trigger as Bob shouted. The bullet glanced along the tawny hide. Nugent and Johnny Bull fired and missed. A bullet from Bob Cherry grazed the tiger's head. The native shikarees poured in a volley, but the tiger, winding among the jungle grasses, escaped most of the bullets. Colonel Wharton,with his rifle to his shoulder, was quietly watching his chance. The ring of his rifle was answered by a scream from the tiger, evidently lard hit this time.

The wounded animal was retreating; but the elephants trampled heavily on his track; and before him, the din of the beaters was loud and incessant, scaring him back. The bewildered, infuriated brute turned once more on the hunters, and there was a shout, as his long, sinuous body was launched through the air in a terrific spring.

Crash!

"Kya! Khabardar! Khabardarraho!" the shikarees were shouting, as the maddened brute landed fairly among them, close by Hurree Jamset Ram Singh's elephant.

Two hunters went sprawling down, under the tiger, shrieking with terror. The rest scattered wildly; and the royal elephant, startled and scared, trumpeted shrilly and trampled back.

From the howdah above, the face of Hurree Jamset Ram Singh looked, his dark eye gleaming along his rifle.

Crack!

The bullet struck the tiger in the neck.

The great brute, roaring and screaming, stood clawing over the two fallen hunters, while the nabob's mahout, playing his goad, urged the royal elephant forward to trample the tiger down.

The striped, sinuous body leaped again, and clutched at the elephant. Like a tawny streak, so swift was the movement, the tiger clambered over the royal elephant's trunk and head.

The elephant trumpeted frantically, with pain and terror, as the sharp claws tore at his rough hide.

The mahout, perched on the elephant's huge neck, slipped off just in time to escape the jaws of the tiger.

The next moment the infuriated animal was on the elephant's back, and clawing at the silken curtains of the howdah, in which the Nabob of Bhanipur was alone.

"Fire!" shouted Colonel Wharton, his bronzed face pale and hard.

The danger of the nabob was terrible.

Hurree Jamset Ram Singh was cool as ice, though the menacing jaws of the tiger were only a couple of feet from him, and it seemed that nothing could stop the terrible beast.

He fired from the howdah, and fired again, and both bullets struck home. But the maddened tiger clung and clambered on, and one stroke of his mighty paw tore out the side of the howdah.

"Fire!" breathed Harry Wharton.

Bullets rained at the tiger clambering on the nabob's elephant. It was impossible to fire without hitting the elephant, too; but that could not be helped. Most of the bullets glanced from the thick, tough hide when they struck, but many of them penetrated, and, between his rounds, and the clawing of the tiger, the royal elephant was mad with excitement, and prancing and trampling frantically. Several of the shikarees were hurled over by the great animal, and the rest scattered from his huge, trampling feet. And still the tiger clambered at the howdah, and Hurree Jamset Ram Singh drove the butt of his rifle at the yearning jaws that threatened him.

Crack, crack, crack!

The Greyfriars juniors pumped bullets at the tiger from their howdah, at the range of only a dozen yards. A shikaree, dodging the trampling royal elephant, ran in with a spear, and drove it into the tiger's ribs. The clinging animal was seen to fall back.

The terrible scene had lasted scarcely a minute. The tiger, torn by unnumbered wounds, weakened by loss of blood hung helplessly on the elephant, unable to reach the nabob's howdah, but still clawing and growling horribly. The elephant, maddened by pain, careered in the jungle, trumpeting with a noise like thunder. Colonel Wharton rushed forward, but had to leap back to avoid being crushed under the huge feet. Mahouts and shikarees gathered round the elephant, but broke and scattered when he neared them. The frantic animal was utterly beyond control, rearing and trampling and careering, and it was death to approach him.

Hurree Jamset Ram Singh, his dusty face set hard, clung to the wrecked howdah to save himself from being hurled to the ground.

The maddened elephant, heedless of the attempts of the shikarees to head him off, trampled away wildly into the jungle. The clawing and growling of the tiger clinging to his flank, seemed to have driven the huge animal insane.

"After him!" yelled Bob Cherry.

A whole mob of shikarees and officers rushed after the elephant as it careered away.

After them trampled the other elephants, driven by the mahouts on that necks, plying the sharp goads.

The tiger, weakened by many wounds, was torn from the elephant's side by thin thickets, as the animal thundered through them, trampling down grass and bush and tree.

The striped body dropped to the ground, but leaped up again, and was surrounded by the hunters. In a few minutes the tiger was dispatched, under a rain of bullets and the thrusting spear of the shikarees.

The tiger had been killed; but the royal elephant, maddened and uncontrolled, was rushing away through the thick jungle at a speed that was amazing in so huge a creature.

Elephants and horsemen and shikarees on foot rushed in pursuit, leaving a wide trampled track in the jungle as they went.

Hurree Jamset Ram Singh clung to the broken howdah, his face calm, but hard and set. To fall was death under the trampling elephant; but the schoolboy nabob did not lose his nerve.

He glanced back as he clung.

The other elephants and their rides had been left far behind, but swift-footed shikarees were keeping pace for the moment. But they could not keep it up and they dropped behind. But a dozen horsemen were riding hard after the run away elephant, among them Colonel Wharton, she had taken a horse froma native subadar. But even the horse men were unable to gain on the fleeing elephant in the difficult jungle, where thick-tangled undergrowths barred the way.

Hurree Singh set his teeth hard.

Beyond the jungle lay a thick forest clothing the slopes of the hills, and the runaway elephant was rapidly approaching the wood. To gain control of the animal was impossible, and to leap from his back was more dangerous than to stay where he was. The schoolboy nabob clung on, waiting for a chance to escape from his perilous position, and the elephant trumpeted on into the forest. Branches of trees swept his back as he rushed on, and the fragments of the howdah were swept away, and the nabob dodged again and again to escape being torn away by a branch. But he took the chance at last, and leaped at a thick bough as the elephant thundered on under a spreading tree.

His grasp closed on the bough, and he hung on, the elephant rushing onward into the depths of the forest, and leaving him swinging.

In a few moments the animal was gone though his frantic trumpeting could still be heard, awakening the choose of the forest.

Hurree Jamset Ram Singh leaped at a thick bough as the runaway elephant thundered on under a spreading tree. Inky's grasp closed on the bough, and he hung on, the terrified animal rushing onward into the depths of the forest.

Hurree Jamset Ram Singh, his brain reeling, clung to the swaying branch, high above the ground. But he clambered on the bough at last—clambered along it to the trunk of the tree, and slid to the earth.

There he stood leaning against the tree, panting for breath.

He had escaped with his life, though he was almost astonished to find himself still alive. He leaned on the tree and panted, waiting for his followers to come up. The trampled track left by the elephant was an easy guide to them, and he had only to wait.

There was a footstep in the trees. The nabob looked round.

It was not one of his own men. They were still distant, though he could hear the hoofs of the horses. A dark face looked at him from the forest, and Hurree Jamset Ram Singh started as he recognized Nally Das. The eyes of the rascally Hindu blazed with triumph.

"Huzoor! Shabash, shabash!" grinned Nally Das.

He gave a shrill whistle.

Hurree Jamset Ram Singh sprang back, his eyes gleaming. He was unarmed, save for the hunting-knife in his girdle. As he grasped the knife, three or four dusky figures rushed from the trees, in response to the signal of Nally Das, and he was seized on all sides.

The schoolboy nabob struggled desperately.

Scarce a hundred yards away, though hidden by the forest, he could hear the trampling of the horsemen, coming on hard. He would have shouted, but a thick cloth was thrown over his head, and wound about his face by strong hands. He was lifted from the ground, and, still struggling, borne away among the thick trees.

A few minutes later, Colonel Wharton and the mounted hunters were riding past the spot; but they rode on the track of the trumpeting elephant, still in the belief that the nabob was on the back of the runaway. There was no sign of the nabob as they passed.

By a devious path in the thick forest, far from the track of the elephant, Hurree Jamset Ram Singh, helping in the hands of his captors, was borne away on the shoulders of Nally Das and his men. Fortune had favored the emissaries of Baji Rao. Chance, and unending watchfulness, had thrown the schoolboy nabob into their hands; and swiftly, swiftly, they were bearing him away to a destination unknown to him.

At long last, Baaji Rao, the ambitious rajah, had succeeded, and Hurree Jamset Ram Singh, who had escaped his enemies at Greyfriars, and on the long journey across half the world, had reached his own kingdom only to fall into their hands.

110

The Missing Nabob!

"INKY! Where is he?"

"Where is Hurree Singh?"

Harry Wharton & Co., mounted on their elephant, hurried along with the crowd of shikarees, beaters, officers, and guards, in the shadow of the forest.

Colonel Wharton and the mounted men had disappeared far ahead; and the juniors suddenly caught sight of Pandy Din, the khitmutghar, riding back. They shouted to him from the howdah.

"Have you found him?"

"Where is the nabob?"

Pandy Din saluted the sahibs in passing, and called out:

"The elephant being found, he falling into a nullah. The colonel sahib send me to tell Jam Bahadur."

And the khitmutghar rode on, heading for the distant camp on the edge of the jungle, where the Jam Bahadur had remained with his retinue during the tiger-hunt.

"Get on!" said Harry Wharton to the juniors' elephant. "Chalo!" he added, having picked up that native word. "Chalo Chalo!" And the mahout drove the elephant on faster.

The chums of the Remove were pale with anxiety. Pandy Din had told them that the elephant was found; but he had said nothing of the nabob. It was not surprising that the maddened elephant, charging blindly through the forest, had tumbled into a nullah—a ravine—but what had happened to the rider? Had he fallen, too—even if he had been killed, it was strange that the khitmutghar had not seen him.

The juniors' hearts were filled with dread as they hurried on, the elephant goaded to speed by the nubout. It was an unexpected and disastrous outcome of the tiger-hunt, though such an accident was not to be unlocked for in so perilous a sport. The hunter of the tiger in the Indian jungle takes his life in his hand.

"There's your uncle, Harry!" exclaimed Bob suddenly.

Colonel Wharton's tall form came in sight. He was on foot, and standing by the edge of a rocky nullah, in an open patch in the midst of the forest. Down in the nullah among the rocks and the plashing water of a stream from the hills, were a score of men searching. The colonel was scanning the interior of the nullah through his field-glasses, and the juniors could see that his face was hard and strained.

They clambered down from the elephant and hurried to join him.

"Uncle!" exclaimed Harry. "What happened? Where is Inky?"

The colonel knitted his brows.

"He is not found yet," he said.

"The elephant—"

"There he lies!" said the colonel, pointing into the nullah.

The juniors stared down into the ravine. Far below, on the rocks by the narrow water-course, lay the gigantic form of the royal elephant. Evidently the animal had rushed blindly over the verge of the ravine, and crashed down to his death; the giant form lay still. But of the nabob there was no sign.

"He must have fallen with the elephant," said Johnny Bull, catching his breath.

"It would seem so," said the colonel. "But—"

"But he isn't found?"

"No. If he fell with the beast, he could not have fallen far from the same spot. There is no trace of him. It would seem that he must have leaped from the elephant before the nullah was reached; but in that case, we must have passed him—and he gave no sign. For the moment I am quite puzzled."

The juniors stared at the still form of the elephant. Fifty shikarees and soldiers were searching the nullah for some trace of the nabob; and they found nothing. It was clear that he had not pitched into the ravine with the frantic elephant. But if he had left the animal before the fall, where was he? The whole troop of hunters must have passed him, and they had seen and heard nothing of him. Even if he had taken the risk of a leap from the thundering elephant's back, and had been killed by the fall, yet he should have been seen by those who followed. And if he lived, why had he not called to his friends as they came?

It was a baffling mystery.

Leaving a crowd still searching in the nullah and along its rocky sides, Colonel Wharton and the juniors turned back by the way they had come. Somewhere between the spot where the elephant had fallen, and the jungle that had been left behind, Hurree Singh was certain to be alive or dead. Colonel Wharton spoke to the nabob's chief shikaree, a grey-bearded old hunter named Mahbub, and Mahbub and his men spread through the forest, searching every nook and cranny on either side of the wide trail left by the runaway elephant.

Perplexed and alarmed, the Greyfriars juniors tramped back, keeping pace with the crowd of hunters on either side of the trampled trail, and they emerged from the forest into the jungle.

The nabob—alive or dead—had not been found. He seemed to have vanished into thin air.

Through the jungle came the tall elephant that bore Jam Bahadur, followed by his retainers, guided by Pandy Din. The little brown face of the Jam puckered with alarm and anxiety.

As he sighted the colonel and the juniors, the Jam stopped his elephant, and leaned out of the howdah, his face full of inquiry.

"You have found him, colonel sahib?"

The colonel shook his head.

The old Jam beat his breast.

"Something unforeseen has occurred, Huzoor," said the colonel quietly. "Hurree Singh cannot be found, and I begin to suspect that in this forest his enemies were watching for him, and a cruel chance threw him into their hands."

The Jam started.

"They have spies in the city, and no doubt the palace itself," said the colonel. "They knew that the nabob would be in the tiger-hunt today. They were on the watch–watching and waiting for a chance. That is the only way I can account for the nabob's disappearance."

"Baji Rao!" murmured the Jam.

"He or his agents," said the colonel. "Luck has favoured them; they had a chance and they have taken it. It seems certain now. But here is Mahbub—"

The chief shikaree came up, salaaming. He spoke hurriedly in his own tongue, the juniors listening eagerly without comprehending. But they were aware that it was news of some kind that the shikaree brought. The Jam's old eyes flashed with fire.

"What does he say, uncle?" asked Harry, when the shikaree finished, and salaamed again and hurried away.

The colonel's face was grim.

"They have found signs where half a dozen men lay hidden in the wood," he answered. "There are traces where a struggle has taken place. Footprints have been found, leading away through the forest and some of the footprints are deeply impressed, as of men who carried a burden. Hurree Singh is if the hands of his enemies!"

Harry Wharton breathed hard.

"Then they were there—watching and—"

"Watching and waiting for a chance sleepless as tigers watching for their prey," said the colonel, gritting his teeth. "In the fifteen or twenty minutes that the royal elephant was out of our sight, they had their chance Hurree Singh must have leaped from the animal's back to save himself—and fallen into their hands. They have taken him—but a hundred skilful shikarees are pressing on their trail through the forest—we must hope for the best."

"Kidnapped!" muttered Bob Cherry.

"Poor old Inky!" murmured Nugent "After escaping the scoundrels so many times—to fall into their clutches here in Bhanipur—with hundreds of guard almost within sight and hearing. Poor old Inky."

"But they will never get clear with him," said the colonel. "All the kingdom of Bhanipur will know what has happened in a few hours—runners are already taking the news to all quarters—the frontiers will be watched every road and path guarded; the whole population will join in the search. Baji Rao has played his last card—too late. There is only one place to which his prisoner can be taken for safety—"

"His castle?" asked Harry,

"Yes. And in a few hours Baji Rao's castle will be surrounded by watchers and the Jam Bahadur will be there with a force that Baji Rao will not dare to resist. Whether the shikarees will be able to follow the trail to the rajah's castle matters little; it is there that Hurree Singh will be searched for.

Pandy Din brought the colonel's horse.

"We return to Bhanipur now," said the colonel. "We return without Hurree Singh—but we shall see him again. Baji Rao will never dare to take his life; and while there is life, there is hope."

He mounted, and rode away, with a grim, thoughtful face. The Jam Bahadur had already started on his return. Harry Wharton & Co. climbed back into their howdah, and the mahout drove on the elephant towards the distant city of Bhanipur.

The faces of the Remove fellows were grave and anxious as they went.

Hurree Jamset Ram Singh was a prisoner; there was scarcely any doubt left on that point now. He was in the power of the plotting rajah; and—as the colonel had said—there seemed to be only one place where the Rajah Baji Rao could hope to keep his prisoner safe. Yet the rajah's castle was certain to be invested and searched; and surely Baji Rao, cunning schemer as he was, must have foreseen as much. If Hurree Singh was found there, it meant the sentence of death to the ambitious kinsman who had dared to lay hands on the reigning nabob. Was it the rajah's intention to defy the Jam Bahadur and his troops, and stand a siege in his castle? Or had he, in this last desperate stage of his dark and tortuous game, placed his rival in a deeper and surer hiding-place than a dungeon of his castle? The juniors could not help fearing so.

"There's only one way that the villain can hope to hide his guilt," Harry Wharton muttered. "If Inky lives, he must be found—and if he's found, what will become of the rajah? The Jam would have had him executed already, but Inky waited for a proof of his guilt. It may be risky for him to kill the nabob; but to let him live is a greater risk."

"Unless—" said Johnny Bull, in his slow, thoughtful way.

"Unless what?"

"Unless they have a safe hiding place for him—some place where he can be kept, at a distance from the rajan's castle. Then Baji Rao could let his palace be searched, and laugh in his sleeve.

"It's possible!" said Herry.

"It's more than possible," said Bob thoughtfully. "It's jolly likely, in my opinion. Somewhere in the forests or the hills—"

"If he lives, he will be found," said Harry.

It was a gloomy party that rode back under the arched gateway of the whitewalled city of Bhanipur. There was gloom in the palace and the city, when it was known that misfortune had befallen the schoolboy nabob. The Indian night had fallen when Harry Wharton & Co. re-entered their old quarters in Hurree Singh's palace. Billy Bunter met them there, with an accusing expression on his fat face.

"Leaving a fellow on his own all day!" he said.

"Oh, dry up, Bunter!" snapped Bob.

"If you think I came here to be treated like this!" exclaimed Bunter warmly.

"Cheese it!"

"Oh, really, Cherry—"

Bunter blinked at the juniors.

"Anything happened?" he asked. "You look about as cheerful as a set of moulting owls."

"They've got Inky!" growled Bob. "Now, shut up!"

Bunter did not seem overcome by the news.

"Have they?" he said. "Who's got him?"

"The kidnappers!"

"Well, if he'd been a bit more decent to me, I'd have come along today, and then it wouldn't have happened," said Bunter. "I came all the way here to protect him, as you know. I've saved him so far. Now—"

"You silly owl, dry up!"

"Oh, really, Wharton! Mind, I'm rather sorry for old Inky, though he's been rather a beast to me," said Bunter And. I'll tell you what—I'll take the matter, in hand."

"What?"

"It's too late tonight," said the Owl of the Remove. "I want my supper now, and then I shall have to sleep early to bed, and early to rise, you know. But tomorrow I'll give the matter my attention."

"You silly chump!" roared Bob Cherry.

"Leave it to me," said Bunter. "You fellows aren't much good, you know Leave it to me!"""

"Oh, sit down!" growled Johnny Bull; and he gave the Owl of the Remove a shove, and Billy Bunter sat down and roared wrathfully as he sat. Long and late into that anxious nigh the chums of the Remove sat, discussing what had happened, and what could be done. Bunter was not included in their anxious counsels. And yet—if they had only known it—it was Bunter who was destined to prove useful in the search for the missing nabob—Billy Bunter, the fat and fatuous Owl of the Remove, who was to be instrumental in saving Hurree Singh from the grasp of this enemies.

PART 10. THE NABOB'S RIVAL!

111

No Go!

"I SAY, you fellows—"

"Can it!"

"But, I say—"

"Oh, run away and play, Bunter!" exclaimed Bob Cherry, looking up from the rifle he was cleaning; and for once, Bob's tone was sharp and irritable. "Don't bother!"

"Roll away, for goodness' sake!" growled Johnny Bull.

Billy Bunter did not roll away.

He remained where he was, blinking at the four juniors of Greyfriars through his big spectacles, with an indignant blink.

It was morning in Bhanipur; the hot Indian morning.

Far off, the white peaks of the Himalayas glimmered against the cloudless blue of the sky, clad in eternal snow. But the white-walled city, und the vast stretches of rice-land, jungle, and forest and nullah, shimmered in the growing heat of the sun.

Harry Wharton and his comrades sat in a balcony under a wide awning, overlooking the palm court of the palace of Bhanipur—the home of their dusky chum, Hurree Jamset Ram Singh.

For the first time since their stay in the Palace of Bhanipur, the chums of the Remove were looking worried and troubled.

Hurree Jamset Ram Singh was not with his comrades; and many hours had passed since the disappearance of the schoolboy nabob. And the mystery of his fate hung heavy on the spirits of his chums.

The juniors were in no mood to be bothered by Billy Bunter just then. It was a time for Bunter to be quiet.

But William George Bunter never could realize that there was a time when his dulcet tones should not be heard. Bunter always found considerable pleasure in the sound of his own voice. He never could realize how quickly it palled upon others.

"Look here—" he recommenced.

"Don't worry now, Bunter," said Harry Wharton quietly. "We're bothered I about what's happened to old Inky. Do dry up for a bit."

"Oh, really, Wharton—"

"Go and have a second breakfast, or a third!" grunted Johnny Bull.

"Oh, really, Bull—"

"Anyhow, dry up!" said Frank Nugent. "Can't you see we're worried, you fat duffer?" Nobody knows what's happened to Hurree Singh."

"That's what I was going to speak about," said Bunter calmly. "Inky hasn't treated me really well since I've been here, though I came all the way to India to protect him. He's not really grateful—"

"Cheese it!"

"But I'm sorry he's been bagged by those natives," went on Bunter. "It wouldn't have happened if I'd come to the tiger-hunt with you yesterday. I suppose you realize that?"

"Go and eat coke!"

"I've been thinking the matter over," said Bunter, unheeding, "and I can tell you, the matter's jolly serious."

"Oh! You can see that, can you?" snorted Johnny Bull. "You can really see that anything is serious, besides sleeping, and guzzling, and wagging your fat chin!"

"It's pretty serious for old Inky," said Harry. "He was kidnapped during the tiger-hunt, Bunter, and it's fairly certain that he's fallen into the hands of dangerous enemies. We may never see him alive again. Goodness knows what may have happened."

And the face of the captain of the Greyfriars Remove clouded. It was terrible to think that perhaps he had looked for the last time upon the dusky, good-natured face of the schoolboy nabob; that perhaps Hurree Singh, in returning to his native land, had returned only to find a terrible doom there.

"It's rotten!" groaned Bob Cherry. "Inky's uncle sent for him to come home from Greyfriars, thinking that fie would be safer here. And it's here that those rotters have got him."

"You fellows listen to me," said Bunter. "I tell you I've been thinking over this, and it's serious."

"Don't we know it, ass? It couldn't be more serious for Inky than it is."

"I mean, serious for us!" snapped Bunter.

"Us!"

"Yes, us," said Bunter. "Now Inky's gone—kidnapped, and perhaps killed where do we come in?"

Harry Wharton & Co. stared at the fat junior.

Certainly, in their distress for their vanished chum, it had not occurred to them to think much about themselves.

But Bunter had evidently taken thought on the subject. There was one important person whom Billy Bunter never forgot for long, if at all; and that person was W. G. Bunter, of the Greyfriars Remove.

"Look how it stands!" said Bunter, as the juniors remained silent, staring at him. "That native, Nally Das, or some of his gang, have bagged Inky that's pretty clear. But Inky thought in fact, we all knew—that Nally Das and his gang were acting under the orders of a relation of Inky's, who wants to take his place as nabob—a chap, named— What is his blinking name?"

"Baji Rao!" said Harry.

"That's it—the Rajah Baji Rao," said Bunter. "It seems that if Inky, pegged out, his cousin Baji Rao becomes Nabob of Bhanipur. Isn't that so?"

"Yes, ass. That is why the rotter has been plotting against poor old Inky, and trying to get him into his hands."

"And now he's got him," said Bunter.

"It looks like it."

"Well, life's jolly cheap in this country," said Bunter. "Now he's got him he will make an end of him. It stands to reason!"

"It's not certain!" said Harry. "There's lots of room for hope yet.

Baji Rao hopes succeed Inky as Nabob of Bhanipur; but he may be afraid to have poor old Inky killed. The British Government may interfere and he may be glad to save his neck by producing Inky alive."

"Anyhow, he will keep him jolly safe!" said Bunter. "It comes to the same thing for us. If Inky doesn't turn up, Baji Rao becomes Nabod of Bhanipur."

"That's so."

"And then, what about us?" demanded Bunter. "We're friends of Inky's. We came here to save him from being kidnapped on the way from England. We've stood by him through thick and thin—me specially. When Baji Rao gets into this place as nabob do you think he will let us get of safe?"

"I haven't thought about it," said Harry.

"You wouldn't?" said Bunter scornfully. "I'm the only fellow in this party that does any thinking at all. I can jolly well tell you that we're in Queer Street!"

"Oh, dry up!"

"Can't you see?" roared Bunter. "I tell you that rajah beast will have his knife into us, and very likely the first thing he will do when he gets the upper hand here will be chopping of our heads."

"Likely enough, if he gets the chance," said Nugent.

"He will get the chance if Inky doesn't turn up; it won't be a chance, it will be a cert!" said Bunter.

"Well, what about it?" exclaimed Harry Wharton impatiently. "Come to the point."

"That's the point—we're in danger! We've got no time to lose!" explained Bunter. "Inky's "uncle, the Jam Bahadur, is still boss here; but as soon as it's certain that Inky won't come back, he will have to stand down for the new nabob. Well, we've got to clear out before then."

"Clear out?" ejaculated Bob Cherry.

"Of course, you ass! I keep on telling you we're not safe here, now Inky's gone!" exclaimed Bunter excitedly. "Once that rajah gets the whip-hand our number's up. What we've got to do is this—go while the going's good! See? It's a day's journey out of

Bhanipur into British territory. We mayn't have any too much time if we start this morning. So, instead of sitting here like a lot of moulting owls, you'd better pack."

"Pack!" said Wharton blankly.

"Yes; and beat it as fast as we jolly well can!"

"Beat it?"

"Just that!" said Bunter. "The going's good, at present, and we'd better go. See?"

The chums of the Remove gazed fixedly at Bunter.

"Go!" repeated Bob Cherry. "Go and leave old Inky in danger? Take care of our own skins, without bothering about what's happened to him? Is that what you mean, Bunter?"

"Well, I'm sorry for Inky, of course," said Bunter "He wasn't grateful for all I've done for him; still, I'm sorry! But our number's up if we stay, and we've got to beat it, sharp!"

"You fat villain!" roared Johnny Bull. "Beat it as fast as you like—and the sooner the better!"

"I can't go alone, of course," said Bunter warmly. "You fellows brought me here, and you're bound to see me safe back! Don't be selfish!"

"Don't be what?" ejaculated Nugent.

"Selfish! I never could stand selfishness!"

"Oh, my hat!"

Bob Cherry rose to his feet with a gleam in his eyes that might have alarmed Bunter, if the short-sighted Owl of the Remove had noted it.

Probably there was a great deal in what Bunter said. Undoubtedly the nabob's ambitious kinsman was at the bottom of Hurree Singh's disappearance; undoubtedly, Baji Rao hoped to succeed his cousin as nabob. And it was extremely probable that if he came into power in Bhanipur, he would deal very shortly and sharply with Inky's English friends, if they were still in the nabob's kingdom. But such considerations, though overwhelming in Bunter's estimation, did not appeal to the chums of the Remove in the very least. Danger to themselves certainly never would have caused them to desert a comrade in distress. Bob Cherry was about to make that clear to Bunter; not in words which would have been wasted on the fatuous. Owl of the Remove, but by a method that even Bunter could not fail to understand.

"That's right—get a move on!" said Bunter approvingly, as Bob rose. "Get going, and—Yaroooh!"

Bunter broke off with a roar as Bob Cherry grasped him by the collar and slewed him round.

"Yow! Leggo! Wharree you at?" roared Bunter, in surprise and alarm.

Crash!

Bob did not explain what he was at. He let his actions speak for him. His boot crashed on Willam George Bunter, and William George fairly flew.

"Yaroooop!"

Bump!

Bunter landed, and rolled over. He turned to blink dazedly at the juniors.

"You—you—you—" he spluttered.

"Get out!" roared Bob.

"You—you burbling ass!" yelled Bunter. "Is this a time for ragging? Is this a time for Lower Fourth larks, you footling chump? I tell you—"

Bob Cherry made a stride toward him.

On second thoughts—proverbially the best—Billy Bunter did not linger to say more. He picked himself up and fled. A lunge from Bob's boot as he went accelerated his flight, and Bunter disappeared, roaring.

Probably Bunter did not understand why, but it was, as least, made quite clear to him that, for whatsoever reason, the chums of the Remove did not intend to go while the going was good.

112

Held by the Enemy!

"HUZOOR!"

The voice of Nally Das was soft and respectful; thought there was a mocking in flection in it.

Hurree Jamset Ram Singh, the schoolboy Nabob of Bhanipur, sat up, with bonds upon his limbs, and looked at him.

It was night in the Indian forest.

In the deep, dense wood, far from any known path, the kidnapped nabob had been set down by the men who bore him on their shoulders, and the blindfolding linen cloth taken from his face.

Nally Das stood before him and salaamed. There was mockery in his look, but respect and fear were strangely blended with it. In the eyes of the Hindu Hurree Jamset Ram Singh was a great nabob, the descendant of a long line of princes, a sacred person of the highest caste. The kidnapper had not hesitated to carry out the orders of his master, Baji Rao; but he was awed by the calm, clear glance of the prince who had fallen into his hands.

Hurree Singh's dark eyes dwelt upon him contemptuously for a few moments, and then he looked round him.

Five or six dusky figures loomed up in the gloom, beyond them the shadowy forest, with faint starlight filtering through the thick branches overhead.

Where he was, the nabob could not tell.

The kidnapper's opportunity had come during the tiger hunt, and he had been seized and borne away; but he had been blindfolded and bound. He was somewhere in the thick forests that clothed the slopes of the hills on the northern side of his kingdom, and that was all new; but he knew that he was far from help and rescue, or the kidnappers would not have halted and set him down.

"Salaam, huzoor!" said Nally Das. "You know me again, huzoor?" He was speaking in his own tongue.

"I know you, son of a pariah dog!" said the nabob contemptuously. "This is done by the order of Baji Rao, as I know also."

Nally Das nodded.

"You have dared to lay hands on a nabob. The punishment is to be trampled to death by an elephant," said Hurree Singh.

The Remove fellows of Greyfriars would hardly have known "Inky, of the Remove" at that moment. He was no longer a junior of the Lower Fourth, he was Nabob of Bhanipur, an Eastern prince to the tips of his dusky fingers. Inky, of the Remove, the best-tempered fellow at Greyfriars, would not have hurt a fly; but undoubtedly the Nabob of Bhanipur would have sentenced Nally Das to death for treason.

"But the power of punishment is not in the hands of the huzoor!" said Nally Das. "I have obeyed my master's orders. It is Baji Rao henceforth who will reign in Bhanipur."

"My friends will find me," said Hurree Singh. "My uncle, the Jam Bahadur, will lead my soldiers to the rescue. The colonel sahib will never rest till he has found me. My shikarees will be seeking me even now."

"But they, who seek you will not find you, huzoor," said Nally Das. "But we waste time in words. The orders of Baji Rao are to treat you with respect due to your rank, huzoor–are you not of his blood and kindred. The huzoor will be blindfolded—but if he will promise not to resist, or to call out for help, he shall be spared the bonds."

"Never!"

"As the huzoor pleases!" said Nally Das indifferently.

He signed to his men, and a dhooly was brought out from a hiding-place under the trees, where evidently it had been in readiness. It was a sort of box supported on a single pole. Hurree Jam set Ram Singh was lifted into the dhooly, his hands and feet still bound, and the linen cloth was wound about his head again serving the purpose both of a blindfold and a gag.

Two of the dusky kidnappers lifted the pole of the dhooly to their shoulders.

A word from Nally Das, and the party moved on again.

Within the dhooly. Hurree Jamset Ram Singh lay silent. still, as he was borne along through the darkness.

That his friends were seeking him that all Bhanipur would turn out to the search, he knew. It seemed impossible that Nally Das and his men would succeed in getting clear with him. Night would have given place to day before they could hope to pass the border of his kingdom; and in the daylight they would be stopped—no dhooly, no palanquin, no car or carriage, would pass on any road or path, or pass unquestioned and unsearched. Every mountain pass, every forest path, every lane through the paddy-field would be watched and beset by eager searchers. They could not be thinking of attempting to take him outside the borders of his kingdom. Beyond, too, lay the territory of the British, where they would be still less secure, if they could reach it. But where, within the borders of Bhanipur, could they have to keep the nabob a secure prisoner?

The castle of Baji Rao was a strong place, manned by his own retainers, but it could never hold out against the force of the Jam Bahadur. Baji Rao's castle would be invested and searched; it was suspected, if it was not known by proof, that the ambitious rajah was the prime mover in the plot against the schoolboy nabob. It could not be in his own castle that the rajah hoped to keep lit prisoner.

It was a strange puzzle, and Hurree Jamset Ram Singh thought it over and over, as he was borne along in the dhooly under the forest trees.

The progress of the bearers was slow.

They were keeping to the thick forest, avoiding all paths, taking every care to elude possible observation. The dhooly brushed by tangled thickets and swishing branches. Hurree Jamset Ram Singh could not see, but he could hear. And all through the strange journey of the kidnapped nabob, he heard sounds that told him that they were still in the forest; that not for a moment did they emerge into a path or a road.

The dhooly stopped at last.

He heard muttering of voices, and then the dhooly moved on again, and his straining ears detected that the bearers were no longer treading the forest; their footsteps were on hard stone. The swishing branches were left behind, he was out of the forest at last. The dhooly was suddenly set down with a bump on stone.

He was in a building of some kind, or at least a paved court. If could not be the castle of Baji Rao, there were many miles of open country between the rajah's castle and the forest where Hurree Singh had been seized. The remembrance came into his mind of the ruined temple of Shiva in the forest. where he had picnicked with his Greyfriars chums. He remembered the face of Nally Das looking from a fissure in the old wall and the strange disappearance of the Hindu when the ruins were searched for him. And it flashed into his mind that it was to the old, deserted temple of Shiva that he had been brought.

Could they hope to hide him there within twenty miles of the city of Bhanipur? He heard a dull, grinding sound, as of a heavy stone moving. Hands reached into the dhooly and lifted him out.

Once more he was lifted on men's shoulders, and he felt himself being carried downward—down a flight of steps.

Above his head, there came the dull, heavy sound again; the sound of is great stone that rolled back into its place.

And now he understood.

Beneath the ruined temple, there was some secret place—doubtless a hiding place for the treasure of the old priests who had been slain in the Afghan raid of a hundred years before. The old temple, haunted as the ryots believed by the spirits of the murdered priests of Shiva, was avoided by all who dwelt in the region; probably it was years since a footstep lad awakened the echoes of the ancient ruins, until the day the Greyfriars fellows came there. It was a safe place for Nally Das and his gang, and Nally Das evidently knew the secret hiding-place of the old priests.

The heart of the kidnapped nabob was heavy.

Here he was safe from discovery. Even if the old temple of Shiva was visited by those who searched for him, they knew nothing of the secret of the moving stone, nothing of the hidden recesses beneath the cracked pavement of the floor.

For the first time, something like despair same to Hurree Jamset Ram Singh, as he was borne down the steps into the darkness below. The dull echo of the great slab falling into its place, struck upon his cars like a knell, shutting him off from light and liberty, and from the hope of rescue.

113

The Castle of Baji Rao!

THE Rajah Baji Rao stood at a high window in a tower of his castle and looked towards the cast.

Far in the distance, beyond forest and plain there was a glimpse of the white walled city of Bhanipur, many a long mile distant.

The rajah's black, glittering eyes were turned incessantly in the direction of the city.

The morning sun was rising higher in the blue sky. For hours the rajah had stood at that high window, gazing to the cast, waiting and watching for what he knew must come.

And now it was coming.

On the road to the castle there was a flashing of lances, a glow of gorgeous uniforms.

High over the horsemen towered a gigantic elephant, with a curtained howdah on its back; and in that howdah, the rajah knew, was the Jam Bahadur, the uncle and guardian of Hurree Jamset Ram Singh.

Five hundred horsemen were riding with the Jam Bahadur, and among the many brown faces the rajah discerned several that were white, though browned by the torrid sun of India.

His eyes glittered as he recognized Colonel Wharton. With the Colonel rode four young sahibs, the school-fellows–as he knew of Hurree Singh at Greyfriars, in far-off England.

Baji Rao's eyes fixed grimly on the brilliant cavalcade.

The Indian rajah, ambitious, hard, ruthless in the pursuit of his ambition, was no coward. But his heart beat faster as he watched the advancing troopers. In the next hour his fate might be decided.

In his castle-palace, and over the few square miles it commanded, he was lord and master. The tiny Principality had been cut out of the kingdom of Bhanipur by his grandfather—the grandfather also of Hurree Singh-and given to a younger son. Baji Rao had inherited castle and lands and the title of rajah; within his narrow borders he wielded the power of life and death.

The ryots who labored in the fields, the villagers and traders of his tiny State, knew him for a hard and grasping despot. All that tyranny could wring from his land he wrung from it, to spend in the reckless profusion of an Eastern palace. But for long years, since the last Nabob of Bhanipur had died, the rajah's eyes had been turned greedily on the kingdom of his cousin, a schoolboy in England. Only that schoolboy stood between the lord of a tiny State and the rich kingdom of Bhanipur. And at last the greedy thought had turned to active plotting, and Baji Rao had determined that he would region in Bhanipur.

But there were spies about him, and he knew it. He knew that the Jam Bahadur more than suspected him. He knew that the British Government of India would have broken him like a reed had it been known at Simla that he had seized his cousin's kingdom by treachery. The way of the plotter was beset by difficulties and dangers.

But the rajah, once he had resolved upon his purpose, had taken the risks, and he had not turned back. The disappearance of Hurree Singh would leave him heir to the nabob's kingdom; and if the worst came, and the British troops marched into Bhanipur to call him to account, it would always be in his power to produce the nabob alive, and save his worthless neck. While, if he could secure himself in his new possession, it would be easy to change the nabob's imprisonment for the surer custody of death. That had been the rajah's scheme; but his many failures had made it more and more dangerous. Now success was his at last; a messenger from Nally Das had reached him in the night with the news that the nabob was a hidden prisoner. But his guilt, if not known, was suspected; and he knew he had to face the ordeal of suspicion and search. The Jam Bahadur was coming to his castle, with a force that could not be resisted, to search for the missing nabob.

The Nabob of Bhanipur was not there; he could not be found

within Baji Rao's castle walls. There was no proof that he had had a hand in what had befallen the nabob. But the rajah knew the ways of the East; he knew that he would not have waited for proof in the Jam's place. He had taken the risk, and he knew that the risk was terrible. With Hurree Singh gone, he was rightful Nabob of Bhanipur; but the missing nabob's uncle was Regent of the kingdom, and in possession of all its forces. Once in possession of the kingdom, he would have ordered the Jam to execution without hesitating a moment. But he was not yet in possession; it was as yet necessary for him to feign ignorance of what had happened; to act surprise at the news that the schoolboy nabob had disappeared. If the Jam did not believe him, or did not choose to believe him, what measures was he likely to take? The scimitar or the bowstring, perhaps, while the power was yet in his hands.

The rajah's heart beat harder as the tall elephant drew nearer and nearer to the castle gates and the clattering of many hoofs came up from below to his ears.

He descended from the tower at last.

The visitors were not to find him on the watch. He had a part to play, which he would play with Eastern cunning.

The rajah was seated upon silken cushions in a gorgeous apartment with tall windows overlooking the castle court, with a silver hookah at his mouth, a picture of Eastern idleness, when there was a clanging at the gates, and a startled officer came to announce the arrival of the Jam Bahadur and his troops.

For a moment the thought was in the rajah's mind to order the gates to be barred, the walls to be manned by his guards, and to bid defiance to the regent of Bhanipur. But such a defiance would have been a confession of his guilt. And in a voice that shook a little, in spite of himself, he ordered the Jam to be admitted.

There was a trampling of many hoofs in the castle court. The tall elephant trod heavily in, and the soldiers crowded the court, looked on grimly by the armed guards of the rajah, a hundred or more in number. The Jam descended from his elephant.

The Rajah Baji Rao came as far as the steps of his palace to greet the visitors, and salaamed low before the Jam.

Harry Wharton & Co. sitting in the saddle, looked curiously at the rajah.

It was the first time they had seen the kinsman of their chum, Hurree Jamset Ram Singh.

In his dark, hard cruel face they could trace no resemblance to Inky of the Remove.

"Looks a tough nut to crack!" murmured Bob Cherry.

Harry Wharton nodded.

"Inky's not here," he said quietly.

"That's what we're going to find out," said Johnny Bull.

"If he were here, we should never have been admitted," said Harry. "If he is here, we shall release him, and Baji Rao will be arrested, if not executed. He's not here, or that rotter wouldn't be facing us with so much nerve."

"I wish I could understand what the jolly Jam is saying to him," said Nugent. "He seems to be jolly emphatic."

The juniors listened; but they understood only a word here and there of the flowing Hindustani.

The Jam Bahadur had not returned the rajah's salute. His little brown face was grim, and his eyes were fixed grimly on Baji Rao. His manner made it quite clear that he had not come to the rajah's castle as a friend.

Baji Rao's face flushed as the Jam went on speaking, and his black eyes gleamed. Then he shrugged his shoulders.

"What is he saying, uncle?" asked Harry Wharton, as the Jam ceased to speak at last.

"He is telling the rajah that Hurree Singh has been taken, and that the castle is to be searched for him," answered Colonel Wharton.

"And the rajah?"

"He says that he knows nothing of it; that the news astonishes him, and that the Jam is welcome to search his castle, stone by stone and brick by brick."

"Some of these johnnies look at if they would like to chip in," remarked Johnny Bull, with a glance at the chaukees of the rajah's guard, who were turning lowering looks on the soldiers from Bhanipur.

"They will not venture to do so, I think," said the colonel. "But the Jam was well-advised to bring a strong force with him."

The juniors realized that that was true. Had the Jam arrived with only a few attendants, it was very probable that a massacre would have taken place in the courtyard. But the force from Bhanipur was overwhelming, and the rajah's chaukees contented themselves with sullen and threatening looks.

Baji Rao, with a sullen brow, stepped back and disappeared from view. The Jam rapped out orders to his troopers.

Two hundred men remained in this great courtyard; the rest of the troopers entered the palace, and the seated, commenced.

114

Still Missing!

"NOTHING doing!"

That was Bob Cherry's comment when the chums of Greyfriars remounted then horses to ride back to Bhanipur in the cool of the evening.

Harry Wharton nodded, with a clouded brow.

He had had little hope that any trace of the missing nabob would be found in the castle of Baji Rao, and what little hope there had been was gone now.

No sign of the nabob had been discovered.

The Jam Bahadur's face was dark and gloomy as he sat in his howdah and the tall elephant bore him back to the city.

Baji Rao had ordered his retainers to place no obstacle in the way of the search-indeed, the servants of the palace had helped in it. Unless there existed some cunningly-contrived hiding place that baffled the searchers, Hurree Jamset Ram Singh was not there.

But the Jam Bahadur was taking no chances. He had left two hundred men in occupation of the castle, with orders o keep on the search, fruitles as it had been, and to keep the rajah under observation.

That was all that could be done.

The terrible thought that Hurree Singh was perhaps no longer in the land of the living haunted the minds of his comrades and clouded their faces.

But they clung to the belief that he was a prisoner in some secure hiding place, and it seemed more probable.

While there was hope that the nabob yet hired, and that he would return, the Jain Bahadur still governed Bhanipur in his nephew's name and all the power of the little kingdom was in his hands. But if Hurree Singh remained absent and undiscovered, his fate unknown,

Baji Rao must succeed to his place as Nabob of Bhanipur, If the Jam did not yield place to him, it might mean civil war in the little mountain kingdom, with the inevitable result of intervention by the British to restore peace-after which the independence of Bhanipur would be a thing of the past.

Baji Rao was the last prince of the line of the nabobs of Bhanipur, and for that reason it was probable that there would be a strong party in his favor. Even the Jam Bahadur hesitated to teal with him as he would have wished, now that Hurree Singh war gone; he knew that if the line of the nabobs failed the annexation of the little kingdom to British India was most likely to follow. While Hurree Singh was stiff in his palace at Bhanipur the Jam would have quite cheerfully ordered the rajah's head to be struck off, to save his ward from peril. But circumstances were altered now.

Billy Bunter had, in fact, been quite right in thinking that the position of the Greyfriars fellows was a perilous one now that Hurree Jamset Ram Singh had disappeared.

For a time—for days, perhaps for weeks—the Jam would continue to keep the power in his hands, while sedulous search was made for the missing nabob.

But when it became certain that Hurree Singh would not return he could not keep the rajah from realizing his ambition. There was no proof of any mind that the rajah had had a hand in Hurree Singh's fate. Suspicion was strong, but it was only suspicion.

"If we don't find old Inky that rascal will score all along the line," Bob Cherry remarked. "What do you think, sir?" he glanced at Colonel Wharton, who was riding with the juniors, with a gloomy brow.

"We must find him," said the colonel,

"You don't think that—that—" Bob hesitated.

Colonel Wharton shook his head.

"I think the nabob still lives," he answered, "His disappearance answers Baji Rao's purpose. If the rajah succeeds peaceably to the throne, no doubt he will make all secure by ordering Hurree Singh's death. But that will not happen yet. In the meantime, we may find Hurree Singh and save him. The rajah has taken long chances in this plot. If the British Government should intervene and call him to account he may have to save himself by producing the nabob alive."

"But is that likely?" asked Harry.

"I think so. Baji Rao is known to be in communication with the Russians, who are very keen to get a footing in these mountains on the Indian frontier. It is quite possible that Bhanipur may be occupied by British troops if the nabob is not found. Baji Rao had to take the chance, and he has taken it; he is like a gambler staking all on a throw of the dice. The outcome is uncertain on all sides; but I think it is fairly certain that the rajah will desire to keep Hurree Singh alive, as a hostage in his hands."

"But where?" said Harry.

The colonel shrugged his shoulders.

"There are a thousand hidden nooks in the hills and forests of Bhanipur where a prisoner might be hidden," he answered. "Perhaps even within a few miles of the city itself. But you may be assured that the Jan will leave no stone unturned to find his nephew."

Dusky night was losing in when the Greyfriars party rode in at the gates of Bhanipur and arrived at the palace.

Billy Bunter fact the juniors as they came into their quarters in the palace, with a discontented frown on his fat face.

"I say, you fellows—"

"Oh, bother!" grunted Bob Cherry.

"Don't worry, Bunter!"

"Oh, really, Cherry—"

"Br-r-r-r-r!"

"Have you found Inky?" demanded Bunter.

"No, ass!"

"You jolly well won't find him!" said the Owl of the Remove, nodding ahead sagely. "That rajah chap will keep him safe enough. Of course, we shall never see him again."

"Oh, cheese it!"

"May as well look facts in the face," argued Bunter. "What's the good of blinking plain facts? We've got to look after ourselves now!"

"Look after yourself as much as you like, fathead!" snapped Harry Wharton. "We're going to look for Inky!"

"Look for a needle in a haystack," said Bunter. "There are a thousand natives or more looking for Inky now. So what good are you going to do? The best thing we can do is to beat it while we've got a chance. If you like to see me safe across the frontier—say, as face as Rawalpindi—you can come back here and let that blinking rajah slice of your silly heads as soon as you like. See?"

"Go and cat coke?"

"I shouldn't mind waiting for yon of Rawalpindi," said Bunter. "That' bungalow we stayed in there was fairly comfortable."

"And that's an important point, I suppose?" said Johnny Bull, with deep sarcasm.

"Yes. The grub was all right, too," said Bunter, blinking at him. "Once I'm safe at Rawalpindi, you fellows needn't worry about me."

"We're likely to worry about you a lot when Inky's missing—I don't think!" growled Bob Cherry. "Shut up and clear off!"

"But, I say—"

"Buzz off!" roared Bob, making a motion with his boot; and the Owl of the Remove grunted and rolled away.

Bunter retired to his own luxurious apartment, in an extremely discontented frame of mind.

He was not really quite indifferent to the peril of Hurree Jamset Ram Singh, but he was chiefly concerned about his own precious skin. Lavish as was the hospitality in the palace of Bhanipur, unlimited as was the tuck, it had ceased to be a happy abode for the Owl of the Remove. The possibility of finding himself at the mercy of the Rajah Baji Rao had a very disturbing effect on William George Bunter's equanimity.

"James!" snorted Bunter as he came into his apartment.

"Salaam, sahib!" murmured Kasi Jee, the naukar who had the privilege of attending Bunter Sahib.

"Take my boots off, blow you!"

"Han, sahib."

Kasi Jee removed Bunter's boots, and was rewarded by a shove of Bunter's foot. He smiled and salaamed, though there was an unpleasant glitter in his dark eyes, But the Owl of the Remove did not notice it; "natives" were beneath his lofty notice.

"Mind you keep the punkah going," growled Bunter, as he turned in.

"On my head be it, sahib."

"If I wake up and find it's stopped, I'll buzz a boot at you, mind."

"The sahib honours his servant," said the impassive Kasi Jee.

Bunter grunted, and laid his head on the pillow. The punkah swayed, cooling the hot atmosphere, and Bunter's deep snore was soon heard. In spite of his misgivings, the Owl of the Remove slept soundly enough.

But sleep did not come so easily to Harry Wharton & Co.

Anxiety for their missing chum troubled their slumbers; and at a very early hour in the morning they turned out; while Billy Bunter still snored serenely, soothed by the swaying punkah.

115

Rivals for a Throne!

"TUM sunte ho, huzoor?"

Hurree Singh started and opened his eyes.

The nabob of Bhanipur had been freed from his bonds; he lay on a thick rug on a stone floor in a little room, or, rather, cell.

Darkness surrounded him.

Through the darkness came the glimmer of a lamp, and in the light of the lamp, as he opened his eyes, he saw the face of Nally Das.

Hurree Singh rose to his feet.

How long he had been a captive in the recesses underneath the old temple of Shiva, he did not know. Day and night were the same, in the darkness of his prison.

But he knew that at least a day must have passed; every hour of it dragging by on leaden feet.

He had lain down to sleep at last, and had slept soundly; the peril in which he lay had not shaken his nerve. His gorgeous apartments in the palace of Bhanipur had been changed for a bare stone cell; his innumerable attendants and officers for two or three sullen gaolers. His rich attire was soiled and torn. But the nabob was calm and impassive as he looked at the kidnapper in the glimmer of the lamp.

"I hear you," he answered. "Why do you waken me?"

His highness the rajah desires to speak to you."

"Baji Rao?"

"Han, huzoor."

A gleam shot into Hurree Jamset Ram Singh's dark eyes.

He had known, he had had no doubt that his ambitious kinsman had been at the bottom of the kidnapping. Now he had proof of it.

"Follow me!" said Nally Das.

The nabob did not stir.

"You are in my hands at last, Hurree Singh," said Baji Rao. "Your life is at my mercy. You will never leave these vaults alive unless it is to leave m e in possession of the throne of Bhanipur." Hurree Singh smiled contemptuously. "Never!" he answered. "I am Nabob of Bhanipur, and I will live or die nabob!"

"Tum sunte ho?" snapped Bally Das impatiently. "Do you hear me, huzoor?"

"I hear you," answered Hurree Jamset Ram Singh contemptuously. "But a nabob of Bhanipur does not obey the order of a son of a pig stitch as you, Nally Das. If the rajah desires to see me, let him come here."

Nally Das eyed him evilly.

But he salaamed, and left the cell; and the nabob stood silent, waiting, in the glimmer of the lamp which Nally Das had set upon the floor.

A murmur of voices came to him from the corridor under the old temple, upon which the cell opened.

Nally Das had left the door open; but Hurree Singh did not think of passing it. He knew that the corridor was guarded.

In a few minutes, Nally Das returned, accompanied by Lazaroff, the Russian. Nally Das was grinning evilly.

"It is the rajah's order that you go to him, huzoor!" he said. "In these vaults you are no longer nabob of Bhanipur; life and death wait at the order of my master, Baji Rao."

The two ruffians pinioned the arms of the schoolboy nabob, and marched him out of the cell.

Between them, Hurree Jamset Ram Singh was taken along the dim corridor of which the old stone walls reeked with damp.

In a large vaulted room, bare of all furniture save a few stools, several lamps had been fastened to the walls; and there the Rajah Baji Rao waited for his prisoner.

The rajah was not dressed in gorgeous raiment he had worn in castle. He was clad in the simple uniform of one of the chaukees of guard.

He was seated when Hurree Jam Ram Singh was brought before his and he did not rise.

His black eyes gleamed at the school boy nabob.

Hurree Singh faced him calmly. In the shadows of the vault lurked four: or five dim figures, and he could discern the gleam of steel. His life was at the mercy of the rajah, and he knew it we enough; the ruffians in Baji Rao's pa would have cut him down at a word from their master. But the school boy nabob did rot falter.

"You are in my hands at last, Hurree Singh," said the rajah, after signing to Nally Das and Lazaroff to stand back, and leave him alone with the prisoner.

"Is that what you have to say to me Baji Rao?"

"Your life is at my mercy."

"What else?"

The rajah compressed his lips. His scimitar lay bared, across his knees and his hand was upon the hilt. But if he had expected that the bares weapon, and his gloomy surroundings would strike terror to the heart of the prisoner, he was disappointed. Not a sign of fear was to be seen in the calm. face of Hurree Jamset Ran. Singh.

"You know why you are here, Hurree Singh," said the rajah at last. "You will never leave these vaults alive unless it is to leave me in possession of the throne of Bhanipur. It is in your power to resign the place of nabob to me, who am better fitted to fill it. Yon have lived in England—you are fond of the White sahibs; swear to leave Bhanipur forever, and never to give tie trouble again, and you shall have a princely fortune in that foreign land What do you say?"

The nabob smiled contemptuously.

"Never!" he answered.

"Your kingdom has shrunk to the size of a small stone cell, hidden under the ruins of a temple in the forest, said the rajah sarcastically. "Do you still cling to it?"

"It is your turn now," said Hurree Singh. "Tomorrow, perhaps, it will be my turn. Who knows?"

"You know that your friends are seeking you, and you hope to be rescued," said the rajah. "But the secret of this temple is known only to me and to my servants. It is known to Nally Das, whose father's father was a priest of Shiva in the old days before the Afghan raid laid the temple in the dust. This is where you would have been brought, had my agents succeeded in making you a prisoner in England—had they captured you on your journey out to India. Do you not understand, then, that it is a safe place, where you will never be found?"

The nabob did not answer.

If there was despair in his heart, he did not allow his face to betray it. His eyes met calmly the savage glance of Baji Rao.

"If you gave the oath, you would keep it," said Baji Rao. "I would dictate an oath that no Hindu prince would dare to break. You shall return to England—you shall have a princely fortune there, and hold up your head among the white sahibs. All in return for giving up what you no longer possess. Is it not worth while?"

"I am Nabob of Bhanipur, and I will live or die nabob!" answered Hurree Jamset Ram Singh calmly.

The rajah made a motion with his bared scimitar.

"You will die, then," he said. "I have staked all upon this cast; and if you are obstinate, these vaults will be your tomb."

Hurree Singh's lips curled.

"You will be called to account," he said. "Do you think that your intrigues with the Russians are not known to the English at Simla? They will never permit you to reign in Bhanipur, and open the passes of these mountains to the Russians. Take my place, and the English will advance from Rawalpindi to dethrone you; and my death will be their excuse for sending you into exile or ordering your execution."

"It is a chance," said the rajah gloomily. "I have taken the chance, I will live or die Nabob of Bhanipur. A castle and a zila of land do not suffice for Baji Rao. And once I have the power of nabob in my hands, the Russians have promised to help—I have many friends at Moscow. That I shall take your place is assured—the Jam Bahadur cannot long deny the rights of the next heir, if you do not return. And think you that you will ever return to your palace?"

"Yes—if the English troops occupy Bhanipur, and their commander shall call you to account," said Hurree Singh. "Then to save your worthless life, you will tell them that the nabob still lives."

Baji Rao gritted his teeth.

"But if the English do not come?" he said. "If I am left in peace to reign in Bhanipur—what then? It is not certain, but it is more than likely. What then, Hurree Singh?"

Again the nabob was silent. He knew what would happen in that case, the bowstring, and a grave in the recess of the old temple.

"Is it not better to accept my offer. than to take such a chance, boy?" said the rajah harshly.

"I bill live and die nabob!" said Hurree Singh.

"Then you will never see the light of duty again. Take him away, Nally Das!""said the rajah.

Nally Das and Lazaroff advanced and seized the nabob by the arms. His eyes gleamed at them, but he did not resist.

"Take him to reflect!" said Baji Rao savagely. "If you change your mind, Hurree Jamset Ram Singh, send a message to me by Nally Das. 'Take the oath of abdication that I will dictate to you, and live. When you come to your senses, boy, send me word."

He waved his hand, and Hurree Jamset Ram Singh was taken back to his cell.

The schoolboy nabob was thrust into the cell, in the darkness, and the teak-wood door closed on him.

He heard the rusty iron bars rattle into their place.

"He will yield!" muttered Baji Rao. "A few more days and nights—and he will yield. By his own act, he shall make the way clear for me to reign in Bhanipur—and then—then that old man's head shall be the first to fall; and the colonel sahib shall find that death lurks in the jungles of Bhanipur. He is safe here, as in the tomb; and he will yield."

But the rajah's dark face was gloomy as he emerged from the hidden recesses of the temple of Shiva, and took his way through the forest. His plans had gone well; but he knew that success was in certain, and that his nay was full of peril. But not for a moment did he think of turning back; the prize was worth the risk. And even if the worst came to the worst, he could always care himself by producing the nabob alive. In his disguise of a common chaukee, the rajah stole lack into his castle in the shadows of the night—leaving his rival to imprisonment, to darkness—perhaps to despair.

116

What Bunter Knew!

"ANY news, uncle?"

Harry Wharton asked the question eagerly.

But the gloomy frown on the bronzed face of Colonel Wharton was a sufficient answer, without his shake of the head.

There was no news.

Two more days had passed, and the search for the missing nabob was still going on; but hope of discovering him was fading.

His comrades still clung to the belief that he was alive; that he could and should be found and rescued. But they know that their opinion was not shared by other occupants of the palace of Bhanipur.

The Jam Bahadur was prosecuting the search with unremitting zeal. From one end of the little kingdom to the other, troops were in motion, and an incense reward was offered for information. But with each day that passed it was growing clear that the Jam Bahadur was not destined to keep the authority in his hands.

The Rajah Baji Rao had claimed the right to occupy the palace of Bhanipur, and to direct the search for his missing kinsman; and the Jam's counselors shook their leads dubiously over the old gentleman's refusal. The situation was growing delicate; for the rajah had friends and emissaries among the palace guards, and his agents were at work among the crowds of the bazar.

"Not bad news, sir?" asked Bob Cherry, as the colonel sat down.

The juniors eyed the colonel uneasily. "No!" said Colonel Wharton.

"But—" He paused. "Bunter has told me that he is anxious to return to British territory!"

"Let him!" said Harry. "Bunter doesn't matter."

Colonel Wharton smiled faintly.

"But I think Bunter is right," he said, "I think it would be wise for all of you to return to Rawalpindi."

"Not before Inky is found!" exclaimed Frank Nugent.

"We can't go and leave him missing sir!" said Bob.

"You must look at the facts as they stand," said the colonel quietly. "Had Hurree Singh been found at once, or within a couple of days, all would have been well. But he has not been found."

"We shall find him yet," said Johnny Bull.

"With Hurree Singh missing, possibly never to return, the situation here has changed," said the colonel quietly. "Already the Jam's orders are no longer obeyed without hesitation. As Regent of the kingdom, he governed in Hurree Singh's name—while Hurree Singh was at Greyfriars, and known to be alive. But it is different now. Already many in Bhanipur are looking to Baji Rao—many of the officials of the government, and the officers in Hurree Singh's troops, are in communication with him—making their peace with him, in the belief that he will reign as nabob."

"Oh!" said Harry.

This was news to the Greyfriars fellows.

"They have little choice," said the colonel. "They are all devoted to Hurree Singh; but if the rajah succeeds him here, they must make their peace with the new ruler. Anyone who posesses him will be sure to be marked out for his vengeance. Many members of the Jam's council are in favor of calling him to the palace, and placing the power in his hands until it is definitely known, what has become of Hurree Singh."

"And he is at the bottom of it, all the time, and could produce Inky if he liked!" exclaimed Bob.

"I believe so, and so does the Jam; but others do not think so, and you must remember that there is no proof," said the colonel. "As matters stand, Baji Rao is heir to a vacant throne and the people and the soldiers will acknowledge him. The utmost the Jam can do is to delay matters for a time, in the hope of discovering Hurree Singh and rescuing him. He is risking his life for it; for if Baji Rao is once installed here as master, the Jam has not long to live. If the rajah does not dare to order his death, there are mainly other way's known to such a man—the poison or the bow-string at the dead of night. It is my duty to remain here, and help the Jam to the last extremity. But you boys—"

"It's our duty, too!" exclaimed Bob Cherry.

"We can't desert old Inky, uncle!" exclaimed Harry Wharton. "We're more than willing to take the risk."

Colonel Wharton shook his head.

"It is not a risk—it is a certainty, if Baji Rao obtains power in Bhanipur," he said, "even those who suspect him of complicity in Hurree Singh's fate, will keep silent, knowing they will be at his mercy. But he is not generally suspected. There are rumors in the bazaar—undoubtedly started by his agents—that the Jam himself is responsible for Hurree Singh's disappearance. It is said to be the rajah's intention to accuse him of making away with his nephew."

"Oh, my hat!"

"That is part of the plot, of course," said the colonel, "and unless Hurree Singh is found, and found soon, I do not see how the rajah is to be kept out. Already the soldiers who occupied his palace have been withdrawn, and he is again master in his own household. It is only a question of a few days, at most, before he is master here also."

The juniors looked at one another in dismay.

"If no news is received of the nabob tomorrow, I must send you to safety," said the colonel, rising. "That is what I came to tell you. I am responsible for bringing you boy, here; and I cannot allow you to, remain at the danger of your lives."

"But, sir—" exclaimed Bob, in dismay. But—you will be staying on—"

"That is my duty," said the colonel quietly. "With you boys it is different If you fall into the power of Baji Rao. I do not think he will spare the friends of Hurree Singh. Once he is in power, he will glut his vengeance upon all whom he regards as his enemies."

The juniors looked at one another when the colonel was gone; and Bob Cherry whistled softly.

"We seem to be in a bit of a hornet's nest," he remarked. "I—I suppose your uncle's right, Harry. But we're jolly well not going to leave Inky in the lurch, all the same."

"I say, you fellows," Bunter rolled in. "I suppose old Wharton—"

What?

"I mean Colonel Wharton," Bunter said hastily "I suppose he's told you we're going tomorrow. I say, you fellows, if you put it to him, he would make it today instead of tomorrow; I can jolly well tell you I'm fed-up with Bhanipur. Blessed if I expect to find my head on my shoulders from one day to another here."

"Blow your silly head!"

"Oh, really, Cherry—"

"We're not going," said Johnny Bull determinedly. "That fat funk can be carted off, but we're not going."

"Oh, really, Bull—"

"We've got to find old Inky somehow," said Bob Cherry desperately. "If fellow only had a clue—"

"They've got him safe enough," said Johnny Bull. "This has been planned a long time ago, and, of course, they had the hiding-place all ready. It, was ready for him when that villain Nally Das tried to kidnap him at Greyfriars, Somewhere in Bhanipur—"

"But where?" said Nugent.

"Goodness knows."

Billy Bunter started a little, and blinked at the chums of the Remove through his big spectacles.

A sudden thought had flashed into the fat, obtuse brain of the Owl of the Remove.

"I—I say, you fellows!" he ejaculated.

"Oh, dry up, Bunter!"

"But, I say—"

"You talk too much, Bunter! Give your chin a rest!" growled Johnny Bull.

"I never told you fellows—"

"Bow-wow!"

"That day you picnicked at the haunted temple in the forest." exclaimed Bunter excitedly. "You left me behind—"

"Bother you!"

"My palanquin broke down, you remember—"

"You fell through the bottom of it, you fat walrus," growled Bob Cherry. "Don't tell us about it now—we're not feeling inclined to laugh just at present."

"I came after you—"

"Did you" grunted Bob. Well never mind whether yon did or not. Run away and play—"

"I've never told you fellows what happened that day," said Bunter. "You know what you are always jawing, and never giving a chap a chance to speak. I came after you, and missed you at the old temple, and—"

"Miss us now!" suggested Nugent.

"That was the day we saw Nally Das," remarked Harry Wharton. "You fellows remember he was hiding in the old temple, and when we looked for him he had disappeared somehow? If we'd only collared him there—"

"He, he he!" chortled Bunter.

"You silly owl!" roared Bob Cherry in great exasperation. "What are you cackling at now? Is this a time for cackling?"

Bunter chuckled, a fat chuckle.

Back into his fat mind had come the recollection of what had happened at the old temple of Shiva, where he had followed the Famous Five, and missed them. He remembered how he had crouched behind the tamarinds, and watched Nally Das emerge from the hidden recess under the temple, watching the great slab of stone rise and father matters had filled Bunter's fat mind since—but now, like a flash, it has come into his fat brain that he held clue to the mystery. Nally Das, kidnapper, had been hidden beneath it haunted temple in the forest; the moving slab of stone gave access to hiding-place. And it came into Bunter mind that the hiding place of the kidnapper was also the hiding-place of kidnapped nabob.

Certainly, it would have occurred Bunter before, had he given the matter much thought—or any thought.

But Bunter's fat thoughts were so entirely occupied by himself, that he had not considered the matter at all; indeed he would not have thought about now, had not the words of the juniors brought it into his mind.

He chuckled.

He, William George Bunter, alone it Bhanipur, held the clue to the disappearance of the nabob!

He was certain of it. He was absolutely assured that he could have guides a rescue-party to the prison of the missing Nabob of Bhanipur!

No wonder he chuckled! It was a case of the "hour and the man" once more Billy Bunter the right man in the right place.

But Harry Wharton & Co., naturally did not understand. They had no ide. of what Bunter knew, and they stared at him in great exasperation as he chuckled.

"He, he, he! If you fellows knew!" chortled Bunter.

"You fat idiot!" roared Johnny Bull.

"Oh, really, Bull—"

"Cheese it, and roll away, you podgy image!"

"Look here—"

"Oh, kick him!" said Nugent.

"You cheeky asses?" roared Bunter. "Look here, if you fellows like follow my lead, and back me up, I'll to my best to rescue Inky. What do you say to that?"

"Fathead!"

"Ring off!"

"You silly cuckoos think a lot of yourselves," said the Owl of the Remove contemptuously. "But I can jolly well tell! you that I'm the man that's wanted now. I could tell you—"

"Give your silly chin a rest!"

Bunter blinked at the juniors through his big spectacles indignantly. He was certain that he held the clue—that he was the only fellow in Bhanipur who held it. He was, as be said, the man who was wanted; and the chums of the Remove would not even listen to him? That was not to be wondered at, worried and troubled as they were about their missing chum, and more than fed-up with Bunter and his "gas." The Owl of the Remove breathed hard.

"All right then," he said. "Go and cat coke! If you fellows think you call hind Inky, go and find him! When you want my help, come and ask for it!"

"That's likely to be a long time, you silly owl," growled Johnny Bull.

"Yah?"

Billy Bunter rolled away. The captain of the Remove glanced after rather curiously.

"That fat idiot can't have thought of anything, I suppose?" Wharton remarked.

"Of course not—only his silly gas, as usual," said Johnny Bull. "Shall I go after him and kick him?"

"We're likely to want his help—I don't think!" growled Bob Cherry. "Oh, bother Bunter. Never mind Bunter What are we going to do about poor old Inky?"

The juniors resumed their discussion, little dreaming of what Bunter could have told them. The discussion was interrupted, by the sound of the trampling of hoofs, the blare of a trumpet, and a rising hubbub of voices from the city.

"Something's up!" exclaimed Bob, jumping from his seat. "If—if it's news of Inky—"

The chums of the Remove ran out eagerly on the balcony. Below, in the court of the palace, was a swarming, excited throng—the whole palace seemed to be in a state of excitement. Wharton caught sight of Pandy Din, the colonel's khitmutghar, below, and called to him:

"Pandy Din! What has happened?"

The khitmutghar looked up. His brown face was very grave.

"The Rajah Baji Rao has entered the city with his guards!" he answered.

"Great Scott!"

"He demands to be admitted to the palace," said Pandy Din. "The Jam Bahadur refusing."

Wharton set his lips.

"This may mean scrapping, you fellows," he said.

The juniors hurried down to the courtyard. The gates of the palace were closed; the guards were at their stations, but the juniors could see that doubt and uncertainty reigned on all sides. They found Colonel Wharton at last; and they found him looking grim.

"Baji Rao is in the city?" asked Harry.

The colonel nodded.

"Yes—he has made a bold stroke," he answered. "It looks as if the tables may be turned on the Jam Bahadur. Baji Rao demands his rights as Nabob of Bhanipur, in the absence of Hurree Singh—and he openly accuses the I am of having made away with his nephew."

"The awful rotter!" said Bob.

"I doubt very much whether the guards will resist him," said the colonel. "The Jam has ordered them to fire, if the rajah attempts to force an entrance. But—" he shrugged his shoulders.

"Where is the rajah now?"

"He has taken up his quarters at the serai, a hundred yards from the palace," said the colonel. "He has given the Jam until this hour tomorrow to yield the palace to him. If Hurree Singh is not found before then, Baji Rao will be master in Bhanipur—the soldiers will not resist the man whom they regard as the rightful heir to the throne. We have twenty—four hours-and if Hurree Singh does not return by then—"

The colonel did not finish; but the juniors knew what he would have said. If Hurree Jamset Ram Singh was not found, and at once, the rascally rajah would take his place as Nabob of Bhanipur—the power of the Jam Bahadur was breaking like a reed in his hands.

And where was Hurree Singh?

117

The Moonshee!

"JAMES!"

Kasi Jee, the naukar, whom Bunter preferred to call James, came up at his master's call.

He did not salaam submissively, as usual.

There was a mocking gleam in the eyes of the naukar. Billy Bunter had not been a pleasant or considerate master. The naukar had received more kicks than halfpence, so to speak, from the Owl of the Remove. Bunter's view apparently was that a mere "native" ought to feel honoured by a kick from Bunter's aristocratic foot. Probably Kasi Jee took a different view—quite a different view. Probably, in the uncertain state of affairs that now reigned in the palace of Bhanipur, the naukar was looking forward to "getting his own back," as it were, upon the fat little sahib. Certainly the respectful humility had dropped from him like a cloak.

Bunter was not observant; but he could not help seeing that there was a difference in the naukar's manner.

He blinked suspiciously, at the naukar.

"What's that row going on outside the palace?" he asked.

Kasi Jee grinned.

"It is the rajah's coming, sahib," he answered.

Bunter jumped.

"That villain Baji Rao?" he exclaimed.

"The great and powerful rajah Baji Rao!" said Kasi Jee. "He has demanded that the palace be given up to him by the Jam, sahib."

"Oh, my hat?"

Bunter starched at the grinning naukar in dismay.

"They're not letting him in?" he exclaimed.

"Not yet, sahib," said Kasi Jee. "But the soldiers are in favour of the rajah, who is now Nabob of Bhanipur, and tomorrow he will be taking possession of palace."

"And what will happen to us?" asked Bunter, with a tremor.

"I thinking the rajah will order execution of white sahibs," said Kasi Jee, with great relish. "Little fat sahib tremble."

Bunter blinked at him. This was quite new language from the naukar, and Bunter realized that the kicks he had bestowed on Kasi Jee had lingered in the native's memory.

"You cheeky native!" exclaimed Bunter.

Kasi Jee grinned derisively.

"Tomorrow Baji Rao being master here," he said. "Already he being master in the city. Little fat sahib see."

Bunter lifted his foot—but dropped it again. The time was past for kicking Kasi Jee.

On the morrow, if Baji Rao became master of the palace, it was probable that the naukar would do the kicking! Bunter, indeed, would have cause to be thankful if nothing worse than kicking came his way. He did not like the look in the naukar's black eyes at all.

"Hurree Singh will be back before tomorrow, though," said Bunter.

"The Huzoor never come back," said Kasi Jee. "They saying in the bazaar that the Jam poison the Nabob. I knowing nothing; but knowing that Baji Rao will be Nabob of Bhanipur." He grinned. "Baji Rao stay now in the serai with his guards—Jam being master of the palace today; but tomorrow all is ended. Already many officers have gone over to the rajah. Little fat sahib see."

From the fact that Kasi Jee ventured to call Bunter a little fat sahib to his face, it was clear that the naukar regarded the game as being up, so to speak, for the friends of Hurree Singh.

"Go and tell the Jam that I want to speak to him!" said Bunter.

"No can see Jam," answered the naukar.

"Take my message to him!" roared Bunter.

The naukar sneered.

"Little fat sahib take him own message," he answered. "I not caring one anna for little fat sahib."

"The great and powerful rajah Baji Rao has demanded that the palace be given up to him by the Jam, sahib," said Kasi Jee, with a grin. "And what will happen to us?" asked Bunter with a tremor. "I thinking the rajah will order execution of white sahibs," said Kasi Jee, with great relish. "Little fat sahib tremble."

And the naukar walked out of the room, grinning. Evidently his allegiance was at an end.

"My hat!" murmured Bunter.

If the naukar was a fair sample, it was not likely to be long before Baji Rao was acknowledged as master by all the swarming attendants of the palace of Bhanipur. The Jam was still holding his own, but desertion was imminent on all sides.

"If those silly chumps would have listened to me, and gone while the going was good, we might have been safe in British territory by now!" growled Bunter. "All the same, it will be all right if Hurree Singh comes back in time—and I jolly well know where to find him."

Bunter rolled out of his room.

He realized that there was no time to lose; matters were very close on a crisis now.

He looked for the juniors; but they were not to be found in the palace. Then he made his way towards the Jain's apartments in another wing of the palace; but he found guards posted there, and they refused to allow him to pass. As Bunter did not understand a word of their language, it was impossible for him to make himself understood; and when he attempted to push by, a scimitar flashed under his fat little nose, and he jumped back and retreated in a great hurry.

Bunter was almost spluttering with dismay by this time. He was certain that he held the clue to the Nabob's hidden prison; but it looked as if his knowledge had come too late.

From a window he caught sight of Colonel Wharton and the juniors in the courtyard. They were mounting their horses, with Pandy Din. Bunter shouted to them.

"I say, you fellows!"

Harry Wharton glanced up.

"Wharton, I say—"

"You had better keep in the palace, Bunter," called back the captain of the Remove. "It may not be safe for you outside the gates now!"

"Where are you going?" shouted Bunter. "Don't leave me alone here, you beasts, among all these beastly natives."

"We're going to hunt for Hurree Singh," answered Wharton.

"Wait for me—"

"Fathead!"

"I tell you—" shrieked Bunter.

With a clattering of hoofs, the colonel and the juniors rode out of the gates, which were immediately closed behind them. Bunter blinked after them in utter dismay.

Harry Wharton & Co. were gone—to make one more desperate effort while there was yet time to discover the missing nabob.

Bunter was left alone with his useless knowledge. He looked round for Kasi Jee, but the nauker—once in incessant and obsequious attendance—was not to be seen. If Bunter could have obtained a word with the Jam Bahadur all might yet have been well; but the Jam was unapproachable.

"If there was just one of these beasts that could speak English!" groaned Bunter. "My hat! The moonshee!"

"Where are you going?" shouted Bunter. "Don't leave me alone here, you beasts, among all these beastly natives!" "We're going to hunt for Hurree Singh," answered Wharton. "Wait for me—" began Bunter. "Fathead!" was the reply; and the cavalcade rode out through the gates.

Bunter remembered the moonshee the wise old man from whom Hurree Jamset Ram Singh had learned his remarkable English in the days before he nabob had come to Greyfriars.

The moonshee had his quarters in the palace somewhere; Bunter had seen him once or twice.

Bunter's fat wits were working at unaccustomed pressure now. Under the spur of danger, even Bunter could do some hard thinking. His fat face cleared as he remembered the moonshee, whose name, he also remembered, was Mook Mookerjee.

He grabbed at the flowing linen garment of a passing Hindu. The man looked at him and shook his arm free. Respect for the white sahibs was failing now; all the palace knew that the new Nabob was no friend of the friends of the missing nabob. This man wore the garb of a jamadar, and belonged to the palace guard..

"I say!" gasped Bunter.

The man stopped.

"Moonshee!" gasped Bunter. "Mook Mookerjee-moonshee!"

"Is taraf!" said the jamadar, understanding that the little fat sahib wished to see the moonshee Mook Mookerjee.

And he led the way.

"Thank goodness!" murmured.

Bunter, in great relief, as he followed the jamadar. "That old ass Mookerjee can speak English—what he calls English—and he can go and tell the Jam. Oh, dear, I wish I was back Greyfriars!"

The jamadar led the Owl of the Remove to a large apartment, windows looking on the palace garden. He spoke to a servant in his own tongue and Bunter was taken into the room where, to his great relief, he found himself in the presence of Hurree Jamset Ram Singh's old tutor.

118

Bunter to the Rescue!

MOOK MOOKERJEE rose and salaamed respectfully to sahib. He was an ancient gathered man, with a flowing white beard and wrinkled and benevolent brown face.

"The honourfulness of white sahib visit is terrific!" he said, and Bun could not help grinning in spite of anxious frame of mind. The old mooshee's English was remarkably like that of Hurree Jamset Ram Singh; it was easy to see whence the schoolboy nabob had derived his remarkable knowledge of the language.

"May I offer the esteemed seatfulness to the sahib?" went on the moonshee.

Bunter sat down.

"I regret terrifically to state the there is at present no newsfulness of the esteemed and absent nabob!" said Mook Mookerjee sadly. "The sadfulness my esteemed self is great!"

Evidently the moonshee supposed the Bunter had come to him in search news of the missing nabob.

"I want to speak to the Jam," said Bunter. "It's important."

The moonshee shook his head.

"His esteemed Highness the Jam Bahadur is in his apartments," he said "He is much troubled with the present terrific state of affairs, and taking counsel with wise and ridiculous counselors. The disturbfulness esteemed Jam is not within bounds possible."

Bunter snorted.

"I know where to find the nabob," he snapped.

The moonshee gave a jump.

"The knowfulness of the little sahib cannot be great!" he said. "This is not subject-matter for ridiculous jokefulness."

"I'm not joking!" howled Bunter. "I tell you I jolly well know where they've hidden Inky—I mean, Hurree Singh! Take me to the Jam and let me tell him before it's too late!"

The moonshee gazed long and earnestly at Bunter.

He could see that the fat junior was in earnest, as well as greatly excited. But he hesitated.

"Can't you understand that we're wasting time?" exclaimed Bunter.

"But howfully does the little sahib know?" asked Mook Mookerjee. "The surprisefulness of the statement is terrific!"

"Well, I do know," growled Bunter, "and I'm jolly well the only chap in Bhanipur who does! If those beasts had been civil I'd have told them. Take my message to the Jam!"

The moonshee rose.

"If the little sahib saying with terrific seriousness that he has valued information to impart to JJam—" he said.

"I tell you that I can lay my finger on Hurree Singh!"

"Let the little sahib follow Mook Mookerjee," said the moonshee. "The understandfulness is not great, but if there is information, the noble and ludicrous Jam will gladfully hear it."

"Buck up, then!" growled Bunter.

The moonshee led the way by the palace corridors, to the entrance to the Jam Bahadur's apartments. There he was stopped by the guards; but he proceeded to explain in flowing Hindustani, which was probably rather better than his English, and was allowed to pass. Bunter, however, was pushed back by the soldiers.

"Little sahib waitfully attend till my esteemed returnfulness," said the moonshee.

And Bunter waited.

In a few minutes the moonshee came back, with the subadar of the Jam's guard, and Bunter was beckoned in. The subadar, Lal Chundar, eyed him very curiously. The bared tulwar in the subadar's dusky hand made Bunter jump, but he followed on into the Jam's apartments.

The Jam Bahadur was alone.

He had dismissed the counselors with whom he had been engaged in discussion. His old brown face was deeply wrinkled with care.

As yet, the Jam's own guards were faithful, but he knew that the contest with the rajah was going against him, and that his power and his life were at hazard.

That did not trouble the old Jam so much as the knowledge that once Baji Rao was in power in Bhanipur the missing nabob's fate was sealed. Only the doubtful chance of the intervention of the British remained; and if the rajah's cunning could contrive to avert that danger, it was certain that Hurree Jamset Ram Singh would never be seen alive again.

The Jam glanced at Bunter, but with little interest.

He had consented to see him; but he had no hope whatever that the fat junior could tell him anything of the missing nabob. Bunter had not stirred from the palace since the disappearance of the nabob on the day of the tiger-hunt.

"Here is the little sahib," said the moonshee, in Hindustani.

The Jam signed to Bunter to come forward.

"What you having to tell me?" he asked, in his own peculiar variation of the English language.

"I know where Hurree Singh is," said Bunter.

The Jam shook his head impatiently.

"You cannot be knowing," he answered. "What is this all meaning?"

"I suppose you know about a ruined temple in the forest, about twenty miles from the city?" said Bunter.

"The old temple of Shiva," said the Jam.

"That's it."

"The temple has been searched, like all other places," said the Jam. "Why you thinking the Huzoor there?"

"There was a picnic, the day before the tiger-hunt," said Bunter. "Those beasts—I mean, my friends—left me behind, and I went after them. They were gone before I got there."

The Jam regarded Bunter a little more attentively.

"That day they seeing Nally Das in the temple," he said. "But he escaped. The Huzoor told me of it."

"Well, he was jolly well there all the time!" said Bunter. "Those rotters—I mean, my friends—were gone, and my naukar was behind with the grub, and I sat down behind some trees in a sort of paved court to rest and wait for him. Then I heard a queer noise."

The Jam nodded.

"The old Temple of Shiva is haunted," he said, "the spirits of the priests slain by the Afghan raiders lingering there.

"It jolly well wasn't a spirit that I saw!" grunted Bunter. "It was Nally Das, the same blackguard who tried to kidnap Inky at Greyfriars. He came up from under the floor of the temple!"

The Jam Bahadur started.

"What you saying?" he exclaimed.

"There's an old statue—a bronze something-or-other—lying there," explained Bunter; "close by it there's a big slab of stone that moved in the floor. It was lifted, and Nally Das came up. There's a secret hiding place under the old temple. That's why they couldn't find Nally Das, after seeing him there—see? He must have dodged into the vault, or cellar, or whatever it is, and lain doggo. He didn't come out till after they were gone—and I was there, though he jolly well didn't see me."

The Jam gazed at Bunter in deep, silence for a moment or two. Then he began to question the fat junior closely.

When he had finished he drew a deep breath.

His old brown face had lighted up.

The existence of the secret recess under the Temple of Shiva was utterly unknown in Bhanipur. But now that the Jam knew of it, he knew where to look for the missing nabob. He had heard from the nabob that Nally Das, the kidnapper, had been seen at the haunted temple, and had vanished and escaped all search. His business there was clear now. If the hiding-place existed under the old temple, unsuspected and unseen, but known to the kidnappers, it was fairly certain that that was the hidden spot to which the kidnapped nabob had been taken.

"It is well!" said the Jam at last. He turned to the waiting subadar, and gave him a rapid order. Then he dropped his old brown hand kindly on the fat shoulder of the Owl of the Remove. "It is well, sahib! It is you who saving the Nabob of Bhanipur. You shall be coming with me and my soldiers to save him, and pointing out to me where to seek."

Bunter grinned cheerfully.

Harry Wharton & Co, were seeking the missing nabob with little hope. While they were engaged on their vain search, Bunter was to lead the rescue party to the right spot. There was much satisfaction in that thought for the Owl of Greyfriars.

"I'm your man!" he said.

"Mook Mookerjee, you order a palkee for the little sahib," said the Jam.

Bunter hurried away with the moonshee, and the Jam made his preparations in haste. No time was lost; in ten minutes the Jam Bahadur was riding out of Bhanipur at the head of a hundred horsemen, and with the horsemen went a palanquin in which sat Billy Bunter.

119

Light at Last!

"HALLO, hallo, hallo!"

"It's the jolly old Jam!"

"And Bunter!"

Harry Wharton & Co. drew rein.

The juniors were riding, with the colonel and Pandy Din, by a path through the paddy-fields, when they sighted the cavalcade. The tall elephant of the Jam Bahadur was recognizable at a great distance, and among the horsemen who escorted the elephant and its rider the juniors discerned a palkee borne on the shoulders of four stalwart, dusky hearers. From the curtains of the palkee looked the fat face and glimmering spectacles of Willian George Bunter, the Owl of the Remove.

The sight of the Jam and a hundred troopers, riding towards the forest, naturally drew the attention of the Greyfriars fellows at once. It looked as if some news had been received of the missing nabob; it was unlikely that anything else could have drawn the Jam from the city at such a time of crisis. What Bunter was doing with the parts was rather a mystery. But the colonel turned his horse at once to intercept the cavalcade, and the juniors followed him.

"Looks like news of Inky!" said Bob Cherry eagerly.

"What ripping luck if that's so!" said Harry Wharton, with a deep breath.

The Jam Bahadur looked from the silken curtains of his howdah and waved a brown hand to the colonel. From the distance the juniors could see the excitement in his old brown face.

Colonel Wharton ranged up beside the tail elephant, and began to speak to the Jam in Hindustani. The juniors fell into pace with the palanquin, Bunter eyeing them very morosely. They were not specially glad to see Bunter, and he was the very reverse of glad to see them.

It was Bunter's idea to rescue the imprisoned nabob while the chums of the Remove were away on a futile quest. and he was not at all keen for them to accompany the rescue-party. He wanted them to find the nabob safe and sound at his palace when they came back, tired and unsuccessful. Bunter was going to produce the missing prince, as it were, like a conjurer producing a rabbit out of a hat. This unfortunate meeting knocked that little scheme on the head.

"I say, you follow, what do you want?" asked Bunter peevishly. "Aren't you hunting for Inky?"

"Yes," said Harry.

"Well, go and hunt for him! You can't expect me to help you, after your cheek and ingratitude!"

"You silly owl!"

"Oh, really, Cherry—"

"Where is the Jam going?" asked Wharton. "And where are you going with him, Bunter? Is he taking you back to Rawalpindi?"

"No—yes! Yes! Exactly!" said Bunter. "Just so! It's an escort—see? The Jam is seeing me off. You follows don't want to come."

"No fear!"

"Well, then, hike off and leave me alone," said Bunter anxiously; "I'm not going to tell you anything."

"What is there in tell, fathead?"

"Nothing, of course," said Bunter. "Nothing at all! I don't know anything about Inky."

"Eh?"

"I can't put my finger on him, you know," said Bunter fatuously. "Nothing of the kind, of course. Won't run away with that idea."

The Co. stared at Bunter. That he was, as usual, lying, was obvious; bit why he was lying was not so clear.

"What is the fat idiot driving at?" asked Johnny Bull, in wonder.

"Oh, really, Bull—"

"Where are you going?" demanded Nugent. "The Jam wouldn't

be escorting you to the frontier at a time like this. That's all rot. Is the Jam hunting for Inky? I suppose that's so; but what the thump are you doing with the party?"

Bunter sniffed.

"I could tell you something if I liked," he answered loftily.

"Well, cough it up then, fathead!"

"Oh, really, Nugent—"

"It's impossible that that fat idiot knows anything about Inky," said Harry Wharton; "but what—"

"Oh, really. Wharton! If you think you're going to bag the credit of rescuing Inky—"

"What?"

"You're jolly well not!" exclaimed Bunter warmly, "You jolly well clear off, and leave the job to me. You're no good, as I've often told you before. You clear off. This is my bizney!"

"Wandering in your mind?" asked Wharton, in amazement.

"The question is, has he any to wander in?" grunted Johnny Bull.

Colonel Wharton backed his horse and joined the juniors, and rode with them. His bronze face was bright.

"News at last!" he said. "It is amazing that it should have been received by means of Bunter—"

"Oh, really, sir—"

"Bunter!" exclaimed the juniors, in astonishment.

"Yes, strangely enough, it was Bunter who gave the Jam Bahadur the clue," said Colonel Wharton. "From what the Jam has just told me, it appears extremely probable that we shall find Hurree Singh hidded at the hunted temple in the forest."

"Great Scott!"

"Oh, how ripping!" exclaimed Bob.

"But what on earth did Bunter know about it, and why didn't he tell us before, if he knew?" exclaimed Wharton.

"It appears to have been by chance that Bunter made a discovery, and he was so obtuse as not to think of it until today, in connection with the disappearance of Hurree Singh," said the colonel. "There is every hope now that Hurree Singh will be found and rescued."

Colonel Wharton pushed on his horse again, to ride beside the

Jam's elephant. The juniors remained with the palanquin, staring at the fat face of William George Bunter. They were astonished, or rather, utterly amazed. "I say, you fellows, it's up to you to clear off!" said the Owl of the Remove peevishly.

"Clear off when we're on old Inky's track!" exclaimed Nugent.

"Well, it's me that's found him, isn't it?" demanded Bunter warmly. "You're jolly well dead in this act. You're jolly well not going to bag the credit, I can tell you."

"You silly ass!" said Harry. "Do you think we're thinking about bagging anything except old Inky himself. Tell us how you knew?"

Billy Bunter proceeded to tell once more of what happened on the day the nabob and his chums had picnicked at the haunted temple of Shiva.

"If that fat idiot had only told us all that before—" said Johnny Bull, when the Owl of the Remove hád finished.

"Did you give me a chance to tell you?" hooted Bunter. "Would you listen to a chap?"

"Yes; if you weren't all jaw, like a sheep's head. How was any fellow to know that you could have talked sense for once?"

"Oh, really, Bull—"

"By Jove! It looks as if we're all right," chuckled Bob Cherry. "We shall bag old Inky, and perhaps the kidnappers, too. Hurrah!"

"Mind, I'm the chap that did it!" said Bunter.

"Bow-wow!"

"I say, you fellows—"

But the juniors were finished with Bunter now. They rode on ahead with the colonel, and the Owl of the Remove was left to waste his sweetness on the desert air.

But Billy Bunter came into his own again, as it were, when the old temple of Shiva was reached.

The party dismounted and entered the ruined temple, which lay silent and still, seemingly utterly deserted in the heat of the afternoon Indian sunshine.

Bunter rolled out of the palanquin and rolled ahead into the paved court, whore the fallen statue of Buddha lay on the cracked flags.

The Jam Bahadur had descended from his elephant in his eagerness in the quest. But the task of descending into the recesses beneath the temple was left to more active persons. Colonel Wharton took the lead. Billy Bunter blinked round him, and stopped beside the bronze Buddha.

"It was just here!" he said.

"Pick out the exact stone, if you can, Bunter," said the colonel.

"I'll jolly soon do that!"

Bunter blinked to and fro, watched impatiently by the juniors. The Owl of the Remove was in no great hurry. He was the important person now; the colonel, even the great Jam himself, were waiting for Bunter to indicate the way. Bunter was not in a hurry to part with his importance.

But he stopped at last at the great slab of stone which he had seen rise from its place on the day he had watched Nally Das emerge from the hiding-place under the temple of Shiva.

"Here it is!" he announced.

"You are sure that is the stone?"

"Oh, really, sir—"

"Are you sure?" rapped out the colonel. He did not seem to notice how important Bunter was, or perhaps he noticed it and did not like it.

"Yes, I am!" grunted Bunter sulkily.

"Stand aside, then!"

Bunter rolled aside, and the colonel bent and examined the stone. At a casual view, it looked like the other stones by which it was surrounded; but as he examined it, the colonel gave a nod. A close inspection showed that, although it touched the adjoining stones, there was no trace of cement between them.

"This slab is detached," said the colonel quietly. "Doubtless there is some hidden mechanism for raising it from below; but of that we know nothing. But we have other means." He spoke to the subadar, Lal Chundar, who called forward a couple of sturdy chaukees, who carried crowbars. A score of men had gathered in the paved court, and at the Jam's order, the rest of the party scattered about the temple, within the ruins, and round the old shattered walls, to keep watch lest there should be another exit from the hiding-place below. Now that the Jam was on the track of the missing nabob, he was leaving nothing to chance.

Harry Wharton & Co. looked on with bated breath while the crowbars were driven in between the great slab and the adjoining stones. Loud blows rang and echoed through the stillness as the crowbars were driven home, and then strong muscles bent to their task, and the great slab was wrenched out of it's place—and the hot sun shone into a deep opening, and upon a flight of steps that wound downwards into deep darkness.

120

The Rescue!

THUD!

Hurree Jamset Ram Singh heard the dull, heavy sound that echoed through the gloom, but without heeding it.

The schoolboy nabob sat on the rug in his prison cell in deep darkness.

The teak door was closed and barred on him; only twice a day did it open to give admittance to his golfers Nally Das, or Lazaroff, or some other of the rajah's servitors.

Then a lamp would glimmer in his cell, and the nabob would eat his spare meal, again to be left in silence, solitude, and darkness.

It was a form of torture that might well have broken down the prisoner's resistance.

But it had no effect on the Nabob of Bhanipur.

With Eastern impassiveness, the prisoner endured the solitude, the deep: chilling silence, the darkness that was like a suffocating cloak.

How many days and nights he had spent in the lonely stone cell, he did not know. He could not follow the passage of time, day and night, sunshine and starlight, were all the same to him, buried from the light of day and the light of the stars. It seemed to him that long years had elapsed since the day of the tiger-hunt, when he had ridden into the jungle so cheerily with his friends.

Despair was in his heart now.

He knew that his friends must be seeking him, that the Jam was striving hard to discover him; that no stone was left unturned. And yet they had failed.

The secret of the temple was unknown—known only to Nally Das, the descendant of the ancient priests of Shiva, and to the kidnapping gang to whom he had confided it. And Hurree Singh did not doubt now that the secret would remain unknown; that he would remain a helpless prisoner at the mercy of his rival.

Still he did not falter in his resolution.

Not by act or word would he help the rajah to realize his ambition; not to save himself from perpetual imprisonment; not to save himself from secret assassination in the dungeon.

When the gaolers visited him, they found him calm and self-possessed, giving no sign.

He knew that his hard usage was intended to break down his resolution, and that if it failed, more active tortures might follow. But his resolution remained like iron.

He saw changed faces among his gaolers; the weariness of the imprisonment under the ancient temple told upon them; one day it was Nally Das, another day the Russian, Lazaroff, and there were others in turn. But the weariness of the gaolers was as nothing to the weariness of the hapless prisoner. Yet every time that he was asked if he had a message to send to the rajah, he shook his head in silence.

Save when his gaolers came in with food, he received no visit and heard no sound. But now, in the deep tomb-like silence of his prison, strange new sounds came to his ears. Faintly through the subterranean spaces came the echoes of distant blows, as though someone were clanging at a distant door.

For some time the nabob did not heed.

But he heard other sounds—a hurrying of feet outside his door, a mutter of voices, in alarm.

Hurree Jamset Ram Singh felt a sudden thrill, and he leaped to his feet.

Was it help at last—help and rescue?

Thud, thud, thud!

Heavy blows, with a metallic clang to then. He thought of the great slab of stone that closed in his subterranean prison. Was it someone who was forcing admittance there? Had his prison been discovered at last by his friends?

His heart throbbed almost to suffocation. For some moments his brain was dizzy with sudden hope, with the thought of rescue and release. But he pulled himself together.

In the cloaking darkness he groped to the door of his cell and placed his ear against the wood, listening.

Thud, thud, thud!

More loudly the blows rang. The sounds, as he judged, came from above; the blows were being struck at the slab of stone.

"Shabash!" murmured the nabob, his eyes gleaming in the darkness of the cell. "Friends at last! Shabash!"

His heart was thumping.

There was a sound outside the teak teak-wood door—the bars were being taken down. Evidently his gaolers were alarmed. Hurree Jamset Ram Singh stepped back from the door; it was thrown open, and the light of a smoky lamp gleamed in.

Lazaroff, the Russian looked in at him with a startled face. Behind the Russian was a dusky Hindu—a chaukee of the rajah's guard. Nally Das was not to be seen. Although Hurree Singh did not know it, the Rajah Raji Rao had that day ridden into the city of Bhanipur and Nally Das, his confidential kamdar, was with him there. Lazaroff and the chaukee were in charge of the imprisoned nabob, and both of them were obviously thrown into utter dismay by the attack on the stone slab above.

Hurree Singh faced the two men quietly, calmly, in the light of the smoky lamp.

Rescue was at hand, that was certain now. But he was still at the mercy of his guards, and it was more than possible that the rajah had left orders for his death should there be danger of his escape. So long as he lived a prisoner, the nabob was a hostage in the rajah's hands; but once he was free Baji Rao was a lost man.

The Russian gave him a bitter look.

"You hear?" he muttered.

"I hear!" said Hurree Singh.

"They are there—at the stone. Do you know who they are? Did you expect this?"

"They are my friends," said Hurree Singh; "and if you value your life you will hand me over to them in safety."

Lazaroff's grasp was on the nabob, his revolver was pressed into Inky's side, as Colonel Wharton approached. "Stand back!" "Death if you harm him," said the Colonel, between his teeth. "Life and freedom for his life," said the Russian,his finger on the trigger.

The Russian made no reply. He bent his head to listen. The thudding blows had ceased; a long, heavy, grinding sound told that the slab had been wrenched from its place. It was a matter of minutes now.

The rajah's chaukee touched the arm of the Russian. His bared tulwar was in his hand, his eyes glittered at the nabob. He spoke quickly in his own tongue, but the Russian seemed to hesitate.

Hurree Singh, his hands clenched hard, waited and watched. It was clear that Baji Rao had left orders that he should be slain if rescue came; and the Hindu soldier was ready to carry out the savage order. But the European hesitated.

Lazaroff, the emissary of the Dolycrits plotters of Moscow, was keen enough to carry out the orders of his master, to place Baji Rao on the throne of Hurree Singh, to range Bhanipur on the side of Russia. But life was dear to him; and he knew what to expect from the Jam Bahadur if he carried out the order of Baji Rao. He did not share the slavish obedience of the Hindu.

Footsteps rang in the subterranean corridors; there was a flashing of lights, a shouting of voices. Echoing from the distance came a voice that Hurree Singh knew well—a voice that made his heart beat.

"Hallo, hallo, hallo! Where are you, Inky?"

The voice of Bob Cherry!

"Here!" shouted the nabob. "Help! Help!"

"This way!" shouted Bob.

"Inky, old man—"

The rajah's chaukee thrust the Russian savagely aside as he hesitated. He turned on Hurree Singh like a tiger, his tulwar flashing aloft the clear steel shining in the lamplight.

Lights flashed and hurried footsteps echoed; the reenters were close at hand now. But the gleaming tulwar was over the head of the schoolboy nabob.

Hurree Singh leaped back, and the slash of the sword missed him by on inch. A revolver was in the Russian's hand; he raised it, and lowered it again. The rajah's soldier followed up the nabob, his tulwar rising for another savage slash.

Crack!

The Russian fired—but not at Hurree Singh. It was the rajah's chaukee who received the bullet at close range, and he rolled over on the floor of the cell, his tulwar falling with a crash.

A tall figure and a bronzed face appeared in the doorway of the cell. Lazaroff's grasp was on the nabob; his revolver was pressed to the side of Hurree Jamset Ran Singh. His desperate eyes glared defiance at Colonel Wharton.

"Stand back!"

"Death if you harm him!"' said the colonel between his teeth. "Death by all the tortures known in the East!"

"Life and freedom for his life!" said the Russian, his finger on the trigger.

"You shall go in peace."

"On the word of a sahib?"

"On the word of a sahib!" said the colonel.

The Russian threw down the revolver.

121

Bunter is Not Satisfied!

"MY esteemed chums—" "Good old Inky!"

"The pleasurefulness of this excellent moment is terrific."

Harry Wharton & Co. chuckled in sheer enjoyment. Never had they been so glad to hear the remarkable English which Hurree Singh had learned from the moonshee Mook Mookerjee.

Hurree Singh was above ground now. In the midst of his elated chums, he had been borne up from the subterranean prison. The chums of the Remove almost hugged him.

The nabob looked worn, almost haggard. His terrible imprisonment had told upon him. But his worn, face was beaming with delight. It was good to see the sunshine again, to breathe the air from the forest.

"Safe again—safe and sound!" said Bob Cherry, smacking the rescued nabob on the back. "Good old Inky!"

"The hopefulness had almost departed," said Hurree Singh. "My esteemed heart was heavy. But now everything in the excellent garden is lovely, and the rejoicefulness is great."

"Ha, ha, ha!

"The jolly old Jam's waiting for you" said Nugent. "This way, Inky, old chap!"

Hurree Jamset Ram Singh ran to the Jam Bahadur with tears in his eyes; the old brown gentleman embraced his nephew. A flood of Hindustani poured from his lips, of which the Greyfriars juniors understood hardly a word, but which evidently expressed the Jam's rejoicing.

"I say, you fellows—"

Bunter, much to his indignation, was unheeded.

Bunter, the right man in the right place, the fellow who had done it all seemed to be overlooked, in the general rejoicing at the rescue of the schoolboy nabob.

"I say, you fellows—"

"Hallo, hallo, hallo! Here's Bunter!" chuckled Bob, Cherry, and he gave the fat junior a terrific smack on the back.

"Yarooooh!"

"What's the row now?" asked Bob.

"Yow-ow! You've broken my back!" roared Bunter. "Whoooop!"

"Ha, ha, ha!"

"Yow-ow-ow!"

Lazaroff, the Russian, came up from the subterranean depths, in charge of Colonel Wharton. The Jam's eyes glittered at him; but the Colonel spoke a few words, and the Jam nodded assent. The Russian was allowed to go; and he lost no time. He vanished at once into the forest, with the warning that if he was found again in Bhanipur his life would be forfeit. But the Bolshevik was not likely to linger long in Hurree Singh's kingdom. The game was up for Baji Rao now—the end was in sight; and the man from Moscow intended to go while the going was good.

The Jam, holding on to Hurree Singh's arm, as if afraid of losing the nabob again, marched him away to the waiting elephant.

"I say, Inky—" bawled Bunter.

But Hurree Singh did not hear, at least, he did not heed.

He mounted into the howdah with the Jam; and the troopers remounted their horses to escort the rescued nabob back to Bhanipur.

Bunter blinked at the chums if the Remove, his very spectacles gleaming with indignation.

"Call this gratitude!" he hooted.

"Can it, old bean," said Johnny Bull.

"After what I've done—"

"Give us a rest!"

"Look here, you fellows—"

But the fellows mounted their horse and rode after the Jam's elephant heedless of the indignant Bunter.

The Owl of the Remove rolled to his palanquin, and rolled into it, and the patient bearers lifted him, and followed on.

It was a joyous procession that took the road to the city.

Ahead of it went the subadar and a dozen men, at full gallop, with news that the nabob was returning, and orders to arrest Baji Rao at the serai in Bhanipur.

"The game's up for that rotter!" Bob Cherry remarked, as the juniors trotted cheerily along under the setting sun. "It was a close thing; but we've jolly well trumped the last trick. What a kindly surprise for him when Inky comes marching in."

"I say, you fellows—" came a fat voice from the palanquin.

"Hallo, hallo, hallo! There's Bunter again. Do you know that you've come in useful for once, Bunter!"

"Oh really, Cherry—"

"You'll never be ornamental, old chap, but you can be useful at times," said Bob. "You're no end of nuisance, old fat man, but I'm not sorry you came out to India with us, after all."

"Fancy Bunter being anything but nuisance and a beastly worry!" remarked Johnny Bull "Queer, ain't it!"

"Uh, really, Bull—"

"Wonders will never cease!" Harry Wharton, laughing. "We'll start you a study spread for this, Bunter when we get back to Greyfriars."

"Yah!"

The juniors chuckled and trotted or Bunter sitting in his palanquin state of great indignation. Hurree Jamset Ram Singh did not yet know he much he owed to the fat junior; an nobody seemed to have taken the trouble to tell him. Certainly, it was quite by accident that Bunter had come in useful; but the Owl of the Remove did not look at it in that light. From Bunter's point of view, he was prime mover in the whole business; he was the fellow that mattered. And somehow or other, the general opinion seemed to be that he did not matter at all. Which was really very hard for a meritorious fellow who was prepared to spread himself as the hero of their hour.

The city of Bhanipur was humming with the news, when the Jam's elephant strode in at the gates; tall buzzing throngs surrounded the returned nabob as he made his way to his palace. At the gate of the palace waited this subadar with the news that Baji Rao had already fled from the city. No doubt a spy of the rajah's had followed the Jam's party to the temple in the forest, and brought back the news of Hurree Singh's rescue in time for the plotting rajah to make his escape.

Baji Rao had left the city by one gate as the subadar and his men had entered it by another—riding for his life.

He was gone—with his long planned schemes in ruins, his life forfeit for his crimes; gone in desperate haste with the emissaries of death on his track.

He had fled to his castle, which was not likely long to protect him. Little hope remained to him of saving his life and his lands; and his dream of reigning as Nabob of Bhanipur was over.

But the Greyfriars fellows, at least, gave little thought to the defeated plotter in their rejoicing at the safe return of their chum. The Nabob of Bhanipar, Inky of the Remove was safe back in his palace, and that was enough for Harry Wharton and Co.

As the nabob entered the palace through salaaming crowds, Bunter rolled out of his palanquin and shouted to him.

"Inky? I say, Inky?"

The nabob did not even glance round.

He disappeared into the palace leaning on the arm of the old Jam. apparently unconscious of the existence of William George Bunter.

Bunter snorted.

"I say, you fellows—"

But the juniors followed the nabob in, and Bunter turned his big spectacles on Colonel Wharton, who had stopped to speak to Pandy Din.

"I say, sir—"

The colonel, apparently deaf, strode away. Bunter breathed hard with wrath and indignation. He was the hero of the hour—the fellow who mattered—and absolutely no one seemed disposed to take heed of his uncommon merits.

"Here, you—" said Bunter to the khitmutghar.

Pandy Din glanced at him, saluted, and went out at the gates.

Even the khitmutghar did not seem to realize the importance of William George Bunter.

"Well, my hat!" said Bunter, in utter disgust.

He rolled into the palace, and went to his own quarters. Kasi Jee was there; and he greeted Bunter Sahib with his deepest salaam. Matters had changed once more; Baji Rao was now a back number, so to speak; the Nabob Hurree Jamset Ram Singh was once more master in his own palace; and Kasi Jee, for his part, was once more the submissive, bowing naukar.

But Bunter had not forgotten. He fixed his spectacles on Kasi Jee with a wrathful glare.

"James!" he snapped.

"Salaam, sahib!"

"You beast!"

"The sahib is angry with his slave!" murmured Kasi Jee.

"You cheeky native!"

"O, sahib!"

"Turn round!" commanded Bunter.

Kasi Jee eyed him apprehensively, but he obeyed. In the belief that Baji Rao would reign in Bhanipur, and that the white sahibs would have their heads cut off, the naukar had let himself go, as it were. He had allowed himself the pleasure of checking Bunter Sahib. Now the tables were turned, and after the feast came the reckoning. Crash!

Bunter's boot, with all Bunter's weight behind it, smote the hapless naukar, and Kasi Jee fairly flew.

"He, he, he!" chortled Bunter, as the naukar rolled on the floor.

Kasi Jee picked himself up, and fled gasping; and Bunter, feeling, rather better, sat down to rest after his great exertions in rescuing the Nabob of Bhanipur.

122

Glory for Bunter!

"HALLO, hallo, hallo!"

"Go!"

"Eh?"

"Go!" repeated Billy Bunter.

The fat junior raised a podgy forefinger, and pointed it at Bob Cherry. His attitude was quite dramatic.

Bob stared at him blankly. He stood in the doorway of Bunter's apartment and stared; and Wharton and Nugent and Johnny Bull stared also.

"What's this game?" inquired Bob.

"Go!"

"But we've come—"

Bunter rose to his feet. He fixed his spectacles on the chums of the Remove, and looked at their feet, and then allowed his glance to travel up to their surprised faces, then to sink down to their feet again. This was what Bunter called looking a fellow up and down, and the effect was supposed—by Bunter—to be crushing.

The juniors did not look crushed. They grinned.

"Go!" repeated Bunter. "I'm fed-up with you! Fed right up to the chin! You lot, and Inky! The whole mob of you! Get out?"

"But—" said Nugent.

"You needn't talk to me, Nugent! I'm sick of you!"

"Oh, my hat!"

"Especially Inky! A sickening lot!" said Bunter.

Harry Wharton & Co. regarded Bunter with growing surprise. The Owl of the Remove was evidently indignant and wrathful. His wrath and his indignation, in fact, knew no bounds.

All the palace, and all the city of Bhanipur, rejoiced over the safe return of the nabob from captivity. In the general rejoicings nobody seemed to remember that Bunter had had anything to do with it. Bunter, who had done it all, according to his own view, was passed over like the idle wind that they regarded not.

Bunter, the fellow whom all Bhanipur ought to have been delighted to honour, was left forgotten in his apartment, comforted only by ample tuck. Tuck was all very well; Bunter did the tuck justice, and more than justice. But tuck, after all, was not everything. Bunter wanted the recognition of his merit, the honour and glory due to his great services. And these details seemed to have been overlooked. Hence the fed-up and indignant state of the Owl of the Remove.

"Sickening!" repeated Bunter emphatically. "An ungrateful lot! In accustomed to ingratitude. That's nothing new. But this is the limit! He travelled all the way to India to protect Inky—"

"Draw it mild," suggested Johnny Bull.

"I've saved him again and again," said Bunter. "This last time, he was fairly done for, if I hadn't weighed in. What do I receive in return? Not even a word of thanks."

"But—"

"But for me," continued Bunter, with growing indignation, "where would Inky be? Where would that fat old Jam be? Where would all you fellows be? I'm not a fellow to push myself forward in any way—"

"Oh, my hat!"

"But there's a limit!" hooted Bunter. "I'm treated with rotten ingratitude. I'm fed-up. I'm going!"

"But—" began Wharton.

"That's enough, Wharton! I'm going!" said Bunter with great dignity. "I decline to remain any longer a guest of Hurree Singh! I refuse to stay in this palace. I am going to shake the dust of the place from my feet, and wash my hands of the whole thing."

"Wash your neck at the same time!" suggested Johnny Bull. "It can do with it."

"Ha, ha, ha!"

"I don't want any cheek!" roared Bunter. "I mean what I say; I'm degusted with all of you, especially Inky. I'm fed-up with you. I shall require a car to take me away, and an escort, and—and plenty of grub for the journey. After that, I'm done with you. You fellows can stay here among the native if you like, and he blowed to you. I'm going!"

Bunter was evidently in earnest. His indignation was deep; he felt that his fat dignity was at stake.

"But—" said Nugent, with a chuckle.

"That's enough, I tell you! Go!"

"But—-" roared Bob Cherry.

"Go!" the podgy foreigner pointed to the door. "Tell Inky that I desire him. That's my last message. When we get back to Greyfriars, I'll thank you not to speak to me. I'm turning you down—the lot of you! Got that? Now buzz off!"

And Bunter turned his back on the grinning juniors.

"Ha, ha. Ha!"

"James!" roared Bunter.

"Salaam, sahib!" Kasi Jee wriggled forward.

"Kick these fellows out."

"Ha, ha, ha!"

"Bunter, you silly ass!" exclaimed Harry Wharton. "We came here to tell you—"

"Go!"

"That we've told lnky it was you that spotted the secret of the old temple, and give us the clue where to find him."

'Oh!" said Bunter.

"Inky wants to see you—" went on the captain of the Remove.

"A reception in state!" grinned Bob Cherry.

"Inky on a golden throne, and all the giddy court standing round to admire!" said Nugent.

"No end of kudos!" grinned Johnny Bull. "Public recognition of your wonderful services!"

"Oh!" repeated Bunter.

The lofty frown faded from the face of William George Bunter. He condescended to smile.

"Come along," said Harry Wharton. laughing. "There's a guard of honour waiting to conduct you to the Hall of Audience."

"Oh! Good!"

"And you can swank as much as you jolly well like."

"Oh, really, Wharton!"

"You can spread yourself all over the show!" chuckled Bob Cherry. "Owl!" mind you don't burst!"

"Oh, really, Cherry!"

"Buck up!" said Wharton. "The court is gathered for the reception; only the great man is waited for. You're the great man."

Bunter's eyes danced behind his spectacles. This was what he wanted—what he deserved! For once he was to get his deserts. His uncommon merits were, after all, to receive due recognition.

"If Inky's really grateful, I'm not the fellow to turn him down!" said Bunter. "I'm ready."

Wrath and indignation had passed like a stunner cloud. Billy Bunter's fat face beamed as he rolled out of the room with the chums of the Remove. In the wide corridor, twenty men of the palace guard waited, with drawn swords. Bunter blinked rather dubiously at the drawn swords; but it was a guard of honour, and the dusky swordsmen saluted him respectfully, and formed up to escort him to the Hall of Audience.

Bunter rolled along with them swelling as he rolled. He felt several inches taller, and his fat chest was puffed out with importance, and his little fat legs strutted. Harry Wharton & Co. followed on, with smiling faces. Bunter was the cynosure of all eyes, and most eyes that regarded him had a glimmer of merriment in them. But Bunter did not notice that. At long last, he was receiving the honour that was his due. He had no doubt that his progress was most impressive; while the chums of the Remove hoped that he would not, in his swollen state, suffer the fate of the frog in the fable.

Dusky guards salaamed to the fat junior, as he arrived at the Hall of Audience, a magnificent apartment, with walls and ceiling decorated with gorgeous arabesques,

At the upper end of the apartment, Hurree Jamset Ram Singh in robes of plate, sat on a golden throne, the Jam on his right hand. Colonel Wharton on his left. Dusky counsellors and officials and guards were grouped round, in their various degrees Bunter advanced up the hall, swelling more and more. Salaams greeted him on all sides.

Hurree Jamset Ram Singh rose from his throne, and descended a step to meet Bunter, an unparalleled honour and distinction. In point of fact, the schoolboy nabob was quite aware of how much he owed to Bunter. True, it was by chance that the Owl of the Remove had been able to help him out. But the fact remained, that but for Billy Bunter, the nabob would still have languished a captive in his hidden prison, in darkness and the fear of death while his rival ascended his throne. It was a fact that could not be gainsaid, and Hurree Jamset Ram Singh was prepared to testify his gratitude in a manner worthy of an Eastern prince.

"My esteemed and ludicrous Bunter!" said the nabob. "I have latefully learned the terrific services you have performed in the rescuefulness of my esteemed self. The thankfulness is truly terrific."

Bunter's fat face expanded in a grin. "All serene, old chap!" he said, "I've mentioned to you several times, you know, that I was the real goods. I've pointed out to you that those chaps were no good-not an earthly. Haven't I?"

"Modesty, thy name is Bunter!" murmured Bob Cherry, and the juniors grinned.

"Now that I am once more upon my throne, my esteemed and ridiculous Bunter, I would testify my gratitude said the nabob. "Anything that it my esteemed power to grant, require only the askfulness."

"Chance for Bunter to get his postal order cashed!" murmured Johnny Bull and the solemn proceedings were interrupted, for a moment, by a subdued chuckle.

Hurree Jamset Ram Singh made a sign, and the Wazir—a gorgeous official—came forward, and draped an enormous gold chain round the fat neck of Billy Bunter. Bunter gasped. The value of the great chain of gold must have been immense. It was a signal honour for the Owl of the Remove; William George Bunter was thinking rather of the intrinsic value than the distinction. His fat grin grew more expansive.

But the Wazir was not finished. A slave brought forward a salver, on lay a collar of glittering diamonds. The Wazir lifted it, and placed it round Bunter's neck.

"I—I say—" gasped Bunter.

More than once during his stay in Bhanipur, had Bunter's eyes lingered on the bronze doors of the placed treasury. His fat thoughts had often, dwelt upon the gold mohurs and precious stones stored up behind the door of bronze. Evidently the nabob he sought in his treasury for a suitable reward for Bunter—a reward that appealed to the fat junior more—much more than the deepest gratitude could have done. Bunter was fairly dazzled by the riches of which he found himself the possessor. His fat face beamed unto a full moon.

"I—I say, Inky!" he stuttered. "I say, old chap, no larks, you know."

"I do not understand the esteemed fat Bunter. There is no larkfulness," said the nabob.

"These trifling gifts are a small testimony of the terrific thankfulness of my esteemed self."

"You—you mean it?" stuttered Bunter. "Let's have it plain you, know." Bunter was a business like youth. "You're giving me these things—I'm to take them home with me, what?"

The nabob grinned.

But his face was grave once again.

"My esteemed and ridiculous Bunter, these small gifts are yours, with all my heart!" he answered. "Keep them in rememberfulness of the service you have rendered to the Nabob of Bhanipur."

He blinked at the glistening gold, that glittering jewels. Visions danced before his eyes of endless spreads in the study at Greyfriars. There was wealth untold in the gorgeous gift of the nabob. Bunter of the Remove was going to be a great man when he was back at Greyfriars. He was going to strut in the old quad, in clothes more expensive than those of Angel of the Fourth; he was going to "chuck" money right and left more lavishly than Lord Mauleverer; he was going to "swank" to the top of his bent It was a prospect full of joy to the Owl of the Remove.

"I say, old chap, thanks," he gasped. "You're a prince, Inky—the genuine goods, and no mistake!"

"My esteemed Bunter—"

"And I'll tell you what," said Bunter, "when we leave Greyfriars, I'll jolly well come with you to Bhanipur. I'll stick to you, Inky. I'm your pal for life. I'll jolly well be your Prime Minister."

"My worthy and ludicrous Bunter—"

"I'll manage the whole thing for you," said Bunter generously. "Rely on me; I'll run the whole show for you, Inky!"

"The thankfulness is terrific," said the nabob. "The generosity of the inestimable Bunter is terrific and unacceptable."

The nabob made a sign, and there was a general movement. The audience was over.

The fat junior rolled away, shining with gold and diamonds, his fat chin held well up, his glance lofty behind his big spectacles.

"Congratters, old fat bean!" said Bob Cherry, grinning in at the door when the guard had gone, and Bunter was left alone in his glory.

Bunter gave a lofty blink.

"Halves!" chuckled Johnny Bull.

"Ha, ha, ha!"

"No jolly fear!" said Bunter promptly. "I say, you fellows, Inky's awfully decent. Jolly docent for a blinking native, what? He knows how to treat a fellow properly. Not like you chaps."

"You fat idiot!"

"Don't give me any check, Bull. I say, Wharton, what do you think these things are worth?"

"Trust Bunter to think of that!" chuckled Bob.

"Oh, really, Cherry—"

"I don't know," said Harry, laughing. "But a good many hundreds of pounds, Bunter."

Bunter grinned gleefully.

"I shall be jolly well rolling in it, when we're back in England," he said. "I say, you fellows, the sooner we start the better. These things will be safer in England than in India. No need to stay here any longer, what?"

"We're staying till Inky has finished with that villain Baji Rao, and then Inky's coming back to Greyfriars with us," said Harry.

"That's all rot, you know," said Bunter. "All very well for you fellows-poverty-stricken bounders like you. It's different with me. I want to start tomorrow morning. Now I'm rich. I'm jolly well going to take care of the stuff. You fellows will have to travel with me to see it safe home. Mind, we start in the morning. Fathead!"

"And I don't want any check!" roared Bunter. "Mind, I'm in favour here now, and Inky will do anything for me—as he ought, considering what I've done for him. You fellows have got to treat me with respect—or it will be the worse for you."

Bob Cherry winked at his comrades.

"Let's treat Bunter with the respect that is his due!" he said. "Eyen Bunter ought to have his due."

"Hear, hear!"

"That's better," said Bunter. "I can jolly well tell you—yaroooh—Leggo—wharrer you collaring me for, you silly asses—yooooooooop!"

Bump!

"Oow, wow, wow!"

"Ha, ha, ha!"

And Harry Wharton & Co, retired leaving William George Bunter sitting on the floor and roaring.

PART 11. FROM INDIA TO GREYFRIARS!

123

Bunter, Too!

"I'M coming!"

Billy Bunter made that announcement in determined tones. He backed it tip with a severe frown.

Billy Bunter was in earnest. Both his tone and his look announced that he was in deep earnest, and that he intended to take no denial.

Harry Wharton & Co. smiled. The chums of the Remove had come cheerily out of the palace at Bhanipur into the sunny courtyard, where the sayces were holding their horses ready for them.

Bunter followed on.

There was bustle and movement in the palace court. Horsemen were mounting there, with a jingle of bridles and accoutrements. Evidently some expedition was toward—and it was not Bunter's intention to be left out of that expedition.

"I'm coming!" he repented. "You needn't grin at me. Wharton—"

"Was I grinning?" asked Harry Wharton mildly.

"Yes, like a Cheshire cheese—I mean a Cheshire cat! I'm jolly well coming—see? Just like you fellows to leave a fellow behind!"

"You see—" began Bob Cherry, with a cheery grin. Bunter held up a fat hand.

"You needn't talk to me, Cherry! I'm coming!"

"But you don't know—" began Johnny Bull.

"I know I'm coming!" said Bunter, with emphasis. "This isn't the first time you've tried to leave me out of things! Do you call it pally?"

"But—" said Frank Nugent.

"You can shut up, Nugent! I don't want any jaw," said Bunter. "The point is, I'm coming! I was left behind last time there was a picnic. I am not going to be left behind again! See?"

The chums of the Remove chuckled. Bunter had seen the preparations for an expedition that morning; he know that provisions had been packed. To Bunter's fat mind, that represented a picnic—merely that and nothing more.

And when Harry Wharton & Co. obviously were going to start without him, Bunter was indignant. Bunter was not taking any, so to speak. Bunter was far too important a personage to be treated in such an offhand way.

"You can cackle!" said Bunter disdainfully. "But I can jolly well tell you you're not treating me here the same as you do at Greyfriars. Who are you, anyway? Nobody! Did you save Hurree Singh when he was kid napped by that blinking rajah? No—I did! Did you have a great reception in your honour, and valuable jewels presented to you in recognition of your services? No—I did! I can jolly well tell you that you fellows are precious small beer here—precious small!"

Bunter delivered this oration with crushing disdain gleaming from his big spectacles. But the chums of the Remove did not appear to be crushed they seemed rather to be entertained.

"Go it, Bunter!" said Bob Cherry encouragingly.

"Bunter is the goods, and we are merely 'also rans'!" remarked Nugent.

"Is that it, fatty?"

"That's it exactly, Nugent! You can cackle as much as you like but that is precisely how the matter stands," said Bunter. "I came out to India to protect Inky. I've protected him. He's grateful—and I admit it. Not so grateful as he ought to be, perhaps—still, he has played up pretty well. As for you fellows, you don't come into the picture at all. Who are you? Nobodies!"

And Billy Bunter turned up his fat little nose—not a difficult task, as Nature had already started it in that direction. Harry Wharton & Co. grinned serenely.

Bunter in a state of swanking self-satisfaction was entertaining; and there was no doubt that Bunter was satisfied with himself those days. Since he bad been instrumental in rescuing Hurree Jamset Ram Singh from the clutches Baji Rao, Bunter had swelled and swelled with importance, till he was in an extremely in-flated slate.

The schoolboy' nabob had testified his gratitude substantially. Bunter had been presented with priceless jewels from the palace treasury—a form of gratitude that Bunter could understand and appreciate. More than that, the nabob had treated him with great distinction; the nabob's uncle, the Jam Bahadur, had honoured him; the nabob's old tutor, Mook Mookerjee, had blessed him, with tears in his eyes, for saving Hurree Singh from his enemies; the guards and officials in the trainee, from the gorgeous wazir to the humblest naukar, salaamed to him with deepest respect when they encountered him. and did not smile till his fat back was turned.

All of which had gone to Bunter's head like wine.

He was a great man in those days—greatest of all in his own eyes.

It was quite different from his old position in the Lower Fourth Form at Greyfriars, where his insignificance and Unimportance had been abysmal.

At Greyfriars he was nobody in particular; and the other fellows were great men in the Remove.

Here in Bhanipur he was a great Man, and the other follows were nobodies—in Bunter's eyes, at least.

Bunter wanted them to understand that clearly; but it did not seem to be quite clear to them, somehow.

Somehow, they still seemed to regard Billy Bunter as a fat and fatuous ass, of no particular consequence.

His lofty airs and graces, indeed, they persisted in looking upon as actually comic.

Which was decidedly irritating to Bunter.

"Nobodies!" he repealed "Nobodies at all! Not even also ran!

'! So just get it into your heads that I don't want any of your cheek! See?"

"Keep it up!" said Bob cheerily. "You don't know how funny you are. Bunter, you really ought to be on the films or in a circus! " Ha, ha, ha!"

There was a stir and bustle in the courtyard; Hurree Jamset Ram Singh was coming out to his horse. Dusky guards and servitors salaamed on all sides as the schoolboy nabob made his appearance. Colonel Wharton came out to his horse, which was held by Bandy Din, the khitmutghar. Harry Wharton & Co. made a movement towards their waiting steeds.

"Where's my horse?" demanded Bunter warmly.

"You're not coming, fathead I"

"I've told you I'm coming!" bawled Bunter. "If you fellows aren't a bit more civil, I'll ask Inky to leave you behind. Inky will do anything I ask him. You fellows have got to learn your place!"

"Ha, he, ha!"

"James!" roared Bunter.

Kasi Jee, the naukar, came up, salaaming. He was Bunter's special attendant, and he treated Bunter with the humility and respect that Bunter considered his due. Every day regularly Bunter kicked him—sometimes twice a day. That was what Bunter considered the best method of keeping a "native " in order. The naukar, no doubt, was accustomed to kicks; bit it was probable that Bunter overdid it a little.

But Kasi Jee—doubtless for good reasons of his own—took it oil with smiling patience and Eastern submission, specially since Bunter had been honored by the nabob, and decorated with priceless jewels, had Kasi Jee displayed a fervent attachment to the fat junior. Indeed, Bunter spoke of him complacently as his "faithful native." "Bring my horse!" ordered Bunter. "Han, sahib."

"And your own. I shall want you to wait on me."

"Kasi Jee is the sahib's slave!" murmured the naukar.

"Get a move on!"

"Look here, Bunter—" began Harry Wharton.

"Cheese it!" said Bunter scornfully.

Can't you understand that we're not in the Remove passage at Greyfriars how! You can swank as much as you like there. Here, you're nobody—less than nobody! Shut up!"

"You silly ass!" roared the captain of of the Remove. "I tell you are not coming! This isn't a picnic or an excursion. We're going into the jungle."

"Rats!"

"We're going into danger!"

"Bosh"

"We're going after Baji Rao—"

"Can it!" said Bunter.

"Take him by the ears, and lead him in," suggested Johnny Bull.

"Good!"

Billy Bunter backed away promptly.

The juniors were far from Greyfriars school now, but some of the manners and customs of the Remove passage survived in the palace of Hurree Jamset Rani Singh at Bhanipur.

Bunter cut across to the schoolboy nabob, who was mounting a magnificent horse. The guards made way for him.

"Inky!" shouted Bunter.

"My esteemed Bunter—" said Hurree Singh, glancing down at the Owl of the Remove.

"I'm coming, old chap!" said Bunter, "those rotters want to leave me behind, same as they did before. I'm sticking to yon, old pal!"

"But—" said Hurree Singh. "Look here, Inky! What do you mean?" demanded Bunter hotly. "You're not going to back up those rotters against me, I suppose, after all I've done for you!"

"If the esteemed Bunter desires to come, the excellent and Ludicrous Bunter is more than welcome," said Hurree Jamset Ram Singh.

"That settles it."

Kasi Jee brought Bunter's horse. The fat junior bestowed a triumphant blink on Harry Wharton & Co., but they did not heed him further. It was clear that Bunter did not understand the nature of the expedition in which he was determined to take part; but as he did not choose to listen to reason the chums of the Remove gave him his head, as it were. With the assistance of Kasi Jee Bunter climbed on his horse, and sat in the saddle with the ease and grace of a sack of coke. The naukar mounted to follow his master.

A trumpet blared.

Hurree Jamset Ram Singh and his chums rode out of the palace gates, with a hundred troopers. From a window the Jam Bahadur waved a brown hand to his nephew. The troop rode out at the city gates, and followed a road through the paddy-fields, towards the jungles and forests that clothed the slopes of the hills to the north, beyond which, range on range, rose the mighty mass of the Himalayas, crowned with eternal snow.

124

Bunter is Fed-Up!

"I SAY, you fellows—"

"Tired?" grinned Bob Cherry.

"Yes!" growled Bunter.

"Look here! It's jolly well time we stopped for a rest! Nobody travels at noon in India. What the thump is Inky thinking of? Besides, I'm hungry."

Bob chuckled.

All through the morning the party had ridden on without a halt. The paddy-fields were left behind, and the troop rode on by a trampled path through the jungle. It was noon now, and the sun sailed high in a cloudless sky, pouring down blazing heat on hill and plain, jungle and nullah. Bunter had been growing more and more discontented for a long time, and now he was fed-up. When Billy Bunter was fed-up, it was time for the whole universe to sit up and take notice. Some of the party had separated and taken different paths. Bunter noticed that Colonel Wharton had disappeared, and with him fifty of the Bhanipur cavalrymen. The subadar, Lal Chunder, had taken another path, with another party of troopers. The thick jungle hail swallowed them from sight. Twenty men still rode with the Nabob of Bhanipur and the Greyfriars juniors. And to Bunter's intense annoyance there was no sign of halting, as the sun reached the zenith, and blazed down with tropical heat.

It was time, for repose, and time for tiffin—two very important matters indeed. No wonder Bunter was fed-up.

"What's this game?" demanded Bunter. "Where are we having the picnic, you follows?"

"Ha, ha, ha!"

"Blessed if I see anything to cackle at!" growled Bunter "Do you think I'm missing tiffin?"

"It isn't a picnic, you ass!" said Harry Wharton. "We're after Baji Rao, and we're not stopping."

"It's no good trying to pull my Wharton. Nobody in India ever travels in the heat of the day."

"Only on special occasions," said that captain of the Remove, laughing. "It is a special occasion."

"I'm hungry!"

"Your own fault, Bunter." said Bob.

"You ate only enough breakfast for Why didn't you pack away enough I dozen?"

"Ha, ha, ha!"

"Beast!"

Under his sun helmet Bunter," fat was crimson and streaming with perspiration.

"I say, Inky!" he bawled.

The Nabob of Bhanipur slackened.

"What is it, my esteemed Bunter?"

"It's time to halt!" The schoolboy nabob smiled and she his head.

"The haltfulness is not the proper, my worthy Bunter," he said. "We ride on till we reach the hills.".

"But that's hours yet!" exclaimed. Bunter, in dismay. "Many hours," assented the nabob. "I'm tired."

"The regretfulness is terrific!"

"I'm hungry!"

"The esteemed Bunter may feed the saddle."

"Look here, Inky—"

"You silly owl!" exclaimed Johnny Bull. "Why didn't you stay behind? You're no use here, and you keep grousing."

"Oh, really, Bull—"

"Give us a rest!"

"You see, my esteemed Bunter!" explained Hurree Jamset Ram Singh, "my excellent and disgusting relative Baji Rao, has fled from Bhanipur, a we are in pursuit of him."

"I told you so, Bunter," said Wharton Hunter snorted.

"Well, let him rip!" he said. "What the thump does Baji Rao matter? I thinking of lunch."

"The matterfulness is terrific," say Hurree Singh. "The worthy Bunter has not forgotten that Baji Rao kidnapped me and kept me a prisoner, and very nearly succeeded in taking my place as Nabob of Bhanipur."

"I'm not likely to forget, as it was I who rescued you, Inky!" snorted Bunter.

"The esteemed Bunter helped, and my gratitude is terrific," said the nabob "But there is no time to lose. Baji Rao is fleeing across the mountains, seeking. to escape to his friends the Bolsheviks I Russia, to wait for another opportunity to oust me from my throne. It not written that Baji Rao shall escape."

"It's a fight to a finish, old fat man," said Bob Cherry.

Bunter blinked at the hills that barred the blue sky ahead, with range on range of the Himalayas beyond.

"Mean to say we're going to follow" the blinking rajah into those beastly mountains?" he ejaculated.

"Exactfully!"

"Look here, I'm jolly well not!" exclaimed. "Let's go back to Bhanipur and let Baji Rao rip!"

The schoolboy nabob shook his head, with a smile. It was a smile that was not much like the good-natured grin of Inky of the Remove. In his own counts Inky of the Remove was an Indian nabob. He had been kidnapped and imprisoned; for days and nights he had lain in the darkness, in the shadow of death, while his rival was seeking to possess himself of his throne.

Baji Rao, defeated at the last moment, had fled for his life. His castle and lands were occupied by the nabob's guards, and confiscated for high treason; but the plotting rajah himself had vanished into the jungles and the hills with the few desperate followers who remained to him. But he was not to escape to renew his plotting at a more favourable opportunity. It was not a Greyfriars schoolboy that he had to deal with; it was an Indian nabob, ruthless to a rebel. Baji Rao had plotted for a crown. He had lost all but his life, and that was to follow. There could be no peace in Bhanipur while Baji Rao lived to scheme and plot, and stern justice waited for him once he was captured.

"Look here, Inky—" recommended Bunter. Bunter was not thinking of the peace of Bhanipur, or justice on the rebel rajah, or any of the interests of Hurree Singh. He was thinking of himself, as usual; and probably he would have given all Bhanipur just then for an ample lunch and a nap under a shady deodar.

"We will ride on," said Hurree Singh curtly.

"But look here—"

"The esteemed Bunter may ride back to the city," suggested Hurree Jamset Ram Singh. "I will send six of my guards with him."

Bunter grunted. Hidden about his fat person were the treasures the grateful nabob had be stowed upon him as a reward for the help he had given in the rescue of Hurree Singh.

Bunter was not likely to trust himself alone among "natives" with those treasures about him.

"I say, you fellows, you ride back with me," said Bunter blinking at the chums of the Remove.

"Fathead!"

"Look here—"

"Don't be an ass, Bunter!" exclaimed Harry Wharton impatiently. "You were warned not to come. Now you've come, make the best of it. We're more than halfway to the hills now; we shall be at our halting place sooner than you could get back to Bhanipur. Make the best of it and don't grouse!"

"Beast! I say, Inky—"

Hurree Jamset Ram Singh shook out his rein and rode on again. Billy Bunter followed, his fat face dark with frowns.

There was no help for it.

Bunter had landed himself, as he often did, from sheer fatuous obstinacy. Now it was too late to retreat.

But he groused and grumbled and groaned dismally as he rode on, perspiring under the blazing sun.

The jungle was left behind; the path lay through a forest, where the big branches interlacing overhead afforded a welcome shade.

By a broad, beaten track they rode on, on rising ground, ever nearer and nearer to the hills. The great branches shut out the blaze of the sun, but the heat was penetrating. Billy Bunter began to wonder whether he would survive that terrible tide, he was aching from one end of his fat person to the other. Kasi Jee rode behind his master, his eyes on Bunter, with a peculiar glint in them. The naukar pushed his pony closer at last and spoke to the Owl of the Remove.

"Sahib!"

Bunter blinked at him wearily.

"If the sahib would return Kasi Jee will guide him safely and swiftly back to the city," said the naukar in a low voice.

Bunter shook his head.

"Keep your pecker up. Bunty, oil bean!" said Bob Cherry encouragingly. "We're all jolly tired; but it's all in the day's work, you know."

"Beast!" said Bunter feebly.

"Hallo, hallo, hallo!" exclaimed Bob, as there was a rustle under the trees, and a dusky man leaped into view in the path.

"Help!" gasped Bunter

"Fathead! It's Mahbub, the shikaree," said Wharton.

"Oh! Sure it isn't a dacoit?" gasped Bunter.

"Ass!"

Hurree Jamset Ram Singh drew rein. Mahbub, the chief shikaree, salaamed to the nabob and spoke in a hurried voice in Hindustani. The face of the schoolboy nabob lighted up.

He turned to his chums, with a grin.

"Mahbub has brought news," he said. "He has been on the track of Baji Rao ever since he fled, and he has tracked him in the forest. He knows where to lay his finger on the rajah."

"Good!" said Bob.

"They are camped by a nullah in the forest, watched by Mahbub's shikaree," said Hurree Singh, "a few miles from here. My esteemed chums, if you choose to share the attack with me—"

"What ho!"

"The colonel sahib and the subadar are seeking in other directions," said Hurree Singh. "We cannot wait for them, or Baji Rao may flee again. But we have twenty men—and ourselves. Muhbub tells me that only six or seven are with the rajah."

"I say, you fellows—"

"He has seen Nally Das, the kidnapper, and the Russian Lazaroff with the rajah," went on Hurree Singh. "The others are chaukees—some of the rajah's retainers who have followed him in his flight. They will fight for their lives. I shall lead my men but you may—"

"Us, too!" said Bob Cherry. "Do you think you're going to have the scrapping all to yourself?"

The nabob grinned.

"Right-ho!" he said cheerily. "We leave the horses here, and follow Mahbub on foot through the forest. The sayces will remain to guard the horses; and Bunter had betterfully stay with them. The esteemed and ludicrous Bunter will be of no usefulness in a scrap."

"Oh, really, Inky—"

"If the excellent Bunter prefers to come he shall come," said the nabob.

Bunter blinked at the rusky sayces. Certainly he did not like the idea of coming to close quarters with the desperate rajah. Still less did he like the idea of being left alone in the forest with a gang of "natives." He groaned dismally.

"I'll come!" he said. "The—the fact is I—I'm rather keen on a scrap. Rely on me."

The party dismounted. For half an hour they rested in the shade of the trees Then, guided by Mahbub through the thick, tangled forest, they proceeded on foot their weapons in their hands, and their eyes open for enemies. And Billy Bunter, in the deepest depths of woe, rolled after them.

125

The Flight of Baji Rao!

BAJI RAO stood in the shadow of a mango tree, with a black brow. The mango grew on the slope of a stony nullah in the midst of the forest. Before the outcast rajah the nullah sloped down steeply to the stream that ran at the bottom. A storm in the distant hills had filled up the water-course, and the stream, usually low and shallow in the summer heats ran deep and swift and strong. Myriads of insects glanced in the sun over the shining, hurrying water that ripped along the bottom of the nullah. Baji Rao was watching the stream, as if in expectation, with a black and savage brow.

At a little distance from him his men were camped. The retinue of the Rajah Baji Rao was small enough now, greatly changed from what it had been on the day when he had ridden into Bhanipur to take possession of the nabob's palace and city.

The rescue of Hurree Jamset Ram Singh from his imprisonment had changed all things for the plotting rajah. Instead of a palace and a crown, it was utter ruin that had fallen upon him. He had ridden out of the city for his life; he had escaped to his castle, but had not dared to linger there, knowing that the messengers of death were on his track. He had stayed only to pack his most precious jewels, and then, with a few followers, he had fled again, and fled through the night and the day following, till from utter weariness the fugitives had been forced to halt.

Now they were camped by the nullah, still fearful of pursuit, knowing that the nabob's shikarees were seeking their trail, knowing that the horsemen of Bhanipur would be searching for them far and wide.

The thoughts of the fugitive rajah were bitter enough.

He had gambled desperately, staking all on a cast—a throne

on one hand, ruin on the other. And he had lost. His only hope now was to escape over the mighty mountain barrier of India, and find his way to Russian territory, where he had friends, or at least confederates. He had spent years of exile in the Muscovite land, and he hoped to find refuge there again now that he had failed in his bid for a throne—it was all the hope that remained to him.

But he knew that the pursuit would be close.

He had been allowed once to return from exile, and he had repaid his pardon with plotting and villainy. He would not be given another chance. Only his life remained to him to save, and a packet of jewels hidden in his bosom; and he knew that the chance was slight. Many a hundred miles of barren mountains lay between him and ssafety; and behind were the pursuers, seeking him, and a price was on his head.

Five ruffianly chaukees were all that remained of the many retainers who had thronged his castle. Ruffians as they were, they were loyal to their master, and they had followed him. With them was Lazaroff the emissary of the Moscow Bolsheviks, whose evil counsels had helped to bring the ambitious rajah to his ruin. Nally Das was also a companion in his flight; but the kam-dar was not to be seen in the camp now.

The chaukees rested under the shade, worn out by the hurried flight. Lazaroff, the Russian, sat smoking cigarettes, with an indifferent face.

The rajah glanced at the Russian, more than once, with a dark glance. He had listened to the counsels of the Russian plotter, and the outcome was—this! Gladly enough would the tyrants of Moscow have placed a puppet nabob on the throne of the mountain kingdom of Bhanipur, opening the passes of the hills to Russian invasion, when at long last the day should come. But the plot had failed; Hurree Singh was still Nabob of Bhanipur, in closest alliance with the British Raj; and the rebel rajah was a fugitive fleeing for his life that was what the Bolshevik counsels had been worth to him.

It was in the mind of the rajah to repay Larazoff for his services, with a stroke of his keen scimitar. But he knew that when he came, at last, a fugitive and a refugee, to Moscow, he might need the rascally agent yet, and he dismissed the thought from his mind.

There was a splash in the stream below, and the rajah turned his glance again down the slope of the rocky nullah.

A tiny boat appeared there, coming down the stream, with Nally Das rowing. Nally Das drew the boat to shore, tied it up, and mounted the rocky slope, to the high bank where the rajah stood.

He salaamed respectfully to the Rajah.

Kidnapper, plotter, assassin, as the Hindu kam-dar was, he was a loyal servant of his master, faithful to him in his fallen fortunes. His manner was as full of slavish respect now, as when he had salaamed to his master in his palace. The rajah gave him a gloomy look.

"I have succeeded, Huzoor!" said Nally Das, in his own tongue. "I have the boat—and the way is open for us to go without leaving traces for the men of Bhanipur to follow."

Baji Rao nodded.

For long hours Nally Das had been absent front the camp; and he had returned successful. The rajah noted that there was blood on the haft of the kam-dar's knife—blood on his linen garments. But he asked no questions The boat had been obtained, and that was all that was necessary. The life of some wretched mountain peasant was not likely to weigh in the estimation of the Rajah Baji Rao.

But his look was still gloomy. Flight only could save him—rapid flight leaving no trail for the pursuer. But the rajah's thoughts were with what he left behind; the fair kingdom and City of Bhanipur over which he had hoped to rule; the castle and lands that had been his own, and which he might have kept had he refused to listen to Bolshevik counsels of evil. Like the dog in the fable, he had snatched at the shadow, and lost the substance. Life was dear; but the prospect before him was dark enough— a fugitive in a strange, half-savage land.

"No time should be lost, Huzoor," said Nally Das. "The horses and the chaukees would be useless in a flight over the great mountains—they must be left here. The boat will carry three."

Baji Rao nodded again.

"Huzoor! " panted Nally Das as Hurree Jamset Ram Singh and his men gained on the two fugitives. "Save yourself! " The rajah rushed on, but Nally Das, tulwar in hand, threw himself in the way of the leading pursuers, and there was a wild clashing of steel.

"There is no help!" he said. "We must go. And yet—" His hand was on the gem-incrusted hilt of his scimitar, and his fierce glance turned back towards the direction of distant Bhanipur.

Larazoff rose, and threw away a half-smoked cigarette.

"You have the boat—good," he said. "Let us lose no time. The chaukees can save themselves—it matters little. Come."

The rajah did not answer, or stir. His fierce glance was still turned back upon the forest, far beyond which lay the white walls of Bhanipur.

The Russian touched him impatiently on the arm.

"Come!" he repeated. "We waste time."

"Chup raho!" rapped out Nally Das fiercely. "Slave! Do you give orders to the Huzoor?"

Lazaroff stared at him for a moment, and then laughed. In the situation of the fugitives, the Hindu's unabated respect for his master roused his mocking derision.

"Fool!" he answered. "There is no more 'Highness' here—we are all running for our lives; and his highness will be fortunate to escape with as much as that and to live on the bounty of my friends in Moscow. Give me no more of that. Let us go—you hear me, Baji Rao?"

Nally Das, dusky hand went to the knife in his girdle. At that moment, there was a sudden exclamation from the rajah.

"Too late!"

"What—"

"Look!" said Baji Rao bitterly.

The chaukees in the camp had leaped up suddenly. From the edge of the forest came a gleaming of weapons, a glimmer of turbans. The rajah's men grasped their tulwars; it was the enemy.

Lazaroff spun round, and stared at the forest, scarce a hundred yards distant, a score of dusky troopers could be seen, and among them, white faces—the faces of the Greyfriars juniors. Mahbub, the shikaree, was pointing.

The Russian gave one rapid glance; and then he went trampling down the stony nullah towards the boat. Nally Das had moored in the stream.

Baji Rao grasped his scimitar.

"Huzoor!" panted Nally Das. "Save yourself!"

He shouted to the chaukees, and the five ruffianly retainers of the rajah shouted back. There was a sudden crackling of rifle-fire. The desperadoes were facing the advancing troopers from Bhanipur.

"Come, come!" breathed Nally Das.

For a second the rajah hesitated; then he rushed down the slope into the nullah, by the side of the Hindu kam-dar. Life was dear.

Behind them came a rattling of rifles, and loud yells, and the clash of steel. Hurree Jamset Ram Singh and his men were coming on fast, and it was only for a few seconds that the rajah's chaukees stood up against overwhelming odds.

Leaving his men to deal with the chaukees, Hurree Jamset Ram Singh passed them, and rushed on the track of the fleeing rajah.

Harry Wharton & Co. followed him fast, and five or six of the soldiers of Bhanipur.

Down the steep, rocky slope into the nullah the rajah rushed, with Nally Das by his side.

Lazaroff had already reached the moored boat; and plunged into it. He was sawing at the grass rope, by which it was moored to the bank, with his knife. The moment the rope parted the Russian would flee—without waiting a second for his associates. Nally Das glanced back desperately.

A dozen yards of rocky slope still separated the fugitives from the boat; and the pursuers were almost in touch. Two of the most powerful of the Bhanipur soldiers were bounding like roes on the track. And they had nearly reached the fleeing rajah and his kam-dar.

"Huzoor! Save yourself!" panted Nally Das.

And he turned back.

The rajah rushed on; Nally Das, tulwar in hand, threw himself in the way of the leading pursuers, and there was a wild clashing of steel. One of the soldiers went down, slashed by the kam-dar's tulwar; and Nally Das engaged the other at close quarters. Kidnapper and rascal as the man was, he was giving his life to save his master. A few moments, and five or six tulwars were flashing round him, and Nally Das, fighting like a tiger, was borne down, under raining blows, and gasped for his life.

But he had gained time for his master; the Rajah Baji Rao leaped into the boat, even as Nally Das fell under the slashing steel.

The grass-rope parted under the knife of the Russian.

The boat leaped out into the rapid, whirling waters, torn away from the bank by the racing current.

Lazaroff seized an oar to steady the rocking boat, the Rajah Baji Rao stared back, with savagely-gleaming eyes, at the receding bank. On the rocks of the nullah stood Hurree Jamset Ram Singh, scimitar in hand, and the fleeing rajah shook a furious fist at the schoolboy nabob. Three or four rifles cracked out, and the bullets splashed into the water round the racing boat; but a minute more, and the winding of the nullah and the overhanging mangoes hid it from sight.

The Rajah Baji Rao had escaped!

126

A Narrow Escape!

"I SAY, you fellows!"

"Tired?" grinned Bob.

"Ow! Yes!" groaned Bunter.

It was night in the jungle.

Hurree Jamset Ram Singh and his followers were still in pursuit of the fleeing rajah and his solitary companion. But as the stars of midnight glistened over the wide-spreading jungle the pursuers had halted for a brief rest.

Mahbub, the chief shikaree, was the guide. Mahbub knew every hill and valley, ghaut and nullah, from Kashmir and the Terai to the great passes of the Himalayas. The rajah had escaped, but Mahbub knew precisely where the fugitives would be compelled to abandon the mountain stream, where great rocks barred the water, and it fell in a cascade in which no boat could live. And for that spot, to cut off the fleeing rajah if possible, Hurree Singh and his party were heading through the jungle. If the rajah and the Russian landed and took to the mountains on foot again the shikaree would be on their trail; relentlessly the pursuit was to go on.

The grim determination of the schoolboy nabob did not surprise his chums. They had already learned that in his native land Hurree Singh was not exactly like old Inky of the Remove.

The rajah was to suffer for his crime, if only to leave Bhanipur in peace when the nabob returned to Greyfriars.

The chums of the Remove did not blame their dusky comrade, though this grim relentlessness was a trait in Inky's character that they liked least. But they knew he was right; justice had to be done. The plotting rajah, whose reckless ambition might have plunged Bhanipur into civil war and bloodshed; the scheming Russian who had sought to carry the evil influence of the Bolsheviks over the Indian frontier, both had to be prevented from working further harm.

The pursuers were proceeding on foot—the thick and tangled jungle was impossible for horses. To Mahbub and his shikarees it was nothing, and the hardy soldiers of Bhanipur tramped on cheerily, while Hurree Jamset Ram Singh, slim and lightly-built as he was, seemed impervious to fatigue. Harry Wharton & Co. were tired, there was no doubt about that, but they stood it out manfully. It was Billy Bunter who groused, and Billy Bunter who, as usual, proved himself a helpless passenger.

Bunter was simply incapable of tramping long miles through the jungle, and he declined to entertain the idea of being sent back to the city under a dusky escort. It was fixed in Bunter's fat mind that no "native " was to be trusted And as he could not be left alone in the jungle—in which case he would certainly have furnished a meal for a hungry tiger before dawn—he had to accompany the party in their prolonged pursuit of the rajah. A dhooly was constructed of bamboos cut in the jungle by the keen knives of the shikarees, and the fat junior was carried in the dhooly, slung on the shoulders of two stalwart natives. Bunter had the easiest time of the party, but Bunter's voice was the only one that was raised in complaint. That, however, was only to be expected.

In the midnight halt Bunter sat with his back to the dhooly and consumed provisions at a great rate. A campfire had been lighted, and it blazed cheerily against the black sky. Night in the jungle was sharply cold after the glowing heat of the day. Harry Wharton & Co. gathered round the fire in cheery spirit. They were tired, but they were enjoying the adventure. At a little distance from the Greyfriars party the Bhanipur soldiers were camped, and round the camp, hidden in the shadows, Mahbub and his shikarees kept watch and ward.

Somewhere in the trackless jungle, probably many a long mile distant, Colonel Wharton and his party were seeking the fleeing rajah. Since they had parted earlier in the day, no word had passed between the two parties of hunters, but at the nullah Hurree Singh had dispatched two of the shikarees to seek the colonel and inform him that the track of the fugitives had been found. But there was no time to wait for the colonel to rejoin them. The pursuit went on under the command of the nabob, and Inky of the Remove showed that he was quite equal to the occasion.

"We shall enjoyfully take an hour's sleep, my esteemed chums," said the nabob. "After that we go on again fully. Perhaps by morning the hunt will be completefully finished."

"An hour?" said Bunter.

"Precisefully."

"You mean twelve hours," grunted Bunter.

"I mean exactfully one hour, my esteemed fat Bunter."

"Look here, Inky—" bawled Bunter.

"Oh, cheese it, Bunter!" said Harry Wharton. "Why the thump didn't you stay in the palace, as we advised you?"

"Yah!"

"Too late now," said Bob. "You can get back to Bhanipur, if you like. Kasi Jee will guide you."

"Rats!"

"Or stay here," suggested Johnny Bull. "Think what a morsel you would be to a tiger who hadn't had his supper Bunter."

"Ha, ha, ha!"

Bunter shuddered.

"Oh, really, Bull—"

"Dash it all, Bunter, you've got nothing to grouse about, when you're carried in a dhooly while we're walking," said Nugent.

"I'm tired."

"Have another supper, old fat bean, and shut up."

"This is what you call gratitude. I suppose?" said Bunter bitterly. "I really expected something better than this from you. Inky, after all I've done for you."

"My esteemed, idiotic Bunter—"

"Shall we bump him?" asked Bob Cherry, looking round at his chums. "Why not give him something to grouse about?"

"Hear, hear!"

"Oh, really, Cherry—"

"Hallo!" said Bob Cherry, with an alarmed look, pointing to a dried twig that lay near the fire. "Yaroooh!" roared Bunter, thinking at once that it was a deadly reptile. "Help!" He plunged round the camp fire and crashed into Hurree Jamset Ram Singh. Clasping the nabob round the neck, he dragged him over in his fall.

"Well, I'm for a snooze," said Johnny Bull, rising and yawning. "If it's only for an hour, let's make the most of it."

And Johnny rolled himself in a blanket with his feet to the campfire and closed his eyes.

"Good egg!" assented Bob.

"Gimme some blankets!" grunted Bunter. "It's jolly cold here. Rotten country—toasting you by day and freezing you by night. I say, you fellows, are there any snakes about?"

"Lots!" grinned Bob.

"Look here, you beasts, you search for snakes!" exclaimed Bunter hotly. "You know I'm short-sighted, you rotters! Not that I'm afraid of snakes."

"Hallo, hallo, hallo! What's that?" ejaculated Bob Cherry with an alarmed look, pointing to a dried twig that lay near the fire.

"Yarooooh!"

It was only a dried twig, but to Bunter it was a deadly reptile. He gave a wild bound to escape.

"Ha, ha, ha!"

"Yaroooh! Help!"

Bunter plunged round the campfire and crashed into Hurree Jamset Ram Singh. He threw his arms round the nabob to keep himself from falling, and dragged Hurree Singh over in his full.

"Ow!" roared Inky.

"Grooogh!"

"Ha, ha, ha!"

Crack!

The sharp ring of a rifle came from the jungle in the midst of the exclamations from Bunter and the nabob, and the laughter of the other juniors.

The bullet whizzed by the campfire and struck the trunk of a mango in a direct line with the spot where Hurree Jamset Ram Singh had been standing.

The nabob's sudden and unexpected fall, in Bunter's grasp, had saved him from the whizzing bullet.

The laughter died away instantly.

"What!" exclaimed Wharton.

"The enemy!"

The camp was in commotion at once. From the shadowy jungle came the shouts of the shikarees. Hurree Jamset was on his feet at once. Bunter remained where he was; he he considered that he was safer on the ground, while shooting was going on; and undoubtedly he was right. In the jungle crack on crack of ringing rifles sounded, and a loud and terrible cry rang from the shadows of the night.

The juniors grasped their rifles and stared about them. In spite of the watchfulness of the shikarees, an enemy had crept near the place in the darkness—near enough to take a shot at the nabob in the glow of the camp-fire. Mahhub came panting from the jungle into the radius of flickering light.

"Huzoor!"

Hurree Jamset Ram Singh questioned the shikaree in Hindustani. He knew how narrow his escape had been; but hardly a muscle of his face flickered. From the jungle came two of the shikarees, bearing a still form—that of one of their comrades, with a deep crimson stain on his garments. They laid the body down; it did not move again.

"What has happened. Inky?" exclaimed Bob breathlessly as Mahbub vanished into the jungle again.

"Someone—an enemy—got through the sentries, creeping like a snake in the jungle grasses," said the nabob quietly. "They did not see him till he had fired. A Englishman, Mahbub says—they saw him as he fled. It must have been the esteemed and execrable Lazaroff."

"He got away?"

"One of the shikarees seized him." Hurree Singh pointed to the still form that lay in the grass. "The man used his knife and fled. He has escaped; but this proves that we are close on them, my esteemed chums. So close to them that we shall not stay here to rest as I intended. But if my esteemed chums would sleep I will leave a guard—"

"Rats!" said Bob Cherry promptly. "We're going on if you do, Inky."

"Yes, rather."

Bunter sat up.

"Are they gone?" he gasped.

"There, was only one, and he has gone," said Nugent.

"Good! As for going on, that's all rot!" said Bunter. "I'm going to sleep, see?"

"The esteemed Bunter must try to sleep in the dhooly," said the nabob gently; and he rapped out orders to his men.

The fire was trampled out, and the men of Bhanipur prepared at once to resume the march.

"You'll be all right in the dhooly, Bunter," said Harry, with rather usual cordiality. "Make yourself comfortable, old bean. We'll shove in the blankets for you."

Bunter blinked at him.

"You're jolly concerned about me all of a sudden," he grunted.

"That's all right; let me help you in."

Bunter was helped into the dhooly and made comfortable there, in a state of great astonishment. The way was resumed, the dhooly swinging on the shoulders of two stout shikaree. Bunter sprawled in it on the blanket wondering, till he realized, at last, that once more he had proved unexpectedly useful. He put his head out of the dhooly.

"I say, you fellows—"

"Hallo, hallo, hallo!"

"I've saved Inky's life."

"Another happy accident!" grinned Johnny Bull.

"If I hadn't pulled him over just then that fellow would have got him," said Bunter. "That bullet was meant for Inky."

"Quitefully so, my esteemed Bunter," said the nabob. "The thankfulness is terrific. Oncefully more the esteemed and idiotic Bunter has turned up trumpfully."

"Jolly lucky for you I came along." said Bunter. "I suppose you fellows thought I was scared about a snake. Well, I wasn't. I pulled Inky over just in time to save his life. My wonderful presence of mind, you know."

"Oh, my hat!" gasped Bob.

"That's me all over—the right man in the right place," said Bunter. "Presence of mind is what does it—you can always rely on me for that."

"Oh!"

And Bunter settled down in the dhooly again, very pleased and satisfied with himself. And Harry Wharton & Co. forbore to tell him what they thought of him. The pursuers marched on, by tangled jungle paths, under the glittering Indian stars, to an accompaniment of deep snoring from the dhooly.

127

The Rajah's Fate!

SERGE LAZAROFF tramped savagely through the jungle, breathing hard. His dark face was wet with perspiration; his clothes torn and rent by thorns. Ahead of him was the sound of falling water, guiding the Russian to the spot where he had left Baji Rao.

He emerged from the jungle at last, and tramped across stony ground, to a spot where a mango tree grew beside the falling stream. Under the tree, wrapped in his cloak, the Rajah Baji Rao lay sleeping.

With footfalls as quiet as those of a cat or a lurking tiger, the Russian approached the tree, and halted, looking down with a grim face upon the sleeping rajah.

The two fugitives were in desperate plight now.

The flight by the mountain stream had saved them, for the time. But the boat had gone over the cascade; and they had barely struggled ashore with their lives. Lazaroff would have pushed on, anxious to put all the distance possible between himself and pursuit. But the rajah was not capable of the exertion.

Baji Rao had lived in ease and Eastern luxury, seldom stirring from his palace save on the back of an elephant, or in a luxurious palanquin borne on the shoulders of his slaves. The hard and wearing life of the jungle was not for the pampered Eastern despot, with his slack and flabby muscles, unused to performing even the simplest services for himself. Baji Rao had stopped to rest; and Lazaroff had stopped also; and while the rajah rested he had turned back on the pursuers.

The hardy, reckless adventurer was no coward; he had taken his life in his hands in a desperate attempt to stop the pursuit, and turn the tables on the enemy, by shooting down the Nabob of Bhanipur.

Fortune had favoured the Bolshevik; he had failed to kill the nabob, but he had escaped from the shikarees with his life.

Now he stood looking down on the sleeping rajah, and the expression on his black-browed, aquiline face might have alarmed Baji Rao had he seen it. But the rajah's eyes were closed in the sleep of utter weariness.

There was a chance yet for the Russian; he was hardy, tireless, resolute, unscrupulous. There was yet a chance for such a man to escape by the mountain passes; but, cumbered with the rajah, there was no chance, and he knew it. The man whose life had been spent in luxurious indolence was not the man for so terrible a journey. Unpursued, escape would have boon difficult, but possible; but with the pursuers close on the track, the days, if not the hours, of Baji Rao were numbered.

The rajah did not realize it; but if was clear enough to the companion of his flight. Neither did the rajah realize that the position was now changed; that he, the once haughty rajah, was now a helpless encumbrance upon the man who had been his spy and scheming adviser and humble sycophant. There were terrible thoughts in the savage mind of the Bolshevik as he stood looking down on the sleeping man.

He stooped over Baji Rao, and softly, quietly, released the scimitar from his girdle. The scimitar Baji Rao's only weapon, was flung far into the mountain stream; it vanished with a light splash into the water.

Light as the sound was, it awakened Baji Rao.

The rajah's eyes opened, and he stared about him, and called out in Hindustani.

Lazaroff grinned savagely.

The rajah, for the moment, supposed that he was in his palace, and that obsequious slaves awaited his call.

But recollection came the next moment, as the mists of slumber cleared away. Baji Rao sat up, leaning against the mango, and stared at the Russian with evil glinting eyes.

"You are not in your palace now, Huzoor!" said the Russian adventurer with grim irony.

Baji Rao read death in the mocking eyes of the traitor whose evil counsels had brought him ruin. He sprang like a tiger, and so swift was his spring that Lazaroff, watchful as he was, was taken almost by surprise. Before he could fire two dusky hands closed on his throat in a savage grip.

"You have seen them?" asked the rajah. He remembered that Lazaroff had gone to scout for the pursuers when he laid down to rest.

Lazaroff nodded.

"I have seen them."

"And where?"

"Five miles from here; and it seems that they know where to seek us," said Lazaroff. "Had luck befriended me, I should have stopped them—my bullet missed the nabob by inches."

The rajah snarled, "Fool! Fool and bungler, as usual! But for your counsels, I should never be here!" he exclaimed savagely. "You have brought me to this—you and your rascally friends in Moscow. I have been a tool in your hands—my lands taken from me, my life in danger, to give the Bolshevik scoundrels a footing on the Indian frontier! A thousand curses—"

The Russian laughed.

"You were willing enough.to make a bid for the nabob's throne," he said. "You opened your ears gladly enough to Bolshevik counsels, Baji Rao. Had all gone well you would be reigning now in Bhanipur as nabob. Would you have reproached me then, weakling that you are?"

"Insolent slave!"

The Russian laughed again.

Even in fleeing for his life Baji Rao was still the proud and domineering despot. The change in his situation had made no change in his nature. Through the flight the Russian had had to listen to bitter reproaches and words of scorn. That mattered little to the adventurer so long as he had a purpose to serve. But the rajah was useless to him now; he had become a danger and an encumbrance. And all the bitter insults, all the lofty scorn and contempt, were stored up in Lazaroff's mind, to be repaid now that the time had come, "Listen to me, Baji Rao," he said.

"Dog! To you I am Huzoor!" said the rajah, his black eyes gleaming at the Russian.

"Fool!" said Lazaroff. "Listen to me! Only a few miles separate us from the enemy, and you—you are helpless burden on my hands. One day more in the jungles and the ghauts, and you will sink down like some helpless infant! I have finished with you, Baji Rao! You will never live to reach Moscow, where you would be useful to us, if only as an agent to stir up discontent in India. You will perish in the mountain passes if you escape the pursuit. I go —but I go alone!"

"Go, then!" said the rajah. "Son of a dog, go!"

The Russian eyed him, with an evil light in his eyes. Lazaroff's hand was in his ragged cummerbund; it grasped a revolver hidden from sight there.

Baji rao staggered to his feet. He was worn with weariness, but he was still the savage-tempered, haughty rajah.

"Dog!" he repeated. "Do you dare to bandy words with me, a prince of India? You, who have crawled at my feet!"

'The Bolshevik knows how to crawl until he can stand and issue commands!" said the Russian, laughing. "It is I who give orders now, Baji Rao!"

The rajah's eyes blazed, and he groped for his scimitar. A change came over his face as he found that his weapon was gone. He made a fierce stride towards the Russian, his hands clenched; but stopped suddenly as Lazaroff's hand came out of his cummerbund with a glinting revolver in it.

Baji Rao breathed hard, showing his white teeth like a tiger at bay.

"I go," said the Russian coolly; "but first hand me the packet of jewels concealed in your breast, Baji Rao!

"You would rob me, then?" hissed the rajah.

"Of what use will they be to you when the jackals and the vultures dispute for your bones?" grinned Lazaroff.

The rajah made a furious movement, and the revolver rose to a level.

"The jewels, or—"

The rajah set his teeth. He understood now—at long last, he knew that the jewels would not save his life.

Lazaroff intended to flee alone, but he did not intend to leave behind him a man who, if by chance he survived, would be a bitter enemy. The Bolshevik was fleeing now; but his treacherous work in India was not done. Baji Rao read death in the mocking eyes of the traitor whose evil counsels had brought him to ruin.

He sprang like a tiger.

So swift was the spring that Lazaroff, watchful as he was, was taken almost by surprise. The rajah reached him before he could pull trigger, and two dusky hands closed on him in a savage grip.

Lazaroff reeled back in the grasp of the rajah, and went heavily to the ground. Baji Rao was upon him, grasping at his throat.

Crack!

The report of the revolver, touching the breast of the rajah as Lazaroff fired, was followed by a deep groan.

Baji Rao rolled from the Russian, and rolled on the ground.

Lazaroff sprang to his feet, panting. The revolver was turned towards the stretched form on the ground, but a second shot was not needed. Baji Rao did not stir again.

The Russian shrugged his shoulders.

He bent over the rajah, and rose again with the packet of jewels—all that remained to the fleeing rajah of his treasures—in his grasp. Then, without another glance at the fallen man, Lazaroff turned, and tramped away—and the night swallowed him.

128

The End of the Trail

HALLO hallo, hallo!" Mahbub, the shikaree, came speeding back. The dusky face of Mahbub was ablaze with excitement as he gabbled Hindustani to the nabob.

Harry Wharton & Co. listened, without understanding. They could see that the shikaree, who had been scouting ahead, had brought back startling news; but the language he spoke was a sealed book to them.

Hurre Jamset Ram Singh turned to his comrades, with a strange expression on his face.

"Our task is done," he said.

"Mahbub has found them?" asked Harry.

"One of them—the rajah," said Hurree Jamset Ram Singh. "Let us go on, my esteemed chums! It was written that my kinsman should not fall by my hand; but Baji Rao's plotting will never trouble my kingdom again."

The Greyfriars party pushed on, asking no more questions. Bunter's deep snore still rumbled from the dhooly.

The sound of falling water came to their ears, echoing through the dim night. They emerged from the jungle at last. Ahead of them a cascade flashed and glittered in the gleam of the stars. Under a mango tree by the water a dozen shirkarees were gathered round some object that lay still on the ground. The shikarees parted respectfully, as Hurree Jamset Ram Singh approached. "Good heavens!" muttered Bob, his face paling. "The rajah!"

It was the Rajah Baji Rao, stretched still and silent under the mango.

Already the jackals had been there, but the hapless rajah was still easily to be recognized.

"Dead!" said Hurree Jamset Ram Singh, and his face was grave as he stood looking down upon his enemy, who was never to trouble him or his kingdom more. "But how?" muttered Nugent.

"Mahbub knows," said the nabob. "He was shot down at close quarters—with a revolver. The Bolshevik—

"The awfull villain!" breathed Bob. "He turned on him then." Hurree Singh nodded.

"But where is the Russian?"

"Fled! But the son of a dog shall not escape!" said Hurree Singh, his eyes gleaming. "He is unworthy of our trouble; but Mahbub and his men shall follow him with a reward of a thousand rupees for his head." Mahbub and a dozen shikarees were already taking the track of the Russian desperado. They vanished along the stream, and the jungle swallowed them from sight; bloodhounds on the track of the Bolshevik, whose face was set towards the North.

Hurree Jamset Ram Singh gave orders to the soldiers. A palanquin was constructed of wood cut in the jungle, and the body of the rajah placed in it, to be borne back to Bhanipur for interment. Rebel and plotter as Baji Rao bad been, he was to sleep with his ancestors in the tombs of the Nabobs of Bhanipur.

The Greyfriars party camped by the edge of the stream.

The palanquin, on the shoulders of half a dozen bearers, bore away the body of the rajah, whose ambition and tortuous plotting and faith in the faithless schemers of Moscow had cost him lands and life. Hurree Jamset Ram Singh sat under the mango tree, enfolded in his cloak, with a thoughtful expression on his face, wakeful long after the other juniors had slept.

From the jungle came the howls of jackals and the deeper voice of a tiger, prowling at a distance, sounds that died away in the dawn. Closer at hand was the undisturbed snore of Billy Bunter, rolled in blankets and sleeping like a top. The Nabob of Bhanipur was thinking as he sat, wakeful thinking of the mission that had brought him to Bhanipur, the danger of losing his kingdom, the plotting of Baji Rao, and of his kam-dar, Nally Das. The Jam Bahadur had called him home from England. But the need was past now. The rajah had paid for all. Nally Das had fallen. The agent of the

Bolsheviks was fleeing for the mountains, with relentless pursuers on his track, his life forfeit for his crimes.

Once more the schoolboy nabob was free to return to Greyfriars, leaving his kingdom, as before, under the governing of his uncle, the Jam Bahadur, untroubled further by plotters and schemers. After many perils the school boy nabob had triumphed over his enemies. Danger had been close, but it was over now, and Hurree Jamset Ram Singh was able to think of his false and ambitions kinsman without bitterness, and to forgive him now that he had paid the last penalty.

The schoolboy nabob lay down to sleep at last. The sun rose higher in the heavens, the jungle day brightened. Hot sunshine streamed down over stream and jungle, and the thousand voices of the day awoke.

Hurree Jamset Ram Singh had been the last of the party to sleep, but he was the first to awaken. He rose and threw aside his cloak and stood in the brilliant sunshine. He looked at the tangled jungle, at the cascading stream in the rocks of the nullah, at the great hills that rose range on range to the north, at the mighty peaks of the Himalayas beyond all..

His brow was clouded with thought. This was his land—his homeland—in England, at Greyfriars, much as he loved the old school, he was a pilgrim and a stranger. He sighed.

"Hallo, hallo, hallo!"

Bob Cherry threw off his blankets and jumped up.

Hurree Singh looked at him, with a smile.

"Jolly near noon, I think," said Bob.

"We have had a long rest," said the nabob. "We needed it, my esteemed chum. We have many miles to go before we reach the camp where we left the horses."

Bob looked at him curiously. He had heard the sigh of the schoolboy nabob.

"Not feeling down, Inky?" he asked.

The nabob shook his head.

"If you're thinking about the rajah, he deserved it, and a lot more," said Bob. "Don't worry about that."

Hurree Jamset Ram Singh smiled faintly.

"I am not worrying about that, my esteemed Bob. It was written that Baji Rao sshould find his death in the jungle."

"What's the trouble, then?" asked Bob.

The nabob did not reply. But again his wistful glance swept the jungle and the hills and the snow-clad Himalayas.

"You want to come back to Greyfriars?" said Bob.

"Ye-es."

"I understand," said Bob softly.

"This country is your home, old chap. You feel about it as we do about. England. But some day you'll come back here to reign as a giddy nabob, and in the meantime it's jolly at Greyfriars. We shall be back in time for the new term and the footer."

Hurree Singh nodded.

"Think of a jolly old rag in the Remove passage!" said Bob. "We'll wake up the Fourth as soon as we get back. We'll jolly well rag Coker of the Fifth—what?" The nabob grinned. "We'll beat Highcliffe at footer and mop up St. Jim's and Rookwood," said Bob. "Won't it be jolly to trot round the old quad again and roll Bunter along the Remove passage?"

The nabob chuckled.

"My esteemed chum is right," he said. "The jollifulness will be terrific."

"I say, you fellows!"

"Hallo, hallo, hallo! Bunter's awake," said Bob. "And I'll bet you two to one in doughnuts that he's hungry."

"The fact is. I'm rather peckish," said Bunter, groping for his spectacles and jamming them on his fat little nose. "What about brekker?"

"Time for tiffin," chuckled Bob. "You can have brekker and tiffin all in one, Bunter. Hallo, hallo, hallo! Turn out you slackers!"

The Greyfriars party turned out and sat down to tiffin under the mango tree. After tiffin they started Bunter in the dhooly, the others walking. Late in the afternoon they reached the camp where the sayecs had been left with the horses, and mounted to ride back to Bhanipur. It was night when they reached the city, where they found Colonel Wharton. The colonel had received news of the end of the trail and had returned to Bhanipur. The old military gentleman was glad enough to see the juniors safe and sound again. The Jam Bahadur beamed on the party when they arrived. Evidently the Jam was greatly relieved by the news that he had received from the jungle, and had no regrets to waste on the ambitious rajah. Billy Bunter rolled away to his apartment followed by the obsequious Kasi Jee. He sat down for the naukar to take off his boots, blinking sleepily at him.

"James!"

"Han sahib!" murmured the naukar.

"I shall be leaving Bhanipur soon now." The naukar placed his hands on his breast in an attitude of deep sorrow.

"The heart of Kasi Jee is heavy, sahib," he said.

Bunter nodded with approval.

Since the Owl of the Remove had received the magnificent gifts of the nabob Kasi Jee had been unalterably attached to him. He received good words and bad words from Bunter with thankful submission, and even seemed to feel honoured when Bunter kicked him. Bunter's impression was that it was the kickings that had done it. That was, according to Bunter, the way to treat "natives," and he had no doubt of the attachment of Kasi Jee. James, as he called him, was, as he had told the chums of the Remove, his faithful native; and Bunter liked the idea of having a faithful native to obey his lightest order and anticipate his lordly wishes. Kasi Jee, on the other hand, doubtless had his own reasons for his faithful attachment to Bunter. But it was easy to pull the leg of the Owl of the Remove.

Bunter only required flattery, and plenty of it, and flattery did not cost the wily Hindu much.

"Don't want to part with me—what?" said Bunter.

"Kasi Jee will mourn when he sees no more the handsome, magnificent sahib!" murmured the naukar.

Quite so!" agreed Bunter. "Well, I'm thinking of taking you with me, James."

"Sahib!"

"I mean it," said Bunter, with a wave of his fat hand. "You're going to be my faithful native. See?"

Kasi Jee's eyes gleamed for a moment. Bunter's experience of India had not yet taught him that the natives did not like being called natives. But the naukar salaamed respectfully.

"Like the idea what?" asked Bunter.

"The joy in the heart of Kasi Jee is immense, sahib."

"Good!"

Bunter rolled to his bed. "Put the mosquito-net over me, James. Fathead! Don't bung your silly elbow in my eyes. Take that!"

"Oh!"

Kasi Jee took it and sat down, his dusky ear ringing with the smack. Bunter rolled into bed and was soon snoring. The naukar looked at him and went softly and silently from the room, smiling.

The following morning, when Harry Wharton looked out of his window into the courtyard of the palace, he caught sight of Mahbub, the shikaree. The man had just come in, tired and dusty from the jungle and the road, and on his shoulder he carried a rice sack. Somehow or other Harry's gaze riveted on the sack. With a grinning face, Mahbub stopped to speak to the guards, and opened the neck of the rice-sack to show them the content. From the distance Harry could not see clearly, but he had a glimpse of something that made his face turn white and brought a sick feeling to his heart. Mahbub shouldered the sack, again and disappeared under the arches towards the shikarees' quarters. Harry was still standing at the window, with a white face, when Bob Cherry clapped him on the shoulder.

"What's the row?" asked Bob, surprised by his look.

"Mahbub has just come in."

"And—"

"He had something in a sack," said Harry, with a shiver. "You remember that a thousand rupees was offered for the head of Lazaroff."

Bob nodded silently, and Wharton turned from the window. When the juniors met Hurree Jamset Ram Singh later in the morning. Johnny Bull asked him if there was any news of the Bolshevik Fugitive. A grim smile for a moment flickered on the nabob's face. "The Russian will never reach Moscow," he said. "He will never plot again among the people of India."

And the juniors made no further inquiry; but Harry knew what had been in the rice-sack on Mahbub's shoulder that morning. The shikaree had earned his reward.

129

The Faithful Native!

"A THOUSAND pounds!"

"Which?"

"A thousand quid, at least."

Billy Bunter sat in his apartment a few days later making up his packages for the road.

Bright days in Bhanipur had followed the end of the long struggle between the nabob and the rajah. Danger was over, trouble had passed like a summer cloud, and the chums of the Remove enjoyed to the full their days in the palace of Hurree Jamset Ram Singh.

But the best of things must come to an end, and the time drew nigh for the juniors to take their leave of Bhanipur. They had enjoyed their stay in the little mountain kingdom; they had had a good time there. But they were looking forward to seeing Greyfriars again, to treading the old quadrangle, ragging in the studies, urging the flying ball on the football field. They had time to reach England for the new term, and they were ready to go. Billy Bunter, indeed, was very keen to get back to civilization, as he politely expressed it to Hurree Singh. For Bunter was a rich man now. Harry Wharton & Co. looked in on the fat junior, having finished their own packing, and found him seated with glittering jewels on his fat knees. Bunter had taken out the massive gold chain and the collar of diamonds that had been presented to him by the nabob, and he was fairly gloating over them. Bunter—involuntarily, but indubitably—had been useful when Hurree Singh had been a prisoner in the hands of his rival for a throne, and the nabob's reward had been princely.

But Bunter had no idea of keeping permanently the nabob's gifts. His idea was to turn them into hard cash as soon as he reached England, and now he was examining them and appraising their value. Kasi Jee, packing clothes for his master, watched him out of the corner of his eye with a greedy look. But he dropped his eyes at once as the juniors came in.

"A thousand quid, at least," said Bunter. "What do you fellows think? These things are worth a thousand quid?"

"Quite!" said Wharton dryly.

Bunter blinked at him.

"You wouldn't sell them, in my place?" he sneered.

"No business of mine what you do with them," said the captain of the remove.

"But you wouldn't?"

"As you ask me—no, I wouldn't!" said Harry curtly.

"Just like you!" said Banter scornfully. "You'd hoard 'em up, what?"

"I should not sell a gift unless I were jolly hard up, anyhow!" said Wharton.

"Well, it's not my way to hoard," said Bunter loftily. "I'm jolly well going to turn them into money as soon as I set foot in a civilised country, see? And my belief is that they'll fetch a thousand quid."

"Just like Bunter!" granted Johnny Bull.

"Oh really, Bull"

"Well, pack them up safely," said Harry. "There are plenty of people about who would like to get their hands on them, Bunter."

"You bet!" grinned Bunter. "I'm going to take jolly good care of them, and I've specially warned James to do the same!"

"James?" repeated Wharton.

"My faithful native." Said Bunter, with dignity.

"But Kasi Jee isn't coming with us is he?" said Bob cherry in surprise."

"I'm going to take him to England with me."

"My hat!"

"But he belongs to Bhanipur," said Nugent. "I fancy that he more or less is the property of Hurree Singh."

"All the better. I shall ask Inky to give him to me," said Bunter coolly. "Then he will be my property."

"You ass!" said Bob. "That's all very well in a native state; and, anyhow, you can't play that game in England!"

"James is attached to me," explained Bunter in an extremely

dignified manner. "I've kicked him into a proper state of mind. He's going to be my faithful nigger, like you read of in story books."

"Ha, ha, ha!" roared the juniors.

"You can cackle," said Bunter contemptuously. "I can tell you, I know how to deal with niggers and make 'em faithfully and attached and all that. My character impresses them."

"Ha ha ha!"

"So I'm taking James home with me," said Bunter. "I shall place him at–at Bunter Court when I go back to Greyfriars. Perhaps I might have him at the school—a fellow of my means ought to have a personal servant even at school. James knows his place and his manners." I've kicked him often enough for that."

"You inspire attachment by kicking him, do you?" asked Bob.

"It's the best way," explained Bunter. "Go easy with them, and they despise you. Kick 'em hard, and kick 'em often, and they'll die for you!"

"Could I make you attached to me the same way?" asked Bob, drawing back his foot.

Bunter dodged round the chair in a great hurry.

"Keep off, you beast!" he roared.

"Ha, ha, ha!"

"Come on, you fellows!" said Bob. "We'll make Bunter attached to the lot of us, as he's shown us the way. First kick to me."

"Yaroooh! Keep off!"

"Ha. ha. ha!"

"You cheeky beasts!" growled Bunter, behind the chair, and eyeing the juniors warily through his big spectacles. "I know you're jolly jealous because I've got a faithful native. Look here! You clear out, or I'll order my native to take his tulwar to you."

"Good old Bunter!" chuckled Bob. "We looked in to tell you we're starting in an hour. If you're not ready, you'll be left behind at Bhanipur with your faithful native. Like me to help pack?"

"My faithful native is doing my packing," said Bunter loftily. "You fellows can clear!"

And the juniors, chuckling, cleared. Bunter's belief that he was able to inspire Kasi Jee, or anyone else, with faithful and loyal attachment, struck them as exceedingly comic. Bunter had no doubts. He was convinced that his manly, masterful character was exactly calculated to inspire loyal attachment in a native." But the other fellows doubted very much whether Kasi Jee was likely to prove a faithful follower of the great William George.

However, they found that it was settled that Kasi Jee was to go. Hurree Jamset Ram Singh was, perhaps, a little surprised by Bunter's request, but he acceded at once.

"My esteemed Bunter," he said. "If you desirefully wish the services of the naukar, the worthy and ludicrous naukar is at your disposal. He can travel as far as Delhi on the way home—or Bombay—"

"I want him for keeps."

"Oh!" ejaculated the nabob.

"I suppose he belongs to you more or less, Inky," asked Bunter.

"Morefully or lessfully," assented the schoolboy nabob. "There is no slavery in India, my esteemed Bunter; but there are certain ancient customs and privileges. If the excellent Bunter desires to keep Kasi Jee, he shall keep him. "

"Then I'll take him to England," said Bunter. "Even if the Head won't let me have him at Greyfriars to wait on me, I can show him to the fellows there, and then send him to my pater's place, see?"

"Ha, ha, ha!" roared the nabob.

"What are you cackling at?" demanded Bunter.

Hurree Jamset Ram Singh had been quite taken by storm, by the idea of Bunter showing off his faithful attendant to the Grey friars fellows. But he became grave again at once.

"My esteemed Bunter, you shall take the naukar, and he shall accompany you faithfully to England, if he does not get lostfully mislaid by the way," he assured.

"That's settled, then," said Bunter.

And when Billy Bunter quitted the palace of Bhanipur, he took with him, not only his gold chain and his collar of jewels, but his faithful native over and above. He kicked Kasi Jee before starting, in order to leave no doubt in the native's mind as to who was who and what was what. But if William George Bunter had been able to discern the thoughts that were going on behind Kasi Jee's submissive smile, he would not have felt quite so assured about the faithfulness of his native.

Fortunately for his peace of mind, Billy Bunter was not a thought-reader.

130

Farewell to Bhanipur!

"HOMEWARD bound!" said Bob Cherry.

In the cool of the early evening, Hurree Jamset Ram Singh, nabob of Bhanipur, cast his farewell glance upon the palace of his fathers.

A splendid cavalcade paraded before the palace, to escort the nabob and the white sahibs as far as the frontier.

Five hundred troopers of Bhanipur, in their most gorgeous raiment, mounted round the towering elephant of the Jam Bahadur. Hurree Jamset Ram Singh mounted into the howdah with his uncle, while Harry Wharton & Co. packed into the colonel's car car, with Bunter and Colonel Wharton. Pandy Din, the khitmutghar, drove the baggage car; and he was accompanied by Kasi Jee, the faithful follower of William George Bunter. There was a blare of trumpets and a clash of cymbals, and the procession started down the street to the city gates amid salaaming crowds.

"We're going off in style!" grinned Bob Cherry.

"We've had a jolly time, take it all in all," said Harry Wharton. "I'm jolly glad we came home with Inky. We'd come along to Bhanipur again some day—what?"

"What ho!" said Bob.

"I mean to," said Bunter. "I've told Inky that I will be his prime minister when he is of age, and reigns in Bhanipur."

"Ha, ha, ha!"

"I suppose Inky jumped at the offer!" chuckled Nugent. "In fact, I think the jumpfulness must have been terrific."

"Ha, ha, ha!"

"Where's your jolly old treasure, Bunter?" asked Bob. "Is Kasi Jee carrying it for you?"

"No jolly fear!" said' Bunter promptly. "Kasi Jee is faithful, of course—deeply attached to his master. But I don't see trusting a thousand quids in his paws."

"Well, that shows a little sense, anyhow," grinned Bob. "It's barely possible that Kasi Jee might disappear over the horizon."

"Oh, he wouldn't leave me for anything," said Bunter confidently. "I don't expect you fellows to understand—there's nothing about you, you see, to inspire these deep and loyal attachments. It's different with me. All the same, I'm keeping the stuff about me; can't be too careful. I've got the things in an inside pocket. Kasi Jee offered to carry them for me."

"Oh!"

"Of course, he's glad to make himself useful in any way he can, being devoted to me."

"Hem!"

"But a fellow can't be too careful!" said Bunter, with a wise shake of the head.

On that point, the chums of the Remove agreed with Bunter. They had no faith whatever in Bunter's system of kicking a native into loyal attachment, and they could not help thinking that Kasi Jee probably had his own personal reasons for his willingness to accompany the Owl of the Remove from Bhanipur to far-off England—if indeed he was willing at all! It seemed to them probable that Kasi Jee had reasons of his own for leaving Bhanipur, and was very likely to drop out of the party before Bombay was reached. But they did not give the matter much thought; and certainly they did not guess what was actually working in the wily naukar's mind.

The cavalcade proceeded by easy stages to the frontier of Bhanipur. That night they camped in a "serai" half way to the frontier; and the next morning, in the cool before the sun was high, resumed the route. At noon they reached the frontier fortress of Bhanipur, and rested there till the heat of the day was past.

At this point, the Jam Bahadur had to part with his nephew, and turn back; beyond the border lay British territory. After that point, Hurree Jemset Ram Singh ceased to be the Eastern nabob, and was to become once more Inky of the Remove, and travel in the car with his chums.

The Jam Bahadur embraced the nabob affectionately and took his leave of him with speeches in flowing Hindustani. Then he remounted into the howdah on his tall elephant, after shaking hands all round with the juniors and the colonel. Then Mook Mookerjee, who had travelled with the party as far as the frontier, took his leave; but Hurree Singh's old moonshee, from whom he had learned English, made his farewells in that language. Harry Wharton &. Co. contrived to keep their faces very serious while the wise old moonshee talked in English.

"Being departful for country beyond the black water," said Mook Mookerjee. "Good fortune and prosper fullness accompany lord and master Nabob. May the sunshine of happifulness banish the cloudiness of adversity, and the hand of friendship avert the kick of calamity."

"Hear, hear!" murmured Bob.

"With friendly and ridiculous respect, I taking leave of white sahibs, friends of noble master and nabob," said Mook Mookerjee. "May you live forever in the shade of the palm trees in your native land; may you be blessed with many beautiful wives."

"Oh!"

"Thanks, old chap!" said Bob Cherry. "The thankfulness of our esteemed selves is terrific."

And Mook Mookerjee salaamed himself away.

There was a blare of trumpets; and the car rolled away on the road to Rawalpindi, and the Jam Bahadur and his troop turned back to Bhanipur. Hurree Jamset Ram Singh looked back, till the last turban of the troopers, and the tall elephant of the Jam, had vanished from sight.

Then he settled down in his seat in the car, with a somewhat pensive expression on his face.

He was silent for a long time, as the car rolled rapidly along the road over the mountain pass, with the Punjabi chauffeur at the wheel. Behind came the baggage cart driven by Pandy Din, with Kasi Jee sitting like an expressionless image of bronze beside the khitmutghar. The sun set behind the mountains; the moon sailed up, streaming silvery light over hill and ghaut and nullah.

A light gleamed by the roadside; the car halted.

"The dak!" said the colonel.

It was the dak bungalow, at which the party had rested for a night on their way to Bhanipur. It was to shelter them once more, on their homeward journey.

The khansama came out bowing and salaaming, beaming with smiles to greet the travelers.

"I say, you fellows, I'm hungry!" remarked Billy Bunter, as he rolled out of the car.

"Go hon!" murmured Bob.

"You fellows remember staying here on our way up to Bhanipur," said Bunter. "You remember what happened?"

"I remember you landed yourself in trouble, as usual," said Bob.

"Eh? Oh! Yes! I don't mean that, ass! I mean we had a ripping supper—topping! A pilau, I think they call it in their frightful language; but it was jolly good!"

"Ha, ha, ha!"

Evidently it was only that important matter that had lingered in Bunter's memory.

The khansama bowed and salaamed his guests into the dak, and there was a supper that satisfied even Bunter, after which the juniors turned into the rooms assigned to them. Harry Wharton had the pleasure—or otherwise—of sharing the room in which Bunter lay down to repose, and for some time he was kept awake by the powerful snore of the fat junior at close quarters.

He slumbered at last, however. Whether it was Bunter's hefty snore so close at hand, or some other cause, Wharton awakened about midnight, and he was conscious that, there was a movement in the room. The starlight glimmered in at the window through the netting and it showed a dim, dusky form that stooped by Bunter's bed.

Wharton sat up abruptly.

"What's that?" he exclaimed sharply.

"Who's there?" .

The dim form by Bunter's bed straightened up at once, and Wharton caught a gleam of glinting eyes.

"Sahib!"

"Is that Kasi Jee?" asked Harry, recognizing the voice.

"Han, sahib."

Harry peered suspiciously at the naukar in the gloom.

"What are you doing here?" he demanded.

"Kasi Jee come to see his master," murmured the soft, submissive voice of the naukar. "Me hearing Bunter Sahib making noise with nose in sleeping, and thinking him ill."

Wharton stepped out of his bed.

The explanation was more or less plausible, but the captain of the Remove was not satisfied. He did not quite trust the naukar; Kasi Jew was a little too submissive and cringing for his taste.

"Well, get out!" said Harry.

"To hear is to obey, sahib."

The naukar glided from the room.

Wharton fastened the bar of the door before he returned to bed. Whether the naukar was anxious about his snoring master, to whom he was so devotedly attached, or whether he had some other motive, he had no further chance that night of bestowing his attentions upon William George Bunter.

131

Bunter Asks for It!

HARRY WHARTON & CO. arrived at Rawalpindi the following day. From Rawalpindi the railroad bore them on their way to Lahore and Delhi. At the railway station Kasi Jee carried the personal baggage of William George Bunter—and the Owl of the Remove strutted considerably. He was the only fellow in the party who had a personal servant, the rest "whacking" out out the services of Pandy Din, the khitmutghar. This was exactly as it should be, in Bunter's opinion.

At the palace in Bhanipur the nabob's hospitably had been boundless; numberless dusky servants had waited on the orders of the sahibs, and Bunter had spread himself to a terrific extent. He missed it all now, but it was a consolation to have retained the special services of a faithful native. Bunter's fat swank made the other fellows smile, but the Owl of the Remove did not mind their smiles. He was, as he said, accustomed to jealousy and envy.

But Wharton had not forgotten the incident at the dak bungalow, and while they waited for the Lahore train he spoke seriously to Bunter on the subject. Bunter listened, with a mocking, fat grin. Bunter was the fellow who knew, so to speak, and he was not in need of advice from lesser intellects.

"Better send that chap back Bunter," said Harry.

"Rats!" said the Owl of the Remove derisively.

"Why do you think he has come with you?" asked Wharton.

"Devoted attachment—"

"You ass!"

"Go it!" said Bunter contemptuously.

"I'm used to this! Jealousy and envy all round!"

"Look here," said Harry quietly, "at the dak bungalow in the hills I woke up and found Kasi Jee in the room groping over your bed."

"Sahib!" murmured Kasi Jee. There was no answer, for the six Greyfriars juniors were sleeping soundly. "Sahib!" repeated the naukar in a louder voice. But still there was no answer. Kasi Jee grinned, and his black eyes glittered as he stooped over Bunter and his thievish fingers groped through the pockets of the slumbering Owl and withdrew something that glittered and sparkled.

"Well?"

"Well, I don't trust him!"

"You wouldn't!" said Binder. "You are suspicious"

Wharton breathed hard.

"Do have a little sense, Bunter'. The man must have some object in sticking to you like this."

"I've told you what it is. He's my faithful native."

"Oh dear!"

"It's character that does it," explained Bunter. "You'd never understand. Wharton; no native will ever become your faithful follower. Character does it—strong, masterful character and—"

"For goodness' sake, Bunter, don't be such a howling ass!" exclaimed the captain of the Remove impatiently. "Are you paying the man any wages?"

"Certainly not!"

"Then why should he stick to you?"

"Faithful natives don't need wages. A kind word from me makes him happy," said Bunter loftily. "Like the old song, you know, about somebody who wept with delight when you gave him a smile, and trembled with fear at your frown. See?"

"Have you got your jewels safe?"

"Eh? Yes!"

"Well, Kasi Jee was not nosing in the room for nothing," said Harry. "He said he thought you were ill, and was anxious about you—"

"Quite right! He's so devotedly attached, you see—"

"It looks to me as if he was after your loot."

"What rot!"

"Well, I've given you the tip," said Harry, losing patience. "The man is a wily fellow, and if you don't get shut of him you'll take your chance."

Bunter sneered.

"Pile it on!" he said. "All superior characters get this envious detraction from common people. I'm used to it."

"Oh, my hat!"

Harry Wharton gave it up at that. Bunter was at liberty to do as he liked, and the captain of the Remove, having warned him, left it at that. He could not help thinking that before he quitted India, Bunter would have a rude awakening on the subject of his faithful native; but it was Bunter's own business, and evidently it was useless to talk to the fat and fatuous Owl.

So Kasi Jee boarded the train with the Greyfriars party and travelled with them to Lahore and on to Delhi.

Bunter, in his fat self-satisfaction, declined to believe that the naukar had any motive but devoted loyally to a noble and magnificent master. But possibly Wharton's warning lingered in his fat mind, all the same, for he was extremely careful of the gift of Hurree Singh, which he kept about his fat person day and night; and at the various places where the party stopped on their return journey to Bombay. Bunter took care never to sleep in a room by himself. If, as Wharton more than half suspected, the naukar had designs on Bunter's jewels, he had no chance of annexing them before the Greyfriars party arrived at Bombay.

At Bombay the party were to spend several days before taking the steamer for home.

Colonel Wharton had engaged quarters at the Palm Tree Hotel, where Kasi Jee was still in attendance upon Bunter. On their previous visit the Grey friars party had been hurried in their movements on their way to Bhanipur. They were more at leisure now, and, under the colonel's guidance, the juniors roamed over the wonderful city of the East, and saw all that was to be seen. Bunter, however, preferred to loaf in the hotel veranda, under the cooling punkah, and to keep Kasi Jee continually busy bringing him refreshments, liquid and solid.

After Bombay, India would be left behind, and if Kasi Jee intended to remain in his native country—as the juniors believed—he would have to quit his magnificent master there. But the fatuous Owl was quite assured that his faithful native was prepared to cross the "black water" with him. and Kasi Jee gave no sign of desiring to go.

When the last evening in Bombay came round even Wharton began to wonder a little. The colonel was spending a few hours that evening at a club with some of his old military acquaintances, and the juniors, tired from a ramble in the city, were taking their case on the hotel veranda till bedtime. Kasi Jee lurked among the great palms in teakwood tubs on the veranda, waiting on the orders of his master. Harry Wharton glanced at him, and glanced at the fat and fatuous face of Bunter.

The Owl of the Remove understood his glance, and grinned.

"You understand now that James is sticking to me, what?" he chuckled.

"The attachfulness of the esteemed Kasi Jee is terrific," remarked Hurree Jamset Ram Singh with a curious glance at the naukar.

"Too terrific to be genuine," grunted Johnny Bull.

"Oh, really. Bull—"

"Is the loot still safe, Bunter?" grinned Nugent.

"Yes, you ass!"

"Then it beats me!"

"Oh, you fellows will never understand the faithful, dog like attachment of a native for a strong, masterful character," said Bunter disdainfully. "It's really the kicking that does it. I kick James every day for his own god. Sometimes I give him a kind word to make him happy. He would go through fire and water for me." Bunter blinked at the naukar.

"James," he hooted.

"Han, sahib?"

"Didn't I tell you to bring coffee?"

"The coffee coming, noble sahib."

"You've kept me waiting two minutes," said Bunter. "Come here!"

"Noble master—"

Biff!

Kasi Jee received the drive of Bunter's boot with his usual submission. He salaamed away.

"That's the way to treat 'em!" said Bunter. "Masterfulness does it. James is attached to me like a faithful dog, you know."

Kasi Jee came back with a tray laden with coffee-cups. He set it on the little table round which the juniors were grouped, screened from the rest of the veranda by spreading palms. With a deft hand the naukar poured out the coffee, and salaamed away again.

"Well, the giddy naukar makes jolly good coffee, anyhow," said Bob Cherry, as he finished his cup.

"I'm going to fix it with the Head to let me keep him at Greyfriars," said Bunter. "He can wait on me in Study No. 7, you know."

"I can see the Head allowing it," chuckled Nugent.

"I say, I'm jolly sleepy," said Johnny Bull. "Are we waiting up till the colonel comes back?"

"He was to be back by nine," said Harry. "May as well wait."

"Pleasant enough here, and those chairs are jolly comfy," yawned Bob," leaning back luxuriously in the long cane chair.

Snore!

"Hallo, hallo, hallo! Bunter's gone to sleep!"

"No need to tell us that," grinned Johnny Bull drowsily. "All Bombay can hear him."

Bob closed his eyes for a moment. They remained closed. Somehow or other a deep drowsiness came over all the juniors. Ten minutes after drinking that excellent coffee made by the naukar they were all nodding off. And silence reigned round the table and the coffee-cups, broken only by Billy Bunter's stertorous snore.

There was a soft footfall, and Kasi Jee glided through the palms.

"Sahib!" murmured the naukar.

No answer. The six Greyfriars juniors were sleeping soundly.

"Sahib!" repeated the naukar in a louder voice.

No answer, and no movement. Kasi Jee grinned. His black eyes glittered as he stooped over Bunter and his thievish fingers groped through the pockets of the slumbering Owl.

A couple of minutes were enough for Kasi Jee.

Something that glittered and sparkled glided from his dusky hand into the recesses of his loose, linen garments. Then the naukar glided softly away. Bunter snored on.

A slinking figure glided through the streets of Bombay, to disappear into a native shop in a bazaar at a distance from the hotel. It was Kasi Jee the naukar who disappeared into the shop, brown-skinned and neatly clad in white linen. It was a black skinned coolie in tattered garments who emerged, to take a seat in a crowded third class carriage in a train that pulled out of Bombay for the north. Kasi Jee, disguised and safe, with Bunter's loot safely hidden in his rags grinned -serenely as the train bore him away from Bombay.

Bunter snored on, regardless.

The Owl of the Remove did not know it yet. But Bunter had lost his faithful native.

132

Alas!

COLONEL WHARTON stepped out on to the veranda and glanced about him, and looked a little puzzled. Among the palms under the shaded electric lights a good many people were smoking cigars and chatting, or sipping coffee and sherbet. The colonel expected to find the Greyfriars juniors there, and he strolled along looking for them. Naturally he expected to hear their voices if they were there, and he was quite surprised when he came on them suddenly. The six juniors were all leaning back in their chairs fast asleep, and of their assiduous attendant, Kasi Jee, nothing was to be seen. Colonel Wharton stopped and stared at the sleeping schoolboys in surprise. Then he touched his nephew on the shoulder.

"Harry!"

The captain of the Remove did not answer. He did not wake. He slept on, oblivious of the touch on his shoulder.

"Harry!" repeated his uncle, more and more surprised. And he shook the junior vigorously. Still Wharton did not open his eyes. All the juniors were breathing steadily. Bunter's snore rumbled among the palms.

Feeling somewhat uneasy, the colonel grasped his nephew by the shoulders and jerked him from the chair.

"Harry, what's the matter with you?"

Wharton's eyes opened at last.

He rubbed them, and stared dizzily at his uncle, and then passed his hand over his head. He seemed dazed.

"I—I—I've been asleep!" he stammered.

"All of you were asleep," said the astonished old gentleman. "There is something very odd about this."

"I—I feel rather queer," said Harry. "I—I think I dropped off after the coffee. Here, Bob, wake up!"

Bob Cherry woke up as the captain of the Remove shook him. He blinked dazedly at Harry.

"Have I been asleep?" he yawned.

"Like a log, old chap," said Wharton. "Look at the others! What the dickens made us all go off like that?"

"Blessed if I know" I've got a headache."

"Same here, and a queer taste in my mouth," said Wharton. "Here, Franky, Johnny, Inky!"

The other juniors were awakened. But it was useless to shake Billy Bunter. He slept on regardless.

Shake, shake, shake, shake!

Bunter only grunted and snored.

"Better help him to bed," said Colonel Wharton. "Where is Kasi Jee?"

"About somewhere. I suppose," said Harry. "I haven't seen him since he brought us the coffee."

"Pandy Din!"

The khitmutghar came up.

"Help Bunter sahib to his room."

Billy Bunter was lifted in the sinewy arms of the khitmutghar, and taken into the hotel, and to his room. The juniors followed, still feeling dazed. Colonel Wharton followed them, puzzled and perplexed. Bunter was laid on his bed. Still snoring stertorously. Harry Wharton & Co. gathered round him.

"My esteemed chums," murmured Hurree Jamset Ram Singh, "I have a taste in my worthy mouth. There was something in the coffee."

"In the coffee?" repeated Wharton.

The schoolboy nabob nodded.

"There was a drug in the coffee, my excellent chum, some decoction of opium was mixed in it. The esteemed Kasi Jee has been playing trickfully."

Wharton started.

"Kasi Jee! He made the coffee!" he exclaimed. "You think that the naukar sent us to sleep on purpose. Inky?"

"The thinkfulness is terrific'"

"But why?" exclaimed Bob Cherry.

Hurree Jamset Ram Singh grinned.

"I fancy you will guess the reason, my esteemed Bob, if you searchfully look through the pockets of the ineffable Bunter. The worthy execrable naukar had his reasons for following the ridiculous Bunter as far as Bombay."

"Oh, my hat!"

Colonel Wharton's face set grimly. The nabob's words were quite sufficient to enlighten him.

"You have been drugged, my boys," he said. "A harmless drug, doubtless; the effects will be gone by tomorrow. But it is probable that Bunter's folly has cos, him a great deal. Pandy Din, find out at once if the naukar is still in the hotel."

The khitmutghar hurried away.

Attention was concentrated on Bunter while he was gone. The fat junior's head and face were bathed in cold water, and he soon showed signs of returning to consciousness. Probably the treacherous naukar had given him a rather stronger dose than the other fellows, to make sure of him while robbing him. Bunter's little round eyes opened at last, blinking dizzily.

"I say, you fellows!" he murmured.

"Bunter— "

"Groogh! 'Tain't rising bell!" mumbled Bunter.

"Fathead! You're not at Greyfriars now," said Bob. "Wake up, Bunter! Sit up, old man."

"Leave a fellow alone! I'm sleepy!"

"My esteemed Bunter—"

"Shurrup! I'm going to sleep!"

"Bunter!" said the colonel's deep voice. "Pull yourself together, my boy! Something was mixed in your coffee to send you to sleep."

Snore!

"Beast! Lemme alone!"

"I think you have been robbed," said the colonel. "You had something of value about you. See if it is safe."

"Eh!"

Bunter started into wide wakefulness.

"It looks as if Kasi Jee has picked your pockets, Bunter," said Harry. "Find out at once."

"Rot!"

"You fat duffer—"

"Oh, cheese it!" said Bunter irritably. "Can't you let Kasi Jee alone? This rotten jealousy because I've got a faithful native attached to me is getting sickening!"

"Examine your pockets at once, Bunter," said Colonel Wharton. "Do you hear?"

"Oh, all right!" said Bunter sulkily.

I know the stuff is safe enough, and Kasi Jee is all right. I—"

Bunter stopped suddenly as he groped in the pocket where he had so carefully stored the gold chain and the diamond collar. A startling change came over his fat face.

"Yarooooh!"

"Well?" snapped the colonel.

"I've been robbed!" yelled Banter.

"I thought so! Make sure that the things are gone, and I will communicate with the police at once. It may be barely possible to stop the naukar."

Bunter went feverishly through his pockets. But the goods were gone. There was no doubt about that. Bunter's visions of wealth had faded; his thousand quids were gone from his gaze like a beautiful dream! He glared suspiciously at the juniors.

"Look here, you rotters, if this is a lark—"

"What?" ejaculated Wharton.

"If you've taken those things out of my pocket for a rotten joke while I was asleep—" _

"You fat idiot!" roared Bob Cherry. "Can't you understand that you were drugged in the coffee Kasi Jee made for you, and that he's picked your pocket and bunked?"

"Rot!"

"Look here, Bunker—" said Nugent.

"Bosh! My nigger is too attached to me to do anything of the sort. Send for him!" snorted Bunter.

"Pandy Din is looking for him now," said Johnny Bull. "I'II lay a fiver to a banana that he doesn't find him."

"Rubbish!"

Pandy Din glided back into the room. Colonel Wharton gave him an inquiring look.

"Kasi Jee is gone sahib. He was seen to leave the hotel an hour ago," said the khitmutghar. "Not being seen to return.'

"He's gone out for something, and he will come back," said Bunter, still not convinced.

"Fathead! Where are the things, then?"

"I suppose somebody picked my pocket while I was asleep, if it wasn't you rotters larking! It wasn't my faithful native!"

"Ass!"

Colonel Wharton went down to speak to the hotel manager, who sent at once for the police. Billy Bunter was not thinking of sleep now. He had a headache; but he declined to believe that it was the result of a drug administered by the wily naukar.

The police-officer who came to inquire to the robbery, however, took quite a different view; and he promised the colonel that every effort should be made to trace and capture the naukar. Bet he held out little hope of success; it was easy for the thief to vanish into the trackless warren of the native town, if, indeed, he was not already outside the city and fleeing for parts unknown.

That evening was not a happy one for Bunter.

It was late when he turned in.

Even when he turned in he did not sleep.

His thoughts were on the jewels he had lost—the price of which was to have made him a rich man at home, and to have provided him with endless feeds at Greyfriars. Those feeds were destined never to be devoured by the Owl of the Remove. Late into the night Billy Bunter groaned dismally over his loss—dismally and dolorously.

The next morning the Greyfriars party had to take their passage on the P. & O. boat for Suez on which their cabins were already booked. Bunter objected strenuously.

"I'm not going without my property!" he howled. "I've been robbed! Look here, let's wait at Bombay at least till Kasi Jee comes back. I am going to take him home with me, as you know."

"You burbling idiot!" said Bob. "Can't you understand even yet that Kasi Jee has bunked with your loot, and that he will never be seen again within a hundred miles of Bombay?"

"Oh, really. Cherry—"

"Our passage is taken on the steamer. Bunter," said Colonel Wharton quietly. "There is no possibility of delay. The matter remains in the hands of the Bombay police, who will do all that is possible; your presence here could give no assistance."

"But—" gasped Bunter.

"If anything is seen again of Kasi Jee or the jewels, we shall be apprised of it," said the colonel. "But you may as well make up your mind that the loss is irretrievable. The man is probably hundreds of miles away by this time, and he has all India to choose from for a hiding-place. You have only your own folly to thank for what has happened; and I hope that the lesson will not be lost on you!"

"But—"

"That is enough!" The colonel looked at his watch. "We start in one hour from now. Finish your packing, and be ready; and say no more."

"Oh dear!"

There was no help for it.

Perhaps even Bunter realized at last, that it really was his "faithful" native who had robbed him, and that there was no chance of ever seeing again either Kasi Jee or the jewels. Anyhow, he had to make up his fat mind to it and at the appointed time he was on board the steamer with the rest of the Greyfriars party. But he sighed deeply as the steamer glided out into the Indian Ocean. Hurree Jamset Ram Singh stood on the deck, looking back at the shores of India till they were lost to sight.

Bunter comforted himself with a second breakfast.

During the long run across the Arabian Sea, and through the Straits of Bab-el Mandeb, and up the Red Sea to Suez, Bunter's fat face wore an almost continuously lugubrious expression.

His riches had taken unto themselves wings and flown away; and he had lost his faithful native! And Bunter, like Rachel of old. mourned for that which was lost, and could not be comforted.

133

Back at Greyfriars!

"HALLO, hallo, hallo!"

"Here we are again!" It was the first day of the new term at Greyfriars. From north and south, east and west, Greyfriars fellows were gathering once more at the old school.

The Famous Five of the Remove strolled arm-in-arm across the old quad, exchanging greetings with old acquaintances. Browned by the burning sun of India, the chums of the Remove were back from their long holiday in Eastern climes. And they were glad to see the old school again.

"We had a ripping time in Bhanipur, Inky old man," said Bob Cherry. "No end of a time. But it's jolly to be back."

"The jollifulness is terrific."

"No end terrific!" grinned Johnny Bull. "Hallo, there's Coker of the Fifth! Give him a yell!"

And the chums of the Remove gave Horace Coker a yell which caused that great man to turn up his nose and walk away in disdain. But the disdain of Coker of the Fifth had no effect on the exuberant spirits of the Famous Five. They walked on regardless.

"You fellows back!" Skinner of the Remove stopped the five cheery juniors. "By Jove! You look brown!"

"Indian sun," said Nugent.

Skinner of the Remove raised his eyebrows.

"Indian sun!" he repeated. "I didn't know there was an Indian sun at Margate."

"Margate!" said Bob "We haven't been to Margate for the summer holidays, fathead!"

"Oh! Was it Southend-on-Sea?"asked Skinner innocently.

"We've been in India."

Skinner nodded.

"Knew a chap once who spent his vac in the South Sea Islands," he said, reminiscently. "But at the time he was seen at Blackpool."

"Bump him!" said Bob.

And the cheery juniors bumped Skinner of the Remove, and walked in leaving Skinner sparing and perhaps wishing that he had not been so funny.

"Hallo, hallo hallo! Here's Bunter! Listen!" chuckled Bob. Billy Bunter was the centre of a little crowd of grinning Remove fellows. Bunter was going strong.

"Danger? Well, some!" said Bunter. "Believe me. I never slept a night except with a loaded rifle by my side, and my faithful native watching tigers! About a dozen. I meant to bring home a tiger for the study Toddy?"

"And why didn't you?" grinned Peter Todd.

"Forgot, you know, in the rush of things," said Bunter. "It was rather a rush all through, I had all the responsibility on my hands. We had a brush with dacoits—"

"With which?" ejaculated Wibley of the Remove.

"Dacoits—that means robbers—Hindustani word, you know. I've picked up a lot of Hindustani at Bhanipur I used to give commands in his own language to my faithful native."

"Ha, ha, ha!"

"Blessed if I see anything to cackle at. My faithful native—"

"Did you bring him home?" chuckled Vernon-Smith.

"Nunno! Lost him in Bombay!—"

"Ha, ha, ha!"

"You can cackle," said Bunter. "But you should have seen me in the scrap with the dacoits. It was some scrap, I can tell you with my trusty rifle and my faithful native—"

"Go it!" chortled Squiff.

"But for me, old Inky would have been killed a dozen times at least—'

"Great pip!" ejaculated the Bounder.

"Inky must have more lives than a cat if be could he killed a dozen times."

"Ha, ha, ha!"

"I—I mean—"

"Pile it on!" said Smithy encouragingly.

"I carried the thing through," said Bunter. "Wharton and those other asses were a good deal in the way; and that old codger, the colonel, was rather a worry. Passengers, the lot of them, you know. Fortunately, I was there. They looked to me for protection, and I saved them over and over again. When there was danger the word was— 'Call Bunter.'

"Ha, ha, ha!" roared Bob Cherry, unable to repress his feelings any longer; and Billy Bunter spun round and blinked at the grinning faces of the Famous Five.

"I—I say, you fellows—"

"Go it, old fat bean!" chuckled Bob Cherry. "Tell the fellows how you squatted on the floor of the car when the dacoits were in the offing—"

"Oh really, Cherry—"

"And how you bunked from a dry twig thinking it was a snake—"

"Ha, ha, ha!"

"And how—"

"Oh, cheese it!" snapped Bunter.

"Ha, ha, ha!"

The Famous Five walked on, chuckling. Bunter was left to continue his thrilling narrative of dangers dire by land and sea, to which the Remove fellows listened with great interest, apparently regarding the narration as Bunter's comic turn.

"Good old Bunter!" chuckled Bob. "He isn't afraid of tigers, or snakes, or dacoits—at Greyfriars. It was rather different at Bhanipur."

"Ha, ha, ha!"

There was a great celebration in Study No. 1 in the Remove that evening.

Most of the Remove fellows were keen to hear the tale of the adventures of the Famous Five in far off India; and No. 1 study was crammed for the occasion, and there was an overflow meeting in the Remove passage.

Billy Bunter, of course, was there, spreading himself as usual.

All the Remove had been asked to the spread, to celebrate the safe return of Hurree Jamset Ram Singh to Greyfriars. Inky's health was drunk in lemonade and ginger beer. Bunter suggested champagne, as it was a special occasion—a very special occasion. He offered to stand the champagne himself, if somebody would make him an advance upon a postal-order he was expecting by the next post. Bunter's offer was not accepted.

Harry Wharton & Co. had to tell the tale of their adventures in the East, and they told it—with amplifications by Bunter. According to Bunter, he, W. G. Bunter, had been the "goods," so to speak, all the time, and his companions had been very small beer indeed. And Bunter was greatly annoyed to find that, so far as he was concerned, the company consisted wholly of doubting Thomases. Skinner, indeed, affected to be a doubting Thomas all along the line, which was one of Skinner's pleasant ways.

"Tell us about that scrap in the jungle again, Cherry," urged Skinner. "That bit's really thrilling."

Bob, who was squirting soda-water into a glass of lemonade, glanced at Skinner.

"You've heard it once," he said.

"You can't have too much of a good thing," said Skinner blandly. "I never knew you had such a splendid imagination, old bean."

Some of the juniors chuckled. "Look here, Skinner—"

"You went through all these deadly perils—dacoits, and tigers, and hissing serpents, and rebel rajahs?" said Skinner.

"We did."

"And then you woke up?" asked Skinner.

There was another chuckle in the study.

Bob Cherry did not reply to Skinner's question in words. He turned the soda-syphon on that doubting youth.

Squi-is-ssh!

"Whoooop!" roared Skinner.

"Ha, ha, ha!"

Skinner scrambled away frantically. The swishing of the syphon followed him.

"Groogh! Stoppit! Yoop!" spluttered Skinner. "Oooooch!"

And Skinner fled from the study, followed by roars of laughter.

134

"Tiger"

"AND I said, 'Buck up, Cherry!'" It was Bunter's voice. Bob Cherry was coming along to No. 7 in the Remove, a few days later, to speak to Peter Todd about the footer. Bunter's voice greeted him as he neared the open door of the study.

Bob frowned.

Ever since the return of the party from India to Greyfriars, Bunter had been going strong on the subject of his adventures in the East. It was an inexhaustible topic with Bunter. And the oftener he told his adventures, the more wonderful they became.

Bunter was not content with blowing his own trumpet. He enhanced his own wonderful performances by derisive descriptions of the doings of the other fellows. Bunter, apparently, had been "IT" all the time; the other fellows were not even also rans. Certainly, nobody in the Remove believed that in the hour of peril, the Famous Five had only been brought up to the scratch by the heroic example of W. G. Bunter. But that was the view of W. G. B. himself, and he enlarged upon it more and more. He was telling the tale to Peter Todd now.

"And I said, 'Buck up, Cherry,'" went on Bunter's fat voice. "He was trembling in every limb, you know—crouching behind me. There was the tiger—only a dozen feet away—"

"Can it!" suggested Peter.

"You can believe me or not, Toddy—but there was the tiger—and Cherry hiding behind me for protection, and Wharton under the table, and the other fellows running for dear life. Did I falter? No fear! I can tell you, that if I had missed then, you'd never have seen any of those chaps again! They were simply paralyzed with fear. Fortunately, I kept my presence of mind. I told Cherry to buck up; I called out to Wharton to pull himself together. And then—"

Bob Cherry changed his mind about calling in at No. 7. He walked on down the Remove passage, leaving Bunter to continue the thrilling yarn to an unbelieving Peter.

"Hallo, what's the trouble?" asked Harry Wharton, as Bob looked into No. 1 Study with a frowning brow.

"Bunter's going it again."

Harry Wharton laughed.

"Let him rip!" he said.

"That's all very well," said Bob. "But he's spinning a yarn about a tiger, which he faced with wonderful presence of mind, while I was hiding behind him, paralyzed with funk—"

"Oh, my hat!" ejaculated Nugent.

"And you were hiding under a table, Wharton—"

"Was I?" exclaimed the captain of the Remove warmly.

"And the other fellows were running for their lives—"

"The silly owl!"

"It's too thick," said Bob, "and I've thought of a wheeze. If Bunter is so jolly bold when tigers are about, we'll give him a chance to show off his jolly old courage. If a tiger looked into his study—"

"Eh? You can't borrow a tiger for the occasion," said Harry. "We're not in Bhanipur now, you know."

"We can borrow the tiger skin from the Head's library."

"Oh!"

"The tiger's head is done up like life," grinned Bob. "It will be enough for Bunter to get a glimpse of it. You fellows come and help me, and then Inky can bring Bunter down to the Rag—"

"Ha, ha, ha!"

For some little time after that, the chums of the Remove were busy. Than Hurree Jamset Ram Singh's smiling face looked into No. 7 Study. Peter Todd had gone down; Billy Bunter was reclining at his ease in the study armchair. He blinked at the schoolboy nabob through his big spectacles.

"My esteemed Bunter, are you staying alonefully here?" he exclaimed.

"Eh, why not?" asked Bunter.

"You have not heard of an escaped tiger from an esteemed menagerie, which has been seen near the school?" asked the nabob.

"Ow!" Bunter jumped out of the armchair as if moved by a spring.

"All the fellows are in the Rag, keeping togetherfully!" said Hurree Singh. "The presence of the excellent and ludicrous Bunter would inspire them with terrific courage."

"I'll come!" gasped Bunter.

He rolled hurriedly from the study. Certainly Bunter did not intend to remain alone if there was an escaped tiger in the neighborhood of Greyfriars. He clutched hold of Hurree Singh's arm, and rolled away with the nabob to the Rag, where he found nearly all the Remove gathered. Bob Cherry was not to be seen there; but Harry Wharton was at the door; he opened it hastily to let in Bunter and Hurree Singh, and closed it again very quickly.

"Lock it!" exclaimed Bunter.

Wharton locked the door.

Bunter gave a hurried glance at the windows—they were all closed.

"I—I say, you fellows, is—is—is it certain that the tiger was seen near the school?" he exclaimed.

"I don't think it's certain," said Wharton gravely; "but you can't be too careful."

"Thank goodness Bunter's here!" said Johnny Bull. "If the tiger gets into the school—"

"Ow!"

"Bunter will face it, while we get clear. We rely on you, Bunter."

Billy Bunter blinked round him. The windows were shut. The door was locked; and if there was an escaped tiger in the neighborhood—which was not certain, by no means certain—the juniors really seemed safe enough in the Rag.

Bunter's confidence revived.

"That's all right, you chaps," he said valorously. "You rely on me. Keep your eyes on me and follow my example. Why, bless you, I'm used to tigers—when I was in the jungle, they roared round me every night, without disturbing me in the least. I was telling Toddy how I faced a tiger, when the other chaps were simply paralysed with funk—"

Grrrrrrrrrrh!

Bunter started.

Grrrrrrh!

It was a hideous growl, and it proceeded from under the big table in the Rag. Bunter spun round towards the table, his little round eyes almost bulging through his spectacles.

"Wha-a-at's that?" he gasped.

"The tiger!" yelled Nugent.

"Help! Save us, Bunter!"

"Yarooogh!" howled Bunter. "Oh, dear! Help! Help! Fire! Murder! Help! Yaroooooooop!" From under the big table, a head emerged—a dreadful-looking head, with glaring eyes and bristling whiskers. Behind it a glimpse could be had of a long striped body.

Grrrrrrrrh!

Bunter made a wild dash for the door. In an instant he was seized in the grasp of Johnny Bull, and dragged back.

"Save us, Bunter! gasped Johnny.

"Yarooh! Leggo, Help!"

"Save us, Bunter!" chorused the Removites.

Bunter struggled desperately to escape. But he struggled in vain. Five or six juniors seized him, and he was held between them and the glaring head of the growling tiger.

"Bunter to the front!" panted Toddy "Keep him in front! Bunter's the chap to face tigers!"

"Save us, Bunter!" sobbed Nugent.

"Yoop! Leggo! Help! Fire! Oh, crumb! Leggo!" shrieked Bunter struggling frantically. "It's coming for me! Leggo! Yooop!"

The tiger was crawling out from under the table. Billy Bunter made a desperate effort and broke loose, and raced for the door. To turn back the key, tear the door open and bolt into the passage, occupied Bunter a moment. He flew down the passage on the wings of the wind.

"Ha, ha, ha!"

A roar of laughter followed him from the Rag. Bob Cherry emerged from under the table, and threw off the tiger skin.

"Ha, ha, ha!"

"Oh, crumbs!" sobbed Bob Cherry, wiping his eyes. "Where's Bunter? Why isn't he facing the tiger? Ha, ha, ha!"

The Removites yelled.

Ten minutes later, Peter Todd tried the door of No. 7 in the Remove. It was locked; and there was a howl of terror within as Peter rattled the handle.

"Ow! Help! Yaroooh! Keep off! Help!"

"You silly ass!" roared Peter. And there was a roar of laughter along the Remove passage.

"I—I—say—is that you, Peter?" gasped Bunter.

"Yes, ass! Open the door!"

"W-w where's the tiger?"

"Gone!" chuckled Peter.

Bunter unlocked the study door, and blinked out into the Remove passage, which was crowded with laughing juniors. Bunter blinked at them in surprise.

"I—I say, sure it's gone, Peter?" he exclaimed.

"Quite!" said Peter cheerily. "Bob took it back to the Head's library."

"Wha-a-a-t?"

"You see, if the Head missed his tiger skin, there would be a row!" explained Bob Cherry

"Ha, ha, ha!"

Bunter gasped.

"Why, you—you—you beast! M-m mean to say it wasn't a real tiger?" he spluttered.

"Ha, ha, ha! Not quite."

"Oh!" gasped Bunter.

Billy Bunter blinked at the hilarious Removites.

"I—I say, you fellows—"

"Save us, Bunter!" chortled Johnny Bull.

"Ha, ha, ha!"

"Of—of course! I know it wasn't a tiger!" gasped Bunter. "I—I knew it was a lark. I—I'll bet I made you fellows think I was scared, he, he, he!"

"You did!" chortled Bob "No doubt about that! You did."

"Ha, ha, ha!"

"But I say—"

"Ha, ha, ha!"

"I tell you—"

"Ha, ha, ha!" roared the Removites.

And Billy Bunter gave it up.

GREYFRIARS SCHOOL
MAIN ENTRANCE
ABBOTS SPINNEY
FRIARDALE
SANATORIUM
PRIORY RUINS
OLD WELL
FRIARDALE
FRIARDAL
VILLAGE
RIVER